Dear Bookmarked Reader,

When we got the news that *The Wednesday Sisters* is your newest book club pick, Frankie, Kath, Linda, Ally, and Brett danced on their fictional desks—which of course they bought at Target. As women with relationships and jobs to tend to, dinners to cook, miles to run, and children to raise, where else would they go for sweatshirts, cookie pans, and the alarm clocks that wake them so they can write in the early-morning silence, before life intrudes?

The Wednesday Sisters is a story about five regular women who, like all of us, have dreams for themselves. At the time they first meet, Linda and Kath have put their dreams on hold to raise children, or perhaps have never really quite mustered the nerve to reach for them. Ally and Brett hit bumps that send them off course. And Frankie has been quietly pursuing her dream for years, afraid to admit even to her dearest friends that she'd like to become something she isn't—at least not yet. These five friends struggle as we all struggle: They laugh together. They cry together, and sometimes alone. And they fail as surely as everyone fails. But they have one another, and through their friendship they gain the courage to pick themselves up from their failures and . . . well, you'll have to read for yourselves to see what they do—what we all can do with the help of friends.

Writing the story of these women was such a joyful experience. Each morning, I wrapped myself in the spirit of my own dearest friends, most of whom live far away but are still close in my heart. I'm absolutely delighted you've chosen to spend your summer with Frankie, Kath, Linda, Ally, and Brett, and I'd welcome the opportunity to share thoughts about the issues their story raises, either by email or—the way I most enjoy connecting with readers—through a phone chat with your book club or any gathering of friends. You can find out more about the book at www.target.com/bookmarked or contact me by visiting my website, www.TheWednesdaySisters.com.

I hope this story of friendship and dreams will leave you as glad of your friends as I am of mine. And I hope that, when you finish reading, you'll pick up your own pen or paintbrush or whatever you might need to head toward your own dream. It's out there, just waiting for you to reach.

Fondly,

Meg Waite Clayton

Praise for *The Wednesday Sisters*

"Clayton captures the evolution of a decades-long friendship in a highly accessible narrative. She grabs the reader's attention early on, hitting on big events of the period while introducing compelling and quirky characters that are easy to identify with."
—Salt Lake City *Deseret News*

"Clayton ably conjures the era's details and captures the women's changing roles in a world that expects little of them."
—*Publishers Weekly*

"Readers will be swept up by this moving novel about female friendship and enthralled by the recounting of a pivotal year in American history as seen through these young women's eyes."
—*Booklist*

"I read *The Wednesday Sisters* in one delicious gulp. With a smart, entrancing voice, Meg Waite Clayton sweeps us into the world of the tumultuous 1960s and beyond and gives us the gift of five young women coming into their own as friends, mothers, wives, and writers. *The Wednesday Sisters* takes their writing group as its core, and up until the last page, I found myself fervently rooting for each of them as if they were my friends, too."
—Lalita Tademy, author of *Red River* and *Cane River*

"This generous and inventive book is a delight to read, an evocation of the power of friendship to sustain, encourage, and embolden us. Join the sisterhood!"
—Karen Joy Fowler, author of *The Jane Austen Book Club* and *Wit's End*

"Meg Waite Clayton's *The Wednesday Sisters* is a heartwarming novel about the joys and complications of friendship, an inspiring story for anyone who has dared to dream big. Clayton's characters are the kind of women you can imagine joining on the park bench—for a good laugh, a good cry, or a spirited conversation about literature and life."

—Michelle Richmond, author of *The Year of Fog* and *No One You Know*

"*The Wednesday Sisters,* a beautifully written story of women's friendship, inspired me the way my closest friends do. It made me laugh. It made me cry. Most of all, it enriched my life. If you've ever had a best friend, buy a copy for her."

—Masha Hamilton, author of *The Camel Bookmobile* and *The Distance Between Us*

"This remarkable group of women demonstrates that no matter what period of history in which we live, no matter what race, creed, or class we are, no matter what pains we endure, our one unifying salvation can be books. And this book reminded me why I love to read."

—Lolly Winston, author of *Good Grief* and *Happiness Sold Separately*

"Richly intelligent, deeply felt, and incandescently original, Clayton's book is a rhapsodic story of female friendship set against wildly changing times and mores. Not only is the book heartbreaking, funny, and undeniably smart, but truly, this is the kind of book you don't just *want* to pass on to all your friends. You *have* to."

—Caroline Leavitt, author of *Girls in Trouble* and *Coming Back to Me*

"A compelling and deeply moving testament to the power of women's friendships. I simply couldn't put *The Wednesday Sisters* down until I'd turned the last page."

—Ellen Baker, author of *Keeping the House*

"I simply could not put down *The Wednesday Sisters*. I gave my heart to Meg Clayton's vivid characters, and I read their intertwined stories breathlessly. Move over, Ya-Ya sisters!"

—Amanda Eyre Ward, author of *Forgive Me* and *How to Be Lost*

What Book Clubs Are Saying about
The Wednesday Sisters

"The Wednesday Sisters are as delightful, insightful, and wonderful a group of women as you could ever hope to meet. This book is about people; about the power of being a woman; it is about you and me, your mother, and your sweetest sister-friend."
—Amanda Waterhouse, Chicks on Lit, Greensboro, North Carolina

"Grab a few bottles of wine when your book club discusses *The Wednesday Sisters* because you're in for a long—and quite interesting—evening. We fell in love with this novel, which uncorked discussions of friendship, marriage, motherhood, writing, and what it was like to live through the changing times of the late twentieth century."
—Jane Schreier Jones, The PageTurners Book Club, Springboro, Ohio

"I laughed, I cried, I learned! *The Wednesday Sisters* is destined to be a book that women give to their girlfriends!"
—Elizabeth Miller, The Literary Ladies of South Jersey, Burlington, New Jersey

"The girls in our book club could relate to so many of the things these women went through, yet reading about it all through Meg's characters was like looking at it through a kaleidoscope of many colors—much more fun!"
—Julie Hardy, The Pulpwood Queens, Tyler, Texas

"*The Wednesday Sisters* brings five women to life—their friendships, their love of writing and literature, and their struggles and triumphs over the years. A book club gem—thought-provoking for all ages."
—Debbie Earl, The Laker Women, Prior Lake, Minnesota

"*The Wednesday Sisters* celebrates the power and strength that a community of women can bring to each other. It is a book that all of us in our book club have treasured and will be passing on to the next generation of 'sisters' of the heart."
—Niki Saxena, The Palo Alto Book Club, Palo Alto, California

ALSO BY MEG WAITE CLAYTON

The Language of Light

The Wednesday Sisters

MEG WAITE CLAYTON

A Novel

BALLANTINE BOOKS · NEW YORK

2009 Target Edition

Copyright © 2008 by Meg Waite Clayton
Reading group guide copyright © 2009 by Random House, Inc.

Published in the United States by Ballantine Books, an imprint
of The Random House Publishing Group, a division
of Random House, Inc., New York.

BALLANTINE and colophon are registered trademarks of Random House, Inc.
RANDOM HOUSE READER'S CIRCLE & Design is a trademark of Random House, Inc.

Originally published in hardcover in the United States by Ballantine Books, an imprint of
The Random House Publishing Group, a division of Random House, Inc., in 2008.

Library of Congress Cataloging-in-Publication Data
Clayton, Meg Waite.
The Wednesday sisters: a novel / Meg Waite Clayton.
p.   cm.
ISBN 978-0-345-51873-6
1. Housewives—Fiction.   2. Housewives as authors—Fiction.   3. Female friendship—
Fiction.   4. Nineteen sixties—Fiction.   5. Palo Alto (Calif.)—Fiction.
6. Domestic fiction.   I. Title.
PS3603.L45W43 2008
813'.6—dc22   2008010627

Printed in the United States of America

www.randomhousereaderscircle.com

2 4 6 8 9 7 5 3 1

Book design by Nancy B. Field

To Jenn, my Wednesday Sister,
   Brenda, my Tuesday one,
   Mac, my 24/7 everything,
      and
   Chris and Nick, fine purveyors of
      tooth fairy magic and squid ink

Where there is great love,
there are always miracles.

—WILLA CATHER,
   Death Comes for the Archbishop

The Wednesday Sisters

THE WEDNESDAY SISTERS look like the kind of women who might meet at those fancy coffee shops on University—we do *look* that way—but we're not one bit fancy, and we're not sisters, either. We don't even meet on Wednesdays, although we did at the beginning. We met at the swings at Pardee Park on Wednesday mornings when our children were young. It's been thirty-five years, though—more than thirty-five!—since we switched from Wednesdays at ten to Sundays at dawn. Sunrise, whatever time the light first crests the horizon that time of year. It suits us, to leave our meeting time up to the tilt of the earth, the track of the world around the sun.

That's us, there in the photograph. Yes, that's me—in one of my chubbier phases, though I suppose one of these days I'll have to face up to the fact that it's the thinner me that's the "phase," not the chubbier one. And going left to right, that's Linda (her hair loose and combed, but then she brought the camera, she was the only one who knew we'd be taking a photograph). Next to her is Ally, pale as ever, and then Kath. And the one in the white gloves in front—the one in the coffin—that's Brett.

• • •

Brett's gloves—that's what brought us together all those years ago. I had Maggie and Davy with me in the park that first morning, a park full to bursting with children running around together as if any new kid could join them just by saying hello, with clusters of mothers who might—just might—be joined with a simple hello as well. It wasn't my park yet, just a park in a neighborhood where Danny and I might live if we moved to the Bay Area, a neighborhood with tree-lined streets and neat little yards and sidewalks and leaves turning colors just like at home in Chicago, crumples of red and gold and pale brown skittering around at the curbs. I was sitting on a bench, Davy in my lap and a book in my hand, keeping one eye on Maggie on the slide while surreptitiously watching the other mothers when this woman—Brett, though I didn't know that then—sat down on a bench across the playground from me, wearing white gloves.

No, we are not of the white-glove generation, not really. Yes, I did wear them to Mass when I was a girl, along with a silly doily on my head, but this was 1967—we're talking miniskirts and tie-dyed shirts and platform shoes. Or maybe not tie-dye and platforms yet—maybe those came later, just before Izod shirts with the collars up—but miniskirts. At any rate, it was definitely not a white-glove time, much less in the park on a Wednesday morning.

What in the world? I thought. *Does this girl think she's Jackie Kennedy?* (Thinking "girl," yes, but back then it had no attitude in it, no "gi-rl.") And I was wondering if she might go with the ramshackle house beyond the playground—a sagging white clapboard mansion that had been something in its day, you could see that, with its grandly columned entrance, its still magnificent palm tree, its long, flat spread of lawn—when a mother just settling at the far end of my bench said, "She wears them all the time."

Those were Linda's very first words to me: "She wears them all the time."

I don't as a rule gossip about people I've never met with other people I've never met, even women like Linda, who, just from the look of her, seemed she'd be nice to know. She was blond and fit and . . . well, just Linda, even then wearing a red Stanford baseball cap, big white letters across the front and the longest, thickest blond braid sticking out the back—when girls didn't wear baseball caps either, or concern themselves with being fit rather than just plain thin.

"You were staring," Linda said. That's Linda for you. She's nothing if not frank.

"Oh," I said, still stuck on that baseball cap of hers, thinking even Gidget never wore a baseball cap, not the Sandra Dee movie version or the Sally Field TV one.

"I don't mean to criticize," she said. "Everyone does."

"Criticize?"

"Stare at her." Linda shifted slightly, and I saw then that she was pregnant, though just barely. "You're new to the neighborhood?" she asked.

"No, we . . ." I adjusted my cat's-eye glasses, a nervous habit my mom had forever tried to break me of. "My husband and I might be moving here after he finishes school. He has a job offer, and we . . . They showed us that little house there." I indicated the house just across Center Drive from the old mansion. "The split-level with the pink shutters?"

"Oh!" Linda said. "I thought it just sold, like, yesterday. I didn't know you'd moved in!"

"It's not sold yet. And we haven't. We won't move here until the spring."

"Oh." She looked a bit confused. "Well, you *are* going to paint the shutters, aren't you?"

As I said, Linda is nothing if not frank.

That was the first Wednesday. September 6, 1967.

When I tell people that—that I first came to the Bay Area at the end of that summer, that that's when the Wednesday Sisters first met—they inevitably get this look in their eyes that says bell-bottoms and flower power, war protests and race riots, LSD. Even to me, it seems a little improbable in retrospect that I never saw a joint back then, never flashed anyone a peace sign. But I had a three-year-old daughter and a baby son already. I had a husband who'd passed the draft age, who would have a Ph.D. and a full-time job within months. I'd already settled into the life I'd been raised to settle into: dependable daughter, good wife, attentive mother. All the Wednesday Sisters had. We spent the Summer of Love changing diapers, going to the grocery store, baking tuna casseroles and knitting sweater vests (yes, sweater vests), and watching Walter Cronkite from the safety of our family rooms. I watched the local news, too, though that was more about following the Cubs; they'd just lost to the Dodgers, ending a three-game winning streak—not much, three games, but then they are the Cubs and were even that year, despite Fergie Jenkins throwing 236 strikeouts and Ron Santo hitting 31 out of the park.

Anyway, I was sitting there watching Maggie on the slide, about to call to her to clear away from the bottom when she did it on her own, and I was just a bit intimidated by this blonde I didn't know yet was Linda, and that occurred to me, that I didn't know her name. "I'm Frankie O'Mara," I said, forgetting that I'd decided to be Mary, or at least Mary Frances or Frances or Fran, in this new life. I tried to back up and say "Mary Frances O'Mara"—it was the way I liked to imagine my name on the cover of a novel someday, not that I would have admitted to dreams beyond marriage and motherhood back then. But Linda was already all over Frankie.

"Frankie? A man's name—and you all curvy and feminine. I wish I had curves like you do. I'm pretty much just straight up and down."

I'd have traded my "curves" of unlost baby gain for what was under her double-knit slacks and striped turtleneck in a second, or I thought I would then. She looked like that girl in the Clairol ads—"If you can't beat 'em, join 'em"—except she was more "If you can't join 'em, beat 'em" somehow. She didn't wear a speck of makeup, either, not even lipstick.

"What are you reading, Frankie?" she asked.

(In fairness, I should explain here that Linda remembers that first morning differently. She swears her first words were "What's that you're reading?" and it was only when I didn't answer—too busy staring at Brett to hear her, she says—that she said, "She wears them all the time." She swears what brought us together was the book in my hand. That's how she and Kath met, too; they got to talking about *In Cold Blood* at a party while everyone was still slogging through the usual blather about the lovely Palo Alto weather and how lucky they were that their husbands were doing their residencies here.)

I held up the cover of my book—Agatha Christie's latest Poirot novel, *The Third Girl*—for Linda to see. She blinked blond lashes over eyes that had a little of every color in them, like the blue and green and yellow of broken glass all mixed together in the recycling bin.

"A mystery?" she said. "Oh."

She preferred "more serious fiction," she said—not unkindly, but still I was left with the impression that she ranked my mysteries right down there with comic books. I was left shifting uncomfortably in my pleated skirt and sweater set, wondering how I'd ever manage in a place where even the books I read were all wrong. I couldn't imagine, then, leaving my friends back home, the girls who'd shared sleepless slumber-party nights and double dates with me, who still wore my clothes and lipstick and blush. Though it had never been quite the same after we'd all married. My Danny had seemed so . . . not awkward, exactly, but uncomfortable with my friends. And they weren't any easier with him. "He's such a brain," Theresa had said just a few weeks before, and I'd said, "He is, isn't he?" with a spanking big grin on my face, I'm sure, and it was only the doubt in Theresa's eyes that told me she hadn't meant it as praise. The conversation had left me feeling fat and desolate and drowning in filthy diapers, and when Danny came home from class that same evening talking about a job in California, I said, "California? I've always wanted to see California," at once imagining dinner parties with Danny's co-workers and their wives and weekend picnics at the beach and a whole new set of friends who would never imagine that Danny was one thing and I was another, even if we were.

Another gal pushed a baby buggy up to our bench just then, a big-haired, big-chinned brunette who had already pulled a book from her bag and was handing it to Linda, saying she'd finished it at two that morning. "No love story, but I liked it anyway. Thanks," she said, her *y*'s clipped, her *i*'s lingering on into forever. Mississippi, I thought, though that was probably because of the book: *To Kill a Mocking-bird.*

Linda, polite as anything, was introducing us, saying, "Kath, this is Frankie . . ." Frowning then, clearly drawing a blank on my last name.

"Mary Frances O'Mara," I said, remembering this time: Mary Frances or Frances or Fran.

"Frankie is moving into that cute little house with the awful pink shutters," Linda said.

"*Linda,*" Kath said.

"In the spring, right?" Linda said.

"Maybe not that house," I said.

"Oh, right. She hasn't bought it yet. But when she does, she's going to paint the shutters."

"*Lin-da!*" Kath blinked heavily darkened lashes straight at her friend's lack of manners. Then to me, "You can see why she doesn't have a friend in this whole wide world except me, bless her cold, black heart."

Kath said how pleased she was meet to me, her head bobbing and her shoulders bobbing along with it, some sort of Southern-girl upper-body dance that said more loudly than she could have imagined that she was an agreeable person, that she just wanted to be liked. I said, "Me, too," nodding as well, but careful to keep my shoulders straight and square and still; probably I'd done a Midwestern version of that head bob all my life.

Kath began to unpack her baby from the stroller, placing a clean white diaper over the shoulder of her spotless blouse first, the careful pink of her perfect nails—the same pink as her lipstick—lingering on baby hair as neatly combed as her own, which was poufy at the top and flipping up at the ends the way it does only if you set it, with a big fat braid wrapped above her bangs like a headband. Not a real braid like Linda's, but a fake one exactly the color of her hair. Still, it was easy to imagine that she slept propped up on pillows so her hair in big rollers would dry through, and that when it rained her hair might revert to disaster like mine did, even when it didn't get wet. She wasn't like my girlfriends back home, exactly, but she was more like them than Linda was. Not Twiggy thin. Not Doris Day blond.

Although Linda had lent Kath *To Kill a Mockingbird*. There was that.

"How old?" I asked Kath, glancing down at my own three-month-old Davy.

"This punkin?" Kath said, admiring her little Lacy. "She's three months. My Lee-Lee—Madison Leland Montgomery the Fifth, he is really—he's three and a half. And Anna Page—"

A young girl with Kath's same chin, her same chestnut hair left alone to fall in its own random waves under a straw hat with a black grosgrain band, tore off across the park, the hat flying back off her head, tumbling into the sand behind her. She tripped and slid in the sand herself, and her dress (this smocked thing with white lace at the cuffs and neck) . . . well, you could see she was not a girl who kept her dresses clean. But she picked herself up without so much as a pout and continued on to the jungle gym, where she climbed to the top cross bar and hung upside down, her sandy dress falling over her face.

"I swear, she'll be drinking bourbon straight out of the bottle before she's eighteen," Kath said.

Linda asked Kath who was coming to her Miss America party that Saturday night, then, and they started talking together about the other doctors' wives they'd met—or the residents' wives, to be precise. Kath had grown up in Louisville, Kentucky, and Linda in Connecticut. They'd both just moved to Palo Alto. They didn't know any more people than I did, really. But they'd spent every Miss America Saturday they could remember gathering with their girlfriends to watch the pageant, like I had, all of us imagining taking that victory walk ourselves even if we were the homeliest things in town. Or Kath had always watched with her girlfriends, anyway, and Linda left the impression she had, too. She didn't say anything that first afternoon about how lonely her childhood had been.

● ● ●

I WATCHED THE PAGEANT in my hotel room that Saturday night, rooting for Miss Illinois while Maggie slept and Davy nursed and Danny was out drinking beers with the Fairchild Semiconductor fellows he would join that spring after he finished school. I lay there on the generic flowered bedspread in the beige-walled room, watching in color—that, at least, was nice—and wondering which contestant Linda and Kath and all the other Stanford doctors' wives were rooting for, and if the Fairchild wives got together to watch the pageant, too. I imagined my girlfriends back home in Chicago watching without me this year. I imagined a future of watching Miss America by myself, rooting for Miss Illinois while all the neighbors I didn't know rooted for Miss California, or for Miss Whatever-State-They'd-Moved-to-California-From.

The winner that year was Miss Kansas, a near twin of the reigning Miss America who crowned her. She looked like a too-eager-to-please Mary Tyler Moore, if you can imagine such a thing, with gobs of brunette hair piled so high it stuck up above her crown. When she walked the Miss America walk, I was afraid that shiny thing would slide right off her head and plaster someone. She played a lovely piano, though. She played "Born Free."

2

W E WEREN'T the Wednesday Sisters when I first moved to
Palo Alto that next spring, of course. We'd only met that
once, when it hadn't been all that hard for me to meet people, when I
wasn't really looking for anything, I was just looking. But it's a harder
thing to do to go out and say, "Hi, I'm new to the neighborhood and
I don't know a soul." The nights were the worst, the hours after Mags
and Davy went to sleep and before Danny got home, while he was
working late or getting to know his co-workers over a beer at the
Wagon Wheel. I'd sit on the front porch reading or simply looking out
at that old mansion, its disrepair softened by the night's darkness,
leaving it looking mysterious and rather romantic. A Miss Havisham
house, that's what Danny called it, and he was right, or nearly right:
the woman who'd built it was not a Dickens character but a real
woman with real sadness to bear, one who'd lost first her husband
and then her only child, her daughter, Eleanor, for whom the park
was named.

No one lived in the mansion any longer. It was a museum of sorts,
and hardly that. It was open to the public only one Sunday a month,
to comply with the provisions of the woman's grant of the property to
the city, to keep it from reverting to her heirs. But staring across the

long lawn that ran beside the playground to the circle of drive in front of the abandoned old place, a circle that connected to nothing, not to the road or to any of the other homes, I imagined the old woman coming out onto the porch in the evening, sitting on the rickety Victorian rocker, looking down the drive that must once have come a long, straight, empty stretch to Center, just across from my house. I imagined her looking across at a lonely newcomer sitting on my front step, looking back at her. I imagined her standing and walking down her drive, crossing the street, saying, "Welcome to the neighborhood, Mary Frances," and telling me about the families that had lived here before me, saying she was sure we'd be happy here. "How could you live in a house with such wonderful pink shutters and fail to be happy?" she'd say.

When I saw Linda and Kath in the park the first sunny morning after we'd moved in, I tripped on the curb hurrying to join them—familiar faces!—and arrived at their bench with grass-stained palms. I introduced myself as Mary as I let Mags head off to the swings.

"Mary Frances," I said, suddenly uncertain—if anyone called me Mary, would I realize they were talking to me? "I met you last fall, didn't I?"

The way they looked at me, I felt I'd interrupted. "Mary Frances?" Kath said. "Oh. Of course." But you could tell by the look in her heavily mascaraed eyes that she didn't remember me.

"You're Kathy, right?" I said, saying Kathy instead of Kath as if I weren't quite sure I remembered right, my hand going to my glasses. "And Linda?" As if I only dimly recalled that she had two daughters who were Maggie's age, twins born in different years, Jamie just before midnight, December 31, 1963, Julie a half hour later, on January 1.

"That's right, I'm Linda." Linda smiled a little, her blond lashes blinking as she shifted her newborn in her lap. "That's right."

Brett, in her white gloves, showed up across the park then, just as I was settling onto a bench that cornered Kath and Linda's bench, putting Davy and his favorite trucks on a blanket in front of me.

"Lordy, I haven't seen that girl all winter," Kath said to Linda. "I thought maybe she'd moved away."

They stared as she settled her daughter into a baby swing—stared at her long, thin nose and her thin little face and her thin legs, stick legs, really. Skinny, you'd call her. Like Twiggy, but without the poise despite the white gloves. Only her hair was remarkable: the most gorgeous strawberry blond, cut into a pageboy that her tiny ears peeked through now and then. Without that hair, she might have disappeared entirely; you might not even have noticed the gloves.

Linda lowered her voice theatrically. "Maybe she slit her wrists," she said to Kath. "Maybe she wears them because her wrists are jagged blue with scars and—"

"I swear on my aunt Tooty's grave, Linda!" Kath glanced in my direction and lowered her voice. "Didn't I tell you not to scare off one more gal before I got in a how-do-you-do?"

I settled back against the bench, the wooden slats more giving than I expected. "Maybe she lives in that falling-down mansion," I offered.

Linda, with a see-I-didn't-scare-her glance at Kath—a glance clearly meant to include me—turned away from the swings to consider the old wreck of a place. For a moment I thought she had in mind to march right up to the front door and demand someone give the poor house a new coat of paint.

Maggie, waiting for her swing to defy all those crazy rules about objects at rest staying at rest, shouted for me. I called, "Pump your legs, for goodness sakes, Mags!" which drew Brett's attention. She said something to Maggie and gave her a little push, all the while smiling toward me.

"She slit her wrists in the old mansion," Linda said, still facing the mansion, her back to Brett, as was Kath's.

Shhh, I thought. *She'll hear us.*

"And she lay in the bathtub bleeding all over the place until her handsome neighbor, wondering why it was so quiet—"

"Came over and whacked that ol' door down with a wood ax to get in!" Kath said just as Brett pushed her daughter all the way through so the little girl was swinging delightfully high beside my Maggie, and Brett herself emerged on our side of the swings, just a few yards away. She ran a gloved hand through her short red hair, leaving it unkempt, then glanced back—her daughter wasn't swinging *too* wildly—and took a tentative step toward us.

I was avoiding eye contact with her, saying, "Linda," meaning to hush her, when Kath said, "You look at her sometimes when she thinks nobody's looking at her. I'll bet she slit her wrists!" and Linda said, "What?"

"*Kath,*" I said, but Kath was already saying, "You know, like 'I'll bet he killed a man'?"

"From *The Great Gatsby,*" Brett said.

Even Linda—who is usually so cool—turned and stared open-mouthed at Brett, no doubt thinking, *Shoot, how much has she overheard?*

I adjusted my glasses, trying to think of something to say.

"Are you partial to the book?" Kath asked—which sounded ridiculous, like a bad pickup line at a Rush Street bar, but Brett just replied that it was an evocative line, wasn't it: " 'I'll bet he killed a man.' "

Kath said, for my benefit in case I hadn't read the book, that the line was from a cocktail-party scene where the host wasn't even at his own party. She'd just read *Gatsby*—or reread it for the fourth time, actually. She's not like Brett. She can't spout lines from novels at will.

It was one of Kath's favorite novels, *The Great Gatsby.* We all loved it, for different reasons. Linda wanted to be the golfer, Jordan Baker, while Brett wanted to be Gatsby—she's never said so, but believe me, she did. I guess I must have identified with Nick Carraway, watching the world from the fringes. And Kath grew up imagining she was Daisy and all the men in the world adored her. Yes, Daisy. She even admitted it, years later. "Of course I wanted to be Daisy. She's what I was *raised* to aspire to be, a nice girl married to a filthy rich man." To which Linda said, "A nice, *vacuous* girl," and Kath said, "Right," and Linda said, "Whose husband kept a *mistress*, Kath," and Kath, to her credit, said "Right" again. But as I said, that was years later.

That Wednesday, Brett gathered Sarah from her swing and settled her with Davy and his trucks, she and Kath already gossiping about old F. Scott like he was a neighbor. We talked about books that whole morning, hiding behind our favorite fictions, revealing ourselves slowly as the children ran on the playground or slept in their buggies or squirmed in our arms.

Kath loved anything by Jane Austen, which Linda said was fine "if you could stand all that happy-wedding-ending nonsense." To which Kath said, without the least hesitation, that she was a happy-ending kind of gal and even Linda couldn't shame her into being anything else.

Linda was decidedly not a happy-ending gal. Her favorite book was *The Bell Jar*. "By Victoria Lucas, which everyone knows is a pseudonym for Sylvia Plath," she said.

"Well I guess I'm just a li'l ol' nobody, then," Kath said, "because I surely didn't know." And Brett and I both admitted we'd never even heard of the novel, though we both loved Plath's poetry.

" 'First, are you our sort of a person?' " Brett said. " 'Do you wear—' "

"The novel hasn't been published here yet," Linda explained. It wasn't, it turns out, supposed to be available in the U.S. even under a pseudonym until after Plath's mother died. "But I found a British copy at a bookstore near my brother's apartment in New York. It's about this girl who's trying to be a writer but her mother and her fiancé just assume it's a dalliance she'll give up when her real life— marriage and babies—begins."

"A writer," I said. "If I could have written anything, it would be *Rebecca*."

"Wouldn't you just die and be buried in a croaker sack to live in a house like Manderley?" Kath said just as Linda said, "Do you write, Mary?" with a hopefulness in her voice that made me look around, confused: *Who in the world is Mary?* In the moment it took me to realize *I* was Mary—of course I was—she said, *"Frankie! You're Frankie. I knew Mary wasn't right."*

"Mary Frances, but sometimes I go by Frankie," I said.

We all looked at each other, and there was a moment when I might have admitted I used to try to write before Maggie was born, when we all might have confessed to dreams we'd once dreamed. We were still just strangers who'd met in a park, though, and so Linda said, "I love that name, Frankie," and she started in on what color my shutters should be painted. "Dark green, like on that house there," she suggested, pointing to a house past the intersection at Center and Channing, one with shutters the green of the circle of pine trees in the front yard, with a bare spot in the middle where the original pine must have been before it died. Just as we turned to look, a curtain dropped to cover the front window of the house—Ally's house, it would turn out—but if anyone else noticed, they didn't say so. They considered color possibilities for my shutters until Linda's girls came squawking over, deep in some four-year-olds' dispute. Then Davy accidentally bonked Brett's Sarah on the head with a truck (at least I hoped it was an accident), and we were all a flurry of realizing it was lunchtime and we needed to get the children home and fed and down for their naps.

Linda, coaxing J.J. into his stroller, looked to Brett and asked, as if it were pure afterthought, "Wherever did you find those gloves . . . what did you say your name was?"

Brett, unfazed, replied, "I'm Brett Tyler."

You could practically see Linda gearing up to ask again about the gloves, but Kath cut her off, saying, "Well, nice to meet you, Brett."

Linda shot Kath a look but said only, "And welcome to the neighborhood, Frankie," leaving me to set off with Maggie and Davy toward the empty front porch of my pink-shuttered house, thinking, *It could be worse, I could be* Fanny, *but still.*

3

I'D BEEN MEETING Linda and Kath and Brett in the park every Wednesday for six weeks by the day we met Ally, the day we learned about Linda's mom. Any other day, it would have seemed the oddest thing, Ally arriving in the park to offer iced tea to strangers she'd never in her life seen before—or that's what we thought, that she'd never seen us. But early that morning, Bobby Kennedy had been shot at the Ambassador Hotel in Los Angeles, and the whole country was waiting with the same held breath, and nobody was a stranger, no one wanted to be alone.

"I'm Ally Tantry," Ally said in a shy, almost whispering voice, and we all turned to see this unfamiliar mom: big brown eyes in a pale-as-white-flour face; full-length batik cotton skirt and sandals; dark hair that fell to her waist in smooth, shiny waves. She wanted only a fresh-daisy headband to look like one of those flower children on the news.

None of us could have said how long she'd been standing there, with her pitcher of iced tea and five matching plastic cups.

We all introduced ourselves: "Linda Mason." "Katherine Claire Montgomery." "Brett Tyler." I said I was Mary Frances O'Mara, not that it did me any good. Then we all looked a little awkward for a minute until Ally offered us tea and filled a cup for each of us, nearly emptying the clear plastic pitcher, leaving only half a cup for herself, but she said she didn't mind.

Over the weeks before that, our conversations had broadened from books to things we'd read in the paper or seen on the news. Linda had gone on and on one week about a woman who'd snuck into the Boston Marathon using her initials, who'd finished only because some men running with her had physically prevented officials from throwing her off the course. That was as personal as it had gotten, though: us saying what we thought about the Columbia student uprising or the Paris peace talks, or what we liked and didn't like in a book—or not saying about John Updike's *Couples* after Kath declared it a "dirty book," which speaks volumes, too. But that morning, by way of explaining ourselves to Ally, we talked about what our husbands did, which was how we defined ourselves in those days: I'm a doctor's wife, a painter's wife, the wife of the president of the United States.

Brett said her husband, Chip, was a small-particle physicist working at SLAC. "The Stanford Linear Accelerator. You know: for experiments in high-energy physics and synchrotron radiation research," she said, and Kath and Linda and I said, "Oh, sure," to which Ally responded in her soft voice, "Heavens to Betsy, you all understood that?" Brett understood it all, though; she'd graduated Phi Beta Kappa from Radcliffe, with majors in math, physics, and English literature, of all things, and she'd done graduate work in physics, to boot.

Linda said Jeff was a doctor at Stanford, and Kath said Lee was, too.

Ally told us her Jim was a lawyer at a new law firm called Wilson, Mosher & Martin. You could see in her puppy-brown eyes that she couldn't help bragging about how he had been editor in chief of the *Michigan Law Review*. Linda, whose brother was a lawyer, asked, "Why didn't he go to a good firm, then? One on Wall Street or in Chicago or San Francisco?" If Ally had had puppy ears to match her eyes, they would have drooped like she'd just been told there would be no walk today, but she said only, "Jim didn't get other offers," with an edge of anger in her voice that left even Linda silent.

They'd all met their husbands in college, except Kath, who'd met Lee in high school but had gone to Vanderbilt with him.

I told them my Danny developed large-scale integrated circuits, throwing the term out as if I had any idea what it meant. He'd started at Northwestern University when he was sixteen, and he'd just finished his Ph.D., I said. I worked in the engineering school recruiting office—that's how Danny and I met, but I didn't say that. I didn't say anything that morning about how invisible I'd felt at my secretary's desk before I met Danny, with the students stopping by to check their interview schedules or drop off more twenty-four-pound linen bond résumés without so much as a "Good morning, Miss Downes," much less a "How about that game last night, Frankie, fourteen innings of shutout lost on one lousy reliever's pitch?" I just went on about Danny's job at Fairchild, making it sound like the job of a lifetime.

We talked about Kennedy being shot then, and about whether the brain surgery he'd had that morning would save him, and what the loss of blood supply to part of his brain might mean. We talked, too, about grandparents and cousins and neighbors who'd died. None of them were parents of young children, though. That broke our hearts more than anything, imagining those poor Kennedy children left without a daddy, like John-John at President Kennedy's funeral with his little hand up in salute and no idea yet that dead meant he'd never see his daddy again.

Then Linda, who'd been strangely quiet, said, "My mom died when I was nine."

"Heavens, you poor thing," Ally said softly, and we all looked to our children, to where Anna Page had a whole crew digging in the sand: our gang and two boys who were often here together, one still in diapers and the other in a Mickey Mouse T-shirt, and a little girl with dark, loose curls and skin as pale as Ally's. Here we were, holding Bobby Kennedy's shooting apart from our own lives—he was running for president, and our own husbands would never run for president—and Linda just brought it right home, right into our safe little lives.

"Nine, gosh. That's hardly old enough to get a whippin'," Kath said, and it was clear that she hadn't known about this before, either, even though she was Linda's best friend.

Breast cancer, it was, and Linda's mother not even forty.

Linda would tell us later that she never saw her mother in the hospital. She didn't know if it was hospital rules or her father's, but she and her brothers weren't allowed to visit their mom. They'd had no warning she was going away the morning of her surgery, either, though in retrospect Linda supposes her mother's voice did crack as she hugged her and said, as she did each school morning, "I hope you have a wonderful day." She supposes her mother even smelled different that morning—not of hair spray, not of lipstick—although she doesn't remember for sure. What she does remember is ducking out of her mother's embrace, afraid she'd be late for school. "But maybe it wasn't like that at all," she says. "Everything about that time is so mixed up in my mind."

Everything except the way her mother looked when she came home from the hospital. It was midafternoon, Linda and her brothers were just arriving home from school, and in their excitement they rushed toward the car in the driveway. Her father intercepted them and ordered them to wait quietly inside until their mother was settled in bed. He ushered them into the kitchen, leaving the nurse he'd hired—a big woman, scary big, Linda remembers—to help her mom upstairs while he poured himself a glass of something from the liquor cabinet. When he caught Linda staring at him—she knew there was something wrong with him pouring that drink even if she didn't quite know what—he said, "Go see your mother now, Linda. Just one at a time. All of you at once will be too much for her."

He drained his glass. "Go on, go," he said. "Don't keep her waiting."

Linda remembers the weight of her legs as she climbed the stairs, the hushed scrape of her leather soles on the wood, the smell as she approached her parents' bedroom, like flowers left too long in a vase. She remembers the terror she felt as she stopped in the doorway, the look of her shoes, scuffed and dirty against the clean carpet, the lines where she'd run the vacuum before school that morning so the room would be nice for her mom.

"My favorite daughter," her mother said, which was what she often called Linda, and it was true of course, because Linda was her mother's *only* daughter. Linda had always heard "favorite child" though, and she'd always felt that, always felt her mother loved her best.

When she raised her eyes to the bed that afternoon, though, the mother she saw didn't match the voice. She remembers thinking they'd taken her mother away and returned something empty, a Coke bottle with the top flipped off, with the sweet liquid drained and nothing left inside. Her hair was flat and awful, and where her bosom had been full and soft and welcoming, it was empty. But it was her arm that frightened Linda most—this grotesquely swollen thing, more the size of a leg. Years later, Jeff brought home an old stethoscope and some booties and hairnets and surgical gloves for the children to play doctor with. He blew two of the gloves up and tied them off, like balloons. One for Julie, one for Jamie. They'd come running to Linda to show her their prizes, and it had been all she could do not to scream. The balloons had been her mother's hand: that colorless, that lifeless, that distorted.

"Climb up here and snuggle with me, sweetheart," her mother had said that afternoon, the way she did when Linda had a nightmare. But her mother wasn't her mother anymore, she was that hideous arm, and Linda turned and ran to her bedroom, where her father found her sometime later, curled up in the closet, sobbing, with the closet door shut.

He kicked some shoes out of the way and sat next to her on the closet floor. He pulled the door closed again, leaving them together in the mothball, dirty-sock semidarkness, the crack of daylight where the door wasn't quite shut falling on Linda. He just sat there, his face staring at the inside of the closet door, not saying a word, not touching her. After a few minutes, he pushed the door open, stood, and without looking at her, said, "I'll need your help with the dinner, honey." And Linda stood and followed him down to the kitchen, where she scrounged in the pantry for a box of macaroni and cheese while her father filled a pot with water from the tap.

Linda didn't tell us any of that in the park that morning, though.

It would come later, not all at once, but in pieces over the years. I came to know the story of Linda's mom the way we came to know everything about each other, I suppose. The way friends who are as close as we are know the important moments in each other's lives, even when we weren't there.

That Wednesday morning, Linda just stared silently out at the playground. We all did, watching our children a little more closely, thinking we didn't want them even to imagine growing up without us to kiss their skinned elbows and applaud their finger paintings and tuck them into their beds.

"When I was a kid, I used to climb up into this big oak tree in our backyard, where no one would see me," Linda said. "I'd straddle one of its fat branches, lean against the trunk, and read until the bark left dents in my skin. *Charlotte's Web.* I read it over and over, a dozen times at least."

"Me, too," Ally said quietly. "Over and over."

"It was like Wilbur, this male pig, was more like me than anyone at school," Linda said, "because he knew about dying."

"'After all, what's a life, anyway? We're born, we live a little while, we die,'" Brett said, just quoting from the book, but her words left us all staring at Linda.

Linda looked away, to the sad old mansion. "Charlotte's children didn't need her," she said finally, quietly.

I think we all leaned more closely together on the park bench then, trying not to think of those poor Kennedy children. Of Ethel Kennedy sitting at the hospital in Los Angeles, wondering if her husband would ever regain consciousness. Of Rose at home in Hyannis Port, facing the loss of a third son. Three sons. How could you bear that, to lose three sons?

$\mathcal{L}$INDA AND KATH and Brett and I left Ally sitting on the park bench that morning. She was just going to stay a bit longer, she said. But even after I put Maggie and Davy down for their naps, called Danny—he was in a meeting—and made myself a cup of coffee, I could see Ally through the plate glass of my living room window, sitting in the same spot on that bench, her plastic cups stacked one inside the other and abandoned in the empty pitcher, her rounded shoulders in her muslin blouse still as death. All the mothers were packing up to take their children home for lunch, but Ally didn't move. And when I looked again, all the mothers were gone except Ally, who sat there alone, one hand absently fingering a lock of long, wavy, dark hair. She got up and left, finally, with only the empty pitcher, the five empty cups. She hurried off with her head bowed, her legs striding the width of her long skirt, and she went into the house with the green shutters, with the cluster of pine trees in the front. You might think I'd have gone running out my door, calling, "Ally, honey, you're forgetting your little one!" But I didn't. There was no child left in the park.

4

THERE WAS A FAINT LIGHT in one of the mansion windows
that night as I settled onto my front-porch steps to wait for
Danny. I'd heard the place was haunted, that when the wind was
blowing just right you could hear the ghost of the old woman who'd
built it playing melancholy organ music, or weeping in the attic, or
calling for her dead child. But there were always stories about places
being haunted, especially old mansions like this one, with tragic tales
behind them. And though I believed in the Holy Spirit and Jesus rising from the dead and visiting the apostles, Doubting Thomas putting
his hand through Jesus' wounded side, I dismissed people who believed in ghosts as overly dramatic and absurd. I figured the light was
the street lamp behind the house coming through the window, the reflection of car lights off a pane, the night watchman or the cleaning
staff. Or maybe I was imagining the light, imagining a ghost to go
with the faint strains of melancholy piano music coming from somewhere in that direction.

Someone checking on the place, I decided. A policeman's flashlight, one of Palo Alto's finest making sure everything was okay
(which was reassuring, given the way hippies and radicals had begun
gathering in downtown Lytton Plaza).

Except that this looked more like . . . well, it looked warmer, more flickering.

The light went out entirely then, just like that, leaving me staring into the glass-window darkness.

A few minutes later, a car came to a stop at the corner. Danny? But it continued straight on Channing and pulled into Ally's drive. A slender, dark-skinned man got out and slipped in through Ally's front door without knocking or ringing the bell that I could tell. I glanced at my watch—*eleven o'clock already?* But I forgot all about Ally then, because Danny came home talking about quitting Fairchild, leaving his nice, stable job at his nice, stable company with its nice, stable salary to join a new company that wasn't even a company yet, just a handful of scientists and engineers putting their heads together at someone's house, with no certain future at all. "NM Electronics, it's going to be called," he said.

And not a month later, my steady, one-job-one-wife-for-life Danny up and gave notice at work.

"You quit?" I said. "Danny! But you just started!" And the job he was talking about now didn't even seem to be the NM Enterprises job he'd been talking about—though it turned out it *was* the same job; the company had just settled on a different name.

"Andy is tired of watching our work languish between development and production at Fairchild," Danny said, "and I'm jumping ship with him. These guys, Frankie, they have a plan to make larger-scale integrated circuits mass-producible!" Words hard enough for me to understand in isolation, much less strung together like that, though Brett, of course, would understand it all. "They're trying to develop a new way for computers to store and access data, something faster and more powerful than ferrite core," she said when I told her the next day, and I said, "Oh, sure, to replace ferrite core," as if that cleared it right up.

Yes, the business was riskier than Fairchild, Danny admitted. They were still meeting in people's houses, though they'd signed a lease for space starting August 1, offices that would turn out to be small and cramped and full of the old tenant's left-behind furniture, with pipes poking out of the ceiling and holes in the floor of the manufacturing space. And the company wasn't even *expected* to make a

profit for a year or more, though there would be money to pay his salary, Danny assured me. A venture capitalist (the first time I'd heard that term) was helping them find investors.

"People are lining up, knocking on the door for the job Andy says *I'm* the perfect guy for, Frankie," Danny said. And Danny is not above liking to be flattered; I should know.

"Silicon-gate MOS," he said. "That's my baby."

I thought I was your baby, I wanted to say. *I thought Fairchild was the opportunity of a lifetime.* Wasn't that why we'd moved so far from home? *I thought we talked about big decisions like this before we made them,* I wanted to say. We *had* talked about it, though, and after five years of marriage I should have been used to the way Danny made decisions when he had to make them: while I was still eyeing the airplane from the ground, he was up above the clouds with the door open, sure his parachute would work.

So many Bay Area parachutes didn't work, though, or didn't work fast enough. The earth shifted beneath them before they could land. Technology-business failures were so common that a *Business-Week* cartoon that fall would parody the risk: crowds piling in and out the doors and windows of an "Integrated Circuits" building while a salesman asks, "Want a beam-leaded MSI Flip-Flop Chip in MOS-Compatible DTL?" and another says, "That went out back in July!" But it wouldn't be funny if Danny's MOS chip was one of the technologies that crashed.

"They're giving me a thousand options," he said. "I'll be an owner, Frankie, without even having to put any money up!" And he started talking about investing our savings in his fledgling company's stock, too, once they'd set up an employee stock-purchase plan. But what about the kids' college fund? What about the mortgage and the groceries and the doctor bills? How would we pay them if the company failed and we were left with no savings to live on while Danny found another position? What if the company was a smashing success but the treasurer absconded to Brazil with all the cash? But to question Danny's decision would make him think I lacked confidence in him. And besides, he'd already quit.

5

WE LAUGH NOW at how nervous I was before our first Miss
America party that September, the first time we moved beyond meeting up at the park on Wednesday mornings. I hurried to finish my curtains and cleaned my kitchen so you could have eaten off
the cabinet floor under my sink, I swear, and I even considered painting my shutters, though in truth I was liking the pink more and more.
That evening, I set up a bar on the kitchen counter and put out
snacks, and I sent Danny off with Mags and Davy for hot dogs and
ice cream at the Dairy Queen, with instructions not to return until the
children were fast asleep in the backseat of the car.

Danny wasn't the least bit disappointed to miss the pageant himself. Funny, isn't it? No fellow I'd ever known would sit through a
beauty contest; the gawking at beautiful women was done by us girls.

Ally was the first to ring my bell that evening. I'd seen no signs of
her child the week after we met: no tricycle left in the circle of pine
trees, no Ally hurrying her little one to the car, no playmates knocking at the door. There might have been toys in the backyard, but it
was wrapped up in a high wooden fence you couldn't see over or
through, and that had seemed to me to mean something, too. But Ally
had turned up the following Wednesday with the hand of two-year-

old Carrie in her grasp. Ally's husband must have fetched their daughter from the park while I was putting my kids down for their naps that first week, I supposed, for a doctor's appointment or some father-daughter something, because Ally and Carrie—a quiet little thing with Ally's dark wavy hair, her chipmunk cheeks—arrived at the park again the next Wednesday, and the next.

Within minutes, Kath and Linda and Brett had arrived at my door, too, and we were settling into my family room with potato chips and sour-cream dip and popcorn made in a pan on the stove, and with gin and tonics or vodka gimlets or, for Kath, a sidecar—not that far evolved from Anna Page's bourbon straight out of the bottle. We felt awkward outside the familiar surroundings of the park, though, unwilling even to take the first chip from the bowl. We started talking about who we would root for, with Bert Parks not even on the TV yet.

What *was* on was special coverage from outside the pageant, hundreds of women picketing like autoworkers without a contract: girls in tidy dresses or skirts and blouses, wearing shoes like we wore, their hair styled like ours. Four hundred women walking up and down the Atlantic City boardwalk, from Florida and from Wisconsin and from California just like the girls inside putting on their makeup and gowns, except that these girls were carrying signs and some were swinging bras like lassos and chanting slogans as they dumped mops and steno pads and girdles into a big trash can.

"Can you imagine not wearing . . ." Ally asked, not saying *brassiere,* a word she spoke aloud only in the lingerie section, and even then she blushed.

I thought of Audrey Hepburn as Holly Golightly in *Breakfast at Tiffany's,* in that black dress with the long black gloves, the five-strand pearls and the tiara in her hair, the extravagant cigarette holder. That dress would have needed a strapless bra, and why would she bother, with nothing for a bra to hold up? And in the movie she'd left her husband behind forever to start a wild life in New York, and I'd loved her for it, and I'd sort of imagined doing something that dramatic myself. Still, I couldn't imagine doing what these real women were doing, leaving their husbands or boyfriends for one day to try to point out that women weren't just for gawking at.

Linda pulled an issue of *McCall's* from my coffee table and, keeping an eye on the protesters and awaiting the start of the pageant, flipped to an article about the balance of power in marriages. "So here's the fifty-dollar question," she said. "Are you the dominator or the dominatee?" And we leaned over the magazine, reading "The Sexual Wilderness" together, glad of the excuse to ignore those girls on the TV.

"The spouse who handles the money has the power?" Brett said. "That's definitely me."

"I'm the wily old gal who foists the money worries off on her husband," Kath said.

"The more powerful spouse chooses the friends?" I said. "Danny wouldn't know a friend if he announced himself on the evening news."

As we laughed, we all glanced at the TV. The camera was focused on a sign showing a brunette in a cowboy hat, her naked back and bottom marked into sections with labels like RIB and LOIN and CHUCK, like a cow about to be butchered. BREAK THE DULL STEAK HABIT, the sign read. The protester carrying it looked young and innocent in her paisley shift, square-necked and falling just above her knee like the one I wore that night, but still the newscaster—his beer gut hanging over his trousers—looked down on her as if *she* were the disgusting one.

We all turned away, back to the magazine. "The one who takes the car to be repaired?" Ally said. "That's an odd sign of power, if you ask me."

"Okay, so which kind of marriage are you in?" Linda asked. "A, 'The Minimal-Interaction Marriage'? That's where you and your hubby basically don't speak." She tipped her head as if to say *Go ahead, admit it, that's you.* "Or B, 'The Peripheral-Husband Marriage'? That means, near as I can tell, that you don't need your man, you just need his *paycheck*!"

"You're skipping all the good ones, Linda," Kath protested. Then to the rest of us, "Don't you know she would?" She grabbed the magazine from Linda and started reading. "'The Fun Marriage'? That's you and Jeff, Linda. I have never heard anyone giggle together like you two. 'The Colleague Marriage'? That's you, Brett, 'cause you're just as clever as Chip is, I'm sure, even if I never have met the fella. 'The Nestling Marriage'—that sounds awfully nice, doesn't it? That's Ally and Jim, don't y'all imagine?" (Ally blushed pink, an admission.) "And 'The High-Companionship Marriage'? That's got to be you and Danny, Frankie."

I faked a loud snore—it really did sound like the most boring of the alternatives.

"Best friends!" Kath insisted. "You do everything together, talk over every little thing in this world."

"So in which bailiwick does your own marriage fall, Kath?" Brett asked.

"Bailiwick?" Linda teased, because Brett was forever doing that, using bigger words than a situation called for.

But Kath simply smiled her big-chinned smile, closed the magazine, and held it away from Brett's reach, bobbing her head so agreeably that you might have thought her answer was E, "All of the good choices above"; you might have forgotten all about the Minimal-Interaction Marriage or the Peripheral-Husband one, you might simply have laughed like Brett and Ally and even Linda did when Kath answered, "Now, that would be telling, wouldn't it?"

The TV cut to inside finally, where Bert Parks was greeting us as if he were oblivious to the goings-on outside, though he'd refused to leave the building between the rehearsal and the show with all those protesters there. It does make you wonder, doesn't it? Was he afraid of being hit in the face with a B cup? And maybe they burned those bras that evening, and maybe they burned Bert Parks in effigy, I'm not really sure because I, like him, pretty much just tried to dismiss them, tried to pretend they hadn't taken this thing I loved watching and made me feel bad about wanting to watch.

Kath, Brett, and I declared for the contestants from our home states, Miss Kentucky, Miss Massachusetts, and Miss Illinois, all of whom were beautiful and thin, of course, and not wearing eyeglasses. Ally chose Miss Hawaii, a cute brunette you could imagine wearing the same long, informal skirts Ally wore, the kind of girl who, in the movies, is completely overlooked by the male lead while he's falling for the statuesque blonde but who ends up with the wedding ring. Only Linda refused to narrow her choices. "Not until the talent competition," she said.

"Talent? It's a *beauty* contest!" Kath insisted, but Linda, her long blond hair not in a braid that night but brushed straight and pulled back with a headband so you could see her clear skin, just raised her straight eyebrows and looked at Kath with those multicolored eyes. No makeup, but you could easily picture her in one of those swimsuits, and it didn't take much to imagine her in a pretty pink gown with a little mascara, her hair swept up in a bun—a chignon, Kath called it. Or maybe not a pink gown; for all Linda looked like a pink-gown girl, she wasn't, not back then. And she was barely even looking at the gowns. *A gown, fine,* she seemed to be saying, *but can she sing? Can she play the piano?* Or—because this is Linda we're talking about, right?—*can she hit a tennis ball like Billie Jean King or run as fast as Wilma Rudolph?* Though of course Wilma Rudolph was black and these girls were white and always had been. Laws barring non-whites from participating were still firmly in place. There was to be a second pageant that night, though, for African-American girls—black girls, we called them—starting at midnight, after the "real" Miss America was over.

"I can run fast and I can write," Linda said, a response, apparently, to Kath's "It's a beauty contest!" "Neither of which would look particularly nifty performed on TV."

Kath said she could play the piano, and Ally said she could, too.

"I'd have to fall back on my baton-twirling skills," I admitted.

"Which would trounce the test tubes or incline planes or star charts I'd be reduced to dragging out," Brett said.

And somehow we were talking about Brett's little sister. Yes, Brett had taught Jenn (and her brother, Brad, too, for that matter) how to focus a telescope, how to mix potassium perchlorate and aluminum powder, how to distinguish a blood cell from one of bone. Still, Brett never imagined Jenn would be applying to medical school. Brad, yes, but her sister?

Ally said she'd thought about being a nurse but she couldn't imagine cleaning bedpans, and I glanced surreptitiously at Brett's gloved hands, wondering if she was afraid of germs.

"Your li'l sis is fixin' to be a doctor?" Kath asked.

"You could still go to medical school yourself, Brett," Linda said, and Brett looked startled, as if Linda had just put her finger on a truth Brett hadn't seen, that she was jealous that her little sister was going to be something Brett had thought girls weren't supposed to be.

"Would y'all ever take your babies to see a lady doctor?" Kath asked. "Lordy, Lordy."

"Jenn doesn't want to be a pediatrician, she wants to be a surgeon," Brett said, which shocked us all; even if you could imagine a woman doctor, you pictured her working with children, like the closest doctor there was to a mom.

And all the while those girls on the TV were walking across the stage in their one-piece bathing suits, not with bathing caps on but with their hair ratted up and sprayed into place, their mascara ready to run dark black the moment they got near water.

Linda said she'd nearly gone to graduate school; she'd applied to the creative-writing program at the University of Iowa, but Jeff had wanted to go to medical school at Johns Hopkins in Baltimore (which had a fine creative-writing program, but Linda hadn't been accepted there). "And then I was pregnant with the twins and they were born and I couldn't get any sleep with them waking each other all night, much less go to school or write."

"I didn't want to be a doctor, I wanted to be an astronaut," Brett said, and we all burst out laughing, even Brett—we were getting a little tipsy. I thought for a moment that she must have been joking about her sister, too—a girl surgeon! But she wasn't kidding about any of it, you could tell that by the sudden look in her leaf-bud eyes, all shaded and down-looking and watery even as she laughed.

"You'd make a great astronaut, Brett," I said. She would have, too. Brett would have made a dynamite astronaut.

"Even before President Kennedy said we'd put a man on the moon—the 'greatest adventure on which man has ever embarked,' remember that?—Brad and I used to imagine it for ourselves," Brett said. "Even before Yuri Gagarin, we used to imagine being the first two people to step on the moon."

We were quiet for a minute then, watching Miss Illinois flip through the air over her trampoline and drinking our drinks and remembering. It had been nighttime when the Russian cosmonaut had flown over Chicago, and my whole family had gone out to watch, to see the reflection of sunlight off his capsule. But I hadn't even felt the awe of it—a man in space! I'd felt only the eerie fear of a Russian flying over me, looking down on my world.

"I'm rooting for this girl even if she is too young to win," Linda said as Miss Illinois finished her routine, and somehow Linda's choosing her seemed almost as if she was saying she thought Brett really could fly to the moon. That we all could. That, as Esther in *The Bell Jar* wanted to believe, a girl didn't have to relinquish her dreams on her wedding day.

"She looks like she walked straight out of the fifties," Ally said, "With her blond hair flipped up at the ends like on Carrie's Barbie doll."

"I expect the judges are partial to that, though," Kath said. "Lee surely is." And she took a big slug of her sidecar, then another, draining the glass.

I was about to offer her another drink—a third—when she went to the kitchen and fixed it herself. We all watched her for a moment, then tried not to watch. "Lee?" I mouthed to Linda, but she only frowned.

"I used to think it would be neat to be a writer, too, a poet or a novelist," I said, the confession spilling out with my own second drink. I'd written one novel already, a mystery set in Renaissance Italy, but I'd buried it in a drawer; even I could tell it was awful. That truth, though, would have to await considerably more alcohol.

Kath, back in the family room, fresh drink in hand, bobbed her head agreeably, but something in the set of her strong chin said *An astronaut and a novelist? You ladies are insane.*

"Or a librarian," I said, backpedaling.

"A novel," Linda said. "That's what I wanted to write, too."

"It's not like I ever really thought I could," I said. "It was just . . ."

"Like wanting to be Miss America," Ally said.

I thought of the bright red A+ circled at the top of the first poem I'd turned in to Sister Josephine, of her urging me to write for the school newspaper, and making me editor in chief. Kath was right, though: I might have been the prom queen of high school English class, but no prom queen from my little neighborhood had ever gotten to the Miss Illinois contest, much less to the Miss America walk.

"If you wanted to, Frankie," Linda said, her voice surprisingly tentative, "we could start writing together."

I glanced at the television (a mother being mistaken for her daughter in the pool because she ate Grape-Nuts), imagining frank, take-no-prisoners Linda wielding a red pen over a poem or story of mine.

"Just you and Frankie?" Kath said, and you could tell from the way she ran a finger over her fake-braid headband that she was feeling excluded.

"We could start a writing group," Linda said. "All of us."

There was a long pause, the only sound a Coke jingle on the TV, before Ally said she couldn't write and Kath said, "How about a book club?"

"But we already talk about books!" Linda said. "Wouldn't you like to try writing one?"

"Just for fun, maybe?" I said. "Nothing serious?"

Kath asked where we'd ever find time to write, and Brett, too, seemed hesitant, but Linda rolled ahead in typical Linda fashion. "You could write a *Pride and Prejudice* set in the American South, Kath—"

"*Mr. Darcy Goes to the Derby!*" I said.

"Just for fun, like Frankie said," Linda said. "It's not as if we're thinking we're going to be the next Sylvia Plath."

From the smile hinted on Brett's bow lips, I figured she was thinking what I was thinking—*Methinks she doth protest too much* (and knowing whom she was quoting, which I did not). But Linda started laying out a plan as if it had been decided: we'd all bring something we'd written to the park Wednesday; we'd move from our bench to a picnic table; we'd read our work and everyone would comment, like they'd done in Linda's college writing class. Never mind that Kath was swearing on her aunt Tooty's grave and Ally was talking about boys in high school sniggering at her poems and Brett had yet to say a single word. And the Miss America Pageant went on at its usual pace for quite some time, and not one of us could have told you what the talent was after Miss Illinois.

By the time we returned our attention to the TV, Bert Parks was announcing the finalists. Kath must have been right about the judges liking that old-fashioned hair because Miss Illinois won despite being a young, blond athlete, more cute than beautiful. "I'm so glad," Judith Ann Ford gushed from under her crown. "I feel like it's a breakthrough." And something made me shift uneasily in my paisley dress. Maybe it was the way she spoke or her silly flipped-up hairstyle, or maybe it was that protester's paisley dress or the bra strap cutting into my own shoulder, or maybe it was knowing Brett had wanted to be an astronaut and Linda wanted to be a writer even still—I don't know. But for some reason I couldn't shake the image of the naked woman on the poster, the stark black capital letters written on her skin: ROUND and RIB and RUMP.

COMMANDEERED the picnic table nearest the playground the following Wednesday, the poem that had seemed so remarkably brilliant that morning before anyone else was awake already losing its luster inside my purse. I brushed away the dried leaves and pulled the worst of the splinters from the tabletop, and I was setting out a big thermos of coffee and a plate of cookies when Kath arrived, defiantly empty-handed, followed by Ally, less defiantly so. I didn't confess to them the existence of my poem—not even after Linda arrived admitting to a few paragraphs and Brett came bearing an entire first chapter. "A whole chapter!" we said more or less in unison. Linda didn't even give her a hard time about the fact that it was a mystery.

"Really, there is no possibility I could read it aloud, though," Brett said.

Linda almost single-handedly got the kids squared away, no small task; Anna Page was back in school, a big second-grader, leaving us nine under-five-year-olds to settle in the sandbox with bowls and measuring cups and sifters. "If everyone is good," Linda promised them, "Maggie and Davy's mommy will get Popsicles for us before we go."

"Before lunch?" Jamie asked. Or maybe it was Julie.

We poured coffee and set to work on Brett then, nudging and cajoling her to read. Even Kath and Ally, despite their resistance to Linda's bludgeoning us all into writing, were dying of curiosity.

"I couldn't even read it to my mother," Brett insisted.

"You couldn't read it to your *mother*?" Linda said.

"Could you?"

There was a stunned silence, Brett's bow lips forming an O as she remembered: while the rest of our teenaged selves were struggling for turf with our moms, Linda was making her own after-school snack in an empty house.

"I couldn't imagine reading anything to my mom either," I said. "It would be like standing naked in front of her, waiting for my flaws to be called out." I looked to Maggie on the swings (the first to abandon the sandbox), wondering if my mom would even *want* to read what I wrote.

Though she would, I thought. It was my father who would have considered my writing foolish.

"I brought a poem," I confessed. "But I just can't read it."

Linda tipped the bill of her cap against the shifting sun. "Some writers we are."

She suggested we could just write instead, and while Kath and Ally were still balking I ran back to my house for paper and pens— actually three decent ballpoints, one respectable pencil, and an eraserless stub of a chewed-up pencil that was the only other writing utensil I could find besides crayons. But what exactly were we supposed to write? How could we come up with stories that hadn't been written before?

"Willa Cather says, 'There are only two or three human stories,'" Brett said, "'and they go on repeating themselves as fiercely as if they had never happened before.'"

Linda said her college writing professor had just dumped a bag of interesting things on the table and told them all to pick one and write about it for five minutes.

"But we don't have a bag of interesting things," Ally said.

"Oh, for Pete's sake." Linda grabbed her purse and upended it over the picnic table, spilling a brown leather wallet with dollar bills sticking out the top and her driver's license showing through its plastic window, an old black leather eyeglass case monogrammed in initials that weren't hers, a blue plastic checkbook, three keys on a whistle key chain, a tampon and diaper pins and change—pennies and dimes and quarters that rolled and scattered, falling through the cracks in the picnic table and landing in the grass at our feet. She stared at the glasses case for a moment, then extracted it from the pile and slipped it back into her empty purse.

"Five minutes," she said. "Just write. And don't worry, we won't read anything. Ready, set . . ." We all looked to the playground, where the kids were happily engaged. Linda's J.J. and Kath's Lacy were asleep in their strollers, and my Davy was pushing his trucks around on the blanket beside the table. "Write!"

I looked at the long blue lines on the white sheet on the wooden table in front of me, all that emptiness. The edge of Linda's wallet nearly touched the paper, the driver's license upside down. I focused on that: height 5'10", weight 139, hair blond, eyes blue because she couldn't check all the boxes for eye color, I guessed, and her eyes did look blue when she wore blue. I thought of my father teaching me to drive, his foot stomping on the brakeless passenger-seat floorboard, his voice booming, "Brake, for Christ's sake, Frankie!" when I was nowhere near the stop sign yet.

I set my eraserless stub of pencil to the blank page, trying to imbue that scene with a humor I hadn't felt at the time. And somehow, the squeals of the children and the smell of airborne sand and the taste of the earthy fall air worked their way into my writing, too, and the urge to look up and make sure Maggie and Davy were okay, and my not wanting to look up, wanting to have this moment for myself.

Linda called "Time!" after what seemed no time at all.

No children maimed or dead out on the playground—that was reassuring. And even Ally and Kath had a little ink on the page, though Kath would admit—*years* later—that all she'd written that morning was "I swear I never met a soul half as bossy as Linda Mason."

"Okay, who wants to read first?" Linda said.

After a good deal of resistance—she'd said we wouldn't have to read! (though Kath, again years later, admitted to thinking she ought to volunteer, it would serve Linda right)—Brett said fine, she'd read first, Linda didn't intimidate her. She read, interrupted only once by her daughter (who was dispatched back to the sandbox with a bucket and shovel). A few paragraphs about a wacky marble-rolling machine she and her brother built when they were in grade school. The rolling coins had reminded her of it.

Kath said she liked how the passage was really about her brother even though it seemed to be about the machine, and Brett, surprisingly, looked for a moment as if she might cry.

I volunteered to read next, saying, "But of course this isn't really anything, I was just—"

"Never apologize, never explain," Linda said. "That's what my writing teacher in college said."

"I don't see you volunteering to read next," I said.

"Oh just shut up and read and I'll read next, okay?"

By the time I'd read about my driving lesson (which did get a chuckle), the natives were getting restless, so I went for the Popsicles—yes, Popsicles at 10:45 in the morning—and while the children dripped melted rocket pops on their faces, on their clothes, on the arms of those of us holding them in our laps, Linda read. Just a few paragraphs that started with the key chain, wondering what doors those keys might open, and ended with a key opening a temple, and inside the temple a thousand people filing past a casket and a little girl in the front wondering why so many people she didn't know were claiming a loss she didn't want to share.

The five of us were silent for a long time afterward as the children licked their treats and giggled and stuck their tongues out to show them blue or green or orange. Finally Linda said, "Okay, Kath, your turn," and you could tell from her voice that she was sure we all thought what she'd written was dreadful.

Kath said what we all would have said: "I can't follow something that good."

"Me either," Ally said. "That was beautiful, Linda."

We spread the children's lunch out on the picnic table, calling it dessert since the Popsicles had been lunch, though that didn't convince them to eat more. While they ate, Linda laid out a plan for the next week: we would reread our favorite books, to see how they were written, and we would buy journals—the nice leather ones she'd seen at Kepler's Books. Ally objected that she didn't even *want* to write, and Kath started to agree, but Linda cut her off. "I'll get journals for everyone," she said. "I'll get them this evening when Jeff gets home, and I'll drop them by." She looked to the playground, almost vacant now, with our nine eating their early lunch. "What we need is a babysitter," she said. "But all mine are high school girls."

"I suppose I could ask my Arselia," Kath said reluctantly.

"Your Arselia?" Brett said.

"My housekeeper," Kath said.

"You, Kath," Linda said, "just ceded any excuse you might have had for not having time to write."

We GATHERED the next Wednesday with our new journals and our copies of E. M. Forster's *Aspects of the Novel,* which Linda had also bought for us, and—best of all—with Arselia, who, for $1.60 an hour, minimum wage, would stay until noon. We set her loose with the children and started to chat until Linda tapped her watch face. "Ten o'clock sharp is writing time," she said.

"Though this is 'just for fun,' isn't it?" Kath said. "'Nothing serious'?"

Neither Kath nor Ally had written anything in their new journals, but Brett and Linda and I had, and even Ally and Kath had started to reread their favorite books. I'd bought a paperback copy of *Rebecca* and cut it—literally—into chapters, which made it easier for me to think about each part.

"*Rebecca*?" Linda said after she'd gotten over the shock of my having cut up a book. "Come on, Frankie. The protagonist is a spine-less dishrag who lets the hired help walk all over her. *Middlemarch,*" she insisted. "You should read *Middlemarch.*"

"Though this is 'just for fun,'" Kath repeated. "'Nothing seri-ous.'" And she started talking about *Pride and Prejudice* in the most insightful way, and they were all talking about the books they'd reread—*Breakfast at Tiffany's* for Brett, *The Bell Jar* for Linda, and for Ally, *Charlotte's Web*—as I sat wondering why I was drawn to *Rebecca*. Because the narrator was an unremarkable girl who'd landed a remarkable man? Because she, like me, imagined other women's lives in great detail, and always imagined those women as better than herself?

"Fitzgerald says, 'All good writing is swimming under water and holding your breath,'" Brett said.

"What's with all the quotes, anyway, Brett?" Linda said.

"'She had a pretty gift for quotation, which is a serviceable substitute for wit,'" Brett said. "W. Somerset Maugham." She just read things and they stuck in her mind, she said. She had no idea why.

I thought Brett might be the only person I knew who was as smart as Danny. And felt the shortcomings of my own education: when I'd read Forster's description of the novel as "most distinctly one of the moister areas of literature—irrigated by a hundred rills and occasionally degenerating into swamps," I'd had to look up *rill* in the dictionary ("a small brook," in case you don't know either). And I'd never read Tolstoy or Dostoyevsky, whom Forster claimed were better than any English novelist, and I wasn't sure I wanted to; they wrote big, fat books that were only slightly less intimidating than those of the other author he recommended, Marcel Proust, whose *Remembrance of Things Past* was several *volumes* even though he was not Russian but a seemingly more reasonable French.

Linda volunteered to read what she'd written that week, and as she read I wondered how to say diplomatically that this new passage—which she'd obviously worked very hard on—was stilted and dull compared with what she'd whipped off in five minutes the week before. Kath jumped in immediately after Linda finished, though, gushing about how "nice" it was, and everyone hopped right onto that "nice" bandwagon. And that's how it would go after that: Brett would bring whole chapters of a mystery that was not particularly mysterious. Linda would bring pages of a short story about . . . well, I couldn't begin to describe it, so what does that say? Ally would occasionally bring a few journal lines about a duck who was not "Some Duck," at least not in the way Wilbur was "Some Pig." And the things I wrote were no better. Still, Kath—who never brought a word—would invariably start off with how nice each was, and we'd all follow suit. We meant to be encouraging each other. We did. And I wallowed in the praise as much as anyone at first. But it began to leave me strangely discouraged. I found myself listening carefully to gauge whether "nice" had any enthusiasm to it, wondering how we'd ever get better if we just sat around whacking each other on the back as if we were the next Monsieur Proust even if we weren't French, or anything close to it.

ONE WEDNESDAY morning that fall we sat sharing what we'd heard about the rock concert "gather-in" at Lytton Plaza that weekend, and trying to fend off Linda's efforts to recruit us to one of her causes (getting a mental-health services bill passed by the California legislature, I think it was that day), and waiting for Ally to show. We weren't worried at first that she hadn't arrived—she went to her sister's for breakfast every Wednesday morning, and frequently pulled back into her drive after the rest of us were already in the park. She and Kath were the only ones who had their own cars. (Ally's was just a white Chevy Nova two-door, but Kath's was a brand-new powder-blue Mustang convertible, with air-conditioning and power windows and seat belts—only the lap belts that had just been made mandatory, but Kath did use them, which was a good thing, it turns out.) By mid-morning, we'd gone ahead and started critiquing our writing, and still Ally hadn't arrived.

"You don't think anything happened with the baby, do you?" I said.

"With Carrie?" Linda said at the same time Brett said, "I *thought* she was pregnant, but she hasn't uttered a word."

"And how can you ask?" Kath said. "I mean, if you're wrong? 'Oh, I see. You're *not* pregnant, you're just getting fat as a porker pie.' "

Which made us all laugh; I had no idea what a porker pie was, but it sounded so funny the way she said it, with the long Southern *i*. Everyone laughed, too, at a story I told about my cousin patting my belly at a family gathering and asking when the little guy was due when the "little guy," my Maggie, was at that moment safely nestled in Danny's arms. It was a story I'd never told before, a humiliation I'd never wanted to recall, but it was funny, it really was. That was something I was beginning to realize: with these new friends of mine, I could laugh at myself.

We considered the possibilities. Maybe Ally had morning sickness? Car trouble? Maybe she'd gone on vacation? (Though wouldn't she have told us?) Maybe a relative was sick or had died?

Her car wasn't in the drive, but we decided Brett and I would go knock on her door anyway. There was no answer even after we knocked and rang a second time. When I tried the doorknob, though, it turned easily.

Inside, the house was dark and stale, the drapes closed against the beautiful day. No radio or TV. No little Carrie chattering to her dolly or throwing a fit over having to eat oatmeal or pulling on Ally's hem and telling her it was time to go to the park.

"Ally?" I called.

No answer.

"Ally?" Brett called a little louder.

The faucet dripped in the kitchen. In the park, the children were screaming the way kids in parks do, all overly excited and dramatic and joyous.

"Ally?" we called a third time, together.

A sound came from upstairs, not a voice or a word, but a human sound. Fear?

Brett and I looked at each other: *Should we call the police?* But this was Palo Alto in the middle of a sunny Wednesday morning, for goodness sakes. I imagined the police showing up and taking one look at Brett's white gloves, the event replayed in the crime column of the *Palo Alto Times* under the heading "No Crime at All" with some long-winded rant about how kooks like us distracted the police from important business. And Brett was already creeping up the stairs, whispering, "Ally? Ally, are you here?"

There was a louder sound then, a sob, and Brett and I bolted up the stairs and started opening doors until we found Ally curled up on a double bed in a dreary, drape-shrouded room, her hair sprawled in a tangle across sheets and blankets and pillows that were a single gray hue in the lightless room.

Brett sat gently on the edge of the bed and lay a white-gloved hand on shoulders so thin they ought to have belonged to a young girl. After a moment, she smoothed Ally's hair from her face, tucked it gently behind her ear, stroked her cheek. "Ally, what happened?" she said.

Ally's shoulders shook soundlessly.

"What's wrong?" Brett insisted, but so kindly that I wondered how this came so naturally to her. "Has something happened to Jim?" she said. "Or to Carrie?"

I sat at Ally's feet and put my hand on the blanket over her calves, trying to echo Brett's ease. We sat there for the longest time, Ally sobbing silently, a tissue buried in her fist, unused. I tried to imagine how long she must have lain like this; there must have been twenty tissues scattered across the carpet, and the basket was full. I imagined Jim—whom I'd never met—picking them up and loading them in the basket, torn between not wanting to leave her that morning and having to get to a court appearance that his job depended on.

"Did something happen to Carrie?" Brett said again, gentle but insistent. "Tell us."

Ally shook her head.

"Was it the baby?" I guessed.

That awful sob again.

"You lost the baby," I whispered.

Brett stayed with Ally while I slipped out to tell Kath and Linda—they wanted to come, too, but we thought that might be too much for Ally, and anyway, someone had to stay with the kids.

When I returned to Ally's house, I put a kettle on for tea. No Lipton's in Ally's cabinet, nothing remotely resembling a tea bag, but there was a copper teapot inlaid with silver at the handle and spout, and on the shelf beside it two cylindrical containers made of thin wood. The first one I opened smelled of spices: cloves and ginger and something else I couldn't identify, maybe a whole bunch of different things. But the other container held a dark, powdery substance that, though it looked finer than tea leaves, did smell like tea.

By the time I came back to the room with the steaming cup, Brett had gotten Ally to sit up. She was leaning against a pile of pillows, and the light on her nightstand was on now, raising the room from dreary colorlessness to chalky blue. I handed Brett the tea, discreetly picked up the tissues, added them to the pile in the basket, and sat back down at the end of the bed.

Brett was trying to be soothing, saying that sometimes a miscarriage happens because there is something wrong with the baby, maybe it was for the best.

Ally's face crumpled in on itself like a dying leaf. "But I always lose my babies. A year ago Easter, and the summer before that, and now."

From Brett's kicked-in expression, I saw she was having as much trouble absorbing this as I was. Three miscarriages in as many years. She set the tea on the nightstand. "But you have Carrie, Ally."

Ally choked back another sob, her chin sinking into her soft neck, her face even paler than usual. She closed her eyes, her lids red at the edges and a weak and veiny blue.

Brett mouthed to me, "It happened Sunday."

"I'm sorry," Ally said. "I'm sorry. It's just that . . ."

"There, there," Brett soothed, setting her hand on Ally's. "There, there."

"It's just that the baby is there, he's my baby, he's my son, I can feel him inside me, and I know . . . somehow I know all about him almost, I *know* him, I can feel his needs, I can feel him saying 'Take care of me, oh please take care of me' just in the way I can't even smell fish and I can't get enough meat and I have to sleep and sleep and sleep. Then I don't, somehow, I don't take care of him. I want to and I try to, I try to do everything so right but I don't and he . . ."

And he dies, I thought. The word she can't say. Her baby dies inside her. He starts dying inside her and she knows it, and there is the awful rushing to the hospital, and the pain, the wrenching of her gut, and the doctors and the nurses and the sterile instruments and then nothing, just emptiness.

"I wake up every morning and there's this moment of . . . of possibility," Ally whispered. "Of maybe it's just a nightmare and the baby is fine."

Brett tilted her head up, blinking back tears. "I know. Getting out of bed is . . . impossible sometimes," she said so gently I was sure she did know, and I wondered again what had happened to Brett, why she wore her gloves, why she never offered a word of explanation, why none of us ever dared ask.

"And Jim, he just curls up around me in bed when he gets home, and he puts his hand on my . . . on my skin, on my belly, and he . . ." She swallowed once, twice, still with her eyes closed, tears spilling from her unparted lids. "He *sings.*" The last word spoken so softly I wasn't sure of what I'd heard. "He just sings, words I don't even understand," she said in the same almost inaudible voice. "He just sings to his baby son as if he's still there."

I set my hand on Ally's foot under the blue blanket. Outside, a car accelerated. A train whistled. One bird scolded and another cawed. Ally pulled her other foot up, tucked it beneath her leg, still under the blanket. She blew her nose and tossed the tissue on the bed. She leaned forward, and for a moment I thought she might get up, but she only pulled another tissue from the box. Something in the way she held herself made me feel she wanted us to leave now, that she'd drained herself and wanted to be alone. That she regretted, already, telling us about Jim. That she felt she'd shown us something about him she shouldn't have shown anyone.

I took a tissue, wiped my eyes under my glasses, blew my nose.

Brett frowned but made no move to leave. After a long silence, she asked where Carrie was, and whether she was okay.

Ally's hand tightened around her tissue, and she looked away from Brett, to the shaded windows. It was a moment before she whispered, "She's . . . she's . . ." In the park, a child called for her mother—not my Maggie. Ally closed her eyes, tears streaming again. ". . . my sister's," she whispered.

I patted the sad hump of Ally's blanket-covered foot encouragingly, giving her space to say more. But it was Brett who spoke, who said, "She's at your sister's. Good. Good." Then, after a moment, "All week?"

W*E ALL CALLED ALLY* that next week to see if we could bring her groceries or take Carrie off her hands for a few hours, or if she just wanted some company, but the answer was always no. We suggested we meet in the park Thursday or Friday, or the next Monday or Tuesday, mornings we had church or school volunteer work or the like that we usually hated to miss. I took her a tuna casserole, which she accepted reluctantly, without asking me in. Kath made fried chicken and potato salad, which is what you do in the South, she said, but she swore she didn't think anyone was eating anything at all in that house. "I wouldn't be eating, either," Linda said, remembering the parade of dishes brought to their door in the days after her mother died—trays of cold cuts, Jell-O molds, pastries, and lemon cake. The dishes had filled the refrigerator, the freezer, the countertops, turning awful shades of green and yellow and brown before her aunt Maud finally threw them into the garbage, casserole pans and all.

Ally didn't show up that next Wednesday, or the next or the next. We went to her door, tried in vain to coax her out, and we talked about it endlessly—wasn't there *something* we could do?

"Maybe she thinks she can't have a baby," I said.

"But she has her li'l Carrie," Kath said. "Of course she can have a baby."

"It may be Rh incompatibility," Brett said as I sat frowning, not sure what more to say. "She wouldn't have had a problem with Carrie, but in that first pregnancy she would have developed an immunity to Rh-positive babies that would cause her to miscarry subsequently.

They have a vaccine for it now—I saw an article about it in *Time* this summer—but it's brand new."

"Three miscarriages," Linda said. "I guess that would make you wonder."

"But she couldn't have had three," Brett said. "Carrie is barely two. I think that was just her being overwrought."

That was the third week Ally didn't show at the park, the week she didn't even answer the door when we rang the bell, even though we knew she was home.

We were at Brett's that morning—a Friday, not a Wednesday. Brett had invited us to her house to watch the *Apollo 7* launch. We sat on the carpet, as close as we could get to the TV screen without blocking each other, our children in our laps or sitting with their noses practically pressed to the screen.

"That's Cape Kennedy, in Florida," Kath explained to Anna Page. "You've been there, though you don't remember. Your daddy and I took you there on vacation one summer, when we lived in Nashville."

"With Lee-Lee and Lacy," Anna Page announced with confidence, and Kath had to say no, little Lee and Lacy had not been born yet.

Anna Page, unfazed, turned to Maggie and the twins and announced that she had gone all by herself to Florida, with her mom and dad and not with Lee-Lee or Lacy. Linda's Julie, not to be outdone, insisted that she had, too, and without Jamie—her twin—or J.J. "Didn't I, Mommy?" she said, and Linda was forced to distract her, turning her attention back to the television, where they were counting down the last few seconds.

A huge bloom of white exploded on the screen, making my heart pound as the rocket disappeared behind all that smoke. I was sure the thing was about to blow—I couldn't help thinking about the explosion of the first *Apollo*—but Brett said that was the way rockets launched. She knew all the crew's names and what they were supposed to do, too, and she talked about them that way—Commander Wally Schirra, Command Module Pilot Donn Eisele, Lunar Module Pilot Walter Cunningham—when the rest of us were just saying "the guy with the Cary Grant hair" or "the fella with the smile the size of Jupiter" or "the goofy-looking one." Yes, we did that. We talked about the astronauts the way we talked about the Beatles or Miss America, as if the sole criterion for sending them into space ought to be how handsome their faces looked through the glass bubbles of their space helmets.

Which were not glass, but rather an ultraviolet plastic. Brett told us that.

As I watched the arms holding that big white monster of a rocket swing away and the thing rise slowly, almost as if it wasn't going to make it more than a few feet, I imagined Brett's face peeking out at me from one of those not-glass bubbles. It seemed as far-fetched as imagining a woman president, or a woman priest, or a woman God.

"Brett," Linda said with a measure of clairvoyance, "have you ever considered *writing* about this space stuff?"

"Miss Marple in *Murder on the Moon*!" I said.

Brett didn't write about "this space stuff" that week, though, and Linda didn't write any more about her mother, and Kath and I didn't tap into our deepest emotions either, though Kath did say she'd written a few lines in her journal—a fact we did not make a big deal about, for fear of scaring her off. Linda didn't write about the Olympics even though she was as wild for them that fall as Brett was for the space race, not even after Brett suggested it and I echoed her, saying, *"Sylvia Plath Goes to the Olympics: A Girl Jock's Guide to Suicide"*—which I could tell amused Linda by the way she tugged at the bill of her Stanford cap. She went on and on the way she does about the state of women's sports, then—"Out of five thousand Olympians, only eight hundred are women." "Only three sports to the men's eighteen." "Only twelve athletics events to the men's twenty-four, with no races longer than eight hundred meters because *fifty years ago,* some woman collapsed in a longer race!"—at which point Kath threw up her arms and asked, "What are you wantin', Linda? For the girls to be boxing? Wrestling? Or, I know, how about weight lifting?" Which cracks me up every time I remember it, because Kath lifts weights at the gym three times a week now—free weights, too; she stands there looking at her muscles flex in the mirror, and she has muscles to flex, too, which she didn't much back then. But as I said, Linda didn't write about any of that. What she wrote was page after page of her amorphous stories (often political rants disguised as fiction, I thought), while Brett wrote chapters of her unmysterious mystery and I wrote beginnings that never seemed to go anywhere. We hadn't yet learned that our best writing comes from pushing our emotional buttons with the kind of force needed to push that rocket ship into space.

And still everything we wrote was "nice," even when I asked specifically for more critical feedback. Which was how I ended up bringing a few pages one Wednesday that I claimed were the start of a novel—pages I knew were, without a doubt, terrible. Maybe they'd be mad at me for this deception, but the point needed to be made.

When the appalled silence after I'd read the thing grew unbearable, Kath said, "Mighty nice," and Linda asked what the novel would be about.

"Oh, *come on,*" I said. "It's absolute drivel. I wrote it to *be* absolute drivel. I wrote it as dreadfully as I could, and I knew you would still say it was just nifty, and here's the thing: we won't ever get anywhere if we aren't honest with each other."

Kath ran a finger over her braid headband. "Are we hankering to get any particular somewhere?"

Linda leaned over the splintered table, frowning down at the pages she'd written that week. "I am," she admitted. "I'd like to publish something someday. Wouldn't you, Kath?"

"Publish?" Brett said so quietly that for a moment I thought it was Ally's voice. It made me miss Ally suddenly, made me wonder if she was still writing about her duck who was not "Some Duck," and what she was doing on Wednesday mornings now, and if she'd ever come back to the park.

"I don't think I could ever publish anything. I don't think I even want to," Brett said. She tucked her hair behind her ear—once, twice, and again; it was too short to stay. "But I would like to improve."

"Publish," I said, feeling the awkward newness of the word on my lips.

It doesn't seem like much now, I know, to admit ambition to your closest friends. I guess you'll have to take my word for it: *it was*. It makes me a little sad when I look back on it, to think how very many women didn't have Wednesday Sisters, to wonder who they might have become if they had.

"Cards on the table," Linda said. "We're honest with each other from now on."

" 'When in doubt, tell the truth,' " Brett said. "Mark Twain."

8

ONE TUESDAY NIGHT that October, I sat on the front porch waiting for Danny and reading *Middlemarch*—despite Linda's insistence that I should read it. I loved the book, maybe because, like Dorothea with Casaubon, part of what I loved about Danny was the prospect of playing a role in what he would accomplish. Fortunately, Danny was no Casaubon. He wasn't much older than me, and he wasn't the least bit pompous. Though he, like Casaubon, spent more and more time on his work, and I, like Dorothea, felt less included than I'd imagined.

Again and again, I looked up from the page, though, toward Ally's house, wondering if Brett was right that Ally just needed time to herself, that she would return to us when she was ready. I was thinking about that—thinking that if I were Ally I'd come to a point where I did want my friends back and I'd worry that they weren't my friends anymore, and I was thinking of Carrie, too, sure she must miss the park—when I saw the dark-skinned man enter Ally's house again. The door closed behind him, and the light came on in the front hall, then went off again just as the window at the upstairs landing lit up.

It seemed so improbable that I hadn't even raised the possibility with Linda and Kath and Brett, for fear of sounding absurd. It made me uncomfortable, honestly, to think of my friend being married to a black man, and uncomfortable to feel uncomfortable. I knew I wasn't supposed to be prejudiced; Martin Luther King had opened our eyes to that. But I'd grown up seeing people of other races as different: They lived in different neighborhoods and they weren't the same things we were—they weren't our doctors or our teachers, congressmen or priests or astronauts—or we didn't see them being what we were. Which was wrong, of course. But while it was easy to see that blacks should go to the same good schools as whites and shouldn't have to give up their seats on the bus, it was a lot harder somehow to imagine a black man married to one of your good friends. Let's just say if I'd come home one day and told my parents I was marrying a black man, my mom would have fainted and my dad would have fallen over dead of a heart attack.

I'd like to think in retrospect that I had some kind of reasonable concerns, like "What about the children, would they be ostracized?" I wouldn't even have married outside the Catholic Church; it would be so hard for the kids, I'd thought, having parents of different faiths. But I suppose the truth is that I was worried about what would happen if I ever, say, invited my friends and their husbands for dinner. A concern that sounds ridiculous now, of course.

It wasn't Danny I was worried about; he's the least prejudiced man in the world. But people are funny. Kath's Lee, for example—Madison Leland Montgomery IV. Would he sit down to dinner with a black man? I'd never met Lee, but I had him pegged as a Southern bigot—another prejudice on my part, yes. It was that "IV" after his name, I think, and the fact that he was from the South. I figured the original Lee Montgomery—Madison Leland Montgomery I— probably owned black men, and it's a long way to go from owning people as property to calling them friends.

The sad truth: I sometimes wonder if I wouldn't have done more for Ally that fall if I'd been sure her husband was white. But maybe I'm wrong about that. Maybe it's just that that was our first crisis, really, and we didn't yet know what to do to help each other in this any more than we did in our writing. We didn't know each other well enough yet to risk mucking around in any real way in each other's lives.

THE NEXT MORNING when I went out to get the paper, Linda blew right by me in pedal pushers and sneakers as if she was training for the Olympics herself, the sweat running down her neck as that blond braid bounced out of her Stanford cap. She showed up the next morning and the next and the next, and by the second Olympic Wednesday she'd changed her pedal pushers for little shorts like the women running in the Olympics wore, and she'd traded her Keds for men's athletic shoes, or boys'. I wondered if she'd had the gall to try on the shoes right there in the men's department at Macy's, but—this is Linda we're talking about—I suppose she didn't think it at all outrageous, or enjoyed it all the more knowing it was. Which was why it surprised me that she didn't say anything about her running when we met at the park that morning—never mind the evidence she wore, the pale white sweat ring around the rim of her cap.

Kath was uncharacteristically disheveled that day; she hadn't worn her headband braid and her mascara was smudged, which would have been par for the course for me, but Kath was always so tidy. She'd been pretty quiet while Linda went on and on about the Olympics again, too, but when Brett asked if she was okay, she said she was fine, just fine.

"It's just . . . these girl athletes, they're just . . ." The word she was looking for was not flattering, you could tell by the tone of her voice. "I *hate* women athletes! Field hockey and gymnastics and basketball. Like Pookie Benton."

"Pookie Benton?" Linda said.

Kath waved her off, saying, "Don't mind me. I put my boots on backward this morning is all."

Ten o'clock came and Arselia arrived and we turned to writing. "Remember: brutal honesty," Linda said, and Brett said, "Maybe not *brutal,* Linda." And we all agreed: "Honesty."

I'd asked for it, of course, but what I read that morning was not something I'd intentionally written as drivel. These were the real first pages of a serious novel—my way of letting my friends into my life, I see in retrospect. My own life dressed up in fictional garb. But Linda didn't know that, and she was hell-bent on starting out right this time, so she began honestly.

"I'm willing to buy that this family *might* exist," she said, "though—"

"Though if your Dritha really can't afford college," Brett interrupted, "she ought to—"

"Do something about it," Linda said. "Her father says an education ruins her for a proper life, and she says, 'Oh, okay'?"

I sat there, looking past them to the new-mown grass and the red-orange-gold trees and the paint-stripped balustrade over the mansion porch, wanting to say, *But that was the way it was.* Maybe that wasn't the way it was in swanky East Coast families like Brett's or Linda's, or rich Southern ones like Kath's, but it was the way it was in blue-collar Midwestern families.

"Maybe she could have gotten a scholarship?" Brett offered.

"But . . ." I looked away to the playground, to Mags, who would go to college if I had to scrub toilets to pay her tuition. "But if she goes to college on a scholarship, she won't make any money, whereas if she takes a job at . . ." *At the Northwestern engineering school.* "If she takes a job and keeps living at home, that's one whole paycheck that can go to paying for her brother's college." One of four brothers in my case, three of whom were younger but all of whom stood ahead of me in the going-to-college line.

I imagined writing the real scene: Sister Josephine calling me into her office one afternoon in the fall of my senior year, all the black-and-white fabric drape of her, the wimple tight across her forehead, the heavy cross at her chest, Christ nailed there in carved wooden detail, and the incongruous sea blue of her eyes, not the peaceful sea you expected on a nun but something more turbulent, a stormy sea that somehow retained its color, that didn't turn white-capped or gray. She sat at her desk in front of a stack of forms, and she asked me to sit in the chair across from her. Then she did something unprecedented: she picked up the forms and came from behind the desk and sat in the empty visitor chair, pulling it close to me. She took my hand and opened it, and she stared at my palm for a moment as if my future might really be found in the lines there—and why not, since God had created my hand and my future both? "God gives us gifts and helps us see fit how to use them," she said, and she set the forms in my hands.

I looked down at the bold black letters: The University of Illinois. It was an application, and below it, forms for financial aid. Underneath them, other college forms, all state schools. She understood my family would never be able to afford a private school for me, not with so many boys to educate.

When I went through the forms at home that evening, I found at the bottom a copy of a recommendation letter for the University of Illinois from Sister Josephine: carbon-blue letters that said I was bright, resourceful, eager to learn, that claimed I would be an asset to any college, that said I was one of the most beautiful writers she'd ever had the pleasure to teach. Allowing me to go to my father with the idea that maybe *God* wanted me to go to college, Sister Josephine had said she thought He meant me to go.

My mom sat quietly at the kitchen table that night, her eyes watering as she read Sister Josephine's recommendation. When my father came home, he sat with us and she passed it to him. He inhaled deeply on his cigarette, scanning the words.

My mother stood and found an ashtray, brown, plastic, and round. "I could find a position to help with the tuition, Jack," she said as she set the ashtray in front of him, her voice its very gentlest.

I started to explain what Sister Josephine had told me, that I could get a scholarship, that if I applied to state schools I might get a full ride somewhere. But my father wasn't listening, my father was smashing out the short stub of his cigarette, extracting another from the pack in his shirt pocket, focusing intently on the match. Not so much angry as ashamed, I see in retrospect—though at the time it seemed only angry.

"You want your sons coming home from school to an empty house?" he said to my mother.

Mom smiled apologetically, and I knew she would say something, and I wanted to tell her *No, don't, not for my sake*. But she was already speaking, saying, "Of course not, Jack. I didn't mean that. I'd work mornings. Mornings and early afternoons. I saw a help wanted sign at the market—"

"The market! No wife of mine—" He took a deep drag on his cigarette, the tip glowing red. "You don't need to be waiting on others for money, Margaret, not while I'm still breathing and not when I'm gone, either, for Christ's sake." He looked down at the linoleum tabletop, tapped his ashes into the ashtray. "I can provide for my family myself."

From my mother's downcast eyes, I knew the discussion was over, I knew she was bending to his will, and I hated that for her—that she was having to bend to him because of me. And I hated that *in* her, too—that she would just bend so easily to his will—and hated what it would mean for me. I couldn't see my father the way she saw him: the mechanic who worked for barely decent pay and little dignity, who buried his ego at work every day so as not to offend anyone; the man who pinned his ambitions on his sons, who wasn't quite sure what to make of the fact that it was his daughter who brought home the straight-A report cards—his daughter who was somehow his wife's child in the same way his sons were his.

"But Sister Josephine—" I protested.

"Those nuns ought to have more sense than to meddle in people's lives." He stood and smashed the new cigarette into the ashtray. "If God wanted women to have a say in anything, He'd have made them priests," he said. "Now, that's enough."

And when I'd gone back to Sister Josephine, the old nun had sighed and started talking about "honoring thy Father," which I was pretty sure meant God, not my dad. "God will have a different path for you, then, child," she said. "He doesn't make children like you without some purpose." Which I can see now she meant as encouragement, but at the time I was left feeling an obligation to do something noble to honor whatever these gifts were that God had given me, with no idea what in the world it might be that I *could* do, much less how to start.

In the park with Linda and Brett and Kath that morning, I just sat there watching Maggie for a long moment, imagining her in a cap and gown approaching my old desk at the university, résumés in hand.

"What do you think, Kath?" Linda said. "You haven't said anything yet."

Kath stared at Linda for a moment, as if trying to remember where she was. "Maybe Dritha's spine is just a little catawampus, Frankie?" she said finally. "You might could pull her up a touch straighter, give her just a pinch more backbone?"

"It could be something as simple as . . . she's dishwater blond, like you are, right?" Brett said. "But you're not just dishwater blond, you have this wildness to your hair that can't be tamed. Give her that, too. Make her one of those 'round characters' Forster likes to talk about, 'capable of surprising in a convincing way.'"

"Exactly," Linda agreed. "If your Dritha is really sacrificing her dreams for the sake of her brothers, we need to see her sticking a black-gloved fist in the air and—"

"*That* wasn't sacrifice, that was radical trash!" I said. A little too loudly, I'm afraid. Mothers around the park turned to stare. Funny how we do that, how when we're losing control of our emotions about one thing, we pop off over something else.

When I look at that Olympics photograph now—of Tommie Smith and John Carlos in that black-power salute—it looks so innocuous, but I sure didn't see it that way then. Those two athletes standing stocking-footed on the Olympic awards podium, thrusting black-gloved fists in the air and bowing their heads as "The Star-Spangled Banner" played in their honor—it scared the hell out of me, as it did much of the world. That's what I'd felt as I'd watched them, before my emotions got all tangled up with my writing: scared as hell. You'd have thought from the world's reaction that those two boys had brought machine guns up to that podium. Those two young men, giving up their own moment of triumph to draw attention to the plight of their race. And do you know what Tommie Smith was doing while he was standing on that gold medal podium? He was praying to God.

We still talk about that moment sometimes, and I think I understand better now than I did then. I can understand being so frustrated with the lot you're dealt that you turn in a direction you never imagined, you explode. That's what happened to me that day in a small way, what would happen to Ally with Linda and the Tylandril three years later, and to Linda the week we didn't call. It's what happened to Kath in a bigger way the next Halloween, and I sure understood it in her, I might have done exactly what she ended up doing—and I might have ended up *killing* Lee since my temper is, on the whole, more capricious. Sometimes you have to stand up for your own dignity. And those boys didn't do anything violent themselves that I ever heard of. They just stood up and said what is wrong is wrong and, as Linda said even then, they sacrificed their futures in the bargain. They were banned from Olympic competition for life. So I guess one part of me likes to think now that if those boys had been my sons, I would have been awfully proud.

Well, we didn't resolve anything about that black-power salute that Wednesday, or about the start of my novel, either. And we were no "nicer" with Linda's piece, a complete short story. She hardly blinked her blond lashes at the criticism, though. She just listened and took a million notes without interrupting or saying a word. Then *she* started asking *us* questions. I watched her, thinking that if any of us succeeded, it would be Linda.

We turned to Kath's work next, two journal pages, which was volumes compared with the few lines she'd brought the week before, and only the second time she'd brought anything in the six weeks we'd been writing together. There was a surprising amount of narrative drive in it—the start of a love story—but it was thin, the characters not the least bit alive.

"One of Mark Twain's rules of literary fiction?" Brett said. "'That the personages in a tale shall be *alive*, except in the case of *corpses*, and that always the reader shall be able to tell the corpses from the others.'"

I was about to ask her to repeat the line so I could copy it in my journal when Kath up and started bawling, big streaks of black mascara cutting a path through the blush on her cheeks. Brett looked alarmed—we all did—and it was Linda who recovered first, who put her arm around Kath in the nicest way.

But Kath couldn't stop crying. "I'm sorry, I don't mean to act ugly, it's not what any of you said, it's just that . . . oh, Lord, I'm afraid Lee's parking his paddy in another wagon."

"You think Lee is"—Linda pulled Kath closer—"is having an affair?"

"He never comes home, Linda."

"But neither does Jeff, Kath. They're residents! And who in the world would he be having an affair with?"

Brett said, "Oh," in a way that somehow suggested Chip and her huddled over a test tube in a science lab when maybe he'd been seeing some other girl.

"He was going to leave me for Pookie Benton," Kath insisted.

"Pookie Benton? Kath, Lee would never leave you for a girl named *Pookie*," Linda said, trying to bring some lightness to the situation.

"But he *was* going to leave me for Pookie. Our junior year in college. He was all over her at the Derby, helping her place her bets like he was just being a gentleman, but it was the very way he first courted *me* when he was still seeing Ada Davidson. And he *would* have left me, he would have been in Pookie's panties as easy as sliding off a greasy log backward, except . . ." She covered her face with her hands. "Except the rabbit . . ."

Brett and Linda and I all looked at each other. "The *rabbit*?" I mouthed. Then, "Oh, I see." A shotgun wedding.

We went from denial to strategy in two seconds flat. Not like girlfriends might now. There was no talk of walking out immediately, no "You can't put up with that." Pride or self-respect? What were those compared with a *husband*? This was all about how she could keep Lee, get him back from this slut of a medical student or nurse or whoever was throwing herself at him. Because the only thing worse than not yet having a husband was being divorced. What man would want used goods?

It never entered our minds that Lee was used goods, too. It never occurred to us that some woman might not want Lee because he wasn't a virgin, just as it never occurred to us that the new girl he was seeing might be anything like us or that Kath might be able to survive just fine on her own, thank you very much. Divorce was shameful, and children needed a father, and the idea of a man being a father even though he didn't live with his children's mother was outside our sphere of understanding. Even Dr. Spock didn't have anything to say about what to do with children when your husband left you; he never once mentioned the word *divorce* in his book.

It scared us, to be honest. You could see it even in Linda. If it could happen to Kath, then it could happen to us, couldn't it? But we didn't want to believe that, so we chose to see it differently. Kath had slept with Lee before they were married; that made her different from me, anyway. It's awful to think of, looking back at it, but Kath's being honest caused us all to lean a little bit away from her that fall. Not that we meant to, or even realized that we were. Not that it was anything, really. We still met her at the park every Wednesday, and we took Anna Page and Lee-Lee and Lacy so she could get her hair done or buy a pretty new dress or go out to dinner with Lee. Still, in some way I can't even explain, we set her apart so that what happened to her couldn't possibly happen to us.

9

WE STARTED COMING to the park early that autumn, in case Ally returned or there was some new development Kath needed to talk about—nothing so obvious as lipstick on Lee's collar, but he'd gotten a phone for the bedroom, one of the new push-button ones with the star and the pound keys no one knew quite what to do with, and he'd taken to making his calls from behind the closed door, saying it was hard to concentrate with the kids screaming in the background and he was making decisions that would affect people's lives, so, really, was it too much to ask for a little quiet? Linda talked, as always, about her causes: she was starting to get involved in environmental issues, and she went on and on about the war, though she wasn't any more involved than the rest of us were in the protests, the thousands of people marching right here in Palo Alto, closing down University Avenue. As the holidays neared, we talked about what the children wanted from Santa (Hot Wheels and Sting-Ray bicycles and the new talking Barbie, who spoke six different and brilliant phrases: "I have a date tonight"; "I love being a fashion model"; "Let's have a costume party"), and about the upcoming *Apollo 8* mission, the first men to leave Earth's gravity, ten orbits around the moon. We instituted a new critique rule: point out something you like about a piece before you launch into how it can be improved. And the second Wednesday of that December—despite how close we'd become, we still met only on Wednesdays—we began to talk about sex.

It was the week after Danny's company Christmas party; I remember exactly because I'd never talked about sex before, not even with my friends back home.

"Chip and I . . . we fooled around up against a fence at a beach club when we were at his cousin's wedding," Brett confessed. "When we got back inside, his brother gave us endless grief about the fence marks all over the back of Chip's shirt. It was mortifying."

Kath raised one perfectly plucked eyebrow. "Fence marks on the back of *his* shirt?"

Brett blushed about as red as her hair, and the next thing I knew we were talking about oral sex. Linda had no more experience with it than I had. But Kath? I couldn't help thinking my friends in Chicago would have called her a slut, though I couldn't think of her that way, not Kath. I thought of her as like me, only a little more reckless, which maybe was a good thing to be, reckless.

I was surprised, then, to find myself starting to confess what had happened to me at the party. Maybe it was Danny's new company—thirty guys who'd just started this enterprise together and had so much hope for what it might become. Or maybe it was the setting, an unpretentious house tucked up against the Santa Cruz Mountains, where the grass was rich green even in December and the host himself was pouring the drinks, where everyone seemed young and enthusiastic and creative, ambitious. Maybe it was the way Danny introduced me to everyone at that party as if I were Miss Illinois of 1968. Or maybe it was the Boston Fish House punch, a stealthy blend of rum, peach brandy, and champagne in a lemon-lime base that was not the harmless little refreshment it was advertised to be. But then these guys were scientists, and every scientist I've ever met likes to explode things.

I was tipsy before long, and the only saving grace was that almost everyone else was, too. And I was surprised to enjoy it so much, and to enjoy the lovemaking afterward, not in bed when we got home but in the backseat of the car on a quiet road on the Stanford campus, with the possibility of being caught.

I eased into telling the Wednesday Sisters about it by talking about what I'd written that night, when I couldn't sleep. I'd gotten up and pulled out my journal, and even though I was still sort of sloshed, I filled a half dozen pages. I wrote about several of Danny's co-workers, including his boss, Andy, who was so logical and straightforward you could listen to him talk for hours about something you knew nothing about without getting bored. I wrote about some of the wives, too. "Like the president's wife, who talks about Maine the way I guess I talk about Chicago," I said, and Brett said I didn't, actually, I rarely talked about Chicago anymore. Which left me wondering if Bob's wife had friends like we did, or if it didn't limit her range of friends to be the head god's wife, because how close can you get to the wives of men your husband might have to fire? I wondered if I'd be happy in that big Los Altos Hills yard I'd envied, where you were so far away from your neighbors you'd have to pack a suitcase to go borrow a cup of sugar.

"I wrote about the president, too," I said. "I said to myself, *Frankie, you are too drunk to write about Bob, put your pen down,* but I didn't. I wrote pages and pages: about his optimism for this new venture, which was contagious; about his insistence that computers would soon be as small as a few chips you could hold in your hand; about the look on Danny's face when he introduced me to this man who had started the company, like a son bringing his girl home to meet his father. Then I just kept writing, spilling into my journal what happened after Bob had poured me yet *another* glass of that punch.

"He's got these eyes that are, I don't know," I told Kath and Linda and Brett. "It was like he was stripping me of my clothes and my skin, too, like he could see everything about me—"

"Lord a'mercy, you didn't sleep with this fella and then write about it for Danny to find!" Kath said.

"No! For goodness sakes! Of course not!" I leaned back from the idea so sharply I nearly fell backward off the picnic-table bench.

Linda tipped her Stanford cap lower, shading her eyes. "I nearly slept with someone else not long before Jeff and I were married," she said. "After we'd already picked silver and china and table linens. My wedding dress. Our rings." She looked to Kath, her pale lashes blinking apologetically. "My creative-writing professor," she said. "He invited me to discuss a story I'd written over coffee one afternoon. Except we . . . we ordered drinks instead. It was almost like we were *both* writers that afternoon, not just him. Then drinks turned into dinner and somehow I wound up sitting in the passenger seat of his car, pulling into his garage."

"His place," Kath said. "So at least the fella wasn't married."

Linda looked to the old mansion, the panes of its tall, rectangular windows reflecting the slanted morning light. "I don't know," she said quietly. "I think maybe his wife was out of town."

I tried not to frown, waiting for the end of the story, how she'd extricated herself. But she kept her gaze fixed on the mansion, and in the silence I wondered if she hadn't slept with him after all, if she wasn't just too ashamed to tell us. I imagined her basking in that professor's confidence the same way I had in Bob's.

I was returning from the bathroom at the party—all that scientist punch—scanning the place for Danny, facing rooms full of people I didn't really know at all: people laughing at raucous retellings of mishaps at work or discussing other people they knew in the valley or talking technical in a way I couldn't begin to understand. Even the other wives seemed to know everyone, to understand everything. And without Danny—where was he?—I was feeling insecure and lonely and a little drunk. Then Bob—this man Danny talked about like he sat at the right hand of the Lord Himself—was standing beside me, handing me a glass of punch I really didn't need and asking how I liked Palo Alto, whether I was settling in and finding friends.

I started talking about Danny, saying how much he was enjoying his job and how sure he was that the company would be a big success.

Bob looked straight into me with those eyes of his. Intense. Hopeful. Encouraging.

"But what about *you*, Frankie?" he asked. "How are *you*?"

He set his hand on my shoulder, and in that one gesture I split open, my insides came tumbling out. Talking to him, I felt I could do things I might never have imagined I could. I felt like I did sometimes when I pushed back from the typewriter after I'd been writing particularly well—or after I thought I had been. And when I walked away from that conversation, I felt wrung out like a sad old rag and unbelievably energized at the same time. I felt like I'd been given a new start—or not *given,* but *found.* A start I'd thought I would have when I married Danny. A start I thought I *did* have after we were first married, but that had somehow slipped from my grasp.

"What were you and Bob talking so intently about?" Danny asked the moment I joined him, stopping the conversation in the group around him, leaving everyone else staring at us and then turning to the buffet table, pretending great interest in the cheese ball. Even as I flushed, I reached down and pulled up that feeling, that new start, and I kissed Danny on the cheek, a kiss that surprised him and made *him* blush, and made him stand up straighter.

I adjusted my glasses, smoothed my hair, looked back across the room. "Who is that woman talking to Bob now?" I asked, addressing everyone, ducking Danny's question, enjoying my husband's suspicion that the head of the company he worked for might be attracted to me. I wondered if he realized as surely as I did that the woman's arrival at Bob's side had marked the end of his conversation with me, if he'd seen how reluctantly I'd stepped away from Bob's warm encouragement.

Danny looked at the woman, but he didn't answer. He left it to the others to lean into the circle and lower their voices, to explain that she was a mask designer, that she and Bob were "quite close." I would learn the details over time: that he liked to take her for flights along the coast to see fireworks on the Fourth of July; that they snow-skied and drank a grape-Tang-and-vodka drink called a Purple Jesus. But that night, Danny only stood looking at Bob and the woman while the guilt rose up in me, guilt and jealousy and something else, too, some uneasiness I couldn't name that left me wondering if it was the entrepreneur in Bob that Danny so admired, or if it was this other thing, this thing with the woman, or if it was both, or something else entirely, something he didn't understand any better than I understood why I couldn't bring myself to tell Danny what I'd so easily told Bob: that I was writing a book.

10

$\mathcal{I}$T WAS TWO DAYS before Christmas when Ally finally returned to the park, and it was not a Wednesday but a Monday. It was one of those funny mornings when the moon appears as a filmy white chink in the sky when you think it really ought to be somewhere else, glowing on the dark side of the earth. I was sitting alone on the bench where we'd all first gathered, watching Maggie and Davy run around with other children on the playground, when Ally sat down next to me.

She was rail thin, her thighs sharp under the patterned cotton of her skirt as she set her hands in her lap. Her hair was carefully brushed, falling in a single dark wavy sheet until it caught between her back and the park bench. And she was as pale as that moon.

She didn't have Carrie with her. I didn't ask where she was. We just sat together, watching the children play for a long moment before Ally looked up at the sky and asked, "Have you been watching?"

I had been. Watching the television coverage of *Apollo 8,* yes. And watching the silent windows of Ally's house, the man I would glimpse occasionally opening the front door in the evening, the same door that never opened to a child going out to play. Sometimes I saw the curtains move, as if Ally was watching us the way I now imagined she'd watched us months ago, before she finally appeared in the park the day Bobby Kennedy was shot. But only the man ever came out.

"Yes," I said.

Ally's gaze remained fixed on the translucent circle of white in the sky.

On the playground, Davy stumbled, and I watched to see if he would pick himself up without me having to go to him, and I tried to imagine what it would be like to be here every Wednesday morning as Ally had been, watching all that love she could not have. And I couldn't imagine it. I couldn't imagine there was anything in this world I would not give up to have Maggie and Davy.

"Ally," I said, wanting to say something but not sure what. Had she thought about adopting? Maybe that. But I didn't know what to say, how to start that conversation, whether she would see my words as an intrusion or pity, or some failure of belief that she could, if she would just keep trying, eventually have a child. So I just looked up at the moon with her, at that circle that seemed so small and uncertain a thing from where we sat but was now, from the *Apollo 8* spaceship, looming larger than the earth itself.

"It must be weird to be up there, free of the earth's gravity," Ally said. "Circling round and round a whole other world."

11

THAT JANUARY, Brett told us she was pregnant—three months already!—and even though Ally wasn't, she and Carrie were again joining us every Wednesday, and Ally was honestly happy for Brett. Linda continued to run by my house each morning. And Kath slipped into a marriage that some days I understood completely and other days I couldn't understand at all. That autumn of tears and anguish rolled into a winter of silence, which settled into a spring of some weird kind of acceptance, or denial, or both. Lee wasn't leaving her, she'd decided—or tried to convince herself she'd decided, though you could tell one part of her still lived with that fear. Not leaving her *yet*, we all worried, but we never said that, not to Kath anyway, because it seemed that what kept her getting out of her antique four-poster bed every morning was the idea that since Lee hadn't left her yet, he wouldn't. He always had burned hot with girls at first, and then he grew tired of them—that was the way it was before he'd married Kath. Which only left me wondering: Had Lee married her because she was different from those others he'd wearied of, or would she have been consigned to the Lee Montgomery heartbreak pile, too, if Anna Page had not been in the works, or if their daddies hadn't been friends?

Still, you could see hope blooming in her as time went on and he continued to come home at night: this was just a passing dalliance, just sex maybe, or the excitement of a new conquest, and when the newness wore off, this other woman would lose her charm for Lee and he would come back. If Kath confronted him, it would just make it worse. And it didn't really matter as long as he didn't love the girl, as long as he still loved Kath, which she'd decided he did. He'd just forgotten a little—which she seemed to think was her own fault.

She worked like the devil to correct that. She dug up new dinner recipes and spent hours in the kitchen; she was forever on a diet; and she was, if possible, even tidier about her clothes. But the effect of all the effort was just awful. She was a little slimmer, yes—even with her new efforts to be a gourmet chef—but it was like watching her shrink into herself, watching her revert to some Southern version of the timid souls so many of us were in junior high school, when all the girls had discovered boys while so very few of the boys had discovered us back.

Writing-wise, we finished *Aspects of the Novel* that April, so that now anyone overhearing us in the park might think we actually knew what we were talking about. We'd say things like "Even when we talk to ourselves we're never completely honest, so our characters shouldn't be either." (That was from Kath's favorite chapter, the one on characters, which she called "people" because Forster did; he was forever using Jane Austen as an example in that chapter, and Kath knew the "people" in the Jane Austen novels about as well as we knew our own children.) We started typing our work, too, and making multiple carbon copies—just stick four carbons behind the original and bang as hard as possible on the keys—and we were taking each other's writing home and reading it, which is a different experience from listening to it being read, believe me. We could reread lines and consider them more carefully, and jot down notes in the margins, which led to much more detailed critiques. And we could take each other's notes home with us, so when we couldn't quite remember what exactly Ally, say, had disliked about a particular line of dialogue, we could turn to her very words.

Our writing was getting better, too. Kath's journal pages were filling, and Ally's "Not Some Duck" was beginning to seem like it might someday actually quack. Linda was integrating Golda Meir's becoming prime minister of Israel and the war protests at Stanford into her stories in a way that enriched rather than overwhelmed; her setting might be the law commune on Alma, where the Shell station is now, or her character might wear a women's lib "brassy" on a chain around her neck (as Linda herself had started doing), but the stories were more and more about the emotions of her characters, rather than their politics.

Brett was at the head of the class in this, as in all things. Late that June, she swore that before the *Apollo 11* astronauts returned from the moon a few weeks later she would finish a draft of her novel— "her *Breakfast*," we called it even though it was a mystery, even though it wasn't anything like *Breakfast at Tiffany's* except that in both books a young woman walked away from her past. By then, she was big-as-a-mansion pregnant, due at the end of July, and she was working so hard to finish you'd have thought she was afraid her free hand for writing would be taken with this second hand to hold, this new baby, and she'd never find time to write again. Never mind that she was quite sure the novel was nothing. It would be "such fun" to have a draft of a novel finished, she admitted, but she wouldn't allow the possibility that it might be published someday. "Such fun." That was all this was, she was quite sure of that.

We all thought she was just being modest.

Then it was July 16—a Wednesday—and Danny and I woke at three-thirty in the morning to follow Neil Armstrong and Michael Collins up the elevator and across the swing arm to their places on the rocket ship, and then Buzz Aldrin, too, and to watch the lines of scientists in white shirts sitting in front of monitors like gamblers at slot machines. I thought of Brett as I watched them—not trying to imagine her with a flag patch on her shoulder and a space helmet securely on her head anymore, but rather picturing her hunched over her typewriter, finishing her novel.

We met in the park that morning, everyone showing up early because we were so excited about going to the moon and we'd been up for hours anyway. Brett was the last to arrive, and we fell upon her like Noah must have fallen on dry land.

"Eight days," she said. "Splashdown, I said. Not launch. I still have eight days."

"Splashdown!" Ally said.

"You better get going, honey," Kath said, "'cause your own water'll be splashing right down your skinny li'l legs before that capsule splashes into the ocean or I'll choke down my best Derby hat!"

The lunar landing was scheduled for Sunday, with the first lunar walk to be Monday morning. "The astronauts have eight hours of work after they land, before they can walk," Brett said. "They land at three eastern time, and another eight hours is midnight—too late for the East Coast to see the walk on TV."

"You think all the Yankees in Manhattan wouldn't be able to keep their li'l Yankee eyes open on a Sunday night for this?" Kath said.

"They want the astronauts to get some rest first, too," Brett said.

"But they'll be sitting on the *moon*, honey!" Kath said. "Can you imagine shutting your eyes for even one minute with your piggy toes dangling out over the moon? You put your chapter break anywhere you want to on this one, no one is turning out the light without turning the page."

We all watched the landing from our homes that Sunday: the cockpit alarm sounding constantly, and you could tell from the astronauts' voices that they didn't know what it was and they sure wanted to know. As that was sorted out (too many signals overloading the computer), they realized it was too rocky to land where they'd planned. They kept talking about how many seconds were left— "They're running out of fuel," Danny said—and finally they landed, just in time. When you read the reports of it, you imagine the first thing they said was, "Houston, Tranquility base here. The eagle has landed." But it wasn't actually the first thing they said. Just the most memorable. Which is something we remind ourselves when we're critiquing: generally, dialogue shouldn't be what people really say, but more like an edited version.

Though that rule—like all writing rules—was made to be broken. The *un*edited version of what Blanche, Kath's family's cook back in Louisville, had to say about those men being on the moon? "They ain't on no moon." And when asked where she thought they were? "I don't know, but they ain't on no moon." Sometimes real life hands you something you simply can't improve upon.

When we learned the lunar walk would be Sunday night after all—the NASA doctors had apparently come to the same conclusion Kath had—we all had the same thought: *Let's watch together.* Ally already had plans to have dinner at her sister's, but the rest of us pulled our half-cooked dinners out of our ovens, gathered our families, and hightailed it over to Linda's. Impromptu potluck. We gathered in Linda's living room, bouncing off the walls with excitement, and introduced our husbands, which was odder than I had imagined, meeting these three men I knew so well through their wives even though we'd never met. Lee was the most surprising to me; I'd pictured a much bigger man, maybe because he was Southern or because he was a doctor or because he was an adulterous bastard (goodness, did I say that?). I had never imagined he would be so charming, either—especially to Kath. Watching him bringing her tastes of all the desserts, and Anna Page sitting on his lap with the wildness seeping out of her almost the moment he wrapped his stocky arms around her, the sweetness filling in under the pretty straw hat that she kept on all evening, I saw why Kath thought he'd never leave his family.

Danny and Chip hit it off immediately, both in their dark, unfashionable but indestructible glasses, both so smart in a way that most of us couldn't really grasp, but there they were finishing each other's sentences like they'd shared a room growing up and did not once lay masking tape across the floor to define their separate, inviolate territories like my brothers had. Jeff was neither as smart as Danny and Chip nor as charming as Lee (though he was plenty smart and plenty charming, don't get me wrong), but he won hands down in the looks category—think Warren Beatty without a hint of arrogance—and he had that same restlessness that Linda had, too, that made you think the things that happened in the world would happen to him because he would make it so. I liked them all. Even Lee. I wished Ally and Jim had been able to come. I wondered if they were really at Ally's sister's house, and if they were having as good a time there as we were here.

We sat on the floor, huddled around Linda's new Zenith Giant-

Screen color television—a twenty-three-inch screen set in an oak-veneer cabinet—watching the footage from Cape Canaveral for the longest time, beginning to despair of ever seeing a man step out of the landing module. When you remember it and you don't think carefully about what you remember, you think Neil Armstrong just stepped down the ladder and onto the moon and said, "One small step for man, one giant leap for mankind," but in reality it was just like "The Eagle has landed": we listened to audio of them opening the door forever, feeling more tension than any thriller movie could ever deliver. We sat watching, and explaining things to the children: "No, honey, the man's name isn't Houston, but he's in a city called Houston, Texas." There was a picture finally, and the fellow in Houston said there was "a great deal of contrast" and it was upside down but they could make out a fair amount of detail. Even knowing it was upside down, though, I still couldn't make out one speck of anything, just gray at the bottom and a band of sunlight cutting diagonally across the top, and something that had to be some part of the landing module but you wouldn't know that if you didn't know.

"I don't see it, Daddy," Anna Page said, and Maggie echoed her, and then all the children were starting to whine that they couldn't see. We couldn't hear either, then, and all we could do was shush them and watch and listen more closely. Linda grabbed a box of cookies finally and said as long as they were quiet they could eat as many as they wanted.

There was movement in one corner of the lighted slash, something blocking the sunlight right by the module. Brett leaned toward the television and touched the screen.

"See that?" she said to the children. "That's the . . ." Her voice faltered, and for a moment there was only the clean white of her glove touching the shadow of the screen, her eyes pooling and blinking.

Watching her, I wondered about her gloves for the first time in months; they'd just become part of her to me, and yet there was something more than that, really. There was some sadness under those gloves that none of us—not even Linda—would ask her to revisit just to satisfy our curiosity. I suppose we all felt she'd share it with us in time.

"That's the astronaut coming out onto the moon," she managed, and Chip pulled her to him then, and linked his fingers with hers.

"It is?" Anna Page said, disappointment thick in her voice.

Lee touched a lock of hair under her hat. "The camera has to send the signal all the way from the moon, punkin," he said. "It isn't as good a picture as the Saturday-morning cartoons because it has to travel all that way."

Linda's Julie said, "And it's real. Cartoons aren't real." And we were all silent then, absorbing that. This was real.

The camera angle changed somehow, which made me wonder where this camera was until Chip explained they'd just flipped the image. We were seeing it right side up now, and closer in. And Houston said, "Okay, Neil, we can see you coming down the ladder now," and then I could see that the thing cutting off the sunlight could maybe be Neil Armstrong's legs making their way toward the moon. You couldn't see much, though. You couldn't see his body or his head. Just darkness at the top of the screen.

"These guys need to do a stint at film school," Jeff said.

In the laughter that followed, Chip pulled Brett closer, her cropped red hair brushing against his black glasses as he whispered something in her ear. *That should be you,* I imagined him saying. *In a more perfect world, Brett, that would be you stepping out onto the moon.*

Houston said something about shadow photography, and the camera view changed again, and there was Neil Armstrong—ghostlike, yes, but you could see the ladder and the whiteness of a huge-headed man in a white space suit, with a big pack strapped to his back. You could make out that he was turning toward the camera, and looking down, and he was talking about the surface, saying it was like powder and the feet of the landing module had sunk into it, but not too far. Then he said he was stepping off "the lam," and it was just as Maggie was saying, "Daddy, he's standing on a baby sheep?" that Armstrong finally said, "One small step for man, one giant leap for mankind." Not until then. His words were all crackling, too, and I wondered if that was the transmission or if the tears were welling in his eyes the same as they were in mine.

"Mama, why are you crying?" Anna Page said, and I saw that Kath's eyes were tearing, too, and Linda's were moist, and Brett was wiping whole streams from her cheeks.

And while Neil Armstrong was talking about his footprints, how he only sank into the surface a little bit and he had no difficulty moving around, Lee put his arm around Kath and pulled her toward Anna Page and him. "It's the first time in history, Anna Page, that man has his feet down on something other than this earth or what was made on this earth," he said. "You watch closely, punkin, this is something to remember your whole long life."

The children, tiring of a picture that was often too wavy or too dark or too fuzzy to make out anything much, began dropping off to sleep. They missed Neil Armstrong half running, half floating across the moon's surface, the sunlight reflecting off his space suit so he looked like the Holy Ghost himself. They missed Buzz Aldrin's joke about being sure not to lock the door on his way out of the module, and the plaque, WE CAME IN PEACE FOR ALL MANKIND, and the raising of the flag—not so much a raising as an opening and planting, the Stars and Stripes sticking straight out as if hung from a taut laundry line.

"No wind on the moon," Brett explained, "so they ran a pole through the top of the flag, to make it look good."

And it did. It looked beautiful, catching the sun, the stripes so clear even the children could have seen they were watching an American flag being placed on the moon. Then President Nixon was saying the heavens had now become a part of our world, and for once all the people of the world were truly one, which seems a little sappy now, and, yes, it was Nixon, but he wasn't Watergate Nixon yet, and it was moving. It was.

As the children slept, we watched the shadow men in their space suits floating back and forth across the screen, taking soil samples and running experiments, negotiating their way back into the capsule, closing the hatch again, all while the camera left on the surface of the moon sent back footage of an unwavering flag posted in front of the silent ship. I remember thinking about Michael Collins, the command module pilot who was destined to become the trivia question, the final *Jeopardy!* even though he spent the same eight days in space that Neil Armstrong and Buzz Aldrin did. Not even able to watch these first steps on the moon that could not have been made without him. I wondered how they chose who did what; if it was alphabetical he got a bad draw, even as a C. I imagined him still orbiting in the spaceship, alone on the dark side of the moon, and how very happy he must be to see the earth rise over the moon's surface each time he came back around.

$\mathcal{B}$RETT ARRIVED at the park by car that next Wednesday morning, and she got out on the passenger side, without Sarah in tow. She grinned bigger than you'd think that little-pout mouth of hers would go as she approached us, holding her very pregnant belly with one hand and four copies of her manuscript with the other. We launched into a big round of congratulations, but she interrupted us, saying she couldn't stay. "I've been in labor since four this morning," she said. "Chip will burst a vessel if I don't hand you these and march right back to the car."

She had the baby forty-three minutes later, a seven-pound, four-ounce boy: Mark Edward Tyler. He was the easiest baby there ever was to spot in the nursery, even through the fingerprint-smudged glass. That child had more hair than any newborn you've ever seen, the same remarkable strawberry blond as his mother's. It would all fall out over the next week, leaving him bald as the moon before the *Apollo* astronauts planted their unflappable flag. But it would grow back improbably thicker, a portent of things to come.

12

THE NEXT WEDNESDAY, Brett arrived pushing little Mark in a baby buggy while trying to hold Sarah's hand—she'd insisted we meet to go over her manuscript even though she'd just had the baby. The novel was a mystery in which a female graduate student, Elizabeth, finds a dead body in the physics lab and, in the course of disentangling herself from suspicion, learns that she is adopted and that her birth mother is a research scientist at the university. But the improbability of that coincidence wasn't even the biggest problem with the book, nor was the fact that only one credible suspect remained after page 42. The biggest problem was the protagonist, Elizabeth, who was, frankly, dull and unlikeable.

We all started with what we liked about the manuscript: the Stanford campus setting, the science (which was surprisingly interesting), the way Elizabeth talked things out with her favorite lab rat. "Ratty! I loved Ratty!" Linda said. "If Elizabeth were half as likeable as Ratty—"

"Y'all can laugh," Kath said, cutting Linda off, "but I swear, Ratty reminded me of Brett's brother in that thing she wrote about the marble machine." And we all did laugh, but she was right, there was a certain charm the two characters shared.

"It's awfully good for a first draft, Brett," Kath said. "A mighty good li'l mystery."

Brett, her watering eyes betraying her earlier insistence that this was just for fun, looked down at her gloved hands. "But it isn't a first draft," she said. "It's a fourth or a fifth or a sixth draft, I don't even know anymore. What is a draft, anyway?"

Kath, not missing a beat, said it was great for a sixth draft as the rest of us sat there, trying not to look incredulous. A *sixth* draft?

Critiquing the manuscript was tough because a lot of what was unlikeable about Elizabeth was what might be unlikeable about Brett, too, if you didn't know her well. But Linda launched us, asking if Elizabeth even wanted us to like her, and Ally said, "Or maybe she doesn't want us to think she *cares* if we like her? Like a defense mechanism?"

Like the way Brett hid behind her smartness, her quotes, I thought.

"She's smart as a whip, sure," Kath said, "but we need to know there's some meat on her skinny ol' bones."

"Meat?" Brett said.

"We need to see she wears gloves," Linda said.

Sudden silence, everyone trying not to stare at Brett.

"I'll bet she killed a man," I said, that line from *Gatsby,* from when we first met Brett. "I'll bet she killed a man over the way he was tearing up her manuscript."

"Justifiable homicide!" Ally said, with a very funny expression on her pale face, as if she'd just been released from the loony bin.

That made us all laugh—even Brett—and our laughter brought us back together, the way only laughter can. It was like admitting we all wore our own little white gloves over some part of us. And the vulnerability of admitting that made us a little emotional, I guess, and it's so much easier to laugh than to cry. Our laughter woke the baby, who'd been sleeping so quietly we'd practically forgotten him. And Brett leaned over to pick him up, but I said, "Let me," because it was too much, to have to tend to a baby and listen to a critique of your manuscript at the same time. And I curled him up in my lap and jiggled him a little, ran a hand over his newly bald little cradle-capped scalp, and like most newborns he didn't seem to care much whose warm arms he was in.

Kath suggested Brett explain what she meant the story to be, and Brett tried, but she lost us by the third sentence of a five-minute explanation that concluded, "I guess it's mostly about . . . beauty versus brains?"

"That's what I thought. That's the big ol' heart of the story, this idea that intelligence in a woman is about as desirable as a trapdoor on a canoe. But that doesn't hardly get a mention until"—Kath flipped through the carbon copy she and Brett were sharing, the faintest copy—"here on page 305, Brett, in this scene with Lizzy and her mama. I was wondering, though, if her mama couldn't be in the hunt from the get-go. You might could split this last chapter, make the first part of it prologue." She turned to one of the last pages. "See here? Couldn't that be the end of the prologue? Then you turn the page to chapter one. Boom: here's Lizzy before she even knows she *has* a real mama, much less how brilliant she is. But the reader *does* know."

Brett nodded after a moment.

Linda, who looked as if she'd been about to bust ever since Kath spoke, said, "I like that idea. I like that," and I silently applauded her for waiting for Brett to like it first. She'd come a long way since that morning she'd bludgeoned us into reading after she'd sworn we wouldn't have to read, that first meeting of what I just that minute began to think of as the Wednesday Sisters.

"The Wednesday Sisters," I said, not meaning to say it aloud.

They looked at me for a moment with puzzled expressions, trying to sort out what in the world I was saying about Brett's book.

"We are!" Linda said. "We're the Wednesday Sisters!"

"The Wednesday Sisters Writing Society!" Ally said.

And we all smiled, seeing even then, I think, that our friendship would change our lives, that it already had.

Linda asked Brett then what she liked about *Breakfast at Tiffany's,* why she'd chosen it as her model book, and Brett, after a moment, said she supposed she liked the way Holly just decides whom she wants to be and becomes that. "And the way she so easily abandons her past without ceasing to love it," she said.

"Think about that when you think about Elizabeth," Linda said.

Brett sighed. "But this will be so much work."

"God doesn't believe in the easy way," Kath said.

"Like you told us Hemingway said, Brett: 'First drafts are shit,'" Ally said.

Kath kicked her under the picnic table—this was a *sixth* draft—but it was too late, Brett's tears spilled over. She looked like I imagined her character Elizabeth looked in the flashback to when she was eight, when her classmates ridiculed her for using words like *paucity* and *atmospherics* and *lithe*.

"Oh, shoot, I didn't mean that, Brett," Ally said. "I just meant even great writers . . ."

But that wasn't why Brett was crying, exactly, I didn't think—or why I would have been crying if I were her, anyway. Which I would have been. Maybe it was just postpartum blues, all those hormones jumping around, but I thought it had more to do with feeling as vulnerable as that girl in her story. It had to do with knowing we were opening ourselves up, cutting ourselves open at our guts and letting the others see inside us in ways we couldn't even see ourselves. It had to do with beginning to imagine opening ourselves up not only to each other, but also to the whole world. Because wasn't that what we were hoping? That someday the things we'd squirreled away behind our little white gloves would be right out there on the bookshelves for anyone to see, our souls so pitifully disguised by our tortured prose.

BRETT SHOWED UP the next Wednesday with new pages. Not a rewrite of the novel—none of us works that fast. Just something she'd banged out on the typewriter the day before. She read it aloud, shyly, a piece that, on the surface, was about watching the lunar landing, and remembering how she and her brother had dreamed of being astronauts, wondering if he watched with the same mixture of awe and pain that she felt, the pain of seeing someone else achieving that dream they'd shared. But underneath that surface, the essay was as much about watching her daughter watching it, too, and somehow it was about the wonder of the landing and the wonder of Sarah and how those two things were the future right there in her living room, and how one day Sarah would go off to school, and then to college, and then to walk on the moon or Mars or on into another galaxy altogether, and how Brett could not imagine letting her go. I watched, riveted by her words, seeing Sarah's bare little hand slipping from Brett's white cotton grasp. Sarah all grown up, the astronaut Brett herself had once dreamed she'd be. Brett removing her gloves to touch her daughter's smooth cheek one last time before she boarded her spaceship, only to find that it was too late, that all her bare fingers could reach was the cold not-glass, the bubble dream of the space suit in which her daughter was now encased.

When she finished reading, there was a long silence.

"What?" Brett said. "I'm splitting my infinitives? Mixing my metaphors? Just tell me! If I can take that drubbing on my novel, I can take anything."

Kath wiped her eyes, and Ally pulled a tissue from her purse and blew her nose.

"Have you thought about where you'll send it?" Linda asked. And we all started talking about where we'd seen anything like this in the magazines we read.

"But it's just a little essay about nothing," Brett said. And despite all our protests—of course Chip would love it, and Sarah did *not* come off as clingy, no one could read it and think Brett didn't love Sarah to the ends of the universe, that's what the whole essay was about—no amount of our saying so could convince her to send the essay out.

13

$\mathcal{E}$VEN AFTER WE PILED into Ally's Nova the next morning, Linda remained mum about our destination. "Special outing, nine A.M., no excuses. I've got a sitter and Ally will drive" was all she'd said on the phone the night before, and this morning all we got was "Turn right here, then right again at the corner." On University, we crossed over the freeway into East Palo Alto, then right again on the frontage road. And let's just say you could have knocked us all over with a light breeze when we made a quick right into the parking lot.

"A funeral parlor?" Kath said. "You're taking us to a wake?"

We stepped through a hushed entryway into a single large room, rectangular and completely silent. The room was split by a center aisle, with slipcovered folding chairs on either side and carpet that was a deep, dark red.

"In case there's some spillage?" I whispered, and we laughed uneasily.

The room was lined with pots of lilies, roses, and freesia, fragrant flowers that did not quite cover a pinch of formaldehyde, a reminder of dead frogs laid out on lab tables and awkward teenagers thrusting frog guts on tweezers into each others' faces. At the front of the room stood an ornate coffin, carved and dark, its lid ominously closed.

A man in a somber suit—vintage funeral-parlor director—stepped through a side door near the coffin and called a startlingly cheery hello to Linda, who introduced him as a friend of Jeff's and hers.

"Don't worry, there's no dead body in the coffin," she said to us as we approached it. "That isn't the point."

"So there is a point here?" Brett said.

"For you, Brett," Linda said. "Especially for you."

The director smiled, nothing somber or sympathetic about him. "This is one of our best models, a toe pincher," he said. Its shape rather more diamond than rectangular, with the head pinched in, the toes even more so, Count Dracula–like. He pointed out its special features: the mahogany carved in crosses and grapevines (all hand-polished, which gave it that luster); the Last Supper depicted on the handle backplates and pietàs at the corners, all in antique gold. He opened the head half of the lid to reveal a diamond-shaped, pleated center panel on the lid, the entire interior done in beige velvet "with full-shirr roll and throwout, and matching pleated pillow." He asked us to knock on the side door when we were finished. No one would bother us until then.

Almost before he was gone, Linda was saying, "Okay, you first, Brett. Climb in."

"Climb in?!"

"Into the coffin."

"*Why?*"

"Brett," Linda said. "I know you always know everything, but trust me this once."

"But I'll get it dirty, for one thing."

Music began to pipe gently through the speakers, a sad trumpet solo at first, joined shortly by other instruments. An oboe. A violin.

"Take your shoes off," Linda said. "Take your shoes off and climb in. Frankie can be next, then Ally and Kath and me. Because that's the order in which we're going to be published."

That, of course, started a flurry of protests. Brett didn't even want to be published, for one thing, and none of us believed Linda would be last. "You're just putting yourself last to be polite, you know you are," Kath said, and Linda said of course she was, but what did it matter?

"What does that have to do with a coffin, anyway?" Brett asked.

"Just get in, Brett," Linda insisted.

She opened the other half of the lid to make it easier, and Brett finally skinned her shoes off and climbed in. At Linda's direction, she lay back on the pillow and closed her eyes. The room was completely silent for a moment, even the trumpet music ceasing, a short pause before the next piece of music began.

"Now," Linda said. "What are you thinking?"

"I'm thinking I do not want to be in this coffin," Brett said.

"Because?"

"Because I don't want to be dead. Because I have my children to raise, for one thing. What would Sarah and Mark do without me?"

"Okay, so now imagine your kids are grown and you're old and you've been sick and in pain and you *are* ready to die. You're dead, in fact. You're ninety years old and your children are in their sixties, they can survive without you, and let's say Chip bit the dust with you, you'd turned your home into an old folks' laboratory, and, *drat,* someone mixed something with something they shouldn't have and blew the whole place up."

Brett bolted upright, startling us, looking directly at Linda.

"You can't be sitting up when you're dead, just forget about that," Linda said, setting a hand on Brett's chest, trying to coax her to lie back on the velvet pillow again. "And even if you manage to die with your eyes open, they'll be closed by the time you're where you are now."

Brett gripped the sides of the coffin, but she did lie back, she did close her eyes. She even folded her hands at her stomach.

I wondered if they would take her gloves off when she was really dead.

"Double funeral here, you and Chip both," Linda continued. "You don't even have to worry about leaving him behind. So here's the thing." She closed the bottom half of the coffin so that Brett appeared only from the waist up. "Thirteen brilliant novels blew up with you. All stuck in a drawer along with one remarkable essay about the lunar landing that was never published because you never sent it out."

The thought of that passed across Brett's thin little freckled face like the shadow of the landing module as it approached the moon. And as Linda closed the other half of the coffin lid, concealing Brett in its darkness, I could see the same shadow passing in her face, and in Ally's, and in Kath's.

"No chance for posthumous publication, even," I said.

"No daughter finding the manuscripts and sending them off to New York," Kath said. "No, ma'am."

"They're gone. That's it. Heavens to Betsy, that's the end of you, the end of everything you might have been, everyone you might have touched with your work."

I wondered if Brett could hear us, or if the inside of that coffin was as quiet as death.

Linda opened the lid again, finally, and Brett sat up.

"You're brilliant, Brett," Linda said. "If you can't do this, how are the rest of us supposed to have any hope?" She was talking about Brett's writing, but she meant more than that. She meant *How are the rest of us supposed to have any hope of becoming whoever it is we're meant to be?*

She pulled a camera from her purse and directed Brett to lie down for another minute. "I'm not letting you forget this moment," she said.

We all took our turns in the coffin that morning, one by one shedding our shoes and confronting our futures, our mortality, our need. Linda took a photograph of each of us—to remind us when the inevitable forgetting began, she said—and when her turn came, I took a shot of her. We would put the photos someplace where we would see them every day, we agreed.

For me, there was a . . . well, a joy, really, in climbing back out of that soft beige velvet, like being reborn. And I said—I don't even know why I said it—that here we had the camera and this lovely setting. "It's high time we had a photograph of the five of us together," I said. "And what better occasion than upon our arising from the dead?"

We were all laughing as we knocked on the director's door, all giddy. He changed the music (to something more appropriate to the occasion, he said), and the Lovin' Spoonful's "Do You Believe in Magic" blared from the speakers as if we were in a high school gymnasium, five young girls dancing together at a sock hop before the rest of the school arrived.

Brett was the one who had the idea about climbing back into the coffin. We crowded around her, still with the music blaring—"believe in the magic that can set you free"—and as the director took that shot of us, we *felt* magical, and we felt young, with our futures ahead of us. Yes, we *were* young then, but we didn't think we were, we hadn't felt we were until that moment. Hadn't felt we were anything other than ordinary, that we all *could* and *would* do whatever we decided to do, that if it would turn out in the end that we'd die without ever achieving our dreams, it wouldn't be because we'd been too afraid to try.

I don't suppose there's a happier funeral photo in all the world.

WHEN THE LIBRARY DOORS opened the next morning, we went straight to the magazine section, and by noon we had a list of twenty publications to which Brett might submit her essay, the addresses and editors' names printed clearly on three-by-five index cards that would become the first entries in a database we keep to this day, though it's computerized now. After peanut butter and jelly sandwiches and chocolate milk for our children and ourselves at my house, we headed off to the park, a little submission army with our typewriters side by side on the picnic table. Brett drafted a cover letter, a "query," while we banged out copies of the essay—in those days, you couldn't just hit your print key again and again, or even photocopy things. Before the post office closed we had ten envelopes stuffed (self-addressed, stamped return envelopes included) and ready to mail.

"Don't tell anyone, not even your husbands," Brett said.

I supposed her reluctance stemmed from the same source mine would, even if she was Phi Beta Kappa from a great college and with three majors to boot. I supposed she, too, thought the only thing worse than failure was having everyone see your disgrace. I was wrong, it turns out. It wasn't failure that Brett feared. But in the time that passed before I would come to learn that, I would take great solace in believing I was in her fine company on this.

The first responses to Brett's essay were discouraging—if that essay could draw return-mail dings, what hope was there for the rest of us? We all started looking at our own writing with increasing doubt. Then one day in late August, as the first coed students were registering for classes at Vassar and Princeton and Yale, Brett's phone rang. *Redbook* wanted to publish her essay, and would pay her a hundred dollars to boot!

We were sitting at our picnic table when she told us, the children tended by Arselia, who had baby Mark in her arms.

"But I can't let them publish it," Brett said.

"I swear on my aunt Tooty's grave, Brett!" Kath said. "Just because a thing comes easily to you doesn't mean it isn't good enough."

Brett looked down at her hands resting on the picnic table. "But Brad . . . my brother . . ."

"He's the most charming person in the essay!" I said. "I'm sure he'll love it."

Brett shoved her hands under the table and met my gaze, as if she wanted to say something but couldn't find the words even with her incredible vocabulary.

"You can't make his dream come true," Linda said quietly.

"You don't know what Brad's been through, Linda," Brett said, speaking even more quietly than Linda had, as if Mark were asleep in her arms.

"You can't make anyone's dream come true but your own, Brett," Linda said. "Only your own. That's it."

Did we buy a bottle of champagne and celebrate? You bet we did. And when that essay appeared on newsstands, we opened a second bottle to celebrate that.

It came as a huge surprise when, just a few weeks later, Linda sold *her* first story—to a small magazine no one had ever heard of, with no circulation whatsoever, but that didn't matter one whit to us. It was that first story she'd given us, a simple thing about a mother putting her children to bed, and I remembered how critical we'd been of it, and how she'd listened and taken notes.

"You never told us you were even fixin' to send it out, Linda," Kath said—not an accusation, but with a hint of feeling betrayed.

I swallowed against the same swelling emotion, the little voice saying Linda must think this was some sort of a competition and she'd just won—or at least come in second after Brett. I remembered a boy I'd dated in high school, who told me I wasn't hurt that he'd broken up with me, I was mad that I hadn't broken up with him first. "Well, it's wonderful anyway," I said.

Linda met Kath's eyes, then mine. "It wasn't like that," she said quietly. "I was afraid you'd say it wasn't ready—which it wasn't, but I guess I needed to get it out there, to get those rejections to see that. After a few revisions, some editors wrote back with personal notes, sometimes even with comments, and I wanted to ask if you guys agreed with them, but how could I when I hadn't even told you I'd sent it? So I just revised again and mailed it back out. Sixty-three times."

"Sixty-three!" In unison, all four of us.

"I have a lot of index cards to add to our collection," she said.

"Sixty-three," Kath repeated. "Lordy, Linda, how in the world could you take that much of a whippin'?"

"Heavens to Betsy, sixty-three rejections," Ally said soberly.

Linda sat back in her chair, crossed her legs. "If I don't believe in my own work," she said, "how can I expect anyone else to? Besides, it was only sixty-two rejections. The last one was a yes."

14

*L*INDA WAS STANDING in front of the bathroom mirror one Tuesday night that August, still smiling over a Woodstock joke Johnny Carson had told in his opening monologue, when she raised her arms to slide on her pajama top and noticed a funny pucker in the skin on her left breast. Her fingers went to the spot, her pajama top dropping to the floor. She could feel something, not in the skin but underneath it. A small hardness, the size of a pea.

She thought of her mother, how she'd run from her mother and her awful arm, how that must have broken her mother's heart.

She felt again, sure she must be mistaken. But the lump was still there.

"Jeff?" she said, a whisper. She opened the door into the bedroom and stood there in her pajama bottoms, still naked from the waist up.

Jeff was propped up against the pillows with a medical journal in his hands, watching Johnny Carson announce the night's first guest: ". . . her new novel is *The Love Machine*. Please welcome the beautiful Jacqueline Susann!"

He looked to Linda, his eyes drawn to her naked breasts. "Hey," he said. "Does this mean I'm going to get lucky?"

"Jeff," she said in a louder voice, more like panic.

He was out of the bed and in front of her in no time, his hands on her arms, looking directly into her eyes. "What, Linda? What is it?"

She swallowed once, twice. "A lump," she tried to say, but her voice didn't come out.

"What!" Jeff insisted. "Damn it, Linda, you're scaring the hell out of me."

Something about his panic calmed her. She focused on the sameness all around her: the medical journal abandoned on the bed; *Portnoy's Complaint* on her own nightstand, bookmarked to the page she'd been reading; the *Tonight Show* audience laughing on the TV. "A lump," she said more surely. "I think I felt a lump. I'm sure it's nothing, but—"

"Oh, shit," Jeff said, turning away from her, running his hand through his dark hair.

"It's probably nothing," Linda assured him. "I was just startled. It's probably nothing."

On the television, the *Tonight Show* band played a few short notes.

"Shit," Jeff said. "Okay. Okay. We'll call Albert. Shit, what's his number?"

"It's nearly midnight," Linda said.

Jeff looked at her as if she'd just insulted him. Suddenly self-conscious, she turned to the bathroom, retrieved her pajama top, pulled it over her head.

In the moment she was turned away from Jeff, he bolted out the bedroom door, down the stairs to the phone in the kitchen. She heard pages flipping, Jeff looking for his colleague's home number, then his voice: "Albert, listen, Linda's got a . . ."

In the long pause that followed, Linda crept down the stairs, peeked around the corner. Jeff sat on the kitchen floor, in the dim light that filtered down from upstairs. He had the phone receiver to his ear, but his head was tucked down to his knees.

He looked up, focusing on the cabinets across from him. He heaved a big breath. "A lump," he whispered. Then after another moment, "Yes."

"Jeff," Linda said.

He stiffened. He'd heard her, but he didn't look her way. He listened into the receiver for another moment and, still without looking at her, handed it over. His hand, she thought, looked like her father's: broad and muscular, and unsteady.

She was chilled all of a sudden.

She took the receiver, answered Albert's questions. The lump was in her left breast. At about three o'clock. Yes, near her armpit. The size of a small pea. Not as hard as a marble, but harder than chewed bubble gum. She listened to Albert for a few minutes, then handed the receiver toward Jeff. "He says there's nothing to do tonight," she said. "He says to call his office in the morning and he'll get Ellie to work me in."

As Linda headed back upstairs she tried to block out the sound of Jeff's voice pleading with Albert, then growing angry. "I could drive Linda over right now, we could be there in ten minutes." And she knew Albert was telling him what he'd just told her, that they would almost certainly have to do a biopsy, that that would take a few days to arrange.

She turned off the television in the bedroom, turned off the lights, climbed under the covers, laid her head flat on the pillow. She stared up at the ceiling, trying not to think, trying to get warm.

From downstairs, Jeff's voice, still badgering Albert. "Okay, seven o'clock, if that's the best you can do. We'll be at your office at seven A.M."

She heard the receiver click onto the cradle. The house was silent for a long moment before she heard the refrigerator door sucking open, ice clinking in a glass. A bottle twisting open. Liquid splashing out. Jeff's scotch.

She was still lying there, awake, when Jeff came upstairs finally. She closed her eyes, able to bear the darkness with him there, and pretended to sleep.

He eased onto the bed and under the covers, but he stayed at the very edge of the mattress, as if he was afraid to get too near her in case she was contagious. She lay awake all night, listening to the sounds of him lying awake, too. She had not felt so alone since before she'd met him, since before he'd first spoken to her at a fall mixer her freshman year at college. She'd been wearing her favorite sweater, a forest-green cashmere cardigan she claimed she liked to wear without a blouse underneath because she loved the soft wool against her skin, although the truth was that a blouse ruined the drape of the sweater, the way the thin green wool accentuated her breasts.

"That's a super sweater you're wearing," Jeff had said, his first words not memorable on their own. But she placed her hands over his eyes without even thinking, without hesitating to touch this boy she'd never met. "Do you really like it?" she asked. "Then tell me, what color is it?" She felt the flush of his embarrassment against her palms, and she knew then it wasn't the sweater, exactly, that he admired, knew it even before he said, "Blue?"

"Most lumps are just fibrocystic tumors or fibroadenomas, especially at our age," Brett said the next morning when Linda told us about finding the lump, having already been to the doctor that morning. She'd persuaded Jeff to stay home with the children while she went to see Albert at seven. She hadn't wanted to alarm the children by dragging them along.

"They don't think it's hereditary, either," Brett said. "Or if it is, genetics play only a minor role, so the fact that your mom—" Her gaze dropped to her gloved fingers tightly intertwined on the picnic table. "We think it's caused by viruses or chemicals or hormones. We know mice can transmit breast cancers to their young through viruses in their breast milk, and researchers have found—"

"I read this article in *Reader's Digest*," I interrupted. You could tell Brett meant to be helpful—if she were Linda, she'd want the scientific facts—but you could see Linda realizing she might have caught cancer from her mom's breast milk, and thinking she'd breast-fed her own children, too. "It said even if it's . . . not good, they do an operation, a mastectomy, and most women live for years."

For five years, that's what the article had said. The five-year survival rate for breast cancer was 80 percent.

"I've Lived with Cancer" was the title of that article, about a woman who was thirty-seven when she discovered a lump in her breast. It had been weirdly upbeat: most lumps were nothing, and for those that *were* something, an operation would likely save you, and your husband would still find you attractive, even without your breasts. But the details were sobering: a permanent form cost fifteen dollars, and they came in all sizes so you could feel "perfectly balanced." I was left imagining taking my kids into the ocean, seawater dripping from my permanent form for hours afterward. I was left picturing myself cowering behind the bathroom door while Danny, in bed, willed himself not to be repulsed. Or worse. In five years, Davy would be only seven, and Maggie ten.

In five years, Jamie and Julie would be ten, like my Maggie. In five years, J.J. would be six.

"Jeff is just flipping out," Linda said, her gaze fixed on the rough wood table in front of her. "It's like he's already imagining me without a breast, already imagining having to climb into bed every night with a *freak*." The word spit out, but with a crack in her voice.

"Linda," Kath said gently.

"Like he's crawling into bed with a corpse," she said more quietly, her eyes shaded by her Stanford cap, but tears making tracks down the arc of her cheek, under her jaw, disappearing into the bold stripe of her turtleneck, the one she'd worn that first day I met her. "It's like he thinks I'm already dead, like he's already drawing away from me so he can bear it like he . . ." She swiped a hand across her eyes. "His mom . . . Like my mom."

Had died, too, she meant, leaving unspoken the details. Was he two or twelve or twenty when she died? Had she been ill long, or at all? Had she been hit by a car and left in a coma? Had she been unstable, taken too many pills?

"What does the doctor think?" Kath asked gently.

Linda tucked her hands underneath herself on the picnic-table bench, straightened her spine. "He thinks it's benign, but he wants to do a biopsy. It's a small lump, so he'll cut out the whole thing and they'll look at it under the microscope, just to make sure."

There was an audible sigh of relief around the table: *Small Lump, Probably Benign.*

"Jeff is trying to arrange a hospital bed for me now." She looked to the empty mansion across the park. One of the front steps had splintered and fallen in on itself. I wondered when that had happened, if it had been hours or days or weeks.

"Good," Brett said. "The sooner, the better."

"They'll put me under, and if the biopsy . . . if it's bad, they won't wait, they'll just do the mastectomy and I'll wake up and . . . Oh, God."

That's what they did back then: they put you under for a biopsy, and if you woke with your chest and your arm all bandaged, you knew—if you could bear to know it—that your breast was gone, that it was cancer, although no one would likely tell you it was until you'd had a chance to recover from the surgery. You trusted your doctor back then. You weren't given any other choice.

"I don't think I can do it," Linda said. "I don't think I can bear to let them put me to sleep knowing when I wake up . . . My mom, you know . . ." She waved a hand in front of her arm. Her gaze found J.J. on the swing, and you could see in her pretty face the little girl she must have been, afraid of her own mother's hug.

"And my kids," she said, "my kids . . ." But she didn't finish the thought; she left it there, left us imagining Julie and Jamie huddled in their closet, J.J. standing at salute, watching his mother's coffin being drawn through the street.

Jeff failed in his effort to get Linda's biopsy done that day; the hospital bed could be arranged, but obtaining an operating room for anything short of an immediately life-threatening emergency was more problematic, even for Jeff. Left with no choice, he allowed himself to be talked into being reasonable with the same rationale we all used to console ourselves—that most lumps were nothing. The biopsy was scheduled for the following Thursday, eight days later. And by the end of that morning Linda had pulled herself together, or pulled herself in, anyway. She insisted in very frank Linda fashion that if we uttered one more word about it before she knew for sure—to her, to anyone else, even among ourselves—she would never forgive us. That if we called her to see if there was anything we could do (there was not, she insisted), if we even just called on some lousy trumped-up excuse to see if she was okay, she would never forgive us. She was not going to think about it, not for another moment, and we weren't to either.

"No point in losing sleep over something that is almost certainly nothing," she said. "I've got to run. I have a committee meeting. We're trying to keep the foothills behind Stanford from being developed. Don't you think they should be kept as open space, for everyone to enjoy?" But the passion that was always in her voice when she talked about her causes wasn't there. She didn't even try to enlist us this time.

"Remember, you promised," she said as she pushed J.J.'s stroller onto the sidewalk. And despite our promise, despite that reminder, the moment she was out of sight we were talking about it amongst ourselves, unable to grant her even this one small request.

15

THAT AFTERNOON, I went to Saint Thomas Aquinas, where I sat in an empty pew looking at the empty altar, wondering if there was a God up there who listened to prayers, and why He was doing this to Linda and had done it to her mom. Wondering why He didn't let Ally carry her babies to term, and why He sat by while Lee hurt Kath, and what He could have allowed to happen to Brett that left her wearing her gloves. Wondering, too, what I could possibly do for Linda other than what she'd asked, which was nothing, which was only not to talk, a task at which I'd already failed.

In bed that night I lay awake worrying about Linda, losing the sleep she didn't want us to lose. Wondering if she was sleeping, or what she was doing if she wasn't, if she, too, was lying awake. I imagined her sitting in J.J.'s room, or in Julie and Jamie's, watching them sleep like the mother had done in her story, the one she'd gotten published, that she'd sent out sixty-three times.

I climbed from bed carefully so as not to wake Danny, and took my glasses from my nightstand. I went to check on Maggie, her face tucked up against her Allo blanket as she mumbled in her sleep, words I never could understand. Then into Davy's room, where I sat on the floor by his bed with my hand on his little leg, trying to remember the details of Linda's story, thinking, *Sixty-three times.*

I thought again of the novel I'd written back in Chicago, the Italian Renaissance mystery. I'd spent so much time writing it, just that one draft, but I'd never done anything with it. I wondered what Linda had written in the years before I met her, what story she might have used to apply to graduate school. Was it in a drawer somewhere, or had she pulled it out, revised it, read it to us, and listened to what we had to say? Then revised again, sixty-three times. Or sixty-two, since the last one was a yes.

I'd so loved the idea of that novel of mine, a whodunit that was also an exploration of religion and the perversion of its purposes—or that was what it was meant to be, anyway. It was one part fascination for me—fascination with Michelangelo and the Sistine Chapel and Pope Julius II, Il Papa Terrible, whose main concern in life seemed to have been to ensure a suitable palace for his own entombment—and one part passion for a church and a religion that were so integral to who I was. But the draft when I'd read it—"Michelangelo's Ghost," that's what I'd called it—was so much less than I'd meant it to be. I'd thought that was all there was to it back then. One single draft. You were a writer or you weren't.

I thought of all the books I'd disliked, or put down without finishing—often books that one or more of the Wednesday Sisters had loved—or books we'd all thought dreadful, that, to our considerable disbelief, made the bestseller list. "Not every book is for every reader." Words Linda liked to say when she'd recommended a book none of the rest of us could stand.

Linda's Ghost, I thought, and I wanted to pick up the phone and call her, even though I knew she didn't want that.

I went to the kitchen. Pulled that old manuscript from the bottom kitchen desk drawer, almost as a way to be with Linda. I looked down at the first few words, the introduction of my character Risa. She was as weak a character as Dritha, the protagonist in my new novel, I could see that now. A smelly old dishrag, Linda would say, with a spine Kath would find catawampus, delivered in prose Ally would find awkward in places, with words Brett would see were not quite what I'd meant.

But if I didn't believe in my work, how could I expect anyone else to?

I pulled the coffin photo from my refrigerator—not the one of just me, but the one of all of us—and I set it in a splash of moonlight on the coffee table. I clicked on the lamp and began making notes in my journal: What is Risa most embarrassed about or ashamed of? What little gesture does she make frequently, and does she realize it, and would she stop doing it if she did? What one thing about her seems to contradict everything else? And why in the world is she out poking into the disappearance of a nun rather than, say, living in a nice home in Palo Alto with two children and a husband, friends she meets every Wednesday in the park—or the early sixteenth-century Roman equivalent?

Because the dead nun was one of Risa's closest friends, that was the answer, of course. A friend who would have done anything for her. One who, if she had given her promise not to talk of a thing, would not go back on it even in the name of trying to help.

In the dark of the night, I made twelve pages of character sketch: what Risa did when she awoke in the morning, her favorite food, what her ideal man looked like, what made her laugh and what her laughter sounded like, which was very like Kath's most uninhibited laugh, and whether she, like me, sometimes laughed so hard she had to cross her legs lest she wet herself. I cut out magazine pictures to help me imagine what she looked like—dark hair like this picture, like Ally's; eyes shaped like this woman's, but the same green as mine; trim and petite like Brett, but with stocky hands and sturdy wrists; freckles on her nose like Brett, too, when the beauty standards of the time demanded none. Then I turned to Risa's friend, the nun, finding no need of magazine photos to imagine her: her face was there in my mind, her eyes the sea blue of Sister Josephine's, the brows above them as straight and expressive as Linda's, the brows of a woman who would put herself smack-dab in the middle of the worst poverty, doing all she could to ease the pain of strangers that Risa, sequestered in her comfortable villa, couldn't imagine how to help. And when I'd finished with the nun, I slid clean paper and carbons into the type-writer carriage, and I typed at the top of the first page "Chapter 1."

That's where I was—sitting with my old manuscript and my scribbles of character sketches, scraping the carbon copies of a misspelled word with a razor to avoid retyping the whole page—when I looked up and saw Danny standing in the doorway, watching me. The sun was coming up already. I'd been working all night.

I looked down at my writing, stark black letters on white. At the coffin photo beside my typewriter, me in my glasses, though usually I took them off the moment I saw a camera.

"I . . . I'm writing," I said.

"I know," he said, and I saw in his expression that he'd stood here before, watching me so lost in what I was writing that I didn't even know he was there.

He smiled slightly. "In that first little apartment back in Chicago, you always sat in my seat, where the edge of the card table was peeling. I thought you'd given it up, though, before we moved here."

He didn't ask why I'd never told him, didn't put me on the spot. He only looked at me like I was a gift he'd just opened, the surprise he'd known was there all along under the wrapping and the bow, but that didn't matter because it was exactly what he wanted. "And what, pray tell, are you writing?" he asked. "If you're willing to tell?"

I didn't say it was my gift to Linda, my prayer for her; I'm not sure I even saw at the time that it was, that the nun had become more and more like Linda in my notes, that I was trying to capture Linda's frankness and her generosity and her fear. But I told him the gist of the story, bungling the description badly. Still, Danny said he couldn't wait to read it. I would let him read it, wouldn't I? And while I was worrying that one—Would he like it? Would he see himself in any of it?—he called me "the future famous novelist, Frankie O'Mara." It was like when I'd told Bob about my novel at the holiday party, only better, and I wondered if this was something Danny had learned from watching Bob, from admiring him, or if he'd always been like this.

I told Danny I wanted to publish under Mary Frances, my way of saying that was my dream, to be published, without having to say it directly. He responded with an easy "What about M.F.? Or

M. Frances? Men won't realize you're a woman. You'll get more male readers that way."

Readers. A word Bob had used, too, in that Christmas-party conversation: "Will you meet your readers, or will you be one of these famous recluses people want so badly to know?"

"It's the weirdest thing," I said, and I hadn't planned to tell Danny this any more than I'd planned to spill my dreams to Bob at that party, but I wanted him to know suddenly, I didn't want to have anything to hide from him. "The first time I met Bob, last December? I told him I was writing. I don't even know why."

"Bob?"

"Bob Noyce."

Danny laughed uneasily, with the oddest expression behind his black-rimmed glasses, an expression that looked so like Maggie when she was about to cry. He focused on my page in the typewriter, the carbons flopped forward where I'd been correcting my mistake.

"Bob has that effect on people," he said, light words, but something in the hesitation before he spoke left me thinking of Bob and his mask designer, the Purple-Jesus-cocktails-and-airplane-views gal. I wondered if she'd fallen in love with Bob, or if it was the image of herself she saw in his mind that had turned her head. I wondered if she was married, if her husband had seen them together. I imagined her husband feeling betrayed by the simple act of his wife having a conversation with Bob, across the room. I wondered if he'd asked what they had talked about, and if she'd answered, and if her husband, seeing how she felt with Bob even if she'd never slept with him, even if she never imagined she would, had gathered his pride and left her, without warning, maybe, without any idea at all why he'd left.

16

*L*INDA WAS THE LAST of us to arrive the following Wednesday, and she looked awful. As little as I'd slept that week, she must have slept even less. We all wanted to say something about it, you could see that by the glances we threw each other, but we had promised Linda we wouldn't, and it was one thing to break that promise among ourselves and quite another to do it in front of her.

No one else had written a word that week.

"Okay, we'll read Frankie's, then," Brett said.

Kath, as always, seemed most to have the pulse of what I was trying to do. "I love the nun," she said. "She just springs to life. She breathes on the page."

The other Wednesday Sisters agreed, although Linda did say, "She's awfully frank, though, isn't she? Is anyone really that frank?"

Kath suppressed a smile. "I like the theme that's developing here, too, Frankie," she said. "How the Catholic Church shapes its congregants, especially women. How it herds women down this narrow little path, ties their corsets so tightly they can't catch a breath."

I nodded as if I had any idea I'd written that.

"And I like Risa, too. I really do," Kath said, her insistence betraying that she did not like Risa one little bit. "But . . . God knows we all wail the wide Mississippi over the wrongs our men do us—look at me, of course—but I'm not sure about the business with the beau. And her friendship with the nun—"

"You call that friendship?" Linda flung her pen on the table. "She's not the nun's friend at all! She doesn't do *anything* to prevent her dying. She doesn't even call her, not once!"

"Doesn't telephone?" Ally said in her hushed voice. "But they didn't have—" Then, "Oh." Followed by, "But you told us not to, Linda."

Before anyone could respond, little Carrie ran up to Ally, incensed beyond consolation. J.J. had taken a shovel from her and said it was his and she couldn't use it. "It's *my* shovel," she wailed—taking us all aback because Carrie rarely said a word, and even when she did it was in the same you-could-barely-hear-her voice Ally had. Then, with a good foot stomp for emphasis, she insisted, "It *is*, Aunt Ally, it *is*."

Silence around the table. Even Linda seemed to have forgotten herself.

Ally inhaled once, deeply, then reached down and tucked Carrie's dark hair gently behind her ears. "It's not your shovel really, honey," she said, focusing on the girl's long-lashed, uncertain eyes, not meeting any of ours. "We didn't bring any shovels, remember? Your mommy accidentally left your shovels at the beach last weekend. But there are lots of shovels. Look, there's a blue one just sitting there, by Arselia."

Carrie, though, wanted the red shovel. No other would do. Even if it wasn't hers, she'd been playing with it and she'd just set it down and J.J. took it. He hadn't taken it from her hand, no. But she'd still meant to be using it.

Ally pulled the girl to her, hugged her, but Carrie, not to be deterred, wriggled from her embrace.

"I'll tell you what, Carrie," Linda said so gently you could not imagine that just a moment before she'd been ready to bludgeon us. "J.J.'s favorite color is blue, so why don't you do this?" She leaned closer to Carrie, her voice an emotional whisper. "You go pick up that blue shovel and start playing with it, and just mention how much bigger it is than the red shovel, how much more sand it can pick up. See if J.J. doesn't offer to trade."

"It *is* bigger!" Carrie said. "*I* want the blue shovel!"

"Well then go get it, honey," Linda said. "And be real quiet about how much bigger it is."

Carrie ran off, leaving the rest of us to our awkward silence.

Ally pressed her palms together, looked up at the sky—a deep blue that day. Not a cloud anywhere in sight. No filmy sliver of moon.

"I used to watch you through my window, before Frankie moved here," she said, "when you two"—Linda and Kath—"used to come and talk together, and watch your children. When I was pregnant, I'd watch you. Then I'd lose the baby and I couldn't watch for a while." Her face clouded over, and I was about to say something, but then she went on. "But I'd always be drawn back to the window. And then Frankie started joining you, and even Brett—" She stopped herself, but it was clear what she meant, that even this weird woman who wore the gloves could find friends in this park, so why not her? "But I didn't have a baby. I kept thinking I would. I'd get pregnant and I'd take every bit of the medicine my doctor gave me to keep from losing the baby, but . . . Then the day Robert Kennedy was shot, I just thought no one would notice. I just thought everyone would be caught up in that and I could bring out tea and say hello and no one would notice I didn't have a child, no one would wonder what I was doing coming to the park alone.

"I even picked out a child to pretend was mine that first day," she said. "I picked a little boy in a Mickey Mouse T-shirt at first, but then there was this girl with loose, dark curls, like my hair was when I was a toddler, like I imagine my baby's hair will be when I allow myself to imagine. Then no one asked, which was a blessing, because what if I'd pointed to that curly-haired girl and she'd gone running off to her real mother?"

There was a low murmur of sympathy from around the table.

"That girl, she seemed almost like a sign that morning." Ally tilted her pale face toward the splintered table. "My babies," she whispered, "they've all been sons."

Kath put her arm around Ally, then, and we all leaned in closer, as if to share our warmth.

"My mother always wanted a son," she said. "I sometimes think if I could have a son, a grandson for her, she and my father both might . . ." She looked again to the sky, to the sharp blue that looked solid and impenetrable hanging over the mansion.

"That first day I just waited till you all left," she said. "It was nice being in the park, even when it was empty. I almost couldn't bear to leave. I think it was only realizing about Carrie that got me up off that bench."

She'd gone home and called her sister, who was delighted at the idea of having one morning a week to herself, without Carrie. Wednesday morning.

"But why didn't you just tell us she was your niece, honey?" Kath said.

"We all have our secrets to hide," Brett said quietly, and we turned to see her looking down at her gloves, at the hands underneath that none of us had ever seen. "'Every man is a moon, and has a dark side which he never shows to anybody.'"

Linda, frowning at Brett, adjusted her Stanford cap. I wondered if she was thinking of the scar she would have on her breast by the end of the next day, if she still had a breast, or if she was wondering about Brett's hands, or thinking about something else entirely, some secret she hadn't yet shared.

"But there's nothing wrong with bringing your niece to the park, Ally," Brett said. "You know we wouldn't have cared."

Ally tucked her hair behind her ears as she'd done with Carrie just minutes before, her eyes as vulnerable as her niece's had been. "I did try to tell you, Brett. You and Frankie. When it seemed nothing would matter ever again anyway."

I took Ally's hand. "She did," I said. "She tried to tell us, but we misunderstood, we thought she was saying her sister was taking care of Carrie for her."

It had been impossible to question her about it that morning in her chalky-blue bedroom, with all those tissues scattered across the floor.

I wondered if I'd have told the others if I had been surer of what I'd heard that morning in Ally's bedroom, if it hadn't been so clear that Brett had heard something else. I thought probably I wouldn't have anyway. I thought probably I'd have let Ally come to telling us herself, in her own time.

"It's just that people ask, you know?" Ally said. "'Are you planning on having children of your own?' And I don't know what to say because I've had *three* babies, three who've died, but people don't understand that, they think a baby who isn't born alive was never a baby, that I shouldn't grieve." She looked across to the mansion, blinking, whispering, "It was comforting even though it wasn't real, to have one morning every week when I could seem like a mom with a living child."

And Linda, who hadn't said a word—had hardly moved since she'd watched Carrie head for that blue shovel—said, "Would you bring my children to the park, too, Ally? If anything happened to me?"

Kath moved closer to Linda, took her hand.

"I felt like I never had a friend in the world after my mom got sick," Linda said.

"You're going to be fine, Linda," Kath said softly. "You'll be fixin' to kick up a ruckus before the sun sets tomorrow, I know you will."

"I can bear anything but the thought of Jamie and Julie and J.J. having to endure that kind of loneliness," Linda said, and you could hear in her voice the child who had not been invited to birthday parties or sleepovers or afternoons of play, you could hear the rustle of skirts as neighborhood mothers leaned down to their daughters, their gentle voices saying Linda's mommy probably wanted her at home today, how about Mary or Joan or Beth? You could see the Linda who'd settled herself on a tree branch where no one could see her and tried to spin for herself a web of imaginary friendships, a world of Charlottes and Ferns and Wilburs. The child who built I-don't-care-if-I-offend-you walls, who decided she didn't *want* friends other than the ones she found in books.

I knew then something I could do for Linda.

"Maggie will always be there for Julie and Jamie, Linda," I said. "And Davy will always be there for J.J."

And as Kath and Brett echoed me, I wondered if Linda hadn't spoken to me that first morning in the park even though I read mysteries because my children were the same age as her children, because I might be someone who kept friends for a lifetime, and my children might be, too.

Not that it mattered. It only mattered that she had told me I was staring or asked what I was reading, whichever it was she'd said first, and that Kath had joined us, and then Brett, and then Ally, too.

17

*L*INDA HAD SAID that she couldn't bear to be put under anesthesia knowing she might wake without a breast, with her arm swollen and hideous. But she did bear it. She hugged her children good-bye—telling them only that she was going on a short trip; she didn't believe it was cancer; it couldn't be—and she went to the hospital and signed the consent form in a shaky hand. When the time came, she climbed onto the gurney and Jeff kissed her and told her he would always love her, no matter what, and she almost believed him, she really did.

It was only when they first put the mask over her face that she realized she was making the same mistake her own mother had. She hadn't told Jamie and Julie and J.J. the truth.

She held her breath against the anesthetic gas, imagining her mother must have felt this, too: the dread of letting go.

She didn't know what happened after that, but Jeff did. No, he wasn't allowed inside the operating room even though he was a doctor, even though he was sure he wanted to be there. He sat in the waiting room like any other husband, and Brett and I sat with him while Kath and Ally took the children to the park. He sat with an untouched cup of coffee, flipping through a stale magazine that neither Brett nor I had the heart to point out was upside down.

"They'll be started now," he told us at 8:06. Not 8:00 or 8:10, but 8:06. He knew exactly what time they were scheduled for the operating room, exactly how long it would take for the anesthesia to put her to sleep. He knew too much for a husband whose wife had to go through this. He knew how sharp the scalpel was and how thick the skin was, how long the incision would be. What a breast looked like with the skin pulled back. What a lump that was not supposed to be there looked like, nestled in healthy tissue, and being cut away. He could almost see the clot of bloody tissue in its sterile container being hurried to the lab. He could imagine every moment: the tissue being spread on a lens, the pathologist leaning his eye to the microscope, peering. They ought to have let him observe, they really ought to have, because he was driving himself crazy, imagining them finding a wide swath of disease lodged in Linda's breastbone, scattered into her lymph nodes, making its way throughout her body to lodge in her liver, her bones, her brain. But there was Brett, armed with the facts: 75 percent of breast lumps are benign; 60 percent of cancers are in women over forty. Statistics that, surprisingly, soothed Jeff in a way that facts had failed to soothe Ally or Linda, even though Brett wasn't telling him anything he didn't already know.

Facts had always soothed her brother, Brett would tell us later, when she told us about Brad finally. She thought maybe men and women were different that way.

When Linda awoke a few hours later, crawling up from the fog of anesthesia, she found she could breathe freely, no heavy push of pressure bandages on her chest, not the least bit of swelling in her arm. She didn't say so, but you know she cried with relief the same way Jeff did when the doctor came from the operating room to tell him it had all gone well, that they'd excised the one lump, that was all there was, and of course they couldn't be certain until the pathologist finished the more definitive tests, but the preliminary results were good, the preliminary results suggested the lump was benign, harmless. Nothing to worry about.

I sure cried when Jeff told us.

Jeff fell asleep in the chair in Linda's hospital room afterward, and slept soundly the whole night that way. It was against hospital regulations, but no one was going to tell him visiting hours were up.

A scar at the side of her breast, that was all. It didn't even show when Linda wore a bikini, which she did later that summer. That physical scar never did show.

THAT SEPTEMBER Maggie, along with Kath's Lee-Lee and Linda's twins, started kindergarten. Linda and I just basically blubbered, and even Kath, who'd been through this before—Anna Page was starting third grade—was as sappy about that as she was about little Lee. Our babies were growing up. But the children were not the least bit nervous. Maggie, dragging along her Allo blanket for her rest-time "friend," let go of my hand as if she'd been doing it for ages. It made me a little sad, realizing how little she thought she needed me.

I would be thirty-eight when she went off to college, I remember thinking that morning. Forty when Davy left. They would grow up and go off on their own in a bigger way, just like in Brett's essay, and though I would always be their mother, I would cease to be their mother in the every-moment way I was now, in the way that Danny would continue to be an every-moment engineer even without the children at home. And who would I be then?

"You should join the AAUW with me, Frankie," Linda said. "The American Association of University Women."

Yes, some women did belong primarily to play bridge, she said in answer to Brett, who said that's what she thought they did. "But doesn't everyone like to play a hand every now and then? You all learned in college, right? And anyway, the Palo Alto branch is much more than a social club." They campaigned for women running for political office, she explained, and they were helping write an environmental handbook and working to get a San Francisco Bay wildlife refuge off the ground. They presented programs on topics such as "Foreign Policy: Dilemmas and Realities" and "Human Use of Urban Space."

"My study topic is 'This Beleaguered Earth: Can Man Survive?'" she said, leaving me to wonder what exactly a study topic might be. "We're trying to show it would be cheaper to preserve the foothills behind Stanford as open space than to develop them. It's a cool group, really. One you can all join. It doesn't matter which college you went to."

I nodded like I'd nodded about the whole bridge-at-college thing when I had no idea how to play bridge.

Linda had met a Northwestern alumna at the AAUW meeting that week. "You must have known her, Frankie. She's just our age, and she was in engineering, which is where Danny was, right? There can't have been three women in engineering. What year did you graduate?"

I didn't know the woman, but I did know that someday Linda would bump into someone who knew me, who'd say, "Frankie? Wasn't she an engineering school secretary?" Or Danny would say something. He had no more idea that these women thought I'd gone to Northwestern than he did that I'd been even chubbier in high school or that I'd once let Sean Casey feel me up even though I didn't like him because I wanted a date to the prom (never mind that he hadn't asked me to the prom anyway).

"I . . ." I adjusted my glasses, not meeting anyone's eyes. "I didn't graduate from Northwestern. Danny. That was Danny."

"But you still had a class, honey," Kath said. "That doesn't make you not part of a class. Lordy, most gals I went to school with never did graduate either. They got married when their husbands were done, and they went and moved with them to whatever sorry town had a job. What year did you start?"

I pulled my sweater closed, too unsure of my hands to venture the buttons. I knew Kath wouldn't care. None of them would care, really. Why hadn't I just told them before?

"I never did start," I said. "I never went to Northwestern. Danny did, but not me."

"Oh," Linda said.

"Where did you go, then?" Ally asked.

The pity in Brett's eyes: she'd understood.

"I didn't go to college," I said. "I was a secretary at the engineering school. That's how Danny and I met."

"Well, shut my mouth," Kath whispered under her breath.

"I just . . . when you assumed I'd been to college, I was too embarrassed to set you straight."

Linda, frowning, adjusted her Stanford cap. Then her eyes lit up, all those colors. "You should apply to Stanford, Frankie," she said.

"Not everyone has to go to college, Linda," Brett said. "Not everyone even wants to."

"Here's one of the greatest universities in the country," Linda said, ignoring Brett, "and you can practically walk to it."

"*Stanford?*" I said. "But I wouldn't know where to begin."

Linda turned her eyes heavenward, a God-give-me-patience look. "You would too, Frankie. You're a smart girl. You just get the application, fill it out, take the SATs. Send it all in. Walk it in!"

As if it were that easy. As if there were no question of my being smart enough. As if the thousands of dollars of tuition were pocket change and she herself had gone off to graduate school when she'd wanted to, never mind the twins.

So, SEPTEMBER 1969. School starting. Leaves falling. Miss America—which the Wednesday Sisters talked about skipping that year. Though the pageant would have higher ratings than the year before, and the following year a record 22 million households would watch, all the controversy—those boardwalk protesters—had taken a toll. Pepsi had withdrawn its sponsorship, saying Miss America didn't represent the changing values of society, which ought to have been true. To the Wednesday Sisters, though, the pageant was more than a beauty contest; it was the anniversary of the day we'd begun to write. Which was what we talked about at Brett's that night, while we fixed our gin and tonics and vodka gimlets and sidecars. A year, it had been, and yes, Brett's essay had been published and Linda's story would be soon, but the rest of us were making no headway.

"Some things just take time," Linda said. "Ruth Spangenberg started the Committee for Green Foothills seven years ago, and we're still fighting development there. And sometimes I think we never are going to get this community to accept teaching minority viewpoints in our schools."

"That fella Sid Walton, he's a Black Panther," Kath said, referring to the district's director of multiculturalism who'd just resigned amidst an uproar over "exchanging" students with the Ravenswood district, where most students were black. "Anna Page's teacher says his house is full of books and bullets."

Bert Parks appeared onstage then, and we turned our attention to the television. Before we'd even seen Miss Alabama, Linda announced she was rooting for Miss New York, who was Jewish, and Kath, without pausing to think why Linda might care what religion a contestant was, asked if she had a nose.

"A nose, Kath?" Linda said. "It would be hard to be voted Miss America without one, don't you think?"

Kath patted her braid headband, then dragged a lock of hair across her ample chin. "Sure, of course. I just meant—"

"Do I?" Linda asked.

"Do you what?"

"I'm Jewish, Kath. Does that make you feel differently about me?"

And I said—I know, unbelievable, but I did—I said, "But you're *blond*."

Miss Iowa, Miss Kansas, and Miss Kentucky walked out, Bert Parks announcing them as I tried to come up with some way to take back my words, to make a joke of them, to break the stupefied silence. But it was Ally's quiet voice we heard first, Ally who said, "My Jim is from India."

"That *was* Jim." I exhaled the words, not meaning to say them aloud but it was such a surprise, somehow, to have it confirmed. And when Ally looked at me in response, I tried to explain. "I saw a dark-skinned—" I started, before thinking better of it. What would I say? *I couldn't imagine you married to a nonwhite even with him right there in front of me?*

Ally's eyes darkened in her pale face. She hadn't needed me to finish my sentence to know what I meant to say; she'd been facing that kind of prejudice since the day she'd started seeing Jim.

Kath, looking from me to Ally, said, "From India like Gandhi? Or from India like the British families who—"

"Jim graduated top of his class at Michigan Law School, and you were right, Linda, he should have had his pick of jobs," Ally interrupted, shutting us all up. "But he didn't get a single offer from the New York firms, or the San Francisco ones, either."

"So that's why he's at a second-tier firm?" Kath said, not meaning anything by it, just registering the answer to the question that had bothered us all. But it came out sounding awful, as if she was suggesting Jim's job wasn't worth having.

"But you never told us, Ally," Brett said.

"Told you *what?*"

"It's *illegal,* honey!" Kath said. "A white girl can't marry a dark man."

"A dark man!" Ally exploded. "He's *human,* just like we all are."

And Linda, speaking at the same time, said, "*Illegal,* Kath? The Supreme Court overturned interracial marriage bans years ago!"

Though Kath wasn't as wrong as all that: at the time Ally had gone to her parents and said she wanted to marry Jim, in states from Texas to her own Maryland, someone who was "white" simply could not marry someone who was not.

It's against God's plan—that's what Ally's father had said when she'd come home to tell her parents about Jim, to tell them he'd asked her to marry him. They sat in the kitchen, at an old wooden table that had been Ally's grandmother's, with a faded black gash at Ally's seat, where her grandmother's toaster had burned the wood.

Ally's response—*But I love him, Dad*—stuck in her throat.

"He'd be touching you, sweetheart," her mother had whispered. *"Touching* you."

And how could she respond to that? Because she'd thought of that at the beginning, too: how dark his hand would look on her skin. It hadn't repulsed her, not the way it did her mother, but she'd thought of it. She'd wondered how she and Jim could look so different when they were so much the same inside.

She hadn't considered back then how their skins would blend in their children. Their features. She hadn't wondered if her children would look like foreigners, or how she would feel if they did. She hadn't thought at all in the beginning. She hadn't imagined a future with Jim. She only talked to him when he came to the law school library desk where she worked part-time to help with her college expenses. They talked quietly; it was a library. They laughed quietly. He always made her laugh.

She was surprised the first time they spoke outside, on the library steps. He wasn't naturally soft-spoken, like she was. But his voice, not hushed, was even more musical.

"Jaiman," she called him, the name she'd watched him print on the checkout cards he pulled from the pockets of the law books, his graceful fingers dark against the lined white paper.

He laughed warmly, and said she could call him Jim, everyone here called him Jim.

"Tell me how to pronounce your name properly," she said. "I can learn." And he smiled, charmed by her willingness to embrace who she thought he was. But he said he preferred Jim, actually.

"Jaiman, that is another world, another life," he said. "A whole other set of expectations." He'd looked out across the campus, bare and dreary gray in the winter light. It made Ally wonder what the world he came from looked like. She imagined it green and sultry, and always warm.

Ally couldn't say when, exactly, she'd fallen in love with Jim. Maybe that first moment she'd heard his lyrical voice—"Excuse me, ma'am"—before she'd even looked up to see his face.

She knew her parents might be reluctant, that they'd worry about the problems she and Jim and their children would face. But she never imagined they would refuse to have Jim in their home, even to meet him. She never imagined that her father wouldn't walk her down the aisle in the end, that she'd be married by a justice of the peace in Ann Arbor, in a dress she'd owned for years.

"I was sure my mom and dad would embrace Jim eventually," she would tell us later. "You can't know Jim and not love him. I never imagined they never *would* come to know him, that when I told them we were married they'd hide their *goddamned* prejudice behind the excuse that Jim wasn't *Christian.*"

And while we were blinking at that—at Ally swearing and meaning it—she would say, "'For I, the Lord thy God am a jealous God, visiting the iniquity of the fathers upon the children unto the third and fourth generation of them that hate me.' Those were the last words my mother said to me, the last time she ever acknowledged I was alive. A quote from the goddamned *Bible,* from Exodus, for Christ goddamned sake."

She would start crying then. She would start crying and we'd all try to comfort her, and she'd shrug us off. "I know it's ridiculous. I know God isn't killing our babies to punish us," she would say. "Jim is the kindest, most loving person in the world. No God would ever punish him even if He would punish me. And I know our children won't be the . . . the mongrels my parents imagine, but a whole of something else, something magical." But the words were her mother's, the voice the one that had sung to her, and read to her, and taught her right from wrong.

Not that we learned any of that at that Miss America gathering, any more than we learned that Ally had never met Jim's parents, either, a fact Jim explained away with the ocean gulf between them, but Ally knew better, she knew they saw her miscarriages as a sign of their own brand of offended gods, and that they, too, thought the offense was hers; their Jaiman could do no wrong.

What we did learn that evening—before the talent competition had even started—was that our quiet little Ally could storm out of a room with the best of them. Which was exactly what she did, but not before she made it perfectly clear—perfectly audibly—that we were "prejudiced morons," "idiots," "fools."

"It's one thing to have to deal with it from strangers," she said. "The policemen who stop us to make sure I'm okay, that I'm not being kidnapped or raped. The maître d's and ticket sellers who pretend they don't see us. The people who *do* see us, who stare at us every time we go anywhere together—and those are the nice people, the people who don't insult us outright. I get plenty of cruelty from strangers. I don't need it from people I thought were my friends. If I don't need my parents, I surely don't need you." And she grabbed her purse and stomped out of the house, and Linda followed her, looking as disgusted as Ally was.

Brett and Kath and I didn't know what to do. We just sat there, watching in silence as those flawless white girls tromped across the stage and back again.

"Ally's husband is colored?" Kath said finally, as if she still couldn't believe it was true.

"*Indian,* Kath," Brett said. "*From India.*"

"My mama's Blanche isn't any darker than I am in the summertime," Kath said, "but that doesn't make her white.

"Ally is such a pretty girl, too," Kath said, giving voice to a thought I hate to admit had crossed my mind, too, even if I never would have said it aloud. She's plenty pretty enough to marry a nice white boy, we meant. So why did she marry Jim?

I'm not saying I'm not ashamed of how I was then. Of course I'm ashamed. I'm not saying I shouldn't have changed sooner, or that we can't change our views about things until we have to deal with them in real life. But I'm trying to get down to the raw truth of it all here, even if it doesn't show me at my best. I'm trying to be as honest as I possibly can.

Well, that was when Brett exploded into a lecture about skin color being just a pigment, nothing more. Which Kath said was a lot of scientific hooey because anybody could tell a person was black just by looking. At which point Brett said Kath was being simplistic and moronic and prejudiced and several other words I didn't know, and she couldn't believe Ally hadn't told us—this was her beef with Ally, that she hadn't told us, which Brett felt meant she didn't trust us to take the news more rationally than her parents had. Which of course we hadn't, but that wasn't Brett's doing, it was Kath's and mine, which Brett pointed out in no uncertain terms. And before I knew it, Brett was shutting her door in my face as firmly as in Kath's, and I was left standing on the porch with Kath, wondering what had happened to the friends who'd sat in the park together every Wednesday morning, helping each other through everything. Wondering how we'd ever get past this and back to that.

19

$\mathcal{T}$HE FOLLOWING WEDNESDAY was an awful, drizzly day—
Chicago weather, not California weather, though it wasn't
raining in Chicago, where the Cubs, having dropped to second in a
loss to the Phillies, were trying to stanch their late-season slide.
Maybe it was the rain, or maybe it was the Cubs' slide or the Wednesday Sisters' explosion and the days of silence that followed, or maybe
it was the squabble I'd had with Danny that morning, I didn't know,
but the abandoned mansion across the park with its cracked windows
and peeling paint, its slanting roofline and side porch, seemed to have
fallen even further into disrepair. And the park, too, was empty, as de-
serted as the house.

A few minutes after the time we usually gathered, Brett trolled by
in her car—she must have taken Chip to work that day so she could
have it. By the time I got to the door, though, she was around the corner. Linda came by, too, but she didn't stop, either, and all I could
think of was how awkward Danny and I had been after we'd argued
that morning, how very hard it is to say you're sorry even when you
are, even to someone you love. Sitting there watching the rain fall on
the empty park, I could not believe our friendship was really this fragile, that it could blow apart over a few ill-considered words. It was as

ridiculous as my aunt Dotty and her brother, my uncle Jojo, who
hadn't spoken in more than ten years, not since Uncle Jojo had said
something derogatory about Dotty's affection for her cat—a nasty little animal, Jojo was right about that, but Dotty had never had children, the cat was all she had. It had been dead for years, though, and
I doubted anyone else could recall what words had been slung, but I
was sure Aunt Dotty remembered, and probably Uncle Jojo did, too.
Memory is an unmerciful thing sometimes.

"I'M SORRY" were Danny's first words when he came through the
door early that evening, a big bouquet of flowers in hand. I said I was
the one who should be sorry, feeling selfish and self-centered and
unredeemable. I'd called him arrogant and self-absorbed, so wrapped
up in his work that he was forgetting his kids—his kids, I'd said, not
me—when all he'd been doing was working his butt off to keep us all
in new Keds.

His company had introduced its first product that May, a sixty-
four-bit random access memory, but it wasn't making them much
money, and their second technology, the multichip memories, kept
popping off their ceramic bases. That left a lot of pressure on Danny's
silicon-gate MOS device. The whole company had gathered in the
cafeteria for champagne in honor of the first one that actually
worked. The yields were dreadful, though; very few of the things actually *did* work, even with Danny's team slaving away past midnight,
tinkering with the kind of water they used, changing the acid dips,
and hanging a rubber chicken over an evaporator for luck—although
how a rubber chicken was supposed to bring them luck I couldn't
imagine. Being completely logical and not the least superstitious myself, I prayed a lot and kept my fingers crossed and, when I found a
penny lying heads up in the park one morning, I practically had it
framed.

Danny was beat to hell when he got home that night—he'd been
at the office until two the night before, and left that morning without

breakfast, with only my accusation that he hadn't seen his children in a week. But we put the flowers in water and kissed and made up, and yes, we still felt a bit awkward with each other that way you do after your feelings have been hurt and you know his have been, too, but we put the children to bed and he poured us each a nightcap and we sat out on the front porch and began to let go of even that.

It had stopped raining but it was chilly as we sat talking about the new friends Maggie was making in kindergarten and how she could already write her name. Then Danny stopped midsentence and just sat there for a moment, staring out across the street.

"Someone's in the mansion," he said quietly. "Someone is wandering around with a flashlight or a candle or something, like the Ghost of Christmas Past."

Dickens. An engineer who reads Dickens. How could I have gotten so mad at him?

"The night watchman, I think," I said.

"A watchman would turn on the lights, Frankie."

I shrugged. "Whoever he is, he's a regular. I've seen the light several times."

"Let's go look," he said with that boyish grin I saw so little of lately. And when I hesitated he said, "Come on, Frankie. It's not like it's going to be a drug drop."

Though it might have been. Teenagers had been arrested for possession of drugs right near this park, I'd heard. But teenagers had drugs everywhere by then.

"Wait! Maybe it's a burglar," he whispered dramatically, "a serial burglar carting off the silver, teaspoon by teaspoon." We'd just be gone for a minute, he insisted. The kids would be fine.

As we crossed the street and headed toward the mansion, Danny carrying the Cubs baseball bat I'd gotten at bat day when I was nine just to appease me, our shoes getting wet in the rain-soaked grass, it did seem almost as though a ghost was wandering the old place. The dim light in one window faded, another window lit a moment later, redder here where the room must be red, bluer there.

"The little girl's room," I whispered. "The daughter's room."

That's the way I'd come to think of the room that was lit now, albeit dimly. I'd finally found the place open one Sunday on our way home from Mass, and I'd quickly changed clothes and returned to look, expecting something grand inside: a butler to greet me at the door and a woman in a silly white cap serving cucumber sandwiches and tea, though how I could have thought that from the dilapidated outside, I can't now imagine. There *had* been a silver tea service and a dramatic candelabra with it, but the silver was tarnished nearly to black and was probably only silver plate anyway, because who would leave real silver in that falling-down house? The place had smelled musty, and there were cobwebs on the wooden balusters of the curving staircase, in the corners of the "little French room," on the portrait that dominated the living room, the stern-faced old woman who'd built the house, her hair coiled in a severe bun. The fabrics on the furniture were rotting, too, and dust lay thick on the marble bust of the daughter, on the framed paintings—the daughter's childhood art—and on the oversized family Bible, which was jammed with old photos and opened to a passage from Job.

But the room lit now, the daughter's room, had been . . . not exactly clean, but better cared for. The bedding was fresher, as if someone occasionally smoothed the spread and fluffed the pillows, ran a dust rag or a sleeve over the dresser, opened the window to let out the stale air. That's why I thought of it as the little girl's room, though there were other bedrooms with wild-rose wallpaper and four-poster beds and looking glasses, and no girl had ever lived there in any event, the old widow had built the house only after her daughter died.

The room had a piano in it, an old upright that was nothing compared with the organ downstairs except that while the organ looked forlorn and forgotten, as if its notes hadn't sounded in years, the piano looked somehow as if a young girl had just slipped off its wooden bench and run outside to play.

That was why I thought of it as the girl's room, I realized. Because of the piano.

"Estella's room," Danny whispered.

"You mean Eleanor?" That was the daughter's name.

"As in Estella and Pip," he said, and I could see what he meant then: the old house wasn't brick, and there were no iron bars over the windows, no walled courtyard, but it was dismal in the way I imagined Miss Havisham's Satis House was. Satis House. Enough House. *Whoever had this house, could want nothing else.*

As we crept up to the front of the house, the light faded from the girl's room, our ghost moving to the back of the house, we thought. We waited and waited, my feet getting wetter and colder, my discomfort at leaving the children escalating. What if one of them woke and found us gone? Still the light didn't appear again.

Danny—leaving the bat with me—went around to the back to see where our ghost was. "The back of the house is dark, too," he said when he came back.

"The servants' stairs," I said. I'd forgotten about the worn, narrow, creaky-steep back stairs that ran down to the kitchen, behind the grand stairway in the front of the house. "They went down the servants' stairs and out the back."

You'd have thought, from the look on Danny's face, that he was Pip himself and old Estella had just told him she was to be Bentley Drummle's wife.

I WANTED TO CALL the Wednesday Sisters every day that week, to patch up this rift, to make it all right again. It would have been easy enough to do: telephone and apologize. Bring flowers like Danny had. Lie prostrate on their front porches and beat my ridiculous breast over the foolishness, the utter wrongness of my ideas about who was supposed to marry whom and, yes, who was better than whom. I did see that. I did see, in my thinking the same thought Kath had voiced even if I hadn't voiced it myself—"But Ally is such a pretty girl"—that I was unforgivably prejudiced.

That's certainly what I would do now: I'd apologize. But I was younger then. I had entirely too much foolish pride to go with my foolish ideas. Enough that, when mixed with my insecurity, left me standing paralyzed, unable to get past the possibility that a repentant me would be rejected as surely as the unrepentant one and I'd be left without a scrap of dignity.

Dignity. How is it that it's most important to us when we're least entitled to it?

Linda drove by the park that Wednesday just as she had the week before. Brett drove by. I was sure Ally was looking out her window, as I was. But no one stopped. It was fifteen minutes after the time we usually gathered when Kath pushed her stroller into the park in the rain, Lacy protected by the stroller top but Kath herself without even a raincoat.

She looked around at the empty park, sat down, and put her face in her hands.

Lacy sat quietly watching her from under the hood of the stroller.

I grabbed Davy and an umbrella and rushed out the door, met Ally hurrying from her house, Carrie only half in her raincoat. Then Linda was there and Brett was, too, and Kath was sobbing, saying, "Her name is *Kathy*."

If we were still mad at each other, we forgot it; the apologies—the self-recrimination and the I'm-such-a-jerk—would come later, along with the worries (Would our husbands mind if we invited Ally and Jim to dinner? Would we be able to treat Jim like a regular person? And what about Linda being Jewish? What did that mean?), and a newfound care for each other's emotions that wouldn't last forever, at least not with the same intensity, but would draw us closer.

"*My* name," Kath wailed. "*My name.*"

She'd picked up the kitchen extension. Heard him call her Kathy. "Kathy, punkin," he'd said, using the same endearment they whispered to their children.

"If he leaves me to marry her—"

"He's not going to leave you, Kath," Linda insisted, retreating from the possibility of "platonic friendship" or "business call" now, hoping only that "Lee won't leave" would prove to be higher ground from which to fight.

"If he leaves me and marries her," Kath insisted, "she'll have everything, even my *name*!"

20

THINGS WENT FROM bad to worse for Kath that October, cul-
minating in what even she now refers to as, like in *Gatsby*, "that
incident with the car"—the hospital Halloween party disaster that occurred the night after the party Danny and I threw at our house. Our
party had a come-as-a-literary-character theme, a mistake in retrospect,
but the Wednesday Sisters all thought it was a terrific idea before it
went so bad on us. It gave people both guidance and a lot of leeway.
You could dress to the nines as, say, Anna Karenina or Mr. Darcy. You
could don a Chinese pigtail and carry an opium pipe for a character
out of *Tai-Pan*. You could put on a hat and tote a violin case for *The
Godfather,* which was all over the bestseller lists that year. Or if you
really hated to wear costumes, you could dress in street clothes and
claim to be Updike's Rabbit or one of his suburban-housewife flings.

Danny and I did Agatha Christie: Danny, with the help of an extravagant mustache and his tuxedo, made a fairly respectable if some-
what thin and nonbalding Hercule Poirot; and I, with my glasses low
on my nose and eyeliner to age my face, made a fine Jane Marple, if I
do say so myself. Brett came as Scout from *To Kill a Mockingbird*—
I swear, she nearly did look seven years old—and Chip came as Boo
Radley, acting in character, too. Kath, who was the first to identify

every one of us (she had an unbelievable talent for guessing who was who), came as Daisy Buchanan from *The Great Gatsby*, in a wispy white flapper dress with sailor collar, a white cloche hat with a gauzy scarf, and a long, long string of pearls that were clearly real, no need to run them over your teeth. She'd joined Weight Watchers (you'd offer her a cookie and she'd say no, she'd already had her free hundred calories for the day, and she could catalogue everything she'd eaten for a day or a week as a number of breads, fruits, fats, and proteins), but I hadn't realized how much weight she'd lost until she showed up in that flapper dress.

Lee came not as Jay Gatsby, as you might have expected, but wearing jodhpurs and knee-high black leather riding boots, and carrying a polo stick: Tom Buchanan, Daisy's rich, polo-playing, washed-up playboy husband. I said nothing about the odd irony of their characters. What was there to say? But it was like the costumes were a bad omen.

The party was going swimmingly, maybe a dozen couples filling our living room and dining room and entry hall, Danny mixing drinks as everyone chatted about the costumes. Some of the fellows Danny worked with were already clinging together, slipping into shop talk, but Danny and I were working hard to introduce people to each other so that neighbors would mingle with Danny's work cohorts and nobody would be hanging at the edges of the rooms. Music was playing on the record player—a Beatles song, "Come Together"—but not too loudly, so people could converse, and we'd launched the first game, an icebreaker called "Adam and Eve" in which each guest has the name of one character from a pair pinned to his back (Dr. Jekyll and Mr. Hyde, say, or President and Mrs. Nixon), and everyone asks each other yes-or-no questions—Am I male? Dead? A movie star?—the object being to be the first to figure out who you are and to find your mate.

The room was buzzing, lively, when the doorbell rang and I opened it to Ally and Jim—he in a long, embroidered white tunic and gathered white pants, she in a gauzy, old-fashioned dress with a sun hat and, incongruously, an umbrella opened over her head. She took one look at the crowded room and said in a bad British accent, "Not much sun this evening, is there, Doctor? Perhaps I shall fold my parasol?" and Jim answered, "I do think that is a fine idea, Miss Quested," the lyrical Indian accent his own. Dr. Aziz from Forster's *A Passage to India,* and his Englishwoman friend-turned-accuser, Adela Quested. Could the English and Indian ever be friends?

I told Jim how happy I was to finally meet him, and I was so busy gathering the next two Adam and Eve labels and some safety pins and explaining the game to them that I didn't realize the lull of conversation around the room, people turning and looking, staring, then remembering their manners and turning away, still stealing glances.

Ally slipped her hand into Jim's as Danny handed one of his coworkers a drink and headed toward us, excusing himself to get through the crowd, intent on defusing the situation although he had no idea how.

Across the room, a neighbor Kath and Lee had been trying to make feel welcome whispered to them, "Is she with *him*?"

Lee, without missing a beat, said, "That's my li'l sis and her husband. Would y'all like to meet them?" The look on the fellow's face, Kath said later, was so dried-apple darn funny she nearly spit out a whole mouthful of bourbon.

The doorbell rang again, and Linda, dressed as Charlotte the Spider, complete with "Some Pig" written on her accompanying web, opened the door herself as Danny was still working his way toward us and I was pinning "Cleopatra" on Jim's back. She stepped inside, looking pretty hot even with eight hairy black legs. Jeff, who followed her in, was the most ridiculous pillow-fat Wilbur you have ever seen.

"Jim!" Linda said, oblivious to the awkwardness they'd stumbled into. "I'm so glad you're here. I'm Linda. And this is my husband, Jeff. But do call him Wilbur tonight." Then to Ally, "Ally, you haven't met Wilbur, either! Wilbur, this is Ally."

Jeff, as if he intuited the tension in the room, looked at them both and said, "Oink."

People all across the room laughed despite themselves.

Jeff shook Jim's hand and cuffed him on the shoulder, as if they'd been pals forever. "Linda tells me you were a first-year at Michigan Law the year my brother-in-law graduated," he said, and you could practically hear the minds in the room reconsidering Jim: he was a Michigan Law grad, and someone like Jeff wanted to be his friend. Even in that pig costume, Jeff was the kind of guy people instinctively admired.

"Oh," Brett exclaimed. "I'm Marilyn Monroe! And Kath, I saw, you're Joe DiMaggio! We win!"

"We're in love, honey!" Kath said.

And again, everyone laughed, and after that we settled into a party that was blessedly lighthearted, blessedly fun.

KATH AND LEE had planned to go to the hospital party the next night in the same Gatsby costumes they'd worn to our party, so Kath was already in her Daisy dress again when Lee called to say there was a problem with one of his patients and he couldn't leave the hospital yet. He didn't think he'd be able to leave for hours. "We'll just skip the party. You don't mind, do you, Kath?" he said, and she said no, of course not, they were his friends anyway. The truth, though, was that she'd been looking forward to showing off her newly Weight Watchered figure to the men with whom Lee worked, to having them admire her in front of Lee.

Lee might have heard the disappointment in her voice, but he was distracted. He told her to hold on a minute, and he covered the phone as if he was talking to someone else. When he came on again, he said he had to run, he'd likely be late, she shouldn't wait up for him. She told him she'd stay in costume for a while in case he freed up, but he said she shouldn't bother, she should let the sitter go, he wouldn't break free before midnight now.

After he hung up, Kath kept telling herself that the person he was talking to was one of the nurses, or maybe another doctor. Medical staff. She repeated that rationalization for well over an hour as she sat there in her Daisy dress, having a sidecar while the sitter played crazy eights with the children. At nine, Kath tucked them into bed herself, asking the sitter not to go yet. Maybe she would just meet Lee for a drink, she said.

When she called the hospital and asked for Lee, she had no idea what she'd say if he came to the phone. The receptionist came back on, though, to say she'd paged Dr. Montgomery twice and he hadn't answered. "I think he went to the Halloween party," the woman said. "The one the nurses organized. I saw him in funny clothes and boots, carrying a golf club or something a while ago."

How long a while? Maybe an hour, maybe two. It had been a busy night, she wasn't sure.

Even then, Kath made excuses for Lee. He'd finished earlier than he'd expected; he was exhausted but he thought he ought to make an appearance at the party and was stopping by for just a few minutes on the way home. Still, she told the sitter she wouldn't be too long, and she got in her little blue convertible and headed for the University Club out on Foothill Expressway. Sure enough, Lee's car was in the parking lot.

She parked a good distance away, turned off her engine, and sat there, trying to figure out what to do. She watched people coming and going for ten minutes, fifteen, a half hour: a nurse in a sexy black cat costume, unaccompanied; a Superman; Albert Einstein and Minnie Mouse walking arm in arm. She was still trying to make up a plausible story to take inside with her when the door opened and Lee came out—alone. She thought she would cry with relief.

He'd just stopped by for a few minutes. Probably he'd arrived just before she had.

He got into the car and just sat there himself, staring through the windshield for the longest time. She was beginning to worry about him—maybe he'd lost a patient, that was always so tough on him. She had to get home and get rid of the sitter, she realized. She had to be changed and ready to comfort him when he got home.

She started the engine and was pulling forward, through to the other parking lot entrance, when the door to the club opened again and a young woman stepped out into the porch light. She was dressed like someone from the 1920s, Kath thought. Not a flapper, but someone substantially less fashionable. She wore a housedress, and she carried some kind of stuffed animal in her arms. A dog? She was pretty, though.

Kath stared at her, trying to figure out who she was supposed to be—Dorothy with her little dog, Toto?

The woman walked down the steps, crossed the parking lot, slipped into Lee's car.

The engine fired and the car pulled out quickly, its lights still off. At the stop sign, Lee popped on the lights and leaned over to kiss the woman. Kath saw their silhouettes in the glow of the streetlight, Lee's face turning the way he used to turn to her at the drive-in movies, when the lovers on the screen were getting romantic. Kath closed her eyes against the other woman, the other Kathy, remembering the baby-rough skin of Lee's cheek just after he'd started to shave, the stiff feel of his varsity letter on his sweater pressing into her cashmere twinset, that first breathtaking moment of his hand sliding up to the side of her breast.

Like any self-respecting jealous wife, Kath tailed them. Surreptitiously at first. But as she drove, as she watched the shadow of Lee caught in the streetlight, his head tipped back in laughter, as she remembered the phone call—she wouldn't mind missing the party, would she?—and imagined him dancing with this slut at the party, with everyone knowing he was there and Kath was not, and all the time their children sleeping in their beds as if their lives could not be touched by this moment, this infidelity, she began to wonder why she cared if he saw her, to think he ought to be the one caring about being seen.

She pressed harder on the accelerator, pulled closer behind him, the lights of her little blue car splashing onto the shiny chrome of his bumper, his black-and-yellow license plate. Tailgating, closer than was really safe, her daddy would have said. She ought to leave five car lengths between her and the car in front of her.

She imagined her daddy finding Lee with this sleazy little white-trash gal. Would he grab his shotgun as he'd done when her mother had told him Kath was pregnant? Kath had gone not to her daddy but to her mother, in a tearful mass of streaked mascara that her mother seemed to find nearly as shameful as the pregnancy. Kath had been almost relieved when she heard about the shotgun. She thought it meant somehow that her father was not so ashamed of her as she'd feared. But he hadn't spoken to her for days, not even at the wedding, a quiet affair in the chapel—not in the main church—on a rainy Thursday morning three days later, with only her parents and Lee's attending. Not even her sisters, who were not to be taken out of school for something like this. No walking down the aisle. No flowers. No giving the bride away. A new dress only because her mother had secretly taken her out to buy it, making her promise not to say a word about it to her daddy. The dress not white, either, but the palest pink.

The moment the ceremony was over, Kath's father strode out of the chapel without a word, stopping only outside on the church steps, to light a cigarette under the roof overhang. He left Kath's mother to hug Lee, to say how happy she was to count him as family. She hugged Kath, too, and pressed a small something into her daughter's hand. Something special, Kath thought. A family heirloom. A single wedding gift.

"Now you make this marriage work, Katherine Claire," her mother whispered in her ear. "Don't you shame us ever again." And with downcast eyes, her mother thanked Lee's parents, without saying a word about what her thanks were for.

The gift had been the small change purse that held her mother's pin money, enough for a crib and diapers and a stroller. Nothing sentimental. Nothing by which to remember the day.

Now, Kath had shamed her parents again; she knew that even if they didn't know it yet. Their daughter, who could not land a boy without sleeping with him before he married her, could not keep him even with her wedding ring.

She pushed harder on the accelerator, less than a car length behind Lee now. She had to jam on the brakes when he slowed for a yellow light.

He leaned over and kissed the slut.

Kath honked the horn.

Lee would have seen her then. He would have glanced up, thinking the light must have changed and, seeing it hadn't, he would have glanced in his rearview mirror and seen her little blue car. Surely his heart would have stopped for a moment. Surely he'd have sworn under his breath or grasped for one desperate moment for some way—any way—to get out of this without being as red-handedly caught as he already was. But he didn't get out of his car. Didn't even acknowledge her.

Kath could see the girl slouch lower in the seat, but Lee turned and said something, and the girl sat up straight again, and actually turned around to look at Kath.

Lee just waited for the light to turn green, then drove on.

Kath wailed on that horn—a high beep that was comic, pathetic—and took off after them again.

Lee was driving faster, already entering the freeway by the time she caught up with him. She did, finally, though, and she honked and honked.

They didn't stop, hardly even slowed.

In this goddamned flapper outfit! Kath thought. *With my face all made up to look like the slut* she *is.*

Myrtle Wilson, Kath realized then. The woman was dressed as the Gatsby character Myrtle Wilson, the car mechanic's wife with whom Daisy's husband had his affair.

It was that thought that sent her over the edge. That's the way she described it. "Over the shameful edge."

She pressed the accelerator, pulled up behind Lee, right on his tailpipe. The chrome of her bumper reflected in his. He sped up, and she sped up. He sped faster. She did, too. She laid on the horn again. What did she want here? What did she expect? Did she think he would stop right here on the freeway and have it out with her? Did she want him to?

She stomped on the accelerator. Flat to the floor.

The crunch of her bumper against his was oddly satisfying. Her pretty blue convertible ramming into the back of Lee's sedan, going seventy miles an hour down the freeway.

Lee just kept driving away, even faster.

She sped up. Rammed him again. Harder this time. Her bumper rode up over his and hung there for a moment, wrenching his loose as the cars again split apart.

You should have seen the front of her car.

Still he didn't stop. Still she chased him, his bumper throwing sparks as it dragged behind him on the pavement, her hood dented upward into her view. When she told us about it, it wasn't any leap at all to imagine: the hard set of the sturdy jaw on this almost demented, newly skinny young Southern girl in a flapper costume as she raced down the highway, bashing into the car in front of her, Tom Buchanan and the cheap woman with the goddamned stuffed dog.

Well, you can see why Lee never did stop that night. Imagine that playing out in the papers: STANFORD DOCTOR IN GATSBY LOVE TRIANGLE RUN OVER BY JEALOUS FLAPPER WIFE. With a photograph. No paper would have been able to resist the photograph.

He was nice enough, at least, to send a station attendant back for Kath after her car died in midpursuit—not long after that second crunch of metal. It took the attendant a while to figure out that the car had simply run out of gas. And by the time he'd poured a jerry can full into her tank and sent her on her way, Lee was long gone. To the girl's apartment, Kath was sure, though she had no idea where that was.

She waited all night for him to come home. Then washed the flapper makeup from her face and changed into day clothes and started pouring Cheerios into bowls so the children would have something that looked like a mother and a home and breakfast when they awoke.

21

W<small>E HELD OUR BREATHS</small> that next week, waiting for the moment Kath would tell us she was leaving Lee. A long silence fell in after she spilled the story of the great car bashing, though, and after a few weeks of not talking at all, she started acting as if the whole episode had never occurred. We discussed it constantly when Kath wasn't there. Should *we* bring up the subject?

"If she didn't know Lee was having an affair, we'd have to say something," Linda said. "But she knows."

"She should leave him," Brett insisted.

"But she isn't," I said. "She won't. It's her choice and she knows what she's choosing. Who are we to tell her she's wrong?"

"I don't like it, either," Linda said. "But you can see the whole rock-and-hard-spot thing. If she leaves him, she's a divorced mother of three young children, with . . . well, with nothing."

"A divorcée." Ally said it the way we were all thinking it, as though it were a terminal disease.

"If she stays," I said, "she's a married mother of three with a nice house and a handsome husband—"

"Not so handsome," Brett interrupted.

"—and if he's a philanderer, well, a lot of women have lived with worse."

Maybe this was just a thing Lee needed to get out of his system. Maybe it wouldn't last. Lord knew, there were enough wives in the Bay Area who looked the other way while their husbands ran around with their mistresses but never did leave their wives.

"Not that many people will know," Ally said.

"Everyone at the hospital," Brett said.

"They're pretty discreet," Linda said.

"But she came to the party as *Myrtle Wilson*," Brett said. "The *mistress*."

"I didn't know that was who she was," Linda said. "Who would ever guess Myrtle Wilson?"

"Kath did."

Linda shrugged. "Maybe Kath just saw Myrtle Wilson because that's who she was looking for. Maybe she was wrong."

"And what?" Brett said. "This girl is a nice girl, just like us only better, gutsier, because she went to medical school?"

"Lee doesn't wear a wedding ring," I said.

"She must know he's married by now," Brett said.

"But maybe not when she fell in love with him," Ally said.

"Time out!" Linda interrupted. "*Which* Kath is our friend?"

We all fell quiet.

"Maybe she *was* supposed to be Myrtle," Linda said. "Maybe it was some kind of bad-girl joke. I could see that. I could see Lee being attracted to a bad girl, someone he's not quite sure he can control. But even if she was, no one knew."

"People will know," Brett said. "People will talk behind their backs." And the rapid blinking of her eyes—very un-Brett—left me imaging her as a young woman, beginning to date her professor or her lab teacher's assistant or whatever Chip had been, someone she knew she ought not to date because he would be grading her. She'd have been sure she was being discreet, that she would have time to figure out if she even really liked him before the whole world knew. Then she'd have realized—words overheard, maybe, or the sudden stop of hushed conversation—that everyone knew. That everyone talked.

"People will talk," I agreed. Even when there was nothing wrong with people seeing each other, people talked. Danny and I had seen that.

Ally cleared her throat. "Like we are?"

"But we're trying to help," Brett said.

"Her mother won't know," I said. "Her father and her sisters. All her friends back in Kentucky."

Everyone nodded, thinking about that, thinking how awful it would be to have your parents know that your husband had a girl on the side.

OUR FIRST REACTION to Jim being Indian was somehow well behind us after that Halloween party, maybe as a result of the profuse apologies we'd all offered after our blowup, or because Ally was right about Jim: you couldn't know him and not love him.

"Strangers—people who don't know him and never will—there isn't anything you can do about them," she told us that first Wednesday in November. "You just have to shrug them off as best you can. The problem for us is our families. Jim's parents—don't tell him I said this, but sometimes I think maybe it's a blessing that phone calls to India are so expensive. They call Jim or Jim calls them once every three months, and they talk for three minutes, it's this limit they've set, as if four minutes would be an unforgivable extravagance. And of course he talks to them, I don't, I've only spoken to his mother once, right after we were married, just long enough to hear the disappointment in her voice. I've never even heard his father's voice. But Jim reads me their letters. They want to know when Jim is going to come home. They remind him it's his job as eldest son to care for them when they're old.

"It's not so much that they care that I'm not Indian. It's more that they can't get over the fact that Jim chose a wife without them. That's something his whole family was supposed to be involved in. Not just his parents but his grandparents and his aunts and uncles, they were all supposed to have a say in choosing a bride for him. Did we even know if our horoscopes matched? That's what they wanted to know. Which, no, we didn't. They were horrified. And his mom, you can tell she worries that I won't know how to wrap a sari and I'll be an embarrassment with visitors when we move to India—"

"You're moving to India?" Brett and I said in unison.

"Of course not. But try convincing them of that. Try convincing them of anything, like even that Jim was already eating meat and drinking alcohol long before I met him. His mother—it's pretty funny, really. Every time she writes, she asks all about our trees. Have we planted a coconut tree yet? Jim had her send his favorite recipes and he translated them into English, but I didn't even know what half the ingredients were, and when I asked for them at the grocery they looked at me like I was loony. But half the recipes call for coconut.

"And do we live near a banyan tree, she wants to know. It's a tree that's sacred in India, Jim says, that represents eternal life because its branches never stop expanding. I keep threatening to plant one even though they grow four times as big as your average Palo Alto yard because, listen to this: it's a wish-fulfilling tree. I'm supposed to—I think this is the way it works—I'm supposed to gather my girlfriends and tie a thread around its bark when the moon is full, and that will keep Jim safe or make me pregnant or both, something like that!"

"Have her send us a branch, honey," Kath said. "It'd be mighty fun to dance a midnight Indian jig!"

"Heavens, no!" Ally said, mock horror on her face. "You can't cut so much as a *leaf* from a banyan tree. It's sacred!" Which had us all laughing that day, though later I wondered why it was any funnier than what went on in my church, people kneeling and crossing themselves in front of manmade altars that women weren't even supposed to stand behind. I wanted to ask Ally what she and Jim did religionwise; I couldn't see back then how a marriage of two different faiths—even two Christian faiths—could work. Though it turns out Jim is Hindu and Ally is Christian and that just doesn't bother them. They feel they're fundamentally the same even if they do pray to different gods.

"I wouldn't laugh if Jim didn't laugh first," Ally said that morning. "But he's sure the minute we have a grandson for them, his parents will be fine. Which is sort of what I hope about my parents, that a grandson will bring them around. My sister says that's all my father talks about with her: When is she going to give him a grandson?"

We all agreed that surely a grandchild would bring everyone around, though Linda, at least, wasn't all that sure. She told us later, after Ally left to take Carrie home, that when her brother's old girlfriend had married a black man, her parents sat shiva for her just as if she had died.

22

WE WEREN'T GOING to *join* the peace march in San Francisco that November, mind you, we were just going to watch, to see what it was all about. As I told Danny, "How can I be a writer if I don't experience the world?"

"You're writing a mystery, Frankie," he said. "One set in Renaissance Italy. And it won't be the world you'll experience, it'll be thousands of irresponsible lunatics bent on causing trouble, shouting for peace as if they could possibly know more about Vietnam than the president does." And when I started talking about the demonstrators lining up coffins outside the Capitol and all those Vietnamese civilians massacred at My Lai, he said, "You don't think we should pull out of Vietnam any more than I do, Frankie. And what if the crowd starts rioting and people are arrested? What if it turns out like the Democratic convention, with people getting killed? What would Maggie and Davy do if anything happened to you?

"If you want to go to a peace march," he said, "I hear there's going to be one right here in downtown Palo Alto." And it seemed impossible to explain the difference: that Palo Alto peace marches rarely drew more than a few hundred people, whereas this San Francisco march might draw a hundred thousand or more.

He wasn't the only husband unhappy about our going. Only Jim and Jeff *didn't* object. Jim thought Ally should stand up for what she believed in—but then, they were childless, they didn't have the same concerns. And Jeff? When Danny tried to enlist his opposition, Jeff said, "I could object from my rooftop, Danny, but Linda is Linda. She'll do what she wants." Which left me wondering why she hadn't gone to the University of Iowa graduate program, why she'd married Jeff and moved to Baltimore instead. It made me think of the way she'd sent her story out again and again—but without telling us. Linda did what she wanted and said what she wanted, but there was more to her than that.

The morning of the rally I slipped out of bed early, and dressed quietly, and walked down to Ally's house in the wet darkness. I sat under my umbrella on the damp bottom step of her front porch, watching the sky over the old mansion lighten to a dull cloud gray. What did I really think about the war? I wondered as I sat there. Not Danny, but me. I read the newspapers. I watched the news. What did *I* think?

Despite the wet chill of the morning, by the time we arrived in San Francisco some two hundred thousand people had gathered at the waterfront, filling the streets and beginning to make their way toward Golden Gate Park. Three men who seemed to belong together only in their size—all big men, though the first wore a suit and tie, the second long hair and lamb-chop sideburns, the third a decorated service uniform—led the way with a large banner that read VETERANS FOR PEACE. There was one woman with them, a nurse in a clean white uniform who walked with a slight limp—a war wound, it dawned on me only later; she, too, was a veteran.

Those three men and the nurse seemed somehow to represent the crowd that day, the diversity. I'd expected . . . I didn't even know, really. Disreputable-looking men with long hair and mustaches? Danny's lunatics? But there were all kinds of men and women protesting—in suit coats and ties, in workmen's clothes, in house-dresses and bell-bottom slacks and skirts and pumps.

It was a long walk—seven miles—to the park.

We Wednesday Sisters walked at the fringes of the crowd, feeling more like the shopkeepers who observed from their doorways than like protesters. Maybe not Linda, but the rest of us. If made to declare one way or the other, Danny was probably right, I probably would have said that Nixon was doing the right thing, that peace through victory was the right path. Yes, I'd watched the footage and listened to Walter Cronkite and Eric Sevareid; I couldn't purge the awful photos from my head. But it wasn't as simple as it sometimes seems in retrospect. I believed—most Americans believed—that the spread of communism would mean loss of freedom and torture and death, and perhaps even nuclear war. We never imagined the communist world would just collapse as it did in the Soviet Union years later. We thought the only way to preserve our lifestyle was to fight theirs. And we couldn't, truthfully, imagine that America might be wrong. We didn't like to imagine that what we were doing as a country could be imperialist or illegal or just plain immoral any more than we liked to imagine an America that could be defeated by a small country of small people we thought of as less intelligent and less compassionate and less worthy than we were. So we just didn't imagine it.

Even Linda, the most vocally antiwar of us, was watching more than protesting with the crowd that morning. "All the disabled veterans," she said. "I never expected to see them here. I never thought about that." And even as she was admitting that, a tall, blond man with his arm amputated at the elbow fell in alongside her, his stump exposed under the edge of his short-sleeved oxford shirt. "Nice to see a pretty girl like you out here with us," he said.

Linda focused on his face—china-blue eyes, slightly crooked nose, freshly shaved chin—listening to him, trying to work up the nerve to touch him. Just a small touch at his shoulder. She veered away from him unconsciously, though, just enough to bump into Brett, who reached a hand out to steady her. Linda looked at Brett's gloved fingers on her elbow but didn't pull away. She turned back to the man, her face solicitous and yet not quite natural. "Did you lose your arm in the war?" she asked, making herself confront it. *See, I can face this. I can do this now.*

"This?" The man thrust the stub of arm toward her, maybe angry at her for seeing his arm rather than seeing the whole of him, maybe angry at what he'd been through, maybe angry at everything.

Linda swayed back from him again, staring at the stump, unable or unwilling to look away. She wanted to tell him that it wasn't him, really. It wasn't him or his arm she loathed. It was herself. She wanted to tell him it was impossible for her to look at him without thinking of her mother, that it was her own guilt that was the problem, the guilt of a nine-year-old who never did embrace her mother. But he was already heading back to rejoin his buddies, who looked toward us as they frowned at something he said.

Brett set her hand back on Linda's elbow, the lightest embrace, and Kath fell in on Linda's other side, where the man had been.

As we walked that morning, we had to squeeze into the crowd when the road narrowed or when we came to a car parked at the curb. We were walking alongside a group of doctors when I stumbled, and I was saved from plastering myself on the pavement by one of them. He and his doctor friends made me stop so they could check my ankle, though I assured them I was okay, I was forever tripping but I'd never once in my life broken or sprained a thing.

They were from Los Angeles, a group called Physicians for Social Responsibility, and one of them—a fellow with the same dark-rimmed glasses and slight build as my Danny—turned out to know people Jeff and Lee knew; he'd interned at Stanford.

Linda told him we were writers.

"Writers?" he said. "That's terrific. What have you written?"

He expected books, you could tell. Books he'd heard of, books on the bestseller list. When you say you're a writer, people always do.

Linda replied, cool as a morning breeze, that Brett had published an essay and she had a story coming out soon. I felt like an idiot even though I wasn't the one who'd proclaimed myself a writer; I hadn't published a thing. Then quiet Ally started asking them questions as if she were a reporter for *The New York Times,* I swear, as if she did not intend to go home until she understood everything that was happening here. Before I knew it, I was asking questions, too. It was so much easier to be a writer with these strangers than it was with anyone I knew, these men who had no preconceptions about me, who wouldn't think that I was just Frankie, the engineering school secretary who'd never been to college, who couldn't possibly have dreams.

It seemed no time before the seven miles were behind us and we arrived at the park. We stayed with the doctors, quite a ways from Black Panther David Hilliard and the other speakers, so it was difficult to see them, but we'd come to see the crowd more than anything and we could hear well enough. As we stood talking, waiting for the speeches to begin, a nun in full white habit and a wimple came and stood near us, holding a sign that read NOT ONE MORE DEAD. Something about her—just the nunness of her, I suppose—made me think of Sister Mary Alice, the head of my high school. Sister Mary Alice was a big barrel of a woman who made things happen, though she'd been nearly eighty when I was in school. I wondered if she was still alive, and if she was still running the school, and if we'd be in this mess in Vietnam if she were in charge of the show. If you'd asked me in the car on the way up if I could imagine Sister Mary Alice— or Sister Josephine or any of the other nuns who taught me— demonstrating for peace, I'd have gotten the giggles so badly I'd have started hiccoughing. But that nun's face held the same measure of compassion those nuns could startle you with when they'd learned your grandmother was sick or your dog had died or you had not been asked to the prom. When they mailed you a note after you'd taken your fiancé to meet them, a note that said, "Danny is clearly a very smart young man, Frances, but don't forget that you are a very smart young woman, too."

It made me tear up, imaging Sister Mary Alice's stooped old body under the weight of a NOT ONE MORE DEAD sign, though I couldn't begin to say why.

The speeches that afternoon were relatively unremarkable, the crowd moderate, enthusiastic but well behaved. When Hilliard tried to stir everyone up, suggesting in the most unpleasant language that we ought to kill President Nixon, the crowd simply drowned him out with shouts of "Peace! Peace! Peace!"

"Peace!" I found myself saying, not exactly shouting but not exactly not, joining Danny's lunatics without feeling the least bit crazy, or even the least bit wrong. And when I looked to Kath and Brett and Linda and Ally, they too were saying, "Peace!" All while President Nixon sat in the White House watching the football game our husbands were watching at home with our children, a game the network didn't even think to interrupt to show live coverage of hundreds of thousands of Americans taking to the streets.

23

ALL THAT FALL, even with so much going on, I worked on "Michelangelo's Ghost," revising and revising. As the Chicago Eight became the Chicago Seven, as two million people participated in the first moratorium against the war, as others were going off to see *Butch Cassidy and the Sundance Kid* or reading *The Godfather* or *The Andromeda Strain*, I sat at my typewriter. The amazing thing was I didn't *want* to do anything else. I didn't want to go shopping or to the movies, I didn't want to watch *That Girl* or *Laugh-In* or even Johnny Carson, which I'd always loved. And I wasn't alone. Brett was revising her novel, Linda started a new story, and Ally traded in her "Not Some Duck" for a porcupine who was at least moving out of her journal onto full pages in a way the duck never really had. Even Kath was writing: gut-wrenching journal entries that were melodramatic and awful, that made me want to talk her into leaving Lee, just dumping him and starting over. But even now, with divorce not the taboo it was back then, it's a hard thing to tell a friend you think her marriage is over. It's impossible, really. What if you're wrong and she leaves him when the next day he might have dumped the girlfriend and, having gotten that out of his system, gone back to life with her and old age and all the till-death-do-us-part happily-ever-after she'd hoped for at the altar on her wedding day? Which was the way Kath's sad melodrama of a story would end if she ever finished it, if she ever got beyond ideas jotted in her journal, you could tell that from the little she'd written. As if by writing it she could make it true.

I'm not even sure now how we'd gotten to the point that we were all writing. I know writers who have a talisman or a ritual to make writing easier: bunny slippers they wear or a certain candle they always burn when they're writing; putting pen to paper at sunrise, or noon, or 11:00 P.M.; sitting in a certain chair in a favorite café or walking their dog on the beach first; playing one song on their iPod on infinite repeat for one novel, then choosing another song for the next. But that always strikes me as dicey. What if that café table is taken? What if the dog you walk on the beach eats your bunny slippers? What if your iPod dies? And the fact is, we were mothers and wives; if we waited for the stars to align just so, we'd still be waiting.

I suppose what we did was park our butts down and write any moment and any place our children were otherwise occupied. We got up early and wrote while our households slept. We carried journals and pens and even manuscripts in our purses, and if the children fell asleep in the car on the way to the grocery store, we sat with our writing propped up against the steering wheel, scribbling quietly, careful not to inadvertently honk the horn. We grabbed every minute we could, hoping it might turn out to be five minutes or ten, maybe an hour if we were lucky. And even when it was frustrating and we didn't like what we wrote, even when we were just jotting down thoughts about a day that had not gone well, there was joy in it, one part the pleasure of feeling creative and one part the way our friendship wrapped around our hopes.

By Thanksgiving, Brett and I—pleased as anything that this new television show, *Sesame Street,* had completely enthralled our children—had completed our manuscripts. By Christmas, we'd put together agent lists and drafted letters describing our books. Brett included a lovely paragraph that said she'd graduated summa cum laude and written for the Radcliffe newspaper, and had done graduate work at Harvard. I put in a sentence reporting that I lived in Palo

Alto with my husband and our two young children and tried not to worry that it didn't look like much.

Kath took one look at our letters and said, "Ladies," in a tone that might have been addressed to Anna Page when she was caught playing in the mud. "Do you think General Motors sells cars with ads that say 'Would you like to see a brown car with seats and wheels and windshield wipers?'"

"You could compare yourself to some famous writer," Linda suggested. "Frankie, you could say something like 'in the tradition of—'"

"Daphne du Maurier," Kath said.

"To name a brilliant example," Linda said, rolling her eyes. "And Brett could say something like . . ." She paused, unable to come up with anyone to whom she could compare Brett's writing. Brett's story ought to have worked, but it didn't, and yet none of us could say there was anything wrong with it exactly.

I wondered if the same thing was happening with my book, if it wasn't really good enough but they were too chicken to tell me "Michelangelo's Ghost" wouldn't fly.

"This is preposterous," Brett said. "We're supposed to boil four hundred manuscript pages down to a single paragraph?"

"Like churning sweet milk," Kath said. "How about this, y'all? How about you start with a question to draw in the reader, then give them a little peek at the story but don't tell the ending? Show them a little ankle, maybe some calf, but don't go sleeping with the boy before the wedding day."

"I heard they're getting copy machines at the library, so you could send a sample chapter, too," Ally suggested. "It's so easy to say no, you don't think you'd like a book, but then you read the first line and pretty soon you've finished a whole chapter and you realize you *do* want to read this story about, say, a middle-aged widow manor owner in thirteenth-century East Anglia."

So Brett and I went back to the drawing board. It's amazing how much time you can spend on a simple one-page letter, but Kath was right: that one page would determine whether anyone would ever read our books.

. . .

D ANNY STUMBLED in the door one night not long afterward to find me working on the same paragraph I'd been working on for days. It was 1:00 A.M. I had a moment of fearing I was in Kath's shoes—or those boots she talked about putting on backward—especially since his initial wave of enthusiasm for my writing seemed to have waned, leaving in its wake a hint of disapproval. I wasn't getting enough sleep, and he missed waking up next to me; couldn't I just stay in bed in the morning?

That night, though, he just started rambling enthusiastically and incoherently—he was definitely a bit sloshed—about chips and wafers and yields. "From two to *twenty-five* good chips per wafer, Frankie," he said. "We popped so many champagne corks that the ceiling needs to be replaced!"

I heard what he was saying then. His MOS dream, his "baby," was becoming a reality, a product they might be able to mass-produce.

"It was the rubber-chicken good luck, was it?" I said, and he laughed, a silly-drunk laugh; he'd started praying to that rubber chicken every morning.

I could get no sense out of him after that—just a bad imitation of his co-worker Les Vadasz jumping all over the place, screaming "Sooooper dip!" in a thick Hungarian accent. I was sure he would wake the children, just as I was sure, in bed not much later that night, that we would both wake them, though we did not.

It wasn't yet dawn when I woke the next morning—no sounds of trash collectors or early traffic yet, but I already had a new first sentence for my query letter in my mind. I slipped out from under Danny's arm, which was draped heavily over me, and reached for my glasses on my nightstand.

"Hey," he whispered. "Where are you going?" He lifted the sheet and blanket and pulled me to him, nuzzling, morning-breathed, into my neck. "Let's do that again."

What would you do if you were Risa Luccessi? I thought. Hold on to the line. Ideas evaporate so easily if I don't get out of bed and write them down.

"It's morning," I said. "Mags and Davy—"

"Shhh," he said, reaching under my nightgown, stroking my thigh. "It's not even light yet."

"My diaphragm," I said, and there was a brief but perfect stillness to him then, him shrugging off his concern about using birth control, one he never voiced in bed.

"Let's make a baby," he whispered. "Let's make a Robert and we'll call him Bobby. Let's make a cute little Madeline who will grow up to be as beautiful as her mom."

But I wasn't ready for another baby, for morning sickness and the overwhelming tiredness that had been bad enough with Maggie and almost unbearable with Davy, when Maggie was already underfoot. And I wanted to steal the quiet of that morning for myself. *Your dream is in reach, Danny,* I wanted to say, *but what about mine?*

He was already lifting my nightgown, though, kissing my breasts. My body was responding even as my mind was thinking *What would you do if you were Risa Luccessi?* and reaching for the next few words that I'd had, the start of the second sentence, the thought that had already dissipated in the morning exchange, leaving me with a question that had no answer, no little bit of ankle, no enticing glimpse of leg.

WHEN I RECEIVED the first positive response to my query letter the second Tuesday in January, my thrill was overrun with panic by the time I got to the agent's bold, blue-ink signature. Before I knew it I'd revised two chapters entirely, screwing up the pagination. I was frantically retyping the whole thing when Danny got home late that night, and yes, he was happy for me, but I'd imagined him more excited. I'd imagined him not caring one whit about his dinner, which, by the time he got home, was three shriveled new potatoes, a pile of dried peas, and a hard lump of chicken left forgotten in the oven. I'd imagined him wrapping me up in a great big hug and calling me "the future famous novelist, M. F. O'Mara" again, saying we ought to open a bottle of champagne.

The next morning, though, the Wednesday Sisters made up for Danny's restraint. They all wanted to touch the letter, as if it were literary spring water from the Sanctuary of Our Lady of Lourdes.

"So, what in the world is a jiffy bag?" I asked. "And what does 'on exclusive' mean?"

By late afternoon, I was standing at the post office window handing over my manuscript, not completely retyped but with two page 34s labeled A and B as Danny had suggested. And even as I pushed Davy's stroller toward home I was holding my breath, sure that at any moment the phone would ring and my literary life would begin.

Minutes turned into hours, days, and weeks, though, my initial euphoria dipping to cautious optimism, souring into apprehension, then rotting almost immediately into massive, Oreo-eating dread. Perhaps the manuscript was so bad that the agent was not even going to grace it with a rejection, too concerned any further correspondence with me might taint him.

WHEN ERICH SEGAL'S *Love Story* was serialized in the *Ladies' Home Journal* starting that February, Kath insisted we'd be fools not to read it. "It's the biggest publishing sensation in a thousand blue moons, y'all. Don't you think we can learn something from this year's May Queen?" She, like the critics, for all the fault they found with the novel, thought it charming. "It's like the bad boy we all fell for at school," she said. "You know you should not even be talking to this fella, he's got a reputation and so does any girl seen with him, but he's charming your bobby socks off and the next thing you know you're unzipping your own skirt without him even having to ask."

Like nearly everyone in America, we did read it, and we argued about every aspect of it, from the story (Oliver Barrett IV defies his wealthy father to marry poor Jenny Cavilleri, only to watch her die) to the prose ("'It skips from cliché to cliché with an abandon that would chill even the blood of a *True Romance* editor,'" Linda quoted from a *Newsweek* review) to the cover, loud red and green and blue letters against a white background (half the copies at Stacey's already looked dirty from people handling it, Ally said, a comment Kath would remember later, about the impracticality of white covers). I was the only one who swallowed the book whole, reading it in one late-night sitting and bawling at the end, having neither the English literature background to call out its flaws nor any idea whether poor Radcliffe music majors really called rich Harvard boys "Preppie," or whether Harvard hockey stars really called their fathers "sir."

"So, what makes it work?" Kath said.

"How can anyone possibly care about this nonsense when hundreds of women are conducting sit-ins at *Ladies' Home Journal?*" Linda said. "When Harvard College and *Newsweek* magazine are being sued for sex discrimination—and with more to come, mark my words." Leaving me imagining Linda holding the book physically away as she read it. Leaving me wondering if any of us could bear to read *Love Story* if Jenny had left behind not just her husband but also two sons and a daughter under the age of ten.

"Okay, what makes it so *popular?*" Kath rephrased.

"Even though it's thin, it's not wrong," Brett said. "Jenny's annoyance that Oliver poaches on the meager Radcliffe library when he can use Harvard's—that's real."

"The quick wedding—no more people than you can crowd into a restaurant booth," Kath said.

"And the way Oliver's father just shuts him out when he marries her," Ally said.

Linda, frowning, said, "You can read it in about thirty seconds; I suppose people like that. No 'The covers of this book are too far apart,' to quote Dorothy Parker."

"Ambrose Bierce," Brett said.

"Really? What's the Dorothy Parker one, then?"

"'This is not a novel to be tossed aside lightly. It should be thrown with great force.'"

"My sentiments exactly," Linda said.

"Love and story, that's what I think makes it work," Kath said. "I don't think people mind awfully a cliché or two—"

"Or two thousand," Linda said.

"—if the plot is bolting down the tracks. High water covers a lot of stumps."

"*Cinderella* meets *Romeo and Juliet*," I said. "The girl we can all imagine we might be—Cinder-Jenny—gets the rich Harvard prince despite the family opposition."

"But why do we want that lump-in-our-throats feeling?" Ally asked. "From the very first sentence, 'What can you say about a twenty-five-year-old girl who died?' we know how it ends."

"'Between grief and nothing, I will take grief,'" Brett said. "William Faulkner."

"Between William Faulkner and nothing, I will take nothing," Linda said. "Do you have to be from the South to understand him?"

"God took special pains creating the South," Kath said.

"And Faulkner wants to inflict that pain on the rest of us?"

That discussion did leave me wondering, though: Why *are* we drawn to sad stories? Why did we all read the book, knowing we were in for the dying-girl ending? Why did we go to the movie that December—Ali MacGraw and Ryan O'Neal—having already read the whole tearjerker book? No one wants to be sad in real life. *You want the sad life behind door number one, Monty, or the happy ending behind curtain number two?* And yet sad plays well in literature. Romance and tragedy. *Romeo and Juliet, Anna Karenina, Madame Bovary.* Why is that?

B RETT RECEIVED no encouragement at all from her first batch of agent queries, so it was pretty hard for me to feel sorry for myself when my mail-battered manuscript came back from that agent with a polite "no thanks." It was like sending a child off to school with such hope, though, then peeking into the lunchroom to see him sitting alone. I cried in the bathtub, with the door locked, despairing of ever being a writer, thinking as I sat in that warm water that I should just give it up.

The truth is, we all thought of giving up at some point that winter, more often than you could imagine. And maybe we would have, if we hadn't had each other, but it was something, having the five of us, knowing we weren't alone.

"He didn't even read to the end," I confessed to the Wednesday Sisters. "The last hundred pages are all nice and tidy, like they've never been touched."

Ally put her arm around my shoulders, and Brett set a gloved hand on mine. " 'Rejections don't really hurt after you stop bleeding,' " Brett said.

At home that afternoon, I studied my two coffin photos, remembering lying alone in the tucked-velvet darkness, listening to the muffled voices of the Wednesday Sisters beyond the polished mahogany. I imagined my tombstone: simple gray marble with perhaps an angel carved at the top; BELOVED WIFE AND LOVING MOTHER; CHERISHED DAUGHTER AND SISTER. It ought to be enough. But all those years I'd watched my brothers go off to college—I didn't know if I could spend my whole life that way, playing the supporting role, having no part of me that wasn't defined by my relation to someone else.

Early the next morning, I pulled out my note-card chapter summaries, scooted Maggie's dollhouse and Davy's train track from the middle of the family room floor, and spread the cards out beside my manuscript. I closed my eyes, inhaled the varnished-wood-and-velvet smell of that coffin. Got up, made a pot of coffee. Sharpened three pencils to a razor tip. And began again.

24

WE ALL SAT GLUED to our televisions that April after an explosion in one of the *Apollo 13* oxygen tanks crippled the rocket. "Houston, we've had a problem." The crew was forced to scrap the lunar landing and swing their damaged ship around to the dark side of the moon, from which they could not even communicate with Earth. There was no live broadcast from the ship due to power limitations, but that didn't deter the newsmen, who used models and animated footage to explain the situation. Brett hardly stepped away from her television for those four days, worrying about those three men crowded into a lunar landing module meant for only two men and only two days. Her sister, Jenn, who'd started medical school the previous fall at the University of California at San Francisco, sometimes watched with her. Jenn had little free time, but she liked to spend what she had with Brett. They spoke the same language. They could talk together about ways the lithium hydroxide canisters from the command module might be modified to fit the lunar module's carbon dioxide scrubbers, and not an eyebrow was raised.

"I'm glad you decided not to become an astronaut, Brett—that could be you," Jenn said as they sat anxiously in front of the television that last morning, waiting for the reentry, praying like everyone else on earth that the command module would work when they reactivated it. And while Brett was considering that—*had* she decided against being an astronaut? Or had it all been decided for her?—Jenn said, "They could sure use your help now, though."

"*My* help?" Brett said.

"I used to want to be an astronaut, too," Jenn said. "Like you and Brad. But I was never smart enough."

Brett laughed. "But you're in medical school, Jenn!"

Jenn looked at her, and something in her sister's green eyes reminded Brett of how she had looked on Brett's wedding day: a fourteen-year-old in a long, silver bridesmaid dress, trying to look grown-up.

Jenn shrugged. "Like that's a big deal, a doctor."

"Of course it is!" Brett insisted. "It would be for anyone, even if you weren't a girl." At the same time still thinking of her wedding day, thinking how her brother had promised not to miss it for the world, how she'd waited at the back of the church for such a long time until finally her father said, "You just have to let Brad go, Brett. We all just have to let him go and hope he finds his way."

"I wanted to be more than a doctor, Brett," Jenn said. "I wanted to be like you."

"Like me? I change diapers, Jenn!" Wondering if it was the eight years that separated her from her sister that made the difference, or if there was more to it than that. Wondering if she, too, would have gone on to become someone if she hadn't met Chip, if she hadn't gotten pregnant before she finished graduate school.

"But you're so *you*, Brett. You do everything easily while I'm pedaling as fast as I can. I swear, one day you're going to be halfway through changing a diaper and the solution to Fermat's Last Theorem will just come to you."

Brett laughed, thinking that seemed like another lifetime, the days when she'd thought she might be the one to solve anything.

"While you're changing a darn diaper, I swear!" Jenn insisted.

On the screen, three bright red-and-white-striped parachutes burst open against the blue sky and the white puffs of cloud, and the capsule splashed safely into the sea.

"A poopy or a wet?" Brett said, and they laughed as they watched the men being lifted by helicopter and the capsule being loaded onto the USS *Iwo Jima,* the crew waving from the deck of the ship.

It wasn't until later, as Jenn's car was pulling out of the drive, that Brett started thinking: *What am I doing? What am I writing, exactly?* Thinking: *Couldn't I write something more meaningful than this failure of a book that is really about nothing at all?*

By the time Chip arrived home from SLAC—he'd worked late that evening—Brett was stooping at the fireplace, watching the flame creep from the match in her hand to the paper under the grate. Stacks of paper littered the coffee table, the couch, the La-Z-Boy recliner, and the new shag rug. Every single page of all twelve drafts of her novel, including all the carbon copies.

"Brett?" Chip said. "What are you *doing?* It's already hot as blazes in here."

She grinned up at him. "I'm burning this rubbish," she said, and she sat on the hearth, crumpled the top page of the stack nearest the fireplace, and tossed it onto the fire. Yes, the fire. The garbage was not permanent enough.

She'd decided everything she'd written to date was utter dross, not worth the paper it was typed on, so much worse than the worst dreck she'd ever read that she would be mortified to see it in print.

"Rubbish?" Chip said.

Brett crumpled a whole fistful of pages and tossed them in with the first page, which was collapsing black into the flames. "Rot," she said. "Tripe. Twaddle."

And maybe Chip thought *Twaddle?* or maybe he didn't, maybe he understood—I rather think he did because what he said was "I see. Well. Do you need some help, then?"

He stacked several of the piles from the coffee table one atop the other and set his briefcase and the evening paper in the space he'd cleared. He sat on the floor in front of the fire, on the other side of Brett's stacks, and picked up the top sheet, pausing to read the first few words.

She wrested it from him, her bare fingers brushing against his. "*Drivel,* that's what Frankie would say," she said. "Linda would say *garbage* because that's about as direct a way of saying it as there is. Ally would say . . . maybe *blather*—that seems like an Ally word. And I can hear Kath now: 'This dog won't hunt.'" She crumpled the page he'd tried to read and tossed it gleefully onto the fire.

Chip looked around dubiously at all those pages. "None of these dogs?"

"They don't even bark," Brett assured him. "They don't even know how to wag the silly little stumps of their tails."

$\mathcal{B}$RETT BEGAN WRITING manically the next morning—the same story, with Elizabeth and Ratty, but completely from scratch. Was it any good? We had no idea. "It's the same novel in a way, and yet not the same at all" was all she would tell us. She didn't want to show us one word until she was far enough along to be certain it wasn't as inconsequential as everything else she'd ever written—that was the way she put it, those aren't my words. But there was this, at least: that draft came pouring out in a great gush she could barely type fast enough to catch.

25

"THE ONLY RULES you've got to follow," Kath said when she invited us to a Derby party at her house that spring, just the Wednesday Sisters and our husbands for some good ol' Kentucky fun, "are that you wear a hat, and you tuck a little money in your pocketbook, to wager, like. Study well on that hat, too, ladies, because sure 'nough it will give you luck with your bets!"

No, Lee had not left Kath yet. And yes, Kath was still clinging to the illusion that nothing was wrong, as if the whole Gatsby car-bashing fiasco had never occurred.

Kath and Lee lived in Old Palo Alto, which was—then even more than now—the most exclusive neighborhood in town (and I mean that in a good way, although a neighbor who was one of the first engineers at Hewlett-Packard did once tell me he moved into the Community Center neighborhood in the 1940s because even Stanford-educated kind-as-anyone-you've-ever-met Asians weren't welcome in the Old Palo Alto, Crescent Park, or Professorville neighborhoods back then). Still, I'd been surprised the first time I saw Kath's house, a great big old thing that looked like a miniature version of the Museum of Science and Industry back in Chicago. It was stone, with huge, frilly columns out front—Corinthian?—and everywhere else those column façades plastered against the house (pilasters, Danny says). It was the kind of place that might have had a fountain out front. Kath said it reminded Lee of the Governor's Mansion back in Kentucky; it was the first house they'd seen in California that looked like a real house, so they bought it even though it cost twice what they'd planned to spend.

Madison Leland Montgomery IV. But they'd been just Kath and Lee, and I'd written off Kath's careful presentation of herself as insecurity. I was glad I'd gotten to know her before I saw her house.

"What does Lee do again?" Danny asked as we stood on Kath's front porch that Saturday afternoon, waiting for the bell to be answered. Before I could remind him that Lee was a surgery resident at Stanford, though, Lee opened the door, cigarette in hand.

Inside, a two-story foyer with a sweeping stairway opened to huge, high-ceilinged rooms with substantial moldings and elaborate chair rails. The furniture was dark and serious, antiques that had been in their families for generations, and on the walls were paintings of their ancestors in heavy gold frames: a forbidding lady in folds of satin, whose chin was Kath's wide chin; a gentleman in judicial robes with the same arc of her brow; a young boy dressed in a lace christening dress, who had Lacy's curls encircling his chubby face.

"You're here and I haven't even got the mint juleps made yet," Kath said when we found her in the kitchen dumping a big slug of Kentucky bourbon into a crystal pitcher. She smiled, but her eyes were red-rimmed, her face pasty. "And they're already running the races back home, too, aren't they, sugar?"

"Not the Derby," Lee assured her. Then to Danny and me, "It's the ninth race this year. I don't quite understand why they only televise the Derby, but who am I to say?"

This was the first Derby either of them had missed seeing live since they were toddlers. Lee's family had a box at the track, as did Kath's. Back home, they'd start the party by midmorning. "With mimosas garnished with strawberries," Kath said.

She pulled a huge jar from the refrigerator—simple syrup: equal parts sugar and water boiled together, then stuck into the refrigerator with six or eight sprigs of mint. She filled the bourbon pitcher with the

syrup and tossed in some fresh mint, and Lee did the honors of pouring, smoothly wresting the job of host from Kath's hands after she'd
done all the work. She'd even put crushed ice in sterling silver drinking cups, each adorned with a row of roses at the bottom, a mono-
gram, and an upside-down horseshoe with a year engraved inside.

My cup—1967—was engraved with Kath's married initials, but
the cup Danny had—1950—was carved with her pre-marriage mono-
gram, a Derby cup from long before she'd have been old enough to
drink.

"Doesn't the horseshoe opening down let the luck run out?" I
asked.

"The horseshoe has always pointed down on the Derby trophy,"
Lee said. "And no one gets a Derby trophy without a little luck." He
predicted even then, though, that Churchill Downs would eventually
buckle to convention and flip the Derby horseshoe ends up, the only
change ever made to the trophy.

The doorbell rang and soon all ten of us were in the kitchen, comparing the five ladies' hats. Ally wore a red one with extravagant blue
flowers, Brett a stovepipe with a pink velvet band and black feathers,
much prettier than it sounds. Linda came in a wide-brimmed to-do
with a sheer flowered scarf wrapped around it and tied in a bow
under her neck; and mine was a simple straw hat with a band of tiny
daisies wrapped around a flat crown. It was Kath—more practiced in
the art than the rest of us—who showed us what a Derby hat should
be: a frothy concoction of sheer silk and linen with a soft navy brim,
an ivory crown, and navy netting—"veiling," she called it—draped
high over the top, all finished with three huge red roses. Real roses
that smelled wonderful.

"It is the Run for the *Roses,* don't you forget it," she said.

Her pearl necklace was real, too—a different strand than she'd
worn at Halloween, with a beautiful clasp that matched her earrings.
"My mama always says if you aren't the prettiest girl at the party,"
she said, "then you just pretend you are."

Lee handed her the last silver julep cup, grinning. "She also says,
'You've got to go lightly with the vices.'"

Kath took a big slug of her drink. "With Mama, you've got to pick and choose which advice to listen to."

Kath hung back as Lee shepherded everyone out to the patio, and I stayed with her.

"This hat fell out of the ugly tree, didn't it?" she whispered. "I should've stuck with the one I wear every year, I know I should have." She grabbed a tissue and blotted her eyes before her mascara could run. "I'm sorry, it's just that she called this morning, that awful slut called. The phone rang and Lee said he'd call back and he shut himself up in the bedroom and I couldn't even get dressed because he'd—"

Lee was at the kitchen door, then, reminding Kath to bring the pitcher.

I whispered that she looked lovely in her hat, and followed her out to the patio, where brunch was set out on a long, smoothly polished wood table: ham with red-eye gravy, made with Kentucky bourbon and coffee, shrimp-and-crabmeat-stuffed tomatoes, piles of eggs and biscuits, casseroles, and coffee cake and lemon bars both garnished with powdered sugar and mint. "There's a sort of theme that runs through a proper Derby brunch," Kath said. "Bourbon and mint." Even the pie, a "Horse-Racing Pie" that looked like a walnut-and-chocolate version of pecan pie, had bourbon in it. "Which maybe I shouldn't tell y'all," she said, "because it's my great-grandmama's secret recipe—every family in Louisville has its own secret recipe, and you're banished from the clan if you spill a word of it. Except it wouldn't be Horse-Racing Pie without bourbon, now, would it? So I'm not really giving out any secrets."

"And that?" I asked, indicating a creamy-looking dish in the middle.

"That? That's just cheese grits, honey. You can't tell me you don't know cheese grits."

"Kath's cheese grits will make you wanna hit your mama," Lee said.

"Don't go bragging on me," Kath said. "It's just the recipe on the box."

"It ain't bragging if you can do it, Kath," Lee said.

While we ate—far too much—Lee and Kath talked about Churchill Downs and its twin hexagonal spires. About the new fellow, Lynn Stone, who'd taken over when Wathen Knebelkamp retired. About Diane Crump, who would ride that day, the first woman jockey ever to compete in the Derby.

"You know your ol' buddy Kath here is a big gambler, don't you?" Lee said. "Plunked down the entire one thousand dollars her daddy gave her for her eighteenth birthday on a horse named Iron Liege. This li'l girl here walked away with almost ten thousand dollars! And the next year, she plunked half of those winnings down again on Tim Tam and walked away with another fifteen grand."

I fingered the five-dollar bill in my pocket. A thousand dollars? That was Danny's take-home pay for an entire month.

"You could do worse than to follow her bets. She hasn't won every year I've known her, but she's never once failed at least to show," Lee said, this so clearly a side of Kath he adored that I wondered if maybe he did still love her after all. Maybe she *wasn't* being foolish to wait around for his affair to blow over, I thought, imagining a smitten young Lee courting a teenaged Kath, this pretty girl from a proper family who'd gone wild, who drank bourbon and bet outrageously and slept with him when she'd barely finished her debutante season. And I remembered what Linda had said about that whole Myrtle Wilson thing, that maybe Lee liked girls he wasn't sure he could control.

Lee kept bringing the mint julep pitcher around, forever topping off our drinks, and throwing them back himself. The only one not drinking much was Jeff. "He's on call," Linda whispered to me, "but Lee doesn't believe a drink or two impairs a real man's ability to do anything. Jeff's decided it's easier just to play along."

Despite how much Lee was drinking, though, when the phone rang an hour into the party he was quick to answer it. Kath's eyes started blinking and blinking, trying to save that mascara, but the call wasn't even for Lee, it was the hospital, for Jeff.

Kath sat frowning at Jeff through the glass doors as if she was annoyed that he was on call, that he hadn't arranged to swap with someone. But he rejoined us a minute later, saying it had just been a nurse with a question about a new patient's medication.

Jim, sitting between Jeff and me, quietly asked Jeff if he knew anything about a medicine called Tylandril. "I read something about it recently," he said. "Is it safe?"

Jeff said it was a synthetic estrogen, that as far as he knew, it was safe. "The issue is whether it actually does anything to prevent miscarriages," he said.

Jim shot a startled glance down the long table at Ally, engrossed in conversation with Lee at the other end. She was pregnant again, and Jim hadn't known—that was all over his face. He must have found the medicine and been reluctant to ask her directly what it was. I wondered if she kept the news of her pregnancy from him out of fear—the more she miscarried, the more she must have worried that Jim would leave her rather than remain childless himself—or if she kept it from him out of love. I wondered if she could bear to hear the heartbreak in his voice again as he sang his Indian lullabies to her empty womb.

"All the studies show that estrogen doesn't prevent miscarriages," Jeff said.

"I see," Jim said, and the way he looked at Ally now, it was hard to imagine she could think he would ever leave her.

Linda would learn more about it from Jeff that night: that studies had consistently shown since the 1950s that synthetic estrogen didn't help women who chronically miscarried; that every major obstetrics textbook but one was very clear that this "wonder drug" did nothing at all. He thought someone should tell Ally that—that she was wasting her money. But it seemed to Linda that Ally got so much comfort from believing the drug *might* help, and what harm could it do?

It was getting on toward post time, after two o'clock, and Lee and Kath were tipping rapidly toward sloshed, several of the rest of us not far behind, when the phone rang again and Lee popped up to answer it. I couldn't help overhearing him—okay, probably I could have, but I listened anyway. He didn't say much, just "sure" a few times (a word that had two syllables in his Southern accent), and "I will."

When he hung up, he said he was very sorry but he was on call and we'd have to excuse him, that was the hospital and he had to go in.

"Lee!" Kath protested, but Lee was already saying, "I know Kath will take good care of y'all," already out the door and gone.

"Is he okay to doctor anyone?" I heard Jim whisper to Jeff.

Jeff just frowned.

On the television, they were announcing the horses for the Derby race, and we turned our attention to picking horses and making our bets. I said I was afraid I didn't have quite a thousand to put down, tendering my five dollars, and Ally admitted that was all she brought, too. Everyone agreed five dollars was the perfect amount to bet among friends. Winner take all.

Linda declared that she was betting on Fathom, the horse Diane Crump was riding. Jeff and Kath lightheartedly squabbled over Dr. Behrman—Jeff maintaining the horse was his by dint of his profession, Kath by relationship. "I'm friendly with one of the Lin-Drake Farm girls," she said. "Her family owns the horse." And Jeff suddenly preferred Terlago and Willie Shoemaker, while the rest of us picked solely on the curb appeal of the horses' names: Corn Off the Cob, Silent Screen, Action Getter, Holy Land, Robin's Bug.

The University of Louisville Marching Band struck up "My Old Kentucky Home," and Kath teared up as she sang along with the crowd, "Weep no more, my lady, Oh! Weep no more today! We will sing one song for my old Kentucky home. For my old Kentucky home, far away."

The horses loaded, finally, and the race began, and there was a flurry of excitement when Silent Screen and Terlago and Robin's Bug all came out fast. Then Brett's pick, Silent Screen, moved into the lead about three quarters of the way through the race, and Brett actually hopped up and down with excitement. Corn Off the Cob, my horse, made a move, and I was jumping with her. Jim's horse, Robin's Bug, was in it, too, and for a moment we were having a ball. Then several horses that had not been in contention came up from nowhere, and Dust Commander was suddenly well in the lead.

"Dust Commander?" Chip said. "What kind of name is that for a horse?"

Then the two minutes were over and none of us had won. Or placed. Or showed. Not even Kath. The best we'd done was Silent Screen, in sixth.

Brett at first refused to accept the winnings—"I'm not taking forty-five dollars for picking the middle of the pack"—but Kath looked so devastated that Brett, thinking it was because of her refusal, said she was just kidding, of course she'd take the money, she'd won fair and square.

With Kath looking so dreadful, and Jim not much better, we started making our excuses to say good-bye as soon as it was reasonable to do so. Linda said she would stay and help Kath clean up and Jeff could let the sitter go.

As the door closed behind us, leaving Linda to comfort Kath, I said to Jeff, "Lee wasn't on call today, was he?"

Jeff sighed, and he didn't answer, but we all knew the truth soon enough.

26

EFORE THAT DERBY PARTY, before Lee moved out late that
summer—1970, this was—the Wednesday Sisters had been
watching the women's movement from the sidelines in the same way
we'd watched the antiwar movement, notwithstanding the San Francisco march we'd attended. We weren't so different from the rest
of the country: a poll in June showed that 60 percent of men and
43 percent of women—college-educated ones—still thought a woman
should be wife and mother first and foremost, a view even we would
have called old-fashioned. But maybe we wouldn't have if Lee hadn't
finally left Kath that August, if he hadn't come home from work early
one evening and put the children to bed rather than assuming Kath
would, then packed a suitcase and told a stunned Kath he'd signed a
lease on an apartment in Menlo Park.

He didn't think they ought to tell the children just yet, what with
school about to start, the specter of homework for Anna Page, who
was going to be a fourth-grader, and Lee-Lee needing to keep a smile
on his face for a full day now that he'd be in first grade. Lee would
come back for breakfast or for dinner sometimes, he said, and since
he was so often at the hospital anyway, they wouldn't know he'd
moved out.

Kath just sat staring at him until finally he waved a hand in front of her face and asked if she'd heard a word he'd said. She said yes—just that one word, yes—and he said, "Okay, then," and walked out the door.

He came home for dinner the next night, and Kath, so hoping he'd changed his mind and come back that she'd convinced herself it was true before dinner was over, was devastated when he gave her his new address and telephone number, as if she were simply one more person who might need to note it in her book.

He still paid the bills and gave her a little money each week—enough for groceries, barely, but what about clothes and toys, medicines and trips to the zoo? She couldn't bear the thought of asking him for more, though, much less taking him to court. She would have welcomed him back in a heartbeat, and she didn't want to do anything that might jeopardize his return. And she wasn't sure Lee had more money to give her, anyway. Yes, they had a big house and plenty of silver, fancy cars, but those were bought with family money, gifts in one way or another from her family or his, doled out at their parents' or grandparents' whim. What they lived on day to day was the same thing Linda lived on, the meager salary of a resident, with only the promise of a doctor's income someday, and though Kath might have gotten help from her parents, that would have raised questions, and she couldn't bear to tell them about Lee moving out.

So that August we started seeing things a little differently, we started seeing a world where any one of us might be abandoned in one way or another by her husband, and where would that leave us? What choice would we have but to get a job, to leave our children in someone else's care while we went off to work?

Linda once said people don't give to causes, people give to people, and I think that's what happened to us. It wasn't so much that our consciousness was raised in any abstract way as that Kath, after a brief and unsuccessful stint trying to get wallpaper-hanging gigs to make a little money, was trying to get a real job. She would step up her job search in earnest after school started that September, while the Cubs were battling for first, getting as close as a half game out, and we would all be incensed on her behalf at what she encountered in her interviews. Men called her "babe" and "honey"—she called people "honey" herself, she knew that, but not in the condescending tone these men used, men who asked why she was looking for a job when she had a husband and children at home.

It wasn't that we thought of ourselves as women's libbers, not for a minute. The media generally dismissed every gathering of women in the name of liberation as a "flop" and stereotyped women's rights advocates as ugly man-haters and left-wing radical lesbians, and I suppose we bought into that as much as anyone did. Our conversation still focused on the breakup of the Beatles and the new Joni Mitchell song (about paving paradise for a parking lot) more often than on the Equal Rights Amendment (though we did cheer when the ERA finally made its way out of the House Judiciary Committee that summer), and the books we read tended toward *The French Lieutenant's Woman* rather than *Sexual Politics*—much less *The Female Eunuch*. Still, we began to see what it was like for women who had to work, and it cast events in a little different light.

Ally had as tough a time that spring and summer as Kath did. Jeff, concerned about the drug Ally was taking, went into the hospital the evening after the Derby party for the express purpose of "bumping into" a colleague in obstetrics, who referred him to a group of doctors in Boston. When Linda telephoned Ally about it that Sunday afternoon, she started slowly, explaining what Jeff had told her about why a woman sometimes miscarried repeatedly: because of an abnormality in her uterus or cervix, or because her reproductive cycle wasn't working right somehow or there were other undiagnosed problems with her health. But Ally didn't want to hear about it. "I'm perfectly healthy, Linda," she said. "I've practically never been sick a day in my life."

That Wednesday in the park, Linda brought it up again, saying, "These Boston doctors Jeff talked to, Ally, they think there's a link between this drug you're taking and some kind of rare vaginal cancer. I'm not sure I quite understand exactly what Jeff was saying, but he definitely thinks you ought to stop taking it." Ally's stare would have turned anyone else away—to Davy barreling headfirst down the slide or Arselia clearing J.J. from the bottom, or to the mansion's porch light burning dimly against the dull morning—but Linda met her gaze.

"What does Jeff know about it?" Ally said. "My doctor says it's a magic bullet, that I'll have a baby."

Linda rolled her lips together, her multicolored eyes kind and sad and determined, still fixed on Ally.

Ally looked away, toward the palm tree to the right of the mansion door, a single dead frond hanging down along its trunk. "How can you know? You have no idea what it's like not to have a baby." Her voice even softer now: "Do you think I care if I might have some higher chance of cancer when I'm eighty?" She met Linda's gaze again, her eyes moist. "Jeff isn't even a gynecologist. He has no idea what he's talking about."

"But the drug won't help," Linda said, so gently you might not even have believed it was Linda. "It's just marketing. The drug companies are making a lot of money on disproved research and false hope."

"You don't know," Ally whispered. "Maybe you just don't *want* me to have a baby."

The tension at that picnic table was palpable, but Kath jumped right in. "We've just got to get us one of those banyan trees and do our midnight jig, ladies," she said, and even Ally laughed.

"Asparagus, mangos, and carrots," Ally said, clearly relieved to take the conversation in a lighter direction. "That's the latest from my mother-in-law. That's what I'm supposed to be eating now. Jim, too. And listen to this: She sent Jim some concoction made from white lilies—Jim thinks you make a tea with it or you blend it in goat's milk or something, even he's not sure. It's supposed to enhance the quality of his output, if you know what I mean!"

Linda let the whole matter of the drugs go that day, but the next week she came armed with a fat medical textbook. Ally wouldn't even look at it, though. And two weeks later, she started bleeding, right there in the park. She didn't notice at first—none of us did. It wasn't until we stood to leave that we saw the red stain on her white slacks.

"Oh Lordy, Ally," Kath said, and Ally looked down at herself, and what little color she had in her face drained away.

I hurried her to her car and drove her to the hospital, leaving Maggie and Davy and Carrie with Linda, telling Ally the whole way that it was going to be okay. The moment they whisked her from the emergency waiting room, I called Jim at his office. By the time he arrived, though, it was too late—the baby was lost.

We took our casseroles and fried chicken again, and wished there was something more we could do. Ally turned away every offer of help, though, and when Kath asked if she wanted to talk about it, Ally answered, "About what?" Which—we talked about it endlessly— seemed like a pretty loud *no*. None of us had any idea what she was going through, we knew that. We couldn't imagine. And poor Linda: you could see her wondering if her warnings had somehow brought this on, if Ally's losing her baby had been her fault.

27

On the fiftieth anniversary of the suffrage movement one warm August Wednesday, while fifty thousand women marched in New York and thousands more marched in ninety cities in forty-two states in a Women's Strike for Equality, the Wednesday Sisters sat huddled at our picnic table, with Arselia watching our children for the same inadequate pay those women were marching about.

"Ladies," Linda kept saying, "you know we really ought to go to town."

The area chapters of the National Organization for Women were staging a noon rally in Lytton Plaza.

"I won't ask you to shed your bras and chuck them in a garbage bin, but aren't you curious?" Linda said. "Aren't you dying to see what's going on?"

There was some discussion about the children. Could we take them to a women's lib rally? Which might have been real worry over their safety: just ten days earlier a mass confrontation downtown had ended with riot police and Mace and more than 250 hippies under arrest. Palo Alto had seen more than its share of violence all through that summer. But I think there was more to it than that. The peace rally we'd gone to, that was pretty easy. It was in San Francisco, where we weren't likely to bump into anyone we knew who might frown on our being there, and no doubt peace was a better thing than war in any event. But this rally Linda was talking about was in our own town, where people we knew ate and shopped. And women's liberation was a little trickier. It was an effort to change the future for women, but we had husbands and homes and children. Too late for Brett to be an astronaut, or Linda an Olympic athlete. So if the future for women *was* to change in any dramatic way, where would that leave us? As the dinosaurs, the last of an unwieldy, dying breed of women who were left to depend on their husbands when that would be seen as weakness, as failure, as shame.

"What if the crowd gets out of hand?" I asked.

"Or the police overreact, like at Kent State," Ally agreed.

"For goodness sakes!" Linda said. "It's Palo Alto!"

"'For goodness sakes' is a Frankie-ism, Linda," Brett said. "You're stealing her line."

"And Palo Alto isn't exactly some quiet little backwater," I said, and even Linda couldn't argue that: in addition to the chaos downtown, there had been bombings at Kepler's Books, at the Free University, and at one of the coffee shops downtown. Still, before we knew it, we were pushing the children's strollers up Center Drive, admonishing everyone to hold hands and be careful as the long, untidy line of us crossed the street.

Hundreds of people had already gathered in the plaza when we got there. Speakers were demanding equal pay for equal work and child care centers and abortion rights. WITH FOUR YEARS OF COLLEGE, I CAN EXPECT TO EARN $6,694 read the sign one woman carried, a woman in a cap and gown who worked, someone said, in the genetics department at Stanford. Half Danny's salary, I thought (though his job was looking more and more tenuous—his company had laid off twenty people at the end of its second quarter, a fact he shrugged off by saying he liked working in a place where the voice listened to was the one that knew the most rather than the one with the highest rank).

A man came out in a Playboy Bunny outfit—black bathing trunks and ears and a tail—unlike anything we'd ever imagined. He was prancing around to entertain women the way women pranced around to entertain men.

"I've got to get one of those for Danny," I said, making a joke to cover my embarrassment.

Brett laughed. "Chip would hate the tail. It would draw attention to his ample derrière."

"Jim's legs in high heels." Ally gave a low wolf whistle, so incongruous that we all cracked up.

"Neither a whistling woman nor a crowing hen ever come to a very good end," Kath declared. "My mama's advice—take it as you like."

A speaker appeared on the podium, saying that the usual channels for women to earn more than ten thousand dollars a year included prostitution, being a Playboy Bunny or a topless waitress, or posing nude for male magazines. I stopped laughing. We all did. We stood soberly as Ava Pauling, Mrs. Linus Pauling, stepped up to the microphone. I'm quite sure I stood straighter after she was introduced, even with Maggie tugging on my skirt, saying how hungry she was. It wasn't so much what Mrs. Pauling said—that women had had the vote for fifty years but we hadn't changed the world as much as we should have—as the fact that she was here. Yes, it was *her husband* who'd won the Nobel Prize, not her, but being married to him granted her a stature we were unsure the other speakers possessed. It made us think, *If Linus Pauling's wife is standing up for women's rights, who are we to be skeptical?*

As we watched the rest of the rally, we found ourselves nodding in agreement, nudging Brett at the antics in a skit about a mother scolding her daughter for playing with her "dirty chemistry set," laughing together at another skit, a "Miss 46-22-36" mock sobbing as she accepted her Miss America crown and thanking "the cosmetic industry and all those cute male photographers" for making her what she was. When the mock Miss America turned around to reveal a "U.S. Department of Agriculture Prime Grade" sign on her back, I whispered to the other Wednesday Sisters, " 'Round,' and 'Rib,' and 'Rump,' " remembering how I'd turned away from that BREAK THE

DULL STEAK HABIT poster on the television the first time we'd gathered to watch the Miss America pageant, when I'd thought the protester carrying it must be so different from me even if her dress was just like mine.

A woman from a group called the Spare Ribs (which would have made us dubious if it hadn't been for Mrs. Pauling) delivered the next speech, which gave us all pause: "We have been told that femininity is being smart enough to be dumb around a man," she said. "For me, femininity consists in being myself, in not putting myself down or my sisters down."

I began clapping then, without having decided to, and I wasn't alone. Linda, on one side of me, and Brett, on the other, were both clapping, and Kath and Ally were as well. Even Maggie, standing in front of me, was clapping, having no real idea what she was clapping for but following my lead. And so were Jamie and Julie, and Sarah and Lacy, and J.J. and Davy and even little Mark. Kath's Anna Page was not just clapping but cheering without restraint, her hair wild around her face, her hat upside down on the pavement behind her, where it would be stepped upon by a passerby too busy staring at the fellow in the Bunny costume to see it there.

W E GATHERED AT LINDA'S the Saturday night of the Miss America Pageant that year, a few weeks after the rally in Lytton Plaza, but we didn't turn on the TV. "No Miss 46-22-36 for us tonight," we said. We planned to enjoy a quiet evening together *not* watching, in part to assure Kath there would be life for her after Lee, if he divorced her, which he hadn't yet. He was, in fact, at their house that very evening, eating the dinner she had prepared as if he still lived there, which was the charade they continued to keep up.

Kath had run through the last of her savings buying school clothes even though she'd economized, letting Arselia go and serving more and more macaroni and cheese. To make ends meet, she'd accepted the first job she was offered, working for an obnoxious accountant who paid her the same $1.60 an hour we paid Arselia, but who let her go every day in time to be home when school got out. Every morning, Kath put on the skirt and hose and high heels required by office rules, saw Anna Page and Lee-Lee off to school, dropped Lacy with one of us, and went to work. When Lacy whined about being left, Kath took it all on her own shoulders, too. She acted as if her job were a fabulous opportunity rather than the sheer drudge it was, and she never once hinted that she was only working so that

Lacy could still have her favorite Lorna Doone cookies and Anna Page could wear patent leather shoes.

You had to admire Kath for that, for never allowing her children a glimpse of what a rat their daddy was. You had to wonder why you'd spend a whole evening admiring Miss Kentucky just because she wore gowns well when no one was admiring the kind of woman Kath was. All that carefully tended beauty, all that apparent faultlessness? You couldn't imagine those girls could be from struggling families, that they might have to work to send their brothers to college, that their husbands might abandon them. You couldn't imagine they would ever find themselves childless, or with lumps in their breasts, or with scars or fears they might need gloves to protect against. They were feminine, beautiful, and so you imagined their lives were all debutante balls and trust funds, that they awoke looking as beautiful as they appeared on the pageant stage, that they would never want for anything, or ever doubt themselves.

No pageant this year, we'd decided. Kath didn't need to stack herself up to Miss Kentucky. None of us did. We would spend the evening together admiring each other instead.

We poured our usuals that evening—gin and tonics, vodka gimlets, sidecars—and we nibbled (long gone were the days when no one would dip the first chip). Ally had brought something that looked like poppy-seed rolls, though not quite. "Rajgira, that's what the seeds are," she said. "The Royal Grain. My mother-in-law sent them. The seeds, not the rolls. They're supposed to give me strength—to carry a baby to term, she means. Although Jim's not sure that baking them into rolls is quite what his mom had in mind." She washed a bite of roll down with her vodka gimlet and grinned. "Much less serving them with alcohol."

We compared mothers-in-law, then, granting Ally's the Most Meddling from the Farthest Distance Award (although the rajgira rolls, with the crusty, nutty-tasting grain sprinkled on top, were actually quite good). Kath's mom-in-law took a close second, while mine came in dead last; Danny's mother was forever saying I was the best thing that ever happened to her son. And when we'd exhausted that subject, we moved on to what kinds of mothers-in-law we would be ourselves when our children married, and what kinds of spouses we hoped they would find. It wasn't long, though, before the conversation turned to the pageant we were determinedly not watching. It's true, I'm afraid. We couldn't help ourselves.

The rules had changed that year, so that nonwhites could participate. How could we not talk about that? Miss Iowa, Cheryl Browne, was competing as the first black contestant. We wondered what it would be like to be a black woman in America—these were the days when George Wallace, who thought blacks should be denied the vote, was the seventh most admired man in America—and how one black woman in a field of fifty could possibly change things. We wondered how it would feel to be her, and whether some of the judges wouldn't refuse to vote for her even if they thought she was the most beautiful and talented. We decided any judge who didn't think black women should participate wouldn't see any black woman as beautiful enough to win. We decided Cheryl Browne ought to win because for her to be named Miss Iowa she had to be super beautiful and super talented. We didn't really believe she could win, but we hoped she would.

As always, the talking was like the eating of potato chips, and the next thing we knew, we'd turned on the TV—just for a minute, we decided. "Just to see Cheryl Browne." "Just till the next commercial break." "Just till her talent, then we'll turn it off." Then the pageant was over and we'd watched pretty much the whole thing. It was the only year we all rooted for the same contestant.

We did watch the pageant differently that year—at least there was that. We weren't so wrapped up in ball gowns and bathing suits. We spent the time talking about what femininity meant and what it should mean—*not* "being smart enough to be dumb around a man," we agreed.

"Though I've done that," I said. "With boys I dated in high school before I met Danny."

"I even put answers I knew were wrong on tests sometimes," Ally admitted, "so the boy I was dating would do better than me."

"Maybe I should have done that," Brett said. "I was great at science, sure, but I never had a date until Chip."

"It's not just us," Kath said. "Do y'all ever watch Barbara Walters on the *Today* show? She waits for the men to finish asking their questions before she says a word."

"She has to, it's in her contract," Brett said.

"Seriously?" Ally said.

"I think my problem is I confuse 'feminine' with 'perfect,'" I said. "My hips are too wide, so I feel like a barking dog even though Danny swears he adores my hips. It's tough being raised with the Virgin Mary as the girl I was supposed to be."

"Virgin, but still she gets the child," Ally said. "The Son of God, no less."

"From a Darwinian standpoint, men are dependent on us, too, though," Brett said. "No women, no babies."

"But men can have identities without babies," Ally said. "Jim wants children even more than I do because family is so important in his culture, but he's supposed to be the breadwinner and he is, and I'm supposed to care for the family and I can't even produce the children I'm supposed to care for."

"I think Frankie is right about this perfection thing," Linda said. "I bet even these girls on the TV see themselves in terms of their shortcomings."

"My knees are too big, my breasts too small," Ally said.

"My little piggy toes are a whopping size nine and a half."

"My glasses." I tipped them for effect. "And my hair is downright goofy."

"Mine is the frizzliest mess—I swear sometimes I might could just shave it all off and be done with it," Kath said.

"Mine flattens before noon and the ends are all split," Linda said. "But I don't know about bald, Kath. It'd be like lacking breasts."

"Without either one you're androgynous," Brett agreed. She looked down at her own flat chest and started laughing, and we all laughed with her.

"At least you aren't overly intellectual," she said when she'd recovered from laughing.

"Or ambitious. God forbid I should be ambitious," I said.

"Heavens to Betsy, I'm just too good a writer to be a girl!" Ally said, and that made us all laugh again.

Okay, our laughter might have had something to do with the cocktails, which also might have been the source of our courage, but we did start talking that night about our own talents in a real way—not the batons we would have twirled in a beauty pageant, but our talents as writers: Linda's graceful sentences, Ally's imagination, Kath's memorable dialogue, Brett's settings, which made worlds spring to life, and my "voice," which I thought was just the way I spoke (exactly, they said). Then, maybe because we were drinking, the fantasizing began.

"Readers in bookstores and libraries," Ally said.

"In recliners, or curled up in bed," Brett said.

"Interviews," Kath said.

"Bestseller lists—why not?" Linda said.

"The Pulitzer Prize," I said.

"How about a big ol' monument," Kath said. "One in our pretty little Pardee Park."

"After we're all in our coffins for real," Brett said.

"Something that says the Wednesday Sisters got their start together, right there," Linda said.

"A fresco," I said.

"All of us huddled over our picnic table, children swinging in the background," Brett said. "Like the oil painting of the Round Table regulars at the Algonquin Hotel in New York, but in a medium that will weather well."

"Not that it's the publishing that matters," Linda said. "It's the writing that matters. Even if we never publish a word."

And we all agreed: it was the writing that mattered. It was through the writing that we were coming to know who we were.

29

WHEN DANNY AND I opened the front door to sit on the porch after the children were sleeping that Monday evening, the girl's room in the mansion across the street—"Estella's room," we'd both taken to calling it—was dimly lit. We smiled at each other and, without a moment of discussion about it, set our drinks on the porch where we would accidentally kick them over when we returned. We didn't even stop to grab the baseball bat.

It was quiet, just the patter of rain starting up as we crossed the street. Then we heard the piano, haunting notes. As we drew nearer, it was unmistakable: the music came from inside the old place.

In the darkness around back, with the streetlights blocked by trees and the moon well sequestered behind rain clouds, the tinkle of piano notes wafted in the stillness, with only the occasional *shhhhew* of wheels on wet asphalt as a car passed on the street, beyond the trees. I started shivering. I was wearing only a light sweater, no protection against the rain and the chill and the tension of waiting. Danny gave me his suit coat, but still I was cold.

It seemed a long time before the piano music ceased and the wandering light appeared at the back of the house, in one of the upstairs rooms. The room grew brighter in the darkness, and then we could see her, a girl with long flowing hair standing at the window, the daughter returning to her piano.

Not a girl, though. A woman. We could see the silhouette of her, though we couldn't see the details of her face.

Danny whispered that he'd never imagined a woman prowling around there at night, but I had. Despite my disbelief in ghosts, I'd come to imagine this person was somehow connected with the widow who'd lived in the house.

The woman disappeared after a moment, and we waited for a long time, beginning to wonder if she'd gone down the main stairs and out the front this time, eluding us again. But a faint light appeared at the top of the servants' stairs, finally, and paused there. Danny tapped my shoulder, silently pointing to what I could see now in the little bit of light was an open window, just by a back door. We moved closer, crouched behind some bushes. It wasn't until the woman began slowly to descend the stairs, the light fading in the upstairs window, growing stronger in the downstairs one, that I imagined my own feet on the worn wooden stairs, my own fingers on the candlestick, my own private sadness being observed.

"Danny," I whispered, and he turned to me just as the candlestick appeared in the window, casting its weak light on a table against the wall. I put my cold hands on Danny's cold cheeks and kissed him, turning us both away from the window.

The candlelight blinked out then, leaving the darkness total, and as our eyes adjusted, we could just make out the lonely shadow of a woman climbing through the window, quietly shutting it and setting off around the corner of the broken-down old place, to the park that had once been its lawn and, beyond it, to Ally's house.

THAT WAS THE FALL we switched from Wednesday mornings at ten to Sundays at sunrise. "Here's the thing," Ally said the third Wednesday after Kath had started working for the accountant. "No offense to the rest of you, but Kath, she's just so . . ."

"She knows when a manuscript is 'just a li'l bit catawampus,'" I said.

"Out of kilter," Linda said.

"She'd like to tell you how you might could fix it," Brett said.

"And she sure can make you laugh when you're just about to tune up," Ally said.

"Or have conniptions!"

"Tell the news!"

"Throw a hissy!"

"*Pitch* a hissy. Not throw. *Pitch*."

We'd just have to find a new time to meet, we agreed. Weekends, because Kath would be "all tuckered out" after work.

But Arselia couldn't sit for us on weekends, there was that problem. And with catechism and Sunday school and church—I'd just signed up to be a lector at Saint Thomas Aquinas—and everything else?

"That leaves Sundays at sunrise," Linda said with a sigh, not really meaning it.

But Brett said, "Sundays at sunrise, then."

"Our Lady of the Park Bench," I said.

I STILL REMEMBER that first Wednesday Sister Sunday: getting up before dawn, moving quietly through the darkened house, trying so hard not to wake Danny or the children. Danny waking anyway, and coming up behind me as I stood watching the coffee bubble up into the clear top knob of the percolator. Him putting his arms around my waist and kissing my neck, whispering in my ear, "Come back to bed."

I felt his warm hands and smelled the coffee and the toast browning in the toaster, and I half wanted to climb back into bed with him, but I said I couldn't. "I'm meeting the girls in the park, remember?"

"Right," he said, exhaling frustration. "Of course."

"Don't go out before the sun rises," he said.

I said I wouldn't, and he went back to bed then, and I peeked in a minute later—he was sleeping again—and I took my coffee mug and my toast and I walked out the front door, into the moonlit park.

As I sat at the picnic table in the moon shadow of the dilapidated mansion, watching for the sun to rise, I thought of Kath. Kath and Lee. I imagined Lee arriving at her house—*their* house? I imagined Kath going to the grocery store after our gathering, Lee helping her unload the bags when she got home, the whole Montgomery clan going off to church as a family, which they planned to do. Lee staying for supper and going back to his apartment only after the children went to bed. I wondered what the other Kathy thought of this arrangement. I wondered if he was still seeing her. Even Jeff, who worked with him, wasn't quite sure. He never saw Lee and the other Kathy together at the hospital.

Not long before sunrise, a slim shadow of darker darkness moved toward me from across the park, but I wasn't scared. Even in the darkness I knew it was Linda. She sat next to me and looked at the mansion too.

"Her daughter died of typhoid," she said, and when I turned slightly toward her, she said, "The woman who built that house. She was from a big political family; her stepson was governor, I think. Her husband died when she was in her early forties, and three months later her fifteen-year-old daughter died of typhoid. Her only child. Like the Stanfords' son. Fifteen. Typhoid. Only child."

We sat silently for a moment, watching the shambles of the house begin to emerge from the darkness as the sky lightened in the east.

"This park always makes me think of my mom," she whispered. "It's what she would have done if any of us had died, I think. She would have made a park for children to enjoy, and named it after us."

She sat beside me, straight-backed and square-shouldered as always. "Even when she was really sick, she used to make herself get out of bed to take us to the park."

I set my hand gently over hers, and she intertwined her fingers with mine.

Across the park, the shadows of Ally and Brett and Kath appeared, approaching us together, side by side by side.

"Someday I'm going to do something like this for my mom,"

Linda said. "I'm going to make something permanent. Something forever. A park in her honor. A college. A library."

"A book," I whispered, as Ally and Brett and Kath reached us, as they slipped onto the picnic table benches as quietly as latecomers slipping into Mass.

"Yes," Linda said just as the first sharp ray of the sun sparked at the horizon. "A book."

"A book," Ally echoed, as if it were right there in a missalette in front of her, her response.

And Kath and Brett repeated after her, "A book." And the dawn broke, the sun cresting the horizon, bringing to life the detail around us: the two brick chimneys rising proudly from either end of the long mansion roof, the sturdy trunks and bright red and orange and gold leaves of the trees all around us, our five faces smiling at each other, not sleepy despite the hour. Kath brushed a dried leaf from the table, then, and Brett pulled the worst of the splinters and tossed them onto the ground, and we set our pages in front of us, and we began again.

30

KATH HARDLY WROTE those next months, not even in her journal. She was emotionally exhausted, all her energy sapped by the demands of motherhood—taking care of Anna Page, Lee-Lee, and Lacy with no real help from Lee—and the drudgery of her work for the accountant. She needed to change jobs, Linda kept saying. "Why don't you find something you enjoy doing, Kath? You could be . . . I don't know. A journalist or an editor or a buyer for a bookstore. You could probably *run* a bookstore." Then one Sunday in November, Linda arrived at the park looking like the canary that ate the cat. She'd met a woman at an AAUW meeting who knew an editor who would be looking to hire someone that spring. She wasn't quite sure of the details, but it was in publishing. Wouldn't Kath love to work in publishing?

"In the spring?" Kath said doubtfully.

"The person she needs to replace is getting married in the spring. I think she's accepting résumés, although she won't interview until after the New Year."

Despite the long lead time, Kath got all in a twist right then. She'd never interviewed for anything, she said. And when we pointed out that she'd interviewed for all those jobs before she started working for the accountant, she said, "Anything that *matters*. Any job I might actually *want*."

$\mathcal{M}$Y OWN LIFE wasn't as complicated as Kath's that winter, but it was complicated enough. For one thing, being a lector at my church was turning out to be more time-consuming than I'd expected. Just a few minutes reading aloud during a Mass I would have attended anyway, I'd thought when I volunteered, and I was thrilled to do it, in part because only men had been allowed to read when I was growing up. I hadn't counted on the psychological energy it took to stand up in front of a whole church full of college graduates, though, their squirming children letting me know just how tedious my version of a Letter from Paul to the Corinthians was.

The first Sunday I read was, shall we say, eventful. I tripped climbing up to the lectern and went sprawling at Father Pat's feet. That got everyone's attention as surely as Sister Margaret's whistle had when I was in grade school—she put her thumb and middle finger to her mouth and shot out a sound that even the boys playing football on the big field couldn't fail to hear. When I was in the third grade, I'd asked her how she did it—I was the only girl ever to ask, she said—and the first time I'd belted out a good one, she'd laughed and said, "Delightfully unladylike! Now you'd best be careful how you use it, Frances, or you'll end up an old nun like me!"

With all those people staring at me from the pews, I picked myself up as gracefully as I could, straightened my glasses, and stood at the lectern. I could hardly find the page where I was to start the reading, even though it was marked with a ribbon. My voice croaked as I began. You could feel everyone suppressing their laughter, or holding their breaths.

The reading was from the prophet Isaiah, and I hadn't yet recovered from my inauspicious beginning when I read, "'None shall be weary nor . . . nor stumble . . .'" I choked up for a minute, too embarrassed to read on. I looked down at Danny, sitting with Maggie and Davy in the second pew, working hard not to laugh. At the whole congregation behind him.

I made a silly face and shrugged, and a rather delightful chuckle rippled through the church.

" 'None shall slumber nor sleep,' " I read on, cutting a glance toward Father Pat, who was known to doze off on occasion when he was assisting rather than saying the Mass himself. That got another chuckle, along with some poking of spouses who were known dozers, too.

When I'd finished reading and sat in the pew again, Danny took my hand and squeezed it, and whispered that I'd done a great job. I closed my eyes, prepared to have a few stern words with my God—privately, of course. But the God that came to me in that closed-eyed darkness looked more like a Wednesday Sister than like a stern old bearded Father, and she was chuckling, too.

All sorts of people stopped me after that Mass to say they'd enjoyed my reading. Even Father Pat had laughed, they said. And though I never did quite feel comfortable up at that lectern, in no time I went from sitting anonymously in the pews every Sunday to knowing so many parishioners that I was forever bumping into them at the parish office and the grocery store.

I was surprised to find myself controversial, too: a woman reader. Just when women had finally found our way to participating in the Mass—not reading the Gospels, that was still reserved for men, just doing the non-Gospel readings—the Vatican issued a revised Roman Missal, which restricted us. The NOW Ecumenical Task Force on Women and Religion burned part of the missal in protest that spring, and that fall it seemed half the nuns in America were in an uproar, the heads of seven orders meeting with Catholic bishops in Washington to demand a stronger voice in the Church. A nun, a woman who'd dedicated her life to the Church, couldn't read the Gospels when a mere deacon could, just because he was a man? That didn't seem right.

We learned that Danny was going to Canada that fall, too. His company was looking precarious—they had rushed to release the 1103, a breakthrough MOS memory product with four times the capacity of the original 1101, but as Danny's boss said privately,

"Sometimes the thing just doesn't remember." Andy feared the chips would all come back in returns and it would be the company's death. But the manufacturing arm of Bell Canada offered an amount equal to the company's entire net worth to be a second source for producing the 1103s, and Danny was being sent to Ottawa as part of the transfer team.

"Just temporarily. A few months, maybe," he said.

"A few months!"

"Six or eight at most, I hope."

I thought we ought to move with him—what would we do without him?—but he insisted that it wouldn't be that long, and that if we moved we'd end up living in a shabby apartment in the heart of one of those dreadful Canadian winters. "You'd be miserable having to bundle up the kids every time you stepped out the door, Frankie," he said. "And with no friends, no park." He'd be working all the time, anyway, he said. It wasn't like we'd ever see each other, even if we all moved.

The first few weeks Danny was away, I called him at his Ottawa apartment each night just before eight—eleven his time—so Mags and Davy could say good night to him, and he was always there. But he started getting back later and later as the weeks dragged on into months. I'd call every half hour, at eight-thirty, at nine; he didn't like to call me lest the phone wake the children, and no amount of assurance from me would convince him it would not.

He's working late, I would tell myself on those nights. He wants to finish up his work there so he can come home. I tried not to imagine him out having fun with his cohorts while the children kept me housebound and exhausted. I tried not to worry that he'd met another woman, that he was drinking his evening scotch with her. But things had been off between us lately—not on the surface but underneath. I can see now that it started that morning he found me writing, the moment I confessed to telling Bob I was writing a novel, but at the time all I could see was the strain that had crept into our lovemaking since I'd gotten my diaphragm, which, with the exception of that morning after he'd had the breakthrough on the MOS chip, I'd been using religiously.

One night when I got no answer at his apartment at eleven, at midnight, at one in the morning—4 A.M. his time—I was sure he was in some other woman's arms. Some mask designer, I thought, who had a life of her own, money of her own, who wouldn't have to turn down the heat in the wintertime to save up for a second car. I don't know why I didn't call his office earlier that night—maybe because I rarely did even when he was here, because I hated to interrupt his work. Or maybe because I, like Kath, didn't really want to know. But when I finally summoned the courage to phone his office, he answered on the first ring, his voice full of that funny croaky roughness it gets when he works intently for a long time.

With all that time alone while Danny was out of town—he came home only for the occasional weekend—I wrote and wrote so that, by the end of 1970, I declared myself "done" with "Michelangelo's Ghost." Again. (There's a wonderful quote by the French poet Paul Valéry—compliments of Brett, of course: "A poem is never finished, only abandoned." We were all beginning to see that "done" was a relative thing, not so much "finished" as "can't bear to read a single word again.") I made a new list of agents, and I was more prepared for rejection this time: Maggie had made me a little squid out of a toilet paper roll, complete with a black piece of paper inside, which, when you blew through the tube, came out as the little guy's "ink." When I got rejection letters, I could just pull out my squid and ink them!

The day I sent off my new batch of queries, Maggie lost her first tooth. She didn't want to leave it under her pillow for the tooth fairy, she wanted to keep it herself. "I don't need money," she said. "I still have my dollar Grandpa gave me for my birthday." She would leave a note under her pillow asking the tooth fairy to let her keep the tooth, she decided. If the tooth fairy promised not to take it, she would put it under her pillow the next night. If the fairy said she'd need to take the tooth to leave the money, no deal. A small thing, that first lost tooth, but I missed sharing it with Danny, missed enjoying together our daughter's odd spin on it.

In mid-February, the phone rang: an agent calling to ask for my manuscript. No need to ink that! One part of me thought it meant nothing, that he liked the idea of the novel but when he started reading he would pass, and another part of me was worried: Who was this agent? What did I know about any of this? Five rejections poured in over the next couple of weeks, only confirming my fears. But then a second request for the manuscript came, another small measure of hope.

One afternoon later that month Maggie and her friend Karen Geisel, along with Linda's Julie and Jamie, proudly informed me they were writing a book together. I made all the right noises—their writing was so neat, and their illustrations lovely. ("Illustrations," I called them, not "stick figure crayon drawings.") Karen, comfortable now, said they were going to send it to her grandpa when it was done, and he would publish it for them.

Me: "Is your grandpa a publisher?" Shamelessly milking this seven-year-old for information, thinking maybe I did have a connection to a publisher, albeit a tenuous one.

Karen: "No, he's Dr. Seuss."

Me (gulping): "Your grandpa is Dr. Seuss?"

Karen: "Yes. And if he likes it, he'll get it published for us."

I just stood there with my mouth open, thinking maybe if I rubbed her head, some of whatever made her grandfather magic would rub off on me.

Two days later the first agent, Fred Klein, called to say he loved my book and he was sure he could sell it. He was utterly charming about the fact that another agent had the manuscript. "It's an important decision," he said. "You need to pick someone you're comfortable with." And within minutes, I'd said I'd withdraw the manuscript from the other agent, and sure, I'd be happy to send him something on my second novel—as if I really did have something to send.

The moment we finished that phone call, I scooped up Davy and twirled him around, singing a tuneless, "Yes, yes, yes, I have an agent!" I called Danny in Canada—he was in a meeting and couldn't be interrupted—and I knew I couldn't tell anyone until I'd told him. So I waited, and called again, and waited and called yet again. Then decided I really ought to tell the Wednesday Sisters first—they were the ones who'd been writing with me. And my mom called just after I'd hung up with Kath, so I told her. And of course everyone who saw me when I went to pick up Maggie from school knew something was up and had to know the news: Maggie's teacher and several of the parents, and, yes, her little friend Karen, whose mother responded to my inquiry about whether Karen's grandfather was really Dr. Seuss with "Dr. Seuss?"

On the way home, Maggie picked me a bouquet of dandelions, which we put in a little pewter vase, and while they ate snacks, Davy made me a picture of a penguin—why a penguin I cannot imagine—and Maggie drew one of me with a cake and candles, my book in one hand and, ever practical, a fork in the other.

A cake is what the Wednesday Sisters showed up with that afternoon, too. A cake and champagne.

I was cleaning up the dinner dishes, exhausted and a little tipsy, when Danny finally called back. The moment the phone rang, I thought, *I can't believe I told Karen's mother—I don't even know her name—and I haven't told Danny yet.* I thought, *This must be something like what it's like to tell your husband you've been unfaithful.* I thought, *But I tried to tell him first. I did.*

"An agent," he said. "That's great, Frankie." No "future famous novelist M. F. O'Mara." No "I'll try to get home this weekend to celebrate." But he had been working so hard, hoping to wrap up things in Ottawa in the next month or so. He was exhausted.

That night, Maggie lost her second tooth. Getting ready for bed, she started explaining the tooth fairy's magic: "She's got this magic that, if you see her, then you get her magic, you get to be the tooth fairy instead of her. So that's why she comes at night." She was up the next morning at 5:18, standing by my bedside with her quarter in her hand and the most wonderful look on her face. She woke me from a dream—my book had sold quickly and Danny had brought me flowers and was calling me "M.F."—and I was so disoriented that for a minute I wondered if she really hadn't seen her tooth fairy, because she sure seemed magical to me.

I never did get back to sleep that morning, a spectacular spring morning that I was certain boded well. I took Maggie and Davy to the park after school and watched them scavenging for the most unreasonable treasures (bottle caps and stubs of chalk and broken crayons they collected in a tennis ball canister they also found), all while I started thinking about my next book, mapping out in my head the details of my new chapter 1.

THE FRIEND OF THE FRIEND of the woman Linda had met at that AAUW meeting, the publishing-job possibility for Kath, turned out to be a Mrs. Arlene Peets, and she was indeed looking for someone to replace a gal who was leaving when she married that March. The day Kath went in for the interview, finally, Mrs. Peets asked her all the expected questions—Could she type? File? Take dictation?—and Kath had to confess she didn't know shorthand. She thought the interview was over when Mrs. Peets said, "Why this particular job?"

"Why this job?" Kath repeated.

"Why do you want it?"

Kath sat there feeling mute and stupid for a moment, as worn out as the fabric on Mrs. Peets's chairs. "All I know is books," she said finally. "I was an English lit major. What do English lit majors know how to do that's practical?"

They'd ended up talking for an hour about their favorite novels, and by the time Kath left that office, she was working for a boss who was not only a woman but also just about the nicest, smartest person she'd ever met. Arlene, she insisted on being called, not Mrs. Peets. Kath would be a copy editor: instead of spending her days typing boring letters with too many numbers in them and fetching coffee and the accountant's dry cleaning, she would spend her days reading. The only catch was that she had to watch for typos, grammatical and factual errors, awkward phrases, deviations from the publisher's style.

"Drop the *ma'am*, too," Arlene told Kath. "You're not in the South anymore, Dorothy. If you want to be taken seriously, don't be calling people ma'am and sir. And don't feel your shoes have to match your bag every day, either. You'll make me look bad, and I'm vainer than you might think."

31

THE FIRST PUBLISHER'S rejection of my novel rolled in a few days after Kath's interview. "A lovely rejection," Fred said. "'. . . Nicely written, with a likeable protagonist. As strong as it is, I'm afraid it didn't keep me turning the pages as I would have hoped. *A close call, though.*'"

No amount of paper squid ink could make it easier to take.

In the following weeks, I mowed the lawn, and painted Davy's room, and recaulked the tub—chores Danny always did but that, with him out of town, fell to me. I listened to Linda's updates on women's rights: the Supreme Court ruled women couldn't be refused jobs solely because they had small children unless fathers of small children were also refused jobs; the Women's Caucus sued every law school in the country for discrimination against women; a Pittsburgh paper was ordered to end the sex segregation of its help wanted ads. I nodded sympathetically as Kath and Linda worried over the sit-in at Stanford Hospital, concerned for Lee's and Jeff's safety should it turn violent. I drove for Maggie's field trip to a park where the class grubbed in the stream, where I talked with other moms about anything but writing while the children ate a picnic lunch and had a water-balloon fight on a playground rich with puddles they couldn't resist. I took Maggie and Davy to the library, despairing of all the books on the shelves—so many books that surely there was no more room for mine.

Nights, I stayed up late reading, and woke early and tired, and started the whole routine again. And the rejections just kept coming: "I'm sorry to say . . ." " . . . not quite right . . ." "I'm sure another editor will . . ." I saw what Fred meant by "lovely," though, when less flattering responses came in: " . . . the more I read, the less enchanted I became."

DANNY GOT HOME from his stint in Canada just in time for us to catch the plane for Kauai that May, for a three-day party paid for by the company, with all the employees who'd been in Canada and their wives. He'd arrived home late that morning, had lunch with Mags and Davy, and repacked his bag while I dropped Davy at Linda's and walked Maggie back to school. We'd barely even spoken ourselves before we boarded the plane, which cast a certain spell of unreality over the whole trip.

"Hawaii, Danny, can you believe it?" I said as he hoisted our hanging bag into the overhead bin and took the seat next to mine, on the aisle.

"You gave Linda the hotel number?" he asked. "And Mags has Allo blanket and Davy has Mutt?"

"They think a three-day sleepover is as big an adventure as going to Hawaii," I said as the stewardess started the spiel about all the things you really don't want to hear when you and your husband are on a plane while your children are at home, ready to be orphaned: oxygen masks, flotation devices, "in the event of a crash."

"I miss them already," Danny said. "I wish we were staying home."

I'd known he would feel this way the minute he saw the children and had to leave them again. I'd offered to skip the trip in a half dozen phone conversations, but he always said he didn't want to disappoint Bob or Andy. I wondered now if that was the problem, or if it was just me he didn't want to disappoint.

He's tired, I told myself. *Cranky. He's been working too hard.*

I looked around at all the familiar faces on the plane. "If this thing goes down, there goes the company," I said.

Though Bob wasn't there, I realized; I supposed as long as he survived, anyone else at the company could be replaced. "Where's Bob?" I asked. "Isn't he coming?"

In the sharp moment of silence before Danny answered, I knew I'd said something wrong. "What?" he said. "Are you dying to tell him your book—"

Didn't sell. He'd stopped himself from saying the words, but I heard them anyway. And while I was recovering from that blow, my face turned to the window, to the long stretch of nothing but deep ocean below, I saw that he was right, that my novel hadn't sold and it wasn't going to, that what Fred Klein had been saying in our last conversation was that "Michelangelo's Ghost" was as dead as the Cubs would be that entire season. Eighteen publishers had passed. Fred might well have been a Cubs fan, though, because he remained staunchly loyal, unreasonably optimistic. "This new one you're working on," he said. "Get it done and we'll send it out." There's always next season, was the idea. But the Cubs hadn't won the World Series since 1908.

"I'm sorry," Danny said. "I shouldn't have said that. It's just that . . ."

He never said what it just was, though. "Bob is coming separately," he said. "Flying himself."

We arrived the way one arrived in Hawaii in those days: greeted by hula-dancing, grass-skirted young women who draped leis around our necks—and we would wear leis every night of that vacation. Corny, maybe, but it was what we needed, or we wanted it to be, anyway: something to break us out of the gloom that had set in between us on the plane. To be honest, I'm not sure we even thought it was corny any more than we thought, consciously anyway, that this was Hawaii, perhaps the trip of our lifetime, that it would be unforgivable to arrive barely speaking to each other, especially after we'd gotten through all those months apart.

I straightened Danny's lei, which had caught up on his collar, and kissed him on the cheek, and I said, "I'm sorry, too," not able to give voice to what I was sorry for any more than he was. I was sorry that I'd told Bob I was writing before I told Danny? If I said that, Danny would have to swear he wasn't jealous of Bob, that he hadn't felt betrayed, and that would leave him feeling the pettiness of carrying that thorn in his paw all this time, and it would leave me feeling that pettiness too, feeling Danny would throw my dream out with the dirty dishwater of his pride.

"It looks like the bags are coming in," I said, relieved for the excuse to turn away.

Our room at the Surf Hotel was ultramodern and stark, its only inviting feature a rope chair that hung from the ceiling. Not at all what I'd expected, none of this was going as I'd expected, as I'd hoped, and we were only just there. And I suppose it's worse to live life without expectation than to live through the pain of expectations crushed, but it never feels that way in the moment, it always feels as though life would be so much easier if only you could stop hoping for things that would never come.

The room did have a glass door opening to a balcony, it did look out over thatch-topped sun umbrellas and sand and waves and an outcropping of land beyond, a view we took in standing side by side, without touching. Standing there with the warm breeze flowing over me, I imagined that if I looked out rather than in all weekend, I would like what I saw, what I was doing. I imagined it would all be okay.

We ate chateaubriand for dinner that evening, and drank umbrella drinks—coconutty pineapply rummy piña coladas I sipped like lemonade while we listened to a jazz band. Around us, everyone was relaxing, unwinding. It was the first time most of these guys had really relaxed since the back-and-forth to Canada had begun. The first time Danny and I had had to really relax, too, though we weren't. We were drinking the same umbrella drinks everyone else was, but we weren't drinking to relax, we were drinking to anesthetize.

You'd think I'd be smart enough to know to avoid those umbrella drinks in that situation.

Everyone else was keeping pace with us, even Bob, who'd arrived just in time for cocktails. After dinner, he made his way around to the tables, thanking the men for all their hard work and their wives for all their patience. As he approached our table, I slipped off my glasses. He sat next to me, took my hand, kissed my cheek.

"Frankie," he said. "I do hope you got some writing done while Danny was in Canada." His voice was so warm and encouraging and enthusiastic that it made me want to spill my guts again, it made me want to tell him I couldn't write a word anymore, my novel was dead, it was never going to sell.

We talked and talked, Bob and I did, while Danny sat back with his arms crossed over his chest, only moving to drain his fourth drink. I was just being the good corporate wife, I'd have claimed, but I knew even as I was laughing with Bob that it was more complicated than that.

Danny and I had sex that night. Not made love. Had sex. Sex that started the moment we closed the door to our hotel room after a silent walk down the long corridor back to our room. "My diaphragm," I said, but he only wrapped his fingers in my hair and held it tight, pulled it tight, and he yanked my lei off and my blouse open, and he squeezed my breast till it hurt. I bit his lip, and he lifted my skirt and took me like that, standing up against the wall of the sterile hotel room, with the sliding door to the balcony closed, the drapes drawn, even the ocean waves crushed into an awful silence that was still with us the next morning when we awoke, hung over and embarrassed and sad.

There's nothing to do but go on pretending in those situations. You can't have a knock-down-drag-out on vacation in Hawaii with all your work cohorts, with your boss. You can't sulk or pout or do anything but pretend to be having as great a time as everyone else is clearly having, to hide the hurt and smile politely and say yes, the pineapple does taste better here, and no, you've never seen an ocean so blue, felt air so soft.

Well into a second night of umbrella drinks, we found ourselves out on the beach—not just Danny and me but the whole expedition, the men stripping off their white shirts, shoes, socks, belts, and pants, stripping down to their undershorts to go for a swim. Never mind that their swimsuits were just a minute away, in their rooms. Never mind that Danny was wearing a pair of embarrassingly frayed-at-the-edges boxers, an orange, monkey-adorned pair I'd tossed into the trash months ago only to have him indignantly fish them out. They were so soft, so comfortable. His favorite undershorts.

"O'Mara, you're sacrificing everything to buy more stock, aren't you?" someone joked. "Even your underwear!"

Danny looked all skinny and leggy and vulnerable standing there in the bright moonlight, dwarfed by the palm tree looming over him, unable to come up with a comeback, witty or not. It reminded me of our wedding night, of Danny slipping his tuxedo shirt off, then inhaling self-consciously, trying to make himself look more manly, as if I needed to be impressed, as if I weren't already madly in love with him.

I wondered if he could see that all the men around him were pulling their stomachs in, too, and trying to flex their arms. That it was as impossible to look comfortable in nothing but your undershorts as it was to stack yourself up favorably next to a Miss America, or even just a Miss Illinois. Even Bob was sucking in his stomach; I wanted to laugh, it seemed so incongruous. I wondered then how I'd failed to see that despite Danny's bravura he doubted himself sometimes, too, just as I did. That everyone sometimes doubted themselves, even if they were college graduates or held swanky positions at swanky companies, even if they'd published a dozen novels and won the Pulitzer Prize.

I climbed up to stand on a teak beach chair, wobbling, nearly losing my balance, but I could see it didn't really matter, no one was looking at me, all the women were looking at their husbands in their boxer shorts (or maybe at the other husbands, what did I know?), and all the men were comparing themselves with the fittest of their colleagues. I put my thumb and middle finger to my lips then, "charmingly unladylike." *Femininity,* I thought as I let that whistle rip, *consists in being myself, in not putting myself or my sisters down.*

The whistle pierced through the crash of the ocean and the drunken chattering of the assembled group, and everyone was suddenly looking at me as surely as they had that morning I'd tripped in church. I took my lei from my neck and wrapped it in a circle just smaller than the circumference of a head, steadying myself again on the beach chair, looking up at the moon, not quite full. I cleared my throat and, in my best Bert Parks imitation, called out, "Mr. Illinois, in shredded orange monkey shorts, hails from Chicago, where he graduated valedictorian at Northwestern University at the age of nineteen." I dropped the lei-crown on Danny's head and started singing, "Here he is, Mr. America . . ." And I'm here to tell you, there is a reason I volunteered to read at church rather than sing in the choir. There's a reason my talent for the Miss America Pageant would have been the baton.

Everyone was laughing then, Danny hardest of all.

"Damn, Danny. Nineteen?" Andy said. "But I knew you were a genius. Wasn't that the first thing I told you, Bob, when I said we should hire him?"

You could practically see Danny's chest expanding. He hopped up on the beach chair beside me, put his arm around my shoulder and, sloshed as he was, still I could feel him standing up straighter, looking as though he'd finally realized he might actually belong with these men after all.

Bob took the opportunity to show off then, plunging headfirst into the ocean—only to discover the tide had gone out. He came up scraped raw and cursing and laughing at the same time. And everyone laughed with him, even harder than we'd laughed before. I watched Danny watching him, laughing as hard as I was, and I thought, *Of course he's jealous, of course he would be, with all the admiration he has for this crazy lunatic boss of his.*

And laughter is a wonderful thing, it really is. It's hard to hold tight to disappointment when your whole body is shaking with laughter, when you're having to stand with your legs crossed so as not to wet yourself.

We were still laughing as we returned to our room late that night, as Danny sat on the chair swing and I straddled him, shrugging off the thought of my diaphragm, maybe not wanting to break the mood or maybe thinking if we made a baby that night, then it was meant to be. We made love like that, with the sliding doors wide open and the warm night breeze on our bare skin, with the moonlight reflecting so beautifully off the white-capped water it would have made you hold your breath if you weren't making love in a swing.

Have you ever made love in a swing? It's not quite as easy as it looks.

And the next night—our last night on the island—I overheard Danny and Bob talking about me, Danny saying yes, it was wonderful that I'd gotten an agent, wasn't it? Saying "Michelangelo's Ghost" hadn't sold yet, but he was still sure it would.

32

T HAT SUMMER OF 1971, the Pentagon Papers were leaked
to *The New York Times*, eighteen-year-olds gained the right to
vote, Danny's company settled into new digs in a pear orchard in
Santa Clara, and Kath and Lee went together to the Outer Banks.

Yes, that was our reaction, too: You aren't even living together in
that big old house of yours anymore; how are you going to do it in the
small confines of a North Carolina vacation? We didn't put it quite so
bluntly to her, but we said it. And it gets worse: they were staying at
his family's summer house, with his parents and his grandparents, his
brothers and even his aunts and uncles and cousins all there, and all
hers a few houses down the beach.

This was where they'd first gotten together, vacationing with
other wealthy Southern families the summer she'd flirted with his
friend Huntley Parker, the year Lee was captain of the football team
at his private boys' school and Kath made the varsity cheerleading
squad at the sister school. And they couldn't *not* go. They'd gone
every summer of their entire lives, and the children had, too, and they
still hadn't said a word about their split to their families *or* to the children. And they weren't either of them ready to do that yet—which
Kath took as a good sign. She thought maybe a return to the place of

that early romance was what was needed to get her marriage back on track.

She dieted even more stringently in the weeks before they left, and lay out in her backyard in a new bikini so she wouldn't be marshmallow pale when Lee saw her in it. She packed the matching powder-blue suitcase and cosmetic bag Lee had given her for their anniversary one year, and she and Lee loaded the children into a taxi like they did every summer and set off for the airport. They flew to Atlanta and changed to a smaller plane that took them to the local airport where the family chauffeur—hers or his, that wasn't quite clear—picked them up.

I'm sure Kath had thought of the room arrangements. She must have. She'd been in that house enough to know that, big as it was, when Lee's whole family was in residence (his parents and grandparents and brothers and sisters and all the little cousins) there wasn't a spare room for spouses who weren't sleeping together. I wondered if she might somehow manage to stay with her family, use the excuse that she didn't see them but this once a year so she ought to stay with them, but I don't think that idea ever crossed her mind.

Did she sleep with him, cuddled together in the bed they'd first made love in one sultry summer night when his parents were at her house for bridge? He hadn't wanted to, he'd as much as said on the plane that he wouldn't do that, that he was in love with the other Kathy and he'd promised her he wouldn't. Kath choked on that. She wanted to whack him across the face, but she only turned to the window—thankful she'd taken the window seat—and looked out at the long stretch of square fields below, fields that looked unreal from this distance, that looked like a play world populated with dolls and toy cars and nothing that could really have any emotion at all.

The vacation was awful, Kath trying so hard every moment to win Lee back. She wooed him by wooing his mother, who'd always seen her as that slut of a girl who'd trapped her sweet Lee by getting pregnant, and his father, who could be wooed by almost any attractive and attentive young woman—at least there was that. She was the perfect sister-in-law; there were servants for the cooking and cleaning, but she watched all the children while the others played tennis or golfed or swam. She tucked her children in at night while Lee sat with the other men on the porch. Mornings, she brought him coffee and the newspaper in bed and made him eggs Benedict—the cook never did make it just the way he liked it—and he ate and read the paper and pretended she wasn't there. But those Southern manners go a long way toward covering up reality. No one had any idea that there was anything amiss.

Kath went to bed with Lee every night like a good wife, too, never once giving even a hint of the fact that, back in California, he was sleeping with someone else. The first night, the second, the third, she stayed up far too late, long after the other wives had gone to sleep, waiting for Lee to finish drinking and telling off-color jokes with his brothers. She wore sexy negligees, and she climbed in next to his turned back, and she didn't say a word about how humiliating it was to be sleeping with a man who'd rejected her, a man who was dreaming of another woman in his sleep.

It was the fourth awful night that she let go. She'd had a sidecar before dinner—they always had cocktails before dinner—and a refill at the table, and another afterward, and when everyone was out on the porch, lost in the kind of summertime laughter that the beach brings out in even the sourest of people, she'd slipped inside and poured herself a good stiff fourth. It wasn't the first time in her life she'd had four drinks in an evening, but she hadn't eaten much, either. She looked great in that bikini—all Lee's brothers had remarked on that, much to their wives' dismay—and she was not about to let go of that attention, that reminder to Lee of what he had in her.

She dawdled in the bathroom that night till Lee was in bed, then went to his side of the bed rather than hers. She stood in front of him, carefully silhouetted in the moonlight so he could see through her negligee. She knelt down on the floor beside the bed, and she touched his cheek, his hip, his leg. He didn't say anything, didn't respond, so she did the only thing she could think to do. She pulled her nightgown up over her head and knelt there, naked and exposed.

"Jesus, Kath," he said, and he turned away.

It seemed impossible even to her that she could humiliate herself further. She knelt there for the longest time, his back to her, telling herself to give up, to go to sleep. "Please, Lee," she said quietly. Pleading. Like a little girl who can't bear to be left out.

He rolled onto his back, said, "Jesus, Kath," again. Then lay there, staring up at the ceiling.

She climbed on top of him.

"I can't, Kath," he said.

She started moving against him, moving, moving until she knew she could slip his boxers off and she would have him. She took him in her mouth, even, which she never had liked, but she knew he loved. She would have done anything he wanted that night.

She faked an orgasm, to flatter him.

He took her angrily after that. He rolled on top of her and banged into her, the bed frame squeaking under them in the quiet of the crowded house.

"Jesus," he said when he'd spent himself, and she felt a small moment of hope. He still loved her. She could still please him.

"Jesus," he said again. "I'll say this, Kath. You still have the warmest pussy I've ever had."

33

I WAS UPSTAIRS getting Maggie a sweater she could wear to
school one Friday morning in September when the phone rang.
I answered it on our new upstairs extension. My agent, Fred: "I have
good news." And the next day, as luck would have it, was the Saturday of the Miss America Pageant. When we gathered—at Kath's that
year—we popped champagne.

"Novelist Frankie O'Mara!" Kath said. "Lordy, Lordy, that beats
the band, doesn't it?"

We hadn't turned on the pageant that evening before we were well
into planning our futures as if this were the very first step for all of us,
as if one of us achieving a dream meant we all could, which was how
we felt. We were all writing pretty regularly by then. Brett was rewriting her novel, and Linda had felt so affirmed when she'd sold her first
story that she'd written several more, having in mind a collection
that could be published as a book. Even Kath was writing, despite
that awful vacation with Lee. Or maybe because of it. Or because the
week after they got back from North Carolina, she "just happened to
drive by Lee's apartment" and found a rent-a-van unloading the other
Kathy's medical books and albums, her bicycle, her pillow and her
childhood teddy bear, her powder-blue cosmetic bag that was identi-

cal to the one Lee had given Kath as an anniversary gift. At any rate, she'd begun writing the novel Linda had urged on her, a *Pride and Prejudice*–type comedy of manners set in the modern South. She'd finished two chapters, both written in her journal—it was less intimidating that way, she said—and she was writing a little nearly every day despite the fact that she was working full-time and raising Anna Page and Lee-Lee and Lacy essentially alone. When we asked how she did it, she said it was better than staying up crying every night. At least she was getting something done when she couldn't sleep.

Ally had reverted to her journal, too, having abandoned her porcupine story. She'd begun writing about the packages that came from her mother-in-law. The latest offering included a length of silk and several pouches of powder: *kumkum,* which was vermilion powder, *haldi,* which was yellow turmeric, and gray ashes called *bhasma.* Jim's parents had taken them to their ancestral place, where they'd offered them as a *pooja* to their *kuldaivat,* their family god. An offering made in Ally's name, Jim said—for a grandchild, Ally knew, although Jim didn't say that. The length of silk, a sari, was so soft that Ally wanted to feel it on her bare skin. She'd wrapped herself in it as best she could, and it hadn't seemed so odd then to have Jim put the red *kumkum* along the part of her hair and on her forehead—just a dot between her eyebrows—and a pinch of the turmeric and ashes on the bridge of her nose. It was like being in costume, Ally wrote in her journal, and yet not: in that sari, she was a more sensual, more exotic version of herself, but still herself. She and Jim had made love the night she donned the sari, the soft silk intertwining with their bodies. And though she hadn't said anything to us about thinking maybe they'd made a baby that night, I imagined the evening had been blessed in the way his parents had meant it to be. I imagined that she would tell us before the pageant ended that she was pregnant again.

What Ally started talking about when the conversation turned away from our writing that night, though, was how thin Linda had become. Which she had. If anyone we knew today got as thin as Linda was back then, we'd worry it was some kind of eating disorder. That term wasn't even in Brett's extensive vocabulary in those days, though. And Linda didn't seem unwell or even the least bit lacking in energy: when it came out that the state of Virginia had turned down *twenty-one thousand* women for admission to state colleges in 1970 while not turning away a single man, she ranted with her usual energy, at her usual admirable volume. But the way Ally was pushing Linda that evening seemed sort of a slap back at Linda for all that pushing Linda had done late that spring over Ally's drugs. Still, Kath agreed with Ally. "You best starting eating better, Linda, or you'll have to stand up twice to cast a shadow," she said.

"I've been running more and more," Linda responded. "I have in mind to run a marathon."

"A marathon!"

"Not this fall, but maybe next. I can run ten miles already."

I'd seen her running by enough mornings to know she was pretty fast, too.

"The New York Marathon is next fall," she said. "I'd run Boston this spring, but they still won't let women enter the race."

It wasn't something women did much then, sports of any kind. That year, fewer than 300,000 American high school girls had taken part in interscholastic sports. Even men didn't run marathons much: only 126 ran the first New York City Marathon, competing for recycled bowling trophies. So I suppose it was a comment on how much the Wednesday Sisters had changed that we didn't think she was loony for wanting to run that far. Or a comment on how well we knew Linda by then. You get to know someone whose writing you critique every week in a way you don't get to know anyone else; you learn things about them they don't know themselves.

We spent so much time celebrating that evening and talking about our own dreams and successes that we forgot entirely about Miss America. Bert Parks was practically naming Miss Congeniality when we turned on the TV. No time for us to pick the winner, Miss Ohio, who looked to me like a brunette version of Linda, with straight hair pulled back from her forehead and a perfect mouth, a perfect nose, perfect eyes. She didn't sound at all like Linda, though. "Now a lot of anxiety is released," she said, the stiffest first words ever uttered by a new Miss America. "Phyllis was a remarkable Miss America," she said. "If I could do half of what she did, then I know I would not be just an image."

Linda would have been considerably spunkier than that even if she'd just finished running a marathon, I remember thinking. Kath would have, too, even if the other Kathy was the one interviewing her. Brett would have even if she'd lost to her sister, the doctor-to-be, and quiet Ally would have, too, even if she'd just been through labor, just given birth. Not one of us would have sounded so ditzy, wearing that Miss America crown or not—that's what I thought that night. Underestimating, I see now, the effect of the stage and lights, the audience. Underestimating the blush of unexpected success.

M<small>Y FIRST PHONE CALL</small> with my editor was a little like a first date: we talked less about "Michelangelo's Ghost" than about where we'd grown up and what we liked to read. I hung up looking forward to working with him. And then . . . nothing. Weeks went by with no contract, no further phone call. I took to asking Danny every once in a while if I hadn't just dreamed it.

All the while Danny was still working nonstop. The second MOS device, the 1103, had turned out to be a brilliant success— memory at less than a penny per bit—which you would think would have given him time to relax. But they were already developing the next-generation product, making something even better, and on top of that, he'd been drafted onto the public offering team, helping the investment bankers and the lawyers take the company's stock public. Near as I could tell, those investment bankers worked all the time, and even after they went home at midnight their poor lawyers stayed on.

That spate of hard work definitely paid off, though. On October 13—a Wednesday—the company went public. The Intel offering was "oversubscribed," a fancy way of saying they had buyers for more shares than they had to sell. Shares sold at $23.50, almost five times what Danny had paid for the stock he'd bought in the employee purchase plan. I didn't know how much that meant for us, but maybe I could get a new oven? Or maybe we could get a second car—a used one—and keep the old oven.

At the celebration that night, Danny fell asleep sitting up in a chair.

He would end up working impossibly hard through mid-November getting the new 4004 ready for release—Intel's first microprocessor, though they didn't call it that; they called it a "micro-programmable computer on a chip." It was something to be a part of, really; I think most company wives felt that way. Yes, sometimes we wondered if it was worth the empty seat at the dinner table, the picnics and baseball outings and family vacations postponed. But we saw ourselves as playing a supporting role in something important, something we were sure would change the world although we didn't quite know how.

That weekend after the company went public, though, there were no problems, only celebration and hope and happiness. Danny went off with Mags and Davy Saturday morning, very mischievously, and came home two hours later driving a brand-new Chevy Malibu convertible, a cherry-red four-seater with "dark saddle" bucket seats, air-conditioning, and a push-button radio and eight-track tape player to boot. *I'd never have guessed him to be a red-convertible kind of guy*, I remember thinking after I'd gotten over the shock of seeing that car in my own driveway. The thing was beautiful, and he clearly deserved it. But what about the kids' college fund? What about putting something away for a rainy day?

He climbed from the car with the biggest grin I'd seen on his face since the day Davy was born.

"Danny!" I said, tamping down my exasperation.

He held open the door, motioning for me to take the driver's seat. "You won't mind driving me back to the car dealer in your new chariot, will you?" he said. "So I can pick up my old jalopy?"

The car was for me. He wasn't a red-car guy. He saw *me* as his red-car gal.

And when I climbed in beside him, he leaned over and whispered a dollar amount in my ear, not the price of the car, but the value of our Intel stock. I remember thinking it was people-might-kidnap-the-children money, your-friends-look-at-you-differently money—though it wasn't, really; it was just more money than I'd ever imagined we'd have. Still, we agreed we wouldn't tell anyone.

The next morning at dawn, I told the Wednesday Sisters.

They told me I'd have to buy the champagne from now on.

34

ALLY CROSSED the three-month mark that November, still pregnant. She was actually beginning to show. It shocked me when I realized that: the children she'd carried before had died before much more than a hint of their existence was visible to the world.

She started writing in a big way, a story for older children about a teenaged runaway who befriends an ancient old soul of a man who dies in the end, she told us, like Charlotte in *Charlotte's Web*—but not before the girl finds herself in his history, his love of her. Kath and Linda and Brett and I could all see that this new manic writing phase had less to do with the story itself than with Ally believing she might actually carry this child to term, as though finishing this book before the baby came would be some kind of good omen, like birds building nests or whatever. As much as she wrote, though, she was always nowhere near the end. I began to wonder if she *could* finish, or if she'd become like that Winchester Rifle heiress who'd built that maze of a mansion down in San Jose, adding room after room for fear that if she ever finished building the house, she would die. Rooms with blind chimneys and double-back hallways, with stairways (always with thirteen stairs) leading nowhere and doors that opened to steep drops—to confuse the ghosts of those who'd died by the Winchester rifle. Sarah Pardee Winchester, that woman's name was. Pardee, like the woman who built the house in our park. Her only daughter had died, too, from a wasting disease not long after she was born.

None of us could imagine saying anything but "nice" about the first pages Ally gave us from her story, but Ally sat waiting the Sunday morning we were to critique them, her back to the mansion and its cobwebs, its dust, its out-of-tune piano. I saw in her expression—her big brown eyes in her pale face expectant in the slant of morning light—that this was exactly what she needed from us, that our taking her work seriously made everything possible. Not just the book—not even the book—but the baby she wanted more than anything.

I cleared my throat awkwardly, began tentatively. There was something haunting about the writing, I said—the first to speak but it started things rolling and before long it was just like any other critique session, or almost like that, anyway. I said what I found compelling in the writing, and then what was slow, what was trite. I didn't use words like *trite*, though, words I might have used with one of the other Wednesday Sisters, or with Ally herself some other time. I called the good parts "fresh," the weaker parts "familiar"—a word I came to use whenever I meant "trite" until one day months later I called something Brett had written "familiar" and she turned to the others and said, "Familiar. That's Frankie-speak for *trite*."

Linda asked that morning what it was about *Charlotte's Web* that Ally particularly liked; maybe it would help to think about that, since it was Ally's model book.

"I like the family that comes together in the barn," Ally said without hesitation. "I like that they aren't all the same thing; one is human and one's a spider and one's a pig. I like that it has nothing to do with blood relations, and everything to do with love."

Ally wasn't alone in clinging to hope for this baby in improbable ways. A few weeks after Jim called his parents and, in one of those three-minute overseas calls, told them Ally was pregnant (the only time he'd told them since the first baby she'd lost, years ago by then), a box arrived from India. Jim was out of town the Saturday it arrived, and Ally didn't want to open it without him; it was no fun to open presents without someone to share the experience. But then she'd awoken Sunday morning in the predawn darkness imagining how much fun it might be to open the thing with us, and she thought, *It's addressed to me, not to Jim, anyway*—usually the packages were addressed to Jim or, more recently, to them both—and so she brought it to the park that Sunday morning.

"It's bigger than usual," she said. "I figure I'll probably need someone to help me eat whatever is inside, and I nominate you!"

We all made faces: the one concoction we'd sampled since the rolls Ally had made with her mother-in-law's rajgira seeds had tasted of mold and paste.

Ally sliced away quantities of brown sealing tape, opened the box, and pulled away the packing paper. The smell of wood—as strong as cedar, but something fresher, almost brighter—filled the air.

Ally looked up with her loony-bin grin. "Heavens to Betsy, you ladies are going to love this!"

She pulled out a statue of some kind—no dainty figurine, this. It was a good foot high and nearly as wide, some kind of deity riding a chariot pulled by ten horses, made of polished wood inexpertly carved. It seemed to want an altar for its display; a coffee table just wouldn't do. And one could only hope that the wood's stiff odor was the result of its months in transit confined to the box, that the smell would die down over time.

"I do declare, even a blind hog finds an acorn now and then," Kath said, and we laughed and laughed, though even as I laughed I wondered if we were laughing at the statue itself, or at our own discomfort at something so foreign touching our friend's life. I wondered if I was the only one who found the thing . . . not beautiful, but oddly moving. Though imagining it displayed in my living room was another thing.

Ally took the statue home that morning and set it on the kitchen table, and she pulled out her mother-in-law's Indian recipes and did her best to duplicate one. She hurried to the door to greet Jim when he arrived back home that evening. "We've got a new offering from your mom," she said as she kissed him. "Something really special this time!"

She made him leave his suitcase in the front hall and close his eyes, and she led him by the hand to the kitchen table, stood him in front of the statue, and said, "Okay!"

He smiled slightly as he looked at it, but he didn't laugh. Ally was glad, suddenly, that she hadn't laughed either, not with Jim.

"It's the Chandra I carved for my mother," he said, his dark eyes watering above the small upward tilt of his lips, the attempt at a smile. "Although my grandfather carved it, actually. I mostly sanded. How did you know it was so special?" he asked, leaving Ally unsettled for a moment—was he teasing her?—and then relieved to see that he wasn't, that he'd mistaken the humor in her voice for delight.

"Chandra. Like my mother, Chandrika," he said. "She used to tell me stories about him when I was a boy. He's just a minor god. A . . . a fertility god, actually." He reached down and touched the wood, his fingers lingering on the god's head, on the chariot, the ten horses. "His chariot is the moon, which he pulls across the sky every night."

Jim put the statue on their dresser when they went up to bed, as if he were just setting it there for lack of anything else to do with it, as if it might be as laughable as Ally had thought it was. They climbed under the covers and turned out the lights, and he curled around her. She was sure he was going to sing to their growing child, as he so often did. But he only smoothed his hand over the stretching skin of her belly, his gaze fixed on the dark shadow on the dresser.

"If the child is a boy," he whispered, "maybe we could name him Rajiv, after my *baba*. If it's a girl, then maybe Chandrika."

Ally, staring at the ceiling, gently fingered his dark hair. The names they'd talked of before were Jonathan, Michael, and Amanda, names unburdened by the weight of the past.

Even after she closed her eyes that night, she felt the statue staring down on her in the thin crack of moonlight peeking through where the drapes were not quite pulled. The gaudy thing worked its way into her dreams: she was in the chariot, and the god was whipping the horses into a frenzy, rushing her to some awful place because she didn't believe. She woke with a start to see Jim standing in the darkness near the dresser. He lifted the idol and held it to his chest, then moved to the bedroom window and pulled the curtain back. He stood there for the longest time, holding the Chandra, looking out at the moonshadowed earth.

The following Sunday, one of those brilliant November mornings when the dawn is the rich red-mauve of early sunlight reflecting around what would become, as the day progressed, bright white cumulus clouds, Linda started in again on the medicine Ally was taking to keep her from miscarrying. The Food and Drug Administration had just released a special bulletin on it. But Ally was not interested in hearing about it. This was none of Linda's business. This was between Ally and her doctor, and she would appreciate it if Linda would keep her bossy nose out of it.

Linda didn't get the least bit ruffled. She simply pulled a copy of the bulletin from her bag and handed it to Ally. When Ally didn't take it, Linda set it on the picnic table in front of her. "Just read it, please, Ally?" she said. "I'm not trying to say I know everything and you don't, but this is important."

Ally hardly tucked her chin toward the paper—one quick glance—before announcing the drug named in it wasn't the one she was taking. Her prescription was for Tylandril.

"But it's this stuff, this diethylstil . . ."

"Diethylstilbestrol," Brett said. "DES."

"Your drug is a brand name for it, Ally," Linda said. "That's what Jeff says."

It was not, Ally insisted, one hand going to her thickening waist. It was not, and she didn't care, anyway. Here she was, three months pregnant, and if it wasn't the drug that was helping her keep the baby, then what was it? "It's the drug," she insisted, "and I am certainly not going to take a chance that it's not."

That drug, like her book, was Ally's Chandra, her seven-story maze of a house meant to keep the ghosts of someone else's dead too confused to get near her unborn child. "I don't care if it hurts me," she said.

"But it doesn't help!" Linda insisted. "It doesn't help! And it's not *you* you're hurting anyway! It's your baby!"

In the silence that followed, the world darkened, the sun slipping behind a soft white puff of cloud.

"The daughters of mothers who took this stuff are getting cancer when they're teenagers," Linda said softly. "Not the moms, but their daughters. Could you bear that, Ally? Could you bear to have this baby and love her to death and then have her die when she's fourteen?"

Linda. Nothing if not frank.

Ally sat staring at Linda, her pale face wedding-veil white now. Three birds flew past behind her. A squirrel looked in our direction, dropped its pinecone, and scurried up one of the old oaks.

I thought of Ally's novel, a book that a fourteen-year-old girl would love.

Ally's doctor called the next morning to tell her about the bulletin. Yes, the drug she was taking was DES, and she had to stop taking it right away, he said. It was like when an alcoholic stopped drinking, though; she'd taken so much comfort in the protection of those pills that it was like giving up her faith.

35

I T WAS EARLY MARCH—a Saturday evening four months
later—when I saw an ambulance pull away from Ally's house.
I knew she was losing the baby, though I didn't want to believe it, I
wanted to think Jim had twisted his ankle or Ally's brother-in-law had
burnt his hand on the grill. I tried calling her house all evening, until
it got too late to call, but there was no answer. And, just after I'd told
the Wednesday Sisters about the ambulance the next morning—
a cold, cold morning, with frost thick on the grass—Jim appeared at
the picnic table to tell us the news.

"She hopes she'll be here next Sunday," he said, lingering on
hopes, the word in his Indian accent a perfect tone. She hadn't lost the
baby, but she was still in the hospital. And yes, he was sure she would
love a visit from us.

We cleared our things from the picnic table—we didn't have to be
asked twice—and piled into my new car. But visiting hours on Sunday, we discovered on our arrival at Stanford Hospital, didn't start
until eleven o'clock.

I called Danny to get him to find someone who could cover my
reading at the twelve-thirty Mass, and we huddled over a yellow
Formica tabletop in the hospital cafeteria, warming our fingers on

Styrofoam cups of insipid coffee until almost eleven, when we made our way through the wide, green-white halls. We found Ally sitting in a railed bed in a shared room, reading her manuscript aloud, but softly, gently. She looked up at us, smiled, and set a hand on her belly as if asking the child to wait a minute, Mommy had to attend to someone else. The book wasn't even meant for babies or toddlers, it was meant for middle-schoolers, but she'd been reading it to her unborn child.

She'd started having the baby early, way too early, but they'd given her some new drug to stop her labor. It looked, at this point, as though she might have to stay in the hospital until the baby was due, another six weeks.

We said we'd meet there on Sundays, then, and we even got permission to meet early, though not quite as early as dawn.

The first week Ally was in the hospital was the week we learned the city was going to tear down the old mansion; the dead woman's heirs had agreed not to object in exchange for half the profits from the sale of a second property the woman had left to the city to fund the upkeep of the place. That week was also the week my editor finally called again, to tell me he was sending edits. Before his letter arrived that Saturday, I'd learned that my mailman had a son Maggie's age, that he'd grown up in the Central Valley, that he was a sculptor who delivered mail to pay the bills. It was a single page, his letter, leaving me wondering how hard my editor had had to work to edit his comments down to a single, unintimidating page.

When I told the Wednesday Sisters the publication schedule the next morning in Ally's hospital room, Linda said, "Early September—that's when the Summer Olympics start!" and Ally said it was the International Year of the Book, that boded well, didn't it?

"So," Ally said as we were leaving later that morning, "only five more weeks of the Wednesday Sisters Writing Society, Sunday Morning, Stanford Hospital Branch."

I hated having to run off to tackle my edits rather than staying the whole day with her, but I had only a few weeks to turn in a new draft. I spent late nights hunched over my typewriter all that week while Danny worked late at the office, almost as if we were working so hard together, rather than in parallel. Still, I visited Ally at the hospital for a little bit every day, meaning to help her through this tough time of hers—though I think she was the one who helped *me* stay sane.

Ally's wait turned out to be not the five weeks needed to bring the baby to term, though, but less than one. The doctors had used up their bag of tricks. There was nothing further they could do.

Babies born prematurely often lack surfactants, soaplike substances that lubricate the surface of the lungs to allow them to inflate and deflate. Jeff explained that to us the day Ally and Jim's baby was born.

"The poor li'l thing can't breathe?" Kath said.

"They've got her hooked up to a machine that gives her oxygen," Jeff said, "and they're treating her with a kind of synthetic surfactant. The hope is they can keep her alive long enough for her lungs to mature."

"We've named her Asha," Ally told us when they let us in to see her, finally, when the four of us crowded into her half of her hospital room to find a frailer, much older Ally sitting with a rough white blanket pulled up almost to her neck although the room was warm. "It means hope," she said. "We're going to call her Hope." She couldn't take us to see the baby, though. Only parents were allowed in the neonatal intensive care unit.

"Hope," Linda said. "That's a beautiful name, Ally."

"A perfect name," I said, but I couldn't help wondering if it was, really, because Ally, in her gray print hospital gown instead of her usual muslin and batik, with her long wavy hair looking tired and limp and her big brown eyes shadowed and sunken, seemed like she had not a hope in the world.

Perhaps my thoughts showed on my face, because Ally's eyes pooled then. "It's all my fault," she wailed, the first tear spilling down her cheek.

"There, there," Brett said, and she sat on the edge of Ally's hospital bed and intertwined her gloved fingers with Ally's. "There, there."

"It's all my fault," Ally repeated. "The marriage, the medicine, I did everything wrong and now it's all my fault, and she's not even baptized, I don't even know anyone to call to baptize my baby."

Brett pulled a tissue from the box on the metal tray by Ally's bed and handed it toward her, but Ally only sank more deeply under her blanket, as she had that awful morning we'd found her in her chalky-blue bedroom, with all those tissues on the floor. "What if my mother is right, what if this *is* God's will?" she said. "What if it is?"

And no amount of anyone saying anything else, no amount of our thinking what we simply could not say—that it was her cold-hearted, prejudiced, religious-zealot mother who didn't deserve to have children—could convince her that it wasn't her fault that her baby was in intensive care.

Ally sat beside her daughter's bed day and night that first week. She put on scrubs and booties and a hairnet, a mask, and she washed her hands to the elbow in a deep sink just outside the intensive care unit, splashing water all over the floor until one of the nurses showed her how to work the foot pedal that controlled the water. All those babies in isolettes, or in open beds like Hope but with wires hooking them up to the monitors and tubes sticking into their little noses and bellies and mouths—they would have broken Ally's heart if it weren't already smashed to bits over Hope. Watching another mother reach through the round holes in the plastic bubble that covered her child just to touch her, Ally said a prayer of thanks to whatever god might be watching. At least she could kiss her baby; at least she wasn't left to press her lips to the glass separating her from Hope.

She took Hope's perfect little fingers in her own hand, trying not to touch the wires and the tubes. "At least she's in an open bed," she said to the nurse assigned to Hope that shift.

"If she ever starts breathing on her own, we'll move her to an iso-lette," the nurse said. "Right now we need her in an open bed in case we need to get to her fast, to revive her."

Ally felt her own breath kicked out of her. She moved back so the nurse could adjust Hope's tubes and change her diaper and draw her blood—once an hour they drew her blood, to make sure Hope was getting enough oxygen from the machine that was delivering it to her.

Ally couldn't watch. She went back to her room, got her manuscript. Came back and put on fresh booties, a fresh hairnet. Lathered her hands and arms with more antiseptic soap than was necessary, and returned to her daughter's side. When she was seated again, she began reading through the mask over her nose and mouth, not caring what any of the others in the neonatal intensive care unit—the doctors, the nurses, the technicians—thought of her story, her voice even more gentle than usual against the beeping monitors, the hard, sterile surfaces, the glaring hospital lights.

She would ask Jim to read, too, wanting her baby to hear her father's melodic Indian accent, her words sounding in his music, which was Ally's music, too, no matter what her own parents might think. Day and night, they read to exhaustion, trying not to think this might be the only chance they would have to read to their little girl.

Hope's first awful week in intensive care—making no progress toward breathing on her own—settled into the beginning of a second week, day eight. Ally did not want to be discharged from the hospital herself; she couldn't imagine leaving her baby there all by herself. She could hardly speak, but it was there in the cut of her cheekbone against her skin, in her stooped posture, in the strands of her long dark hair falling out in clumps.

Jim finally convinced her she had to come home, to get a good night's sleep in her own bed, to keep up her strength. "You can't do anything the doctors and nurses aren't already doing," he said. "Hope needs you to be strong for her. She needs you to get some rest."

Ally relented, finally, and Jim checked her out of the hospital, eased her into the passenger seat of her white Chevy Nova, and brought her home. He helped her up the stairs and tucked her into bed, climbing in next to her. He woke at 3 A.M., though, to find Ally's side of the bed empty. She had pulled her clothes back on quietly in the darkened bedroom, climbed into her Nova, and returned to the hospital. She'd bought a stale cup of coffee from a machine in the waiting room and drunk it on the way down the hall, tossing what she hadn't finished into the trash outside the neonatal intensive care unit. She'd donned the scrubs and booties and hairnet again, and washed to the elbow, working the foot pedals easily, used to anything by then.

"I just couldn't bear to leave her all alone in the cold, bright lights of this awful room," she told Jim when he found her there. Leave her alone to die, that's what she was thinking, or what she was not allowing herself to think. If she left the hospital, went home to sleep for even a few hours, Hope might die there, all alone, with no one to hold her tiny hand.

36

$\mathcal{T}$HAT WAS THE WEEK Arlene Peets announced she was moving to one of the big New York publishers. Kath was devastated, of course. She loved that job, loved working with Arlene, who'd moved her from copy editor to assistant, which hadn't sounded like much of a move in the right direction to us, but Kath said if it got any better, she'd have to hire someone to help her enjoy it. "I'm busier than a moth in a brand-new wool mitten," she said. Instead of finding typos and double-checking facts, she was reading through manuscripts, making the first cut, sitting down with Arlene over lunch to recommend which manuscripts she ought to read herself.

"I just can't believe she's up and moving to New York without so much as a how-do-you-do," Kath told us.

It wasn't as if there were a million publishing jobs to be had in San Francisco back then, either. But Kath put together a résumé, then knocked on Arlene's door, and went in and sat down, gathered her courage, and asked for a letter of recommendation.

"A recommendation?" Arlene asked.

Kath, sure she sounded ridiculous, said, "So I can apply for a new job."

"To work for the competition?" Arlene said. "I can't let you do that, Kath."

Kath looked to the piles of stacked manuscripts—manuscripts she'd spent hours on, often taking them home, reading late into the night, working her butt off for Arlene. An eye for an eye leaves everyone blind, she reminded herself. But all of a sudden she didn't much care about leaving the whole world blind if it came to that. She'd like to start with that little bitch of a medical student.

"Well, that really cocks my pistol, Arlene," she said. "Here I am working my wide rear off for you and thinking you like my work, and . . ." She stood up. She didn't even realize it. She towered over Arlene at her desk. "You *do* like my work, you can't tell me now you don't! You're just being ugly here, for not a reason in the whole damned world. You're walking away from this place yourself, but you're going to leave me in the lurch, with no recommendation to—"

"But I want you to come *with* me," Arlene said.

Kath felt herself sinking into her high heels. "*With* you?"

"With me," Arlene said. "I'm glad to see you've learned to stand up for yourself, by the way, Kath. *Literally.*"

Kath sat back in her chair, remembering her daddy's voice: *You keep letting your mouth overload your tail, Katherine Claire, and you surely will live to regret.*

"Don't look so sheepish," Arlene said. "I still want you to come with me. Yes, even after that. Good thing I stopped you before you started telling me what you really think of me, eh?" She laughed her genuine laugh, the one Kath would sometimes hear when Arlene was reading a manuscript that Kath, too, had found laugh-out-loud funny, which was the rarest of finds.

"On second thought, go ahead, look sheepish," Arlene said, still laughing. Then a moment later, "'Cocks my pistol'? Damn, Kath, if only my authors could express themselves half as colorfully as you!"

Kath was flattered, she really was, but she couldn't possibly move to New York, not with Lee here. True, part of her thought that might be a great solution—move to New York and start over by herself. Leave Lee behind. But she couldn't bear to move Anna Page and Lee-

Lee and Lacy away from their daddy. And how would she survive without the Wednesday Sisters?

"Gosh, I would just about move a mountain to keep working for you, Arlene. But I can't move to New York. I just can't."

"New York?" Arlene smiled, not the professional smile she pasted on when she met with the most unpleasant of her authors, but a genuine one that went with her laugh. "I'm not going to New York," she said. "I thought you knew that. I'm opening a West Coast office. Here. And I have plans for you, Kath. Plans that do *not* include letting you go off to work for someone else."

$\mathcal{I}$T WAS IMPOSSIBLE to celebrate anything that spring with Hope's fragile little future overshadowing everything in the Wednesday Sisters' lives. How can you bear to feel good for even a moment when your friend is in so much pain? Still, when I received the *Michelangelo's Ghost* galley proofs—my typeset novel, the way it would look between hard covers—I did feel something. I turned to the dedication page: "to Danny and Maggie and Davy, and to the Wednesday Sisters." Then to the first page: "Chapter One." I read the opening sentence. It read like a novel.

I thought of Ally as I sat wiping my face to keep tears from dripping on the pages. I imagined her sitting at the hospital with Hope, reading quietly to her. I imagined what her book would look like when it was set, too, after it had sold, which I decided then it had to, it really had to. And I imagined Brett's book, too, and Linda's stories gathered into a collection, and even something by Kath. I imagined walking into Kepler's or Books Inc. or Stacey's and finding our beautiful books all on the shelves. I imagined the five of us on the bestseller list, numbers one through five. I imagined myself at the top first, but then I put Ally there instead, and my own name second. I wondered if I'd be jealous. I wondered if the other Wednesday Sisters were really, deep in their hearts where they wouldn't even admit it to themselves, jealous. I knew I would have been. I knew I would have felt the same way I'd felt watching my brothers drive off to college. Not jealous as in wanting to take it away from them, but jealous as in wanting it for myself as well.

I began to read aloud, my words in my voice like Ally's words in hers. It's a surprisingly different way of reading. You become more focused on the rhythms. You find all sorts of places where you stumble. You even see typos you never saw before. I remember how silly I felt at first, how I closed myself in the bathroom and turned on the fan lest Danny or the kids hear me and think I'd gone off my rocker. But then I imagined Ally reading in that intensive care unit, and I read on.

THE SURFACTANT the doctors were giving Hope would not help her breathe, though no one knew that then; it would be another ten years before effective artificial surfactants were developed, far too late to help Hope. But she was one of the lucky ones. Slowly, gradually, she turned the corner, needing less and less oxygen from the machine until, finally, she was breathing on her own.

Ally had not yet done anything to get ready for the baby when she found out Hope was going to be released. She didn't have a crib or a changing table or even diapers. We'd thought we'd have a baby shower for her, but then she'd gone into the hospital and it wasn't clear the baby would be born alive, then if she would survive. So the minute we learned Hope was coming home, we all just started bringing things to Ally's house. Brett brought her changing table, because she was done with it, or if it turned out she wasn't, she could always get it back. I loaned her my crib and my baby buggy. Kath had the most beautiful little antique bassinet that she insisted Ally use for this special child of hers. We all chipped in money, too, and Linda and I went out and bought everything you could need for a baby: diapers and baby powder and pacifiers, a receiving blanket, pajamas, a cute little baby hat. And bottles. We knew Ally's milk would have come in while Hope was in intensive care, and it would have dried up. But most mothers used bottles then, anyway. We didn't know things like how very good that first stuff that comes before the milk, the colostrum, is for babies. We assumed the formulas developed by male scientists in jackets and ties must be better for our babies than anything we girls could produce.

So Hope came home, and Ally and Jim settled her into that antique cradle, and as you can imagine they just couldn't stand not holding her. They picked her up again, and wondered over her the entire morning, watching her clear eyes watching them. They called her "princess" and gave her their fingers to grasp, laughing at the sounds and expressions she made. They kissed her nose, her belly, her toes. And they said over and over again, to her, to each other: "Mommy," "Daddy," "Hope."

Late in the afternoon of the day Hope came home, a crane with a wrecking ball drove up over the curb and across the grass of the park to the circular drive in front of the old mansion. The driver got out, lit a cigarette, and stood looking up at the place. A second truck, a pickup, pulled up beside it a few minutes later. Two men joined the first and began talking and pointing at the trees and at the park around them. They disappeared around back, reappeared several minutes later, stood talking for another moment before all three loaded into the pickup and set off over the grass again. They left the crane squatting on the cracked asphalt of the circular drive that went nowhere, its wrecking ball looming over the poor old mansion's grand columns, its peeling paint, its already-falling-down porch.

The children wanted to bring a present to Hope—her first teddy bear, they decided, since Hope hadn't been allowed stuffed animals in the intensive care unit (too many possibilities for germs). So that Wednesday we piled everyone into Kath's and my convertibles—Kath joining us since she had a few days off while the movers packed up Arlene's furniture and personal files and moved them into the office space for the new publisher—and we headed for the Stanford Mall.

Of course, the children wanted to deliver the bear to Hope themselves, but even at home Hope wasn't allowed visitors yet, especially not child-sized visitors with their runny noses and dirty hands. Linda, though, had an idea. While we were at the mall she bought one of the new Polaroid Instamatic cameras, the kind that spit out pictures you could watch develop right before your eyes, and the following morning, bright and early, we brought the children over to Ally's front porch and waited while Ally took Mr. Pajamas—that's what the children had named the bear, because Hope couldn't talk yet and the poor bear needed a name—and put him in the cradle with Hope, and shot off ten pictures, squandering the entire picture pack so we could see them right away. Ally stayed with Hope to rock her to sleep afterward, but I brought the camera out to her front porch, where Linda pulled the film pack from it. We sat on the steps with the children, all of us eating Popsicles and watching the images of Hope and Mr. Pajamas arise from the little gray squares.

"She sucks her thumb," Linda said. "I sucked my thumb when I was little."

I had sucked my thumb, too, and carried my blanket everywhere I went. My mom used to joke about it sometimes, when I wouldn't let go of something I wanted—a new pair of shoes that were too expensive, or an inappropriate boy I wanted to date. I wondered if Linda's mother told her those same kinds of stories before she died, and if they would have meant as much to a nine-year-old.

"Hope sure does favor her daddy, doesn't she?" Kath said. Which she did: she had her father's narrow face and full mouth, and her skin was a creamy light brown that was warm and lovely even marred with newborn acne, as Davy's had been.

"But she has Ally's huge eyes," I said. "Except they're blue."

"All newborns have blue eyes," Brett said.

"Even Indian babies?" Kath asked.

Brett frowned to herself. "Hope is only half Indian," she said, and I sat wondering if that would be hard for Hope, to be neither entirely one thing nor entirely another.

"She looks like Mr. Pajamas," Brett said.

"She looks like Mr. Magoo," I said. "But all babies look like Mr. Magoo."

"Bless her iddy-biddy li'l heart, she's just about nothing," Kath said. "My babies were whoppers compared to her."

"She looks like a miracle to me," Linda said, and we all agreed: that child lying in Kath's antique bassinet in Ally's room with Mr. Pajamas, covered with the softest blanket Linda and I could find, was definitely a miracle.

An engine rumbled to life across the street as Ally joined us, leaving the front door open so she could hear Hope if she woke. Quite a few trucks had gathered around the mansion that morning, with men in hard hats smoking cigarettes and kicking at the earth. Before we knew it, the crane was swinging its heavy ball at the top story of that poor old mansion, at the windows of the room with the faded-rose wallpaper, where the piano had been. The sound of shattering windows and splitting boards joined the rumble of the crane.

The children had to be told no, they couldn't watch from any closer, it would be dangerous, something might fall on their little heads.

"How'll that rascal mansion ghost of yours occupy herself now, Frankie?" Kath said.

"She'll have to find another home to haunt," Linda said.

"Maybe she's done haunting," I said. "Maybe she's found whatever she was searching for."

"Maybe she has," Ally said. "Maybe she can be at peace."

We sat silently for a moment, watching the heavy ball swing back again in a long arc, almost in slow motion. It was shocking how quickly the sad old house succumbed to the tyranny of that wrecking ball. Within minutes, only a few walls of the lower floor were standing, and I was left wondering what had been done with the house's contents, hoping the tuneless piano had found a home in a house with a little girl who would just be learning to play. Then the lower walls, too, were down, the once glorious old home reduced to a pile of rubble. It didn't even kick up much dust in its last gasp.

37

DESPITE ALL THE DISTRACTIONS that spring (Hurricane Agnes hit the East Coast, George Wallace was shot, Title IX steamed toward passage, and the Cubs . . . well, never mind the Cubs that year), Brett presented us with her revised novel one Sunday in late May. She seemed excited about the prospects of this new version, though what she said was, "It's changed. I'm just warning you. It could be atrocious, I don't even know. I have no perspective on it anymore, if I ever did." And when the rest of us showed up in the park at dawn the next Sunday to discuss it, she did not.

We'd just decided we'd have to go drag her out of her house when she showed up, finally, her tiny face flustered under that glorious red hair, full of hope and dread. The minute we saw her, Kath stood and started clapping wildly, and we all followed suit.

In the prior versions—all those drafts that had ended up in the fireplace—the book had been a mystery, or tried to be, but the mystery element had failed to add narrative drive to the story. Brett, astonishingly, had simply abandoned it altogether. No murder in the book anymore. And where the earlier version had been set in the present, this new one was set in the future. It was funny, because this wasn't a book I'd rush off to the bookstore for, although the original version had been. A short description of it now would read something like "as the destruction of Earth looms, fifteen women set off in a rocket ship with frozen sperm and insemination technology, to start a new world." No men. Men couldn't give birth, so they'd have wasted precious seats on the rocket. And yet by page 3, before you even realized you were reading science fiction, you were so charmed by Elizabeth and Ratty that you were *not* putting the book down. Charmed and intrigued, and sympathetic to Elizabeth's plight, which was the same plight Kath had identified in the earlier draft, the mother-daughter story.

"I bawled like a babe at the end," Kath said.

"But I was laughing out loud, too," Ally said.

"How did you make it so funny and so touching at the same time, Brett?" I asked. "It's a little bit of magic, that."

"There's just this one iddy-biddy li'l thing about this novel," Kath said. "I do love it to death but—"

"More than one," Linda said. "We *all* loved it, right? But that doesn't mean we don't have comments."

We all agreed: yes, we had comments.

"But this is *important*," Kath said. "*Mighty* important. This title? *Populating Paradise Galaxy*?"

Brett groaned.

"Titles are crucial, though," Kath insisted. "Would y'all have read a book called *The High-Bouncing Lover*? That was what Fitzgerald wanted to call *The Great Gatsby*. It's not just the reading public it matters a big ol' mess of greens to, either. Agents with heaps of manuscripts on their desks? Editors with big piles on theirs? Poor li'l assistants like me? I'd just stick a nice letter in an envelope saying no thanks, and Arlene would never see page one of this book."

Kath had an idea, though: How about *The Mrs. Americas*? It hit on the theme of the book, the relative importance of beauty and brains in women. And in that time of Miss America being so popular still, and yet also so controversial, the title was both appealing and intriguing. We all agreed that, yes, we would at least pull that one off the shelf and read a page or two.

• • •

A FEW DAYS AFTER we'd all given our last little comments on Brett's new, retitled draft, Kath took *The Mrs. Americas* into her office and handed it to Arlene. When Arlene handed it back to Kath the next morning, she said, "Tell your friend we'd like to buy this. We'd like to publish it in September—not this year, but next."

"Lordy, Arlene," Kath said. "Just like that?"

"And when she asks her editor's name, you can say 'Kath Montgomery,'" Arlene said. "Or would you prefer Katherine? No rush, but I'll need to know eventually so I can order the nameplate for your door."

Kath was pleased as punch to be made an editor, of course, but she was reluctant to start with Brett's book. Brett was her friend, and this was business. She didn't want to do anything that might jeopardize the Wednesday Sisters. But Arlene insisted. She was not about to take her hands completely off this one, she assured Kath. Kath shouldn't worry about that.

"Is she young, your friend?" Arlene asked. "Is she attractive?"

Kath said she had remarkable strawberry blond hair. "She's just this tiny little slip of nothing, near 'bout every bit of her is thin as bone, bless her heart. She'd be a wallflower without the hair, but her hair, it's the berries."

"Little is okay," Arlene said. "Little is memorable."

Kath winced at *memorable,* thinking of Brett's gloves, trying to figure out how to put a little lipstick on that pig. Could Brett be talked out of wearing them? And how could Kath even ask?

"She's a pistol when it comes to smart," Kath told Arlene. "She went to Radcliffe, she graduated top of her class with degrees in English lit and math and chemistry—or maybe it was physics—and she took graduate classes at Harvard. She knows more about the space program than the astronauts do, I swear, and she wears gloves."

That last tacked on as if it might have something to do with knowing about space, or might be entirely missed.

Arlene sat back in her chair, the same worn chair she'd had in the old office, but it looked even shabbier here against the freshly painted walls. She frowned, a hand going to her chin. "Gloves?"

Kath heaved a big sigh. "Little white cotton ones," she admitted. "Like girls used to wear to church."

"Like Jackie O?"

"I don't have one guess in paradise why she wears them, I really don't. I might could—"

"How marvelously eccentric! Gloves!" Arlene's chair creaked as she leaned forward, grinning at Kath. "Excellent. Perfectly excellent. It will get people talking and get her name out there. Mark my words, Kath: those gloves will generate more attention than anything we could do."

KATH RODE THAT HIGH of being made editor for the rest of the week. She showed up Sunday morning more chipper than ever, and offered her suggestions on our writing with a newfound confidence. She floated through the whole day that way: through church services with Lee and the children, through her solo outing to the grocery store. She was so happy that even Lee seemed affected. He offered to help with dinner—very unlike him—and she assigned him the worst tasks: peeling the potatoes and the garlic for the garlic mashed potatoes and slicing berries for strawberry rhubarb pie.

"She's making you an editor?" he must have said a dozen times that day, as if it shed some new light on Kath he never had seen before. And the way he looked at her made her feel like the young girl who'd placed all those wild bets again, the girl he'd fallen for.

He stayed as always after Sunday dinner, helping Anna Page with her homework and reading the children a story. Anna Page was quite sure she was too old for story time whenever Kath was doing the reading, but Sunday nights she snuggled right up next to her father. That night Lee tucked them into bed, too, and after they were down he came back into the kitchen. He fixed Kath a nightcap and stood talking with her while she finished the dishes. They spoke of the children, of things that needed to be taken care of around the house, that was all, but still it left Kath feeling hopeful.

She'd just put the last plate away when he reached up to close the cabinet door, close enough for her to smell the scotch on his breath.

"An editor," he said, not a question this time.

Kath thought he was going to kiss her and she didn't know if she wanted him to or not. One part of her wanted him to scoop her up and carry her to their bed and close the door and make love to her, as he had their first time, at his family's beach house all those long years ago. But another part of her wasn't so sure anymore.

"Well, I suppose you'd better be getting on home," she said. Home. Which wasn't where Kath lived anymore.

They both turned at the same time, then, to see Anna Page standing in the doorway, watching them. "Punkin," Lee said without missing a beat. "What's the matter, punkin? Why aren't you asleep?"

The way Anna Page smiled up at her father, her eyes sleepy and her nightgown misbuttoned at the top, Kath knew her daughter didn't understand what she'd just heard, but that she would someday.

While Lee took Anna Page back upstairs, and sang softly to her, staying until her breathing slowed and her thumb settled beside her lips but not in her mouth, Kath tried to imagine how she ever would explain the scene to Anna Page. What kind of example was she setting for her daughters? Or for her son, for that matter? A woman who looked the other way while her husband lived with another woman, who clung to the charade of a happy marriage—sitting together in church, Sunday dinners, even weekday breakfasts and dinners sometimes—when the truth was something entirely different. The truth was he slept in another woman's bed every night, and still Kath wanted him back. She didn't even have the dignity to say enough was enough.

Anna Page would see the truth someday, Kath knew, even if she didn't that night. Lee-Lee and Lacy would, too, and what would they think? They would grow up believing this was the way men and women were: Men were philanderers and women put up with it. That was the example they would take from watching her.

And yet what was the damned alternative? To divorce Lee, or to publicly separate? Kath couldn't imagine how that could be better for Anna Page and Lacy and little Lee. Would they go to his apartment to visit him, then? Would they sleep there, with the other Kathy there as well? Would that awful woman fix their breakfasts and brush their hair and drive them to school, or would Lee do that himself? Would their classmates find out about it and call them names? And how could they possibly understand that their daddy loved them even though he didn't want to live with them? How could she put them through the shame of that? Shame that was her fault, or Lee's, that had nothing to do with them but would hurt them all the same.

38

THREE MONTHS BEFORE *Michelangelo's Ghost* was scheduled to be released, my editor was offered a better position at a competing house. I was happy for his good fortune, but his move left me orphaned—I could see that even before we'd hung up the phone. He'd bought my novel because he loved it, but what if no one else at the publisher loved it as much as he did? What if the editor who took over thought it was a dog of a book that deserved to be left home on a Saturday night?

My new editor, when he called, couldn't even get my name right. He asked for M.F.—that was my name on the book jacket, so that was fine—but when I said he could just call me Frankie, he said, "Fine, Fanny."

"*Frankie,*" I said, and he said, "Oh yes, right, sorry"—but then proceeded to call me Fanny again and again.

When my first review came in—just dreadful—Kath said not to get riled up about anything in that rag, they were just meaner than a cottonmouth to every poor soul in this whole world, and Linda said she was sure the reviewer hadn't even read the book. "He's got Risa's name wrong!" she said. "He calls her Rosa." Still, it's amazing how one scathing review can deflate your confidence. I began to wonder if the book really was as bland as the reviewer suggested, if it really was "familiar"—not the word he'd used, of course. He, sparing no one's feelings, had outright called it trite.

That was the week Linda flew to New York to run her first race. She'd been shooting to run a marathon—the Amateur Athletic Union had finally permitted women to run in its sanctioned marathons, and eight had run Boston that May, with Nina Kuscsik finishing ahead of some eight hundred men. But Linda's training had not been going well, and she'd settled instead on running the country's first official all-women's race, the Crazylegs Mini Marathon. Mini, after the miniskirt.

It was "just a little six-mile race."

Six miles? The rest of us could barely *walk* six miles.

"I'm not going all the way to New York just to run," she said. "I'm taking the children back east to visit my brother in Manhattan, and the timing worked out well. But running with a whole race full of women? Can you imagine that? If enough women show, maybe we'll convince the Olympic Committee that women *are* physically capable of running long distances." The longest race women ran in the Olympics that year was fifteen hundred meters, the "metric mile"— Linda was disgusted with that. Though not half as disgusted as she would become. Women who ran the New York Marathon that year would go so far as to stage a sit-down protest for ten minutes after the starting gun went off, and still the first women's Olympic marathon wasn't run for another twelve *years*.

Seventy-eight women showed up with Linda that June of 1972, to run that first mini-marathon. Really nice women, Linda said. Never mind that there were Playboy Bunnies at the start, a publicity stunt she found insulting (especially as they hopped off into the bushes rather than run the race). Never mind that after the race two of the co-founders, Nina Kuscsik and Kathrine Switzer (the woman who'd run Boston posing as a man), were asked to hike their dresses over their knees for a photograph at a press event. They refused; Linda was really happy about that.

The winner ran the six-mile race in just over thirty-seven minutes, almost six-minute miles all that way. Linda finished less than two minutes behind her. It was the fastest she had ever run, but she was sure she could run faster.

T WELVE WEEKS AFTER Hope was born, her doctors finally gave Ally and Jim permission to start bringing her out into the world. They took her for a walk around the neighborhood that evening, stopping at each of our houses, leaving Maggie and Davy, who'd not yet been allowed to see her in person before, awake long past their bedtimes, still talking about little Hope. We all agreed to meet Ally and Hope at ten the next morning—a Wednesday, but Kath arranged to have the morning off so she could join us—to share Hope's first outing to the park. Ally had been imagining this moment ever since she first stood alone inside her house, watching us through her window, wishing she belonged. None of us was going to miss this.

Ally was already there, just sitting down on our old Wednesday bench, when Mags and Davy and I came out the front door. Three mothers sitting together on the next bench were talking to her as she gathered Hope from her buggy and began to unwind her blankets, to settle in. The moment we'd crossed the street and I let go of Maggie's hand, she took off like a shot for Ally and Hope, shouting, "Hope!" I hurried after her with Davy, and arrived to find Maggie dancing around Ally, begging, "Can I hold her, please?" In her excitement, she'd practically careened into Ally.

Ally had just finished extracting Hope from her wrappings, and there was just the briefest pause as the other mothers registered Hope's skin color before one of them said, "Isn't she a cutie?" and another said, "She's so tiny. How old is she?"

"She isn't yours, is she?" the third, a dumpy brunette, asked.

"She's my daughter," Ally said. "Yes."

"Can I hold her, please can I?" Mags repeated.

"She's your daughter?" the dumpy brunette said to Ally.

"Her name is Hope," Maggie informed the woman in no uncertain terms. "Her birthday is March seventeenth, and we gave her her first teddy bear, Anna Page and Julie and Jamie and me did."

"Me, too," Davy said.

"And Lee-Lee and Lacy, too," Maggie said.

"We named him Mr. Pajamas," Davy said.

The woman frowned at them.

"*Please* can I hold her?" Maggie begged.

Ally looked so nervous that I said, "Not yet, Maggie. Hope is still awfully little."

"But I can hold Davy and he's bigger," Maggie said.

Ally patted the bench next to her and said of course Maggie could hold Hope, and Maggie hopped right up between Ally and the women on the other bench.

"You have to hold her really carefully, especially her head," Ally said. "See how I'm holding her? With her head on the crook of my elbow?"

"That's the way Mommy taught me to hold Davy," Mags said, and Ally said that's right, of course it was.

Jamie and Julie came running over at full speed as Maggie scooted right up next to Ally and Ally slid the baby over into Maggie's lap, quickly looping her arm around Maggie's waist to secure Hope herself even though the baby was now, as far as my daughter could tell, completely within her control. Maggie's round face was so full of delight that it made me wonder what she would look like when she held her own daughter someday, my granddaughter. It made me a little sorry for Ally's mother: despite Ally's sister Ruth's efforts to sway their parents, her mother had only hesitated a moment when Ally had called to tell them Hope was born, before she'd hung up on her.

"I get to hold her first," Maggie crowed, "because I know how to hold babies."

"I want a turn! I want a turn!" the twins insisted as Linda arrived with J.J.'s hand in her grasp.

"Easy, girls," Linda said. "Hope is a baby, not a toy."

The women on the bench watched this all, the first two smiling indulgently, but the dumpy one frowning. "Why did you adopt a colored baby?" she asked.

Ally stared at the woman for a moment, still with both hands on her daughter, then looked off to the empty spot where the mansion had been, where all that was left was a bare scrape of rocky earth run through with tractor-tire marks.

"She's half Caucasian and half Indian," Ally said. "And she isn't adopted."

"Couldn't you get a white baby?" the woman said.

Linda turned and gave the woman her most withering look.

"Linda, don't," Ally said. And as Brett and Kath and their children, too, arrived at the bench, Ally said, "I'm taking Hope down the baby slide. Anyone want to come?"

The whole lot of us, without so much as a backward glance at the obnoxious woman on the bench, swarmed together onto the playground. I held Hope as Ally climbed the three little steps up the baby slide and sat at the top. I handed her daughter to her then, and we all cheered wildly together as Ally, with Hope firmly in her lap, slid down the little slide.

39

THE ARRIVAL OF *Michelangelo's Ghost* in bookstores did not make the headlines for Saturday, September 2, 1972—that honor went to Bobby Fischer, who beat Boris Spassky to become the first American world chess champion—but it sure was exciting for me. Kath and Linda were at the Stanford Mall that afternoon when Linda spotted it, right there on the front table by the door at Books Inc. She screamed, literally screamed, so that everyone in the store turned to look, and she picked up the book and held it high over her head. "This is a great book," she said, loud enough for half the mall to hear. "A really great book. You all should buy it."

"It was so dried-apple darn funny I nearly wet my drawers," Kath said. "It's a good thing Linda's about kin to Doris Day or they'd have called the police to haul her away."

They called me from the pay phone outside Macy's—the twins in the background asking if they couldn't get ice cream now and Linda shushing them, saying yes, ice cream in just a minute, but girls, that's Frankie's book, that's Mrs. O'Mara's book! When I arrived, with Danny and Mags and Davy in tow, I was too excited to see the book right in front of me. When I did, finally, I just started bawling, tears streaming, and there was nothing I could do to stop them. Danny, tearing up, too, wrapped me up in a big hug and spun me around the way he had on our wedding day, while everyone in the store turned to stare.

"It's her first novel," Kath explained. "It's the first time she's seen it. You folks sure would tune up, too, if you were lucky enough to be her."

"Dream-come-true time," Linda said.

Two newspaper reviews of my novel came out that week. The *Chicago Sun-Times* called me "a writer to watch," and my dad's hometown Iowa paper said I "deftly explored the dark underside of religion in general and the Catholic Church in particular, while delivering a compelling story about the redeeming power of friendship." My dad started carrying his copy of *Michelangelo's Ghost* with him wherever he went, and I got a lovely note from Sister Josephine saying, "I'm so very proud to see you are using those gifts we once spoke of" and mentioning nothing about any dark underside of anything, religious or otherwise.

As the weeks passed, though, I watched my books move from the tables at the front of Bay Area stores to the O shelf in general fiction, buried between a slew of O'Connors (Frank and Flannery) and *Animal Farm*. By the time Nixon won reelection in a landslide that November despite Watergate (it was just too incredible to believe the president himself might have been involved), I despaired of my book ever selling more than a few copies to my mother's friends and my own. Even my agent had gone from saying more reviews would come, just be patient, to saying he couldn't imagine how my book had slipped through the cracks. Slipped through the cracks, it had, though. By Christmas, *Michelangelo's Ghost* was gone from bookstore shelves everywhere.

Danny tried to console me, tried to pull me up with his own joy, which was one part having a little breathing time at work and one part the soaring Intel stock. He brought me flowers, and pretty new clothes purchased on his lunch hour, and a brand-new IBM Selectric II typewriter. He took me out to dinner and started talking about taking a vacation together, just the two of us. And one morning, after he'd left for work very early, I came down to the kitchen to find the coffee made, some fancy pastries under plastic wrap on a plate, and several piles of paper that were, on closer inspection, applications to Stanford and the University of California at Berkeley.

And all the while I listened with fascination to what was going on with Brett's book. Kath and Arlene—who insisted Brett hire an agent—flew with Brett to New York to lunch with agents Arlene thought Brett might particularly like. Within weeks she'd sold rights for publication in England, Germany, and Japan, of all places. Then *The Mrs. Americas* caught the attention of one of the biggest film agents in Hollywood.

Movie rights? It wasn't even a book yet!

Even her author photo was nothing like mine. She was sent to a professional photographer who used a stylist who painted more makeup on Brett's face than she'd worn all the days of her life put together. Kath was sent along, too, with a single instruction: make sure the photographer got Brett's gloves in the photograph.

"Well, it's not the coffin photo," Linda said as we sat hunched over the picnic table one Sunday morning, admiring the result. "You know what I was thinking when we took that coffin photo, Brett? I was thinking if you really were dead, I would definitely peek under your gloves to see what was there."

"Linda!" I said.

"I swear on my aunt Tooty's grave," Kath said.

"But I would," Linda said. "All of us would, wouldn't we?"

Brett ran a gloved hand through her cropped red hair as visions of that long-ago Wednesday Sisters blowup flashed through my mind, that Miss America gathering when we'd learned that Linda was Jewish and Jim was Indian, and that we could hurt each other even when we weren't trying to, and that none of us was as perfect as we liked to pretend.

Was Linda right? Would we all peek? Would we all want to?

I thought she probably was.

"Well then," Brett said, "I'd better be sure to leave instructions for a closed-coffin wake."

40

I ARRIVED AT THE PICNIC TABLE one Sunday morning the following April to find Linda just sitting there, looking off into the empty space where the mansion had stood. I said good morning, but she only nodded, leaving me to sit with her in silence until everyone had arrived. When they had, Linda told us she'd found another lump in her breast.

"Oh, Linda," Kath started, but Linda cut her off.

"I'm sure it's nothing," she said. "But I've got an appointment to have it looked at next month."

"Next month!" Brett said. "But—"

"In three weeks," Linda said.

"But three weeks is—"

"The last one was benign, and they told me then that I shouldn't be surprised to find another one. They told me not to panic. Women who get lumps get lumps."

"Linda!" Kath said.

"Heavens to Betsy," Ally whispered.

"I probably couldn't get in to see anyone here for a few weeks anyway," Linda said.

"Here?" Ally said, and Kath started, "But Jeff could—"

"I'm running the mini-marathon in New York again," Linda interrupted. "I'm having it looked at back there. I can't do it here. Jeff knows everyone here."

She didn't want Jeff to know about it, didn't want him to worry about it, not like he had the last time. That's what she was saying without quite being able to say it. Still, we all understood. And we understood, too, that we were sworn to secrecy, which felt wrong to me, but I wasn't Linda, it wasn't my choice.

Then Linda dropped another bombshell on us: Jeff was taking a position at a hospital in Boston, starting the next week. It was just for the summer, but he was pretty sure that if it went well, they'd make him a permanent offer, a better one than he could get out here.

"What am I supposed to do?" she said. "Say he can't accept a job in Boston because I have friends here?"

"We're staying in Palo Alto for the summer—the kids and I are," she said. "We decided it would be less disruptive for them."

"We always knew this wouldn't be a permanent home, right, Kath?" she said. "We've been lucky to get to stay as long as we have."

"God, I don't know what I'll do without you guys," she said. "You'll still have each other, but I won't have anyone."

WHEN LINDA CAME BACK from New York a month later, she was depressed as hell. No, the lump was nothing, just a cyst, she assured us that Sunday at dawn, the morning after she returned. She'd run poorly in the race, though. Slower than last year. "A fourteen-year-old girl won in under forty minutes," she said, but without enthusiasm, as if she'd read about it in the paper rather than tried to keep up. "Maybe I'm overtraining," she said.

Maybe that was it: she was running too much. Maybe that was why her shoulders looked so angular, why the skin under her eyes was translucent blue and her hair seemed in need of a good old-fashioned scrub.

"But you had the lump whacked out?" Kath said. "By someone who knows a fur coat from a frying pan?"

Linda sat silently for a moment, staring off at the empty playground as if watching J.J. pump high on a swing and leap forward off it, planting his palms in the sand as he landed. She gathered a smile from somewhere in the red morning light, then, as if to give her son a big thumbs-up, and she turned that newly gathered smile to us. "They did something called mammography," she said. "They smushed my breasts flat between plates of glass they must keep stored in a freezer, they were so damned cold. And then they told me to stand stock-still up on my toes the way they had me hooked to the machine, and to hold my breath until I just about burst."

"It's like an X-ray," Brett explained. "It takes a sort of picture of the breast tissue, like an X-ray takes a picture of bone."

"Anyway, the lump is gone, 'whacked out' by a nice New York surgeon," Linda said; though mammography technology existed, it didn't save you from a biopsy back then. "And it was nothing," she said, that gathered smile somehow deepening the circles under her eyes. "Really. It was just a cyst."

41

BⵃⵃRETT'S PUBLISHER had big plans for *The Mrs. Americas,* including a substantial first printing. The only pothole in her smooth, wide, newly striped road was her first review—like mine, a real stinker, and from the same trade magazine, too. Within a week, though, *Woman's Day* called, and then *Cosmopolitan.* Could they send interviewers? Photographers? By late July, still more than a month before her book was to be released, her publisher went back for a second printing. Then the clincher came: *The Tonight Show* with Johnny Carson.

Johnny wanted Brett to appear on his show—or his scheduler did, anyway. The exact date was a little up in the air, but it would be either the Friday night before or the Monday night after the Miss America Pageant, playing off the book title.

"I swear, my hair is going gray with worry," Brett said. We were sitting in the park Sunday morning, already long after dawn.

Linda, next to Brett, tugged at the brim of her Stanford cap and peered closely at Brett's cropped red hair. "It really is, isn't it?" she said. "Just a few little grays at the temple, but you're barely thirty, right?"

"I read somewhere that stress can cause you to go gray practically overnight," I said.

"You should dye it, honey," Kath said.

"Dye it?" Ally and I said.

"She can't go on Johnny Carson with gray hair," Linda said. "Don't be ridiculous. She'd look . . ."

Like an elderly twelve-year-old, wearing her grandmother's gloves.

Like the weedy ground that reminded you, by its emptiness, of how haunting the dilapidated mansion had been. They'd seeded the dirt finally—without removing the rocks or the weeds—and for a while it had become the neighborhood's most popular bird breakfast café. But already the seed was gone, the only trace of it a few little shoots of grass trying to survive.

"You could just wear a hat, like Linda," Ally said, and she pulled Linda's Stanford cap off and put it on Brett's head.

In response to the astounded looks on the rest of our faces, Brett said, *"What?"*

Linda's braid had come off with her hat. Just come off completely. Gone with the hat to Brett's head, an incongruous plait of blond against her red hair. All that was left on Linda's head was a short bob of blond hair, flattened and chaotic from being tucked up under her hat.

"Lordy, Lordy, Linda, you whacked your hair off?" Kath reached up and touched her own hair, trying to make some sense of Linda's braid being removable now, like the braid headband Kath rarely wore anymore.

"But . . ." Brett reached to Linda's Stanford hat perched on her own head and fingered the long blond braid coming from the back. "Why is the . . . What is it"—she pulled the cap off hurriedly, as if she'd just realized she was wearing someone else's underwear—*"sewn* to your hat?"

"I . . . I felt naked without it." Linda's eyes started pooling—a real shock because Linda never cried, only that once when she'd found her first lump. "I've never had short hair, but I wanted a change, and . . ." She glanced at the playground, which was empty, all our children safe in their beds at home. "God, I hate it!"

"But you look as pretty as a speckled pup," Kath said.

"She means that as a compliment, as improbable as that seems," Brett assured Linda, and we all laughed a little nervously. Linda did look good, really. She always looked beautiful, but in some ways she looked even more so now. Short hair brought out those stunning eyes of hers, and masked the persistent thinness of her face.

"I know how you feel, though, Linda," I said. "What is it with hair? A bad cut—one I think is bad—can put me in a funk for days." And we talked for a long time then about how important our hair was to how we saw ourselves, how much money we wasted on hair products, how ridiculous we were to sleep in those big curlers and to sit under the hot hoods of our hair dryers, how great the new handheld blow-dryers were supposed to be. All with our writing set on the picnic table in front of us, uncharacteristically ignored.

"Who'd think we could make such a big fuss out of a bunch of dead protein," Brett said.

"Do go on," Kath said. "How pretty I feel depends on how well my thick skull sprouts *dead protein*?"

"Hey, sweetheart, you want to run your fingers through my dead protein?" I joked, a lame attempt to cheer Linda up.

"It *is* easier to wash short hair," Linda said, pulling herself together, beginning to pretend she hadn't cried. "And I wash it so much more now. I get so sweaty running."

And while Kath assured Linda that ladies never sweat, they "glisten," I sat trying to remember if I'd seen Linda running since she'd returned from New York, thinking I had not.

"WHAT IF I SOUND like a blithering idiot?" Brett said the following Sunday, a foggy morning that made it impossible to tell when the sun had actually risen. Each great new development on her book—she was going to be in the Book-of-the-Month Club, and her publisher was planning to run ads—was no longer cause for celebration but rather cause for more anxiety. She was so stressed that it was hard to imagine she'd ever thought she might be calm enough to make it all the way to the moon, much less to sleep before sticking her little piggy toes out. Not that you couldn't fall off a cliff when everything seemed to be going your way. Look at the Cubs that season: first place going into the All-Star break, and they ended the season in fifth, a late-season slide if ever there was one. Which I supposed could still happen to Brett, though I couldn't really imagine it would.

"What if I make a complete fool of myself right there on national television?" Brett said. "What if I open my mouth and nothing comes out?"

We leaned in closer over the rough wood table, the fog moist against our faces.

"You're going to be a star, Brett," Linda said. "I know you are."

Which was what I wanted to say, but the words were stuck deep in my gut, beside my disappointment over *Michelangelo's Ghost*.

"You are," Kath agreed. "You're one of the most articulate people I know. And your book is wonderful. It's going to sell like hotcakes at the county fair. How could such a fine li'l book not sell like hotcakes?"

Brett's green eyes under that strawberry hair flicked to me, and just as quickly flicked away.

"You're going to do great," I said, working the words over the thick clay of my tongue. That look of Brett's was the closest any of the Wednesday Sisters had ever come to confronting the fact that my novel had bombed. And my college applications were faring no better: I'd been wait-listed at Stanford, and UC Berkeley somehow had failed to receive my second recommendation until after the deadline. ("I'm sorry, Mrs. O'Mara, but our deadlines must be firm.")

"Just be yourself and we'll all be bumping along on your coattails, Brett," Linda said.

"If you start to get the jitters, just remember the coffin photo," Ally said.

"Just think of that big ol' memorial that will be standing right here in this park someday," Kath said. "The one that says the Wednesday Sisters first started scribbling in this very spot."

42

JUST AS THE SUN was lightening the horizon a few Sundays later, with the park still deep in shadow, Kath said, out of nowhere, "The lady's stepson, her husband's son? He hauled that poor lonely ol' widow right into the courtroom." She was staring off into space, to where it seemed you could almost see the mansion still standing there in the dim morning light, behind the majestic palm. "With her husband, his own father, barely cold in the grave," she said. "And her daughter barely dead, too. He liked to left her without a penny."

Linda, sitting next to Kath, put her arm around her and rested her head on Kath's shoulder. She'd abandoned the braid but still wore the cap, her hair perfectly cut underneath. "Lee's not going to leave you with nothing, Kath," she said. "And even if—"

But Kath was already pulling away, shrugging Linda's friendly head from her shoulder. Linda's hat shifted. And so did her hair.

Brett said, "Oh," her small mouth puckering as she stared, startled, at Linda, who was grabbing at her shifted hair as if Kath had wounded her.

Kath, not noticing, looked wounded, too, her face screwing up so that her big chin stuck out bigger, almost as though she wanted someone to take a swing so she could swing back. "You don't have any idea, Linda!" she said. "You and your perfect relationship with your perfect husband, you don't—"

She stopped as suddenly as she'd started, and, like the rest of us, stared at Linda still grasping her cap.

"Linda?" Kath said. "Oh, Linda."

The first hint of sun cut through the branches of the trees lining the east side of the park, subtle red across the eyesore of rocky dirt. It was Linda's hair under that cap, but it wasn't. It sat not quite straight on her head.

I saw then how gaunt her face had become, how hard her cheek-bones jutted against her skin.

She straightened her cap and her hair together, then crossed her arms in front of her. "It's from the chemotherapy. It makes you lose your hair sometimes."

She didn't cry. She just sat there, a defiant look in her blue-green-purple-gold eyes.

I didn't cry, either. None of us dared cry.

"So," she said. "So."

The lump hadn't been nothing; she'd lied to us about that.

Yes, she knew she ought to have had it looked at immediately, she ought not to have waited the three weeks until her trip, but she'd found a doctor in New York who wouldn't make her consent to a one-step, who wouldn't insist on doing an immediate mastectomy while she was still under anesthesia from the biopsy.

"I couldn't face that again," she said. "I did that last time, going under knowing I might come out with . . ." She looked away to the empty playground, to the jungle gym where Anna Page had hung up-side down that day all those years ago now, her sandy dress falling over her face. "With no breasts at all," she said. "With no chest mus-cles. With arms that might be swollen and achy the rest of my life. And I couldn't tell Jeff until I knew what we were dealing with. I just couldn't put him through that again." Turning to Kath now, her eyes searching. "Every doctor in this whole town knows Jeff. Word would have gotten back to him, you know it would have, Kath.

"I wanted to make the decision myself. I couldn't imagine leaving it up to some man I'd never met before, who would have no idea what it would feel like to . . ." She swallowed hard. "To lose a breast."

She'd read the same *McCall's* piece we'd all read about Shirley Temple Black, who'd refused to consent to a mastectomy before she knew what the biopsy showed: *I wouldn't have it that way*—that's what she'd written, and that's how Linda had felt, too.

"And I couldn't know for sure what I'd want to do until I knew how bad it was," Linda said.

She'd read that most doctors thought any woman who had anything less than a radical mastectomy was being unforgivably foolish. Unless they took out the whole breast and the surrounding muscles and lymph nodes, they couldn't be sure they'd gotten all the cancer. But she'd read, too, about a doctor in Cleveland who thought a lumpectomy—cutting out only the lump and leaving the rest of the breast alone—was as effective as a radical for some women. "More effective, even, because he thinks the lymph nodes help your immune system fight the disease."

"Dr. George Crile," Brett said. "There was a piece on him in *Reader's Digest,* about studies in Finland and Canada showing five-year survival rates for lumpectomies equaled those for radicals. It discussed a new study just beginning here in the U.S., twenty-two hospitals participating in randomized pools."

"I think I saw that fella on the *Today* show," Kath added nervously.

"Randomized?" Ally whispered.

"You're blindly assigned to one of the treatment groups," Brett explained.

I looked off to the palm tree still standing in the old mansion yard, wanting to say *Don't do that, Linda, don't let your treatment be decided randomly, luck of the draw.* Wanting to say this couldn't be helping Linda, all this talk. But they *were* talking at least, while I sat mutely imagining Linda in that coffin for real, Jamie and Julie and J.J. in the front pew, having no idea that *dead* meant they'd never see their mommy again.

Linda had gone to Memorial Sloan-Kettering on the Upper East

Side of Manhattan, not far from where her brother and sister-in-law lived. Her sister-in-law kept J.J. and the twins while she went to the hospital for the preliminary tests: X-rays and blood samples, an electrocardiogram, a lung-capacity test. She was evaluated by a surgeon, a radiologist, and a chemotherapist. They agreed to go in and do the biopsy, tell her what they found, and let her participate in the decision about what to do about whatever it turned out to be.

"One lump," she said. Like the first one, but not.

She'd been saying no to herself all along: No, it's not a lump I'm feeling, it's just fibroid tissue or something, like the last time. No, I'm fine, really, even if it is a lump; look how well I'm running. When they said yes, it was malignant, she wanted to say no again, but she was all out of denial.

"I had them"—she waved a hand in front of her chest—"take out the whole thing. But not the muscles, not the nodes."

She couldn't tell Jeff about the lump at first. She didn't tell him until the night before the biopsy. He was in Boston, but she called him that morning from her brother's apartment and told him he had to come to see her in New York. She couldn't even say why over the phone, but he hadn't questioned her. He'd been up all night at the hospital, and still he didn't hesitate. "I have a gunshot wound in post-op, but I can get someone else to cover," he'd said, and she'd told him if he could get there that evening, that would be soon enough.

"It's just a breast, right?" she told us, her voice cracking. And it had been bottled up inside her for so long that it all came out in a gush. "A breast," she said. "Just a breast. You wouldn't think it would be so . . ."

I thought she'd cry then, but she didn't.

"So hideous," she whispered. "There is nothing sexy about me at all anymore. I'm just hideous.

"I grew up the child of the sick mother, and then the child of the dead mother. I couldn't imagine going back to that. I couldn't imagine putting my kids through that. I couldn't take that chance. I'm healthier, though. I'm so much healthier than my mother was to start with. I could run ten miles. And I caught it earlier. My mom, she was . . . When they cut her open, it was just . . ." She waved her hand again, a gesture that said *everywhere,* her mother's cancer had been everywhere.

"They said consider chemotherapy. They don't really know if it will help, but they're having success with it in treating other"—she closed her eyes and took a deep breath—"other cancers."

Fast-growing cancers, where a high percentage of the cells are always in some phase of division, Brett explained later. The drugs had to hit the tumor cells while they were dividing; that was when they were most vulnerable, easiest to knock out.

"I was past no by then," Linda said. "I said of course I'd have the chemotherapy. Sure, I'll have this first poison on the menu, and the third one, too, thanks. And I just decided I wouldn't have any of the bad side effects they talked about, the nausea and depression and . . ." She touched her head. "And this."

She cut her hair off the night she got home from New York, while Jeff was back in Boston explaining what had happened, telling the folks at the hospital that he could stay only until they could find a replacement for him. She took the scissors and sliced her braid across at her neck. She went to a hairdresser the next day and had it fixed so it looked nicer, and she attached her braid to her hat. It wasn't until her hair started falling out in clumps that she took the braid to a wig maker, a woman who, when Linda entered the upstairs shop in San Carlos, was fitting a Hasidic Jew for a wig to wear after she married, because only her husband was allowed to see her hair after her wedding day. "I guess they know how often a man falls in love with a woman's hair," Linda said to us. "The girl had eyebrows and lashes," she said. "I was jealous of that, of her dark eyebrows, her dark lashes, of her knowing they wouldn't fall out."

She felt sick after the chemo—which was being supervised out here; Jeff had lined her up with the best doctor at Stanford—but she'd been given a drug to help curb the nausea. She wasn't living days with her head over the toilet; she wasn't unable to get out of bed. Maybe J.J. and the twins were watching more television than she'd like, maybe dinner too often came from a box—"Let's hear it for Hamburger Helper," she said—but some things just couldn't be helped.

"The doctor said some people think smoking marijuana helps,

but I couldn't imagine explaining that to a neighbor stopping by to borrow a cup of sugar," she said, and with a break in her voice, "much less to my kids."

Brett handed Linda her cap back, and Linda put it on.

"Jeff didn't fall in love with me," she whispered. "He fell in love with my hair."

And you could see it all then, like the aha ending we are always striving for in what we write, the of-course-I-should-have-seen-that. The braid first. The cutting off of the braid and yet holding on to it, too. Gaining control over this thing she couldn't control, or trying to.

"He won't leave you," Kath said quietly.

It was clear from the pooling in Linda's eyes that this wasn't a new idea to her. Worse, she believed he *would* leave her, he would want to every time he saw the gash across her chest where her breast had been. Maybe he wouldn't move out right away because that would be unseemly, but he would want to and he would do it eventually, he wouldn't be able to help himself.

"Jeff won't be going anywhere," Kath insisted. "Lee would, but not Jeff."

There was no discussing it, though. Linda was ashamed: her body had betrayed her. She was terrified that Jeff would come home one day and announce he'd rented an apartment, just as Lee had. And as much as I wanted to assure her otherwise, I knew I would feel as she did if all that was left of my breast was an ugly scar.

Brett, beside me, had not said a word in a while, I realized then; she'd hardly looked up from her lap. She had taken her gloves off. It was a shock to realize it—as shocking as if she'd stripped off her navy sweater and bell-bottom slacks and stood stark naked before us.

The conversation halted, everyone looking at Brett now. Linda looking at Brett's hands, though the rest of us quickly looked away.

We'd seen, though: her fingers all there, but the skin warped, as if it had melted and run, like candle wax or a lava flow. Her left hand more scarred than her right, the little finger bent slightly, as if she couldn't quite straighten it all the way.

"I burned them in a chemical explosion when I was twelve. I

hadn't thought through what would happen if . . ." She blinked once, twice, her leaf-bud gaze fixed on Linda, who alone still stared at Brett's bare hands. "I guess it was an accident," she said.

She was silent for a long time. We were all silent, the only sound the flapping wings of the birds, big ugly black crows landing, gathering to peck at the grass seed that had, once again, been spread across the scar of dirt.

"Not even an accident, exactly," Brett said, her voice uncertain, as if this was something she'd only just realized, something she'd stuffed deep inside herself and kept hidden there, even from herself, all these years. "My brother dared me. He never dreamed I could make such a dramatic bang." She intertwined her scarred fingers. "He's as badly scarred as I am. In a different way."

Linda's gaze lifted from Brett's hands to her thin little face.

"Chip says he loves my hands," Brett said, seeming to be speaking only to Linda now. "He loves me more for my hands. He says he can see that twelve-year-old girl I was, showing her brother she was so much smarter than anyone could imagine.

"Jeff loves you, Linda," she said. "It isn't your hair or your breasts he loves. It's the person you are. Just like Chip loves me."

It seemed we'd been sitting there for an hour, for two, for a lifetime, but the sun had not yet crested the tree line. The sky was still the soft color of dawn.

"But Chip fell in love with you *and* your hands," Linda whispered. "Jeff fell in love with a blond Jewish girl with"—her hand went unconsciously to her wig—"with perfect C-cup breasts, in a sweater that wasn't blue."

She adjusted her wig, her cap, almost surreptitiously, while Brett sat there with her hands free, touched by the fresh morning air.

I wondered if people would stare less at Brett's bare hands than they had always stared at the gloves. I wondered if she'd ever thought about having plastic surgery, or if there was anything they could do. If she could afford it if there was. I imagined her watching the medical news, waiting for the day to come when they could fix her up, when they could give her new hands.

I wondered if it was more complicated than that, if she didn't on some level cling to the gloves as a kind of protection against the world. It was just her hands people were rejecting, then. They weren't rejecting the odd girl who could talk about science better than most scientists, the girl who had wanted to be an astronaut when most of us had no idea what an astronaut was, when most of us aspired only to be the homecoming queen. I imagined her as a young student at Harvard, not belonging in that man's world but belonging no better at Radcliffe. One of the very few women who'd crossed into that world. I imagined her thinking they all would love her—the Harvard boys and the Radcliffe girls and everyone who had ever made fun of her in the school yard or sniggered behind her back in class—if only they could get past her hands.

She would tell us more later. She would tell us that her brother was so good at science that he really could have been an astronaut. His eye had been injured in the explosion, but he'd had an operation and she'd sat through the recovery with him, even as a girl laying out the facts for him. But Brad never took another science class beyond what he was required to take in high school. In college, he majored in history even though he'd never liked history, and he flunked out. And when he was twenty, he had a breakdown. He couldn't get out of bed for weeks. He spent several months at Sheppard Pratt outside Baltimore, and he was better after that, but he never was the same. "It's as if he can't do anything but relive the past," Brett said. "He thinks my hands are his fault, because he dared me. But it was my fault, really. I knew what I could do." And I would remember then Brett's reluctance to send out that first essay, and see it for the first time as what it was: not fear of failure but fear of success. I would wonder what it was like to love a brother so selflessly, to give up your own success lest it make your brother's failure worse.

That afternoon when we first saw Brett's scarred hands, though, I thought only that those hands were her hands, that she wouldn't be Brett without them, with or without her gloves. I took one scarred hand in mine, and Kath, across the picnic table from her, did, too, and then we had all joined hands, even Linda. We just sat there, not saying anything, just sitting together as the sun rose above the trees, as the sky lightened from pink to blue and the shadows shortened and the day became just another Sunday to the people waking in the houses around us. Men strapping on running shoes to run marathons. Toddlers dragging stuffed bears they'd cuddled since the moment they were born. Husbands and wives spooning together. Little girls placing their fingers on white piano keys, then reaching up for the black.

43

*L*INDA CAME TO THE NEXT Wednesday Sisters meeting with a piece of writing she wanted to share with us, something she'd written before she'd gone to New York. I took it home and read it, then read it again: Linda packing up J.J. and Jamie and Julie the morning she found the new lump, loading them into the car to search through bookstores. She knows what a radical mastectomy is, but what does it mean, really? How does it look? It's what they did to her mother, a double radical; they cut both her mother's breasts off, she knows that, but she doesn't know, she has never seen.

There are alternatives now: a modified radical mastectomy and radiation therapy. But what do *they* mean? How is she to have any idea which choice to make if she has to make a choice? None of it sure to save her life, anyway. A double radical, and still her mother died.

She wanders through Kepler's Books on El Camino, through Stacey's on University, through Books Inc. at the mall, but there is no book on breast cancer that she can find, nothing that shows her what a breast looks like when it's gone.

Back home, she calls the American Cancer Society, but the disembodied woman on the line is curt. Severe disapproval in her voice: Books with photos like that for anyone but medical personnel? But

Linda grabs on to that one phrase, "medical personnel," and she is already hanging up the phone, already loading the children into the car again, promising them just a few more minutes looking at books and then ice cream as she heads for the Stanford bookstore, where Jeff gets his medical texts.

The volume of books at Stanford is overwhelming, though. She doesn't know where to start, and she can't ask anyone, she simply can't. But she won't have time to do this after she's in the hospital, so she starts paging through volumes: photos of children with cleft palates, children with measles and mumps, children with unspeakable diseases of the skin. She puts that volume back, moves to another aisle, finds old people with gout and kidney disease. She fumbles her way to books on oncology, where she finds photos and drawings of diseased lungs, small spots on skin that are not good news, polyps in colons and tumors on ovaries. Still, she cannot find a photo of a breastless chest. And the children are insistent now: It's time for ice cream, she has promised no more than fifteen minutes and it has been twenty-five, Julie says. Linda is sorry the twins have learned to tell time, sorry she has given them her watch.

She turns to Lee Montgomery. Yes, to Kath's Lee. She feels the guilt of it, the disloyalty. Lee will know and Kath won't. But he is the only person she knows who can and *will* sit and explain to her the options and what they mean. He will let her take all night to get the words out if she needs to. He will tell her where she should go to have it looked at. And Lee, she knows, is discreet. He will never tell a soul, not even Jeff. Especially not Jeff.

I wept as I read, and as I reread, and then I called Kath.

"We've got to do something directly," Kath said. "And I'm not talking about making casseroles."

But what? That's what the conversation came down to. But what?

THE NEXT WEEK, Linda wrote of the sterile, obsolete-magazine anonymity of the surgery waiting room, of imagining this would be the way she would spend the rest of her life, what little rest of her life there might be. She remembered how her father had never looked at her mother after her surgery. How her father hadn't looked at any woman after that, not even his daughter.

The third week, five exquisite pages of Linda sitting naked and alone at her makeup mirror, watching in the soft light of the frosted round bulbs as her own hand raised the sharp silver blades of her sewing scissors to the long twist of her hair. I wept as I read. As I reread. The simple act of cutting a braid off—what it meant to take control of this thing before it took control of her.

And the fourth week: eight heartbreaking pages that started with the alarm going off the morning of the mini-marathon, Linda waking and realizing that she couldn't run, that she couldn't bear to spend a moment away from Jamie and Julie and J.J. on this last day before her biopsy. Realizing, too, that she had to tell Jeff.

It was early, but she picked up the phone and called him, found him at the hospital, working the overnight shift. She asked him to please come to New York, it was important. Then she went into the bedroom the twins were sharing at her brother's apartment and woke them. "We're in New York," she said. "Let's go explore!"

She gathered J.J., and she took them all for breakfast at the Plaza Hotel: waffles with strawberries and whipped cream. And she told them. First thing, over the waffles and whipped cream, she told them so they would have the whole day to ask questions. She waited until the waiter had served them, until they'd eaten and it didn't look as if they could handle another bite. She waited till the waiter refilled her coffee cup and took the check and the money away, returned with the change, so that they wouldn't be interrupted. She made them all look at her, then. She made Julie and Jamie put their forks down; they were playing with the uneaten strawberries, threatening to begin flinging them across the room. She supposed they sensed something was up. She wished, as they set the silver forks on the edges of their plates, that she had three sets of silver, that if anything happened to her they would each have that, a set of silver that had been their mother's, that would touch their fingers every day of their lives.

"Listen," she said. "This is important. I want you to listen for a minute while I tell you something, and then you can ask anything you want. I want you to ask anything you want."

"Can we go to the toy store?" J.J. asked; they'd passed FAO Schwarz on the way.

"After we're done talking," Linda said. "Maybe it will be open by then."

She pulled J.J. into her lap and leaned closer to the table, the twins on either side of her. She looked at each one of them, at Julie and Jamie, who had Jeff's sober brown eyes, at J.J., whose eye color couldn't quite be described, like her own.

"Mommy has to go to the hospital early tomorrow morning for an operation," she said. "I hope it will be just a little operation, but I don't know. If it is, I'll be home in two days. I might have to have a second operation, though, and if I do, I'll be in the hospital longer."

"Will you bring a baby home, like Hope?" Julie asked, her face so expectant that Linda had to look away. Her eyes met her own reflection looking back at her from the mirrored wall, her children's smaller faces focused on hers, fear edging its way into their eyes.

She held J.J. more surely, leaning closer to the girls. She set her hand on Julie's hair, on the little bit of ear that peeked through the sheet of blond. "Not this time, honey," she said.

"Can we come visit you?" Jamie asked.

"Yes, you can visit me there," Linda said. "Daddy will be here tonight, and he'll bring you every day." She touched a finger to her daughter's neck, pushing away the thought that she might never see how lovely it would look on the woman her daughter would become. "I might look kind of weird after the second operation, if I end up having two," she said. "Grandma did."

Her mother must have known Linda loved her even as she was hiding in the closet, Linda realized. Julie and Jamie and J.J. would always love her: she knew that as surely as she knew anything.

She took a sip of her coffee, cold already. She didn't want to scare them, but she wanted them to understand. "Honestly," she said, "it's okay to be afraid if you think I look weird. I'll probably be afraid, too. Everyone is."

And when Julie said, "But Grandma died, Mommy. Are you going to die?" Linda thought: *This is why Mom and Dad never told us, because how do you answer this?*

She met each of their eyes before she spoke again—all those straight-across eyebrows, like hers—so they would see that she was telling them the truth. "I don't think so," she said. "I don't think I'm going to die, but I can't promise I won't." The earnest way they looked back at her. Could they even begin to understand this? "If anything happens to me," she said, "I want you to always remember this: No mommy in this whole wide world has ever loved her children more than I love you guys. And always, always, you make me the happiest mommy in the world. No matter what happens, I want you to remember that. Okay? Promise me that?"

They all did. They all promised her, no matter what.

"Forever?" she said, working to make her voice lighter. "Even when you're a hundred and two?"

They all giggled.

"Even when I'm a hundred and *ninety*-two," Julie said, and Jamie, not to be outdone, said, "Even when I'm two *thousand*!"

Linda wrapped them in a big group hug then, not able to get out the one last thing she'd wanted to say, not able to tell Jamie and Julie they might have to remind J.J., that he might not remember his mother at all, he was so young.

They rode the carousel in Central Park that morning. At the zoo, the children laughed at the gorillas (Linda trying not to think about the poor mother gorilla who'd been so sad to be separated from baby Patty Cake and now might never get him back), and J.J., at least, *eeeewww*ed with real glee at the two-headed snake. They rented a little rowboat and the twins took turns at the oars, making a crazy zigzag across the water, putting them in the path of other rowboats again and again, but no harm ever came to them.

When they got back to her brother's place, Jeff was there, and she told him, and when she leaned into him once the awful words were out, he wrapped his arms around her and kissed the top of her head. "It's going to be okay," he whispered, and for a moment she thought maybe it would.

They all slept in the same bed that night, the five of them together, so that if the children woke in the middle of the night she and Jeff would be there. She snuggled up with them, and when they were all breathing easily—even Jeff, who'd been up all the night before at the hospital—she eased out from under the covers and found some of her sister-in-law's heavy stationery. She settled on the floor in the hallway outside their room, and she wrote Jamie and Julie and J.J. each a long letter, recalling the moments they were born and their first words, their first steps, describing in detail what she loved about each of them and imaging the wonderful futures she knew they would have, the things they would do and the love they would find, the love they would give along the way.

The next morning, she and Jeff got dressed quietly, not wanting to wake the children before they had to. When she was ready, she climbed back into the bed, woke them gently, hugged them and said again how much she loved them.

"Always remember that," she said. "How much I love you. And remember: it's okay if you're afraid, even if you're afraid of me, if you think I look gross."

They giggled at the word *gross*.

"Mommies can't look gross!" J.J. protested.

She wiped the sleep from his eyes. "Remember that two-headed snake we saw yesterday?" she said.

"*Mommy*, you won't have *two heads*!" J.J. howled delightedly, and they all laughed.

"No," Linda promised them. "I won't have two heads, I can promise you that."

She hugged them again, and she told them one last time that she loved them, and she said good-bye, and she went to the hospital and signed the consent to surgery, the you-may-die stuff. She held her breath as she had that first time, when they put the mask over her face. And she said a prayer not to God but to Jeff, to take special care of them if anything happened to her, to hug them every morning and kiss them every night and always always to remind them how much she had loved them, how much she still loved them even if she couldn't be with them as they grew up.

44

Anyone who saw Jeff with Linda that summer could see he would never leave her. I hoped she could see it herself. He commuted to Boston until they could find someone to replace him, but he'd already gone back to the people at Stanford, already said whatever they could give him, he'd take. And still we Wednesday Sisters were saying to each other that we had to do something for Linda. But what?

We could take the children for a weekend or even a week, we told Jeff the week Linda was finishing the chemotherapy. She would be feeling better physically, at least. What she needed now, we decided, was some time without worries, to have fun, to remember who she was. "Why don't you two go on a vacation together?" we said to Jeff.

He ran a hand through uncharacteristically unkempt hair, and for a moment I thought he would cry, and I pictured Linda, how she never cried. I imagined how hard that must be for Jeff, to feel he couldn't cry because she wouldn't.

"She isn't comfortable with the physicality of being with me," he said, his mouth heavy. "She will be. I know she will be. But she isn't yet." He did not sound convincing.

"What about you girls all going somewhere?" he said. "A

Wednesday Sisters weekend away." And something in his handsome, exhausted face made me remember him in that Wilbur the pig costume at our Halloween party, made me think, *Some Husband.*

"Not too far away," he said, and you could see the struggle in him, the need to make Linda happy fighting against his own need to keep her within his grasp, to help her himself.

"The Miss America weekend, a Miss America retreat," Kath said, and the rest of us rang up in an echo chorus before the utter ridiculousness of it splashed across our expressions, Ally blinking, looking down, Kath's eyes startling with the realization that this dog certainly would not hunt. How could we imagine Linda would want to watch those perfect women in bathing suits when she'd just lost her breasts, her hair? When she was fighting for her life?

Brett sat rubbing one gloved index finger over her other gloved palm. "I've got the Carson thing that Friday," she said, and you could see she could barely stand to mention it, that she was mortified to be talking about promoting her novel on television at such a time.

"Linda's really excited about that," Jeff said. "I'm so glad you're doing it. It gives her something to look forward to. And Carson always makes her laugh, even when his jokes aren't funny." He smiled a little, and you could almost see him sitting in bed beside Linda, tucked under the covers with her. Ten-thirty. Watching Johnny's opening monologue, basking in her laugh.

"The Tonight Show."

I think we all said it at the same time.

We'd talked about getting tickets when we first found out Brett would be on, but we hadn't known the date yet, and then with Linda being sick it had slipped our minds. Or perhaps we'd pushed it out, the fun we'd once imagined seeming far beyond our reach.

Could we still get tickets?

"Maybe I could get them, as a guest," Brett said. "I got one for Chip."

"I might could get them through the office," Kath offered.

I thought, but didn't say, that if all else failed, Danny could get them for us, through the investment bankers, I was pretty sure of that. They were always offering tickets to the opera and weekends in

Napa, dinners at trendy new restaurants you couldn't get reservations at for months. Four *Tonight Show* tickets couldn't be that hard to come by, if you knew how to go about it, if you had strings to pull.

A *Mrs. America* weekend in L.A., with Johnny Carson, we agreed. *The Tonight Show* Friday night. And Saturday? Something other than Miss America, we decided. Who could spend a wild weekend in Los Angeles staying in a hotel room and watching an outdated beauty pageant, anyway?

We booked rooms in the hotel Brett was staying in—four rooms, because we couldn't imagine Linda would want to share a room, and it seemed wrong for any of the rest of us to exclude her by doing so ourselves.

"And we'll cut our hair," Ally announced.

"Cut our hair?" Kath said.

"Cut it off," Ally said. "Cut it all off, heavens to Betsy. It will give us some idea of what she's going through, shrugging off that one crutch we rely on to feel we're feminine."

I thought of how Ally had felt all those years, doubting her femininity because she wasn't able to have a baby. I tried to imagine myself without my mop of unruly dishwater blond hair—not gorgeous, but still so much a part of who I was.

"Shave it off?" I said quietly, trying to imagine walking out my front door with my skull showing, bald and free.

No one answered, though everyone had heard me.

I tried to imagine all of us standing before Linda, pulling off wigs or caps to reveal that we, like her, were smooth as our newborn babies' little bottoms had been. I would cry if the Wednesday Sisters did that for me. I would cry at their choosing to go through what I had no choice but to endure myself.

But I wasn't Linda.

I found a smile creeping up from the pit of my stomach. "She'll laugh," I said. "Somehow I know it will make her laugh. I'd do it just for that."

"She could sure stand to laugh a spell," Kath said. "And it's what she'd do for us, sure enough."

It was what she would do for us, we all agreed. Everyone except Brett, who sat silently looking down at her gloves.

Kath reached over and put a hand on Brett's. "But Brett can't," she said. "She'd be nervous as a long-tailed cat in a room full of rocking chairs fixin' to go on Johnny Carson with a shaved head."

"I could wear a wig?" Brett said, but the rise in her voice told everything. This was her big moment, and she was dreading it already. She could no more appear on *The Tonight Show* with her head shaved than she could with her gloves off.

"You can't do that, Brett," I said.

"It will be hot enough under the lights without a wig on," Ally agreed.

Brett nodded, but there was something unconvincing in it, as if she couldn't stand to have hair if the rest of us were bald.

"Henry Adams said, 'One friend in a lifetime is much; two are many; three are hardly possible,'" she said. "What is it we've done so right in our lives that has made us five?"

"We'll be your big ol' bald fan club," Kath said, "the good Lord willin' and the creek don't rise." And we all, again, agreed. There wasn't a hint of conviction in our voices, though. I was sure when the time came we would talk ourselves out of this. We'd justify our cowardice or convince ourselves it would embarrass Linda. Or maybe we'd just plain lose our nerve.

45

WHEN THE BIG EVENING CAME, we were seated side by side, Kath and Ally and Linda and I together on the aisle in the third row, with Brett waiting backstage. I felt as if I were in a dream, as if none of this could be happening. I could not possibly be that little girl who grew up in suburban Chicago, who went to Catholic school and played the French horn and went on to be a secretary. I could not possibly have married the smartest guy at Northwestern and moved to a place I'd never heard of, two thousand miles away from my family, with my two children in tow. Most of all, I could not be the woman who'd just been accepted to Stanford—my admissions letter had come in the mail that morning, just before we left!—and made these wonderful friends with whom I was now sitting, and published a novel myself and helped my friend who was now here, waiting to sit next to Johnny Carson and talk about *The Mrs. Americas* as if she were Harper Lee.

I could not possibly be sitting here with a wig scratching against my shaved scalp, knowing that Kath and Ally were bald underneath their wigs, too.

We'd thought we would buy wigs that looked like our hair, but that turned out to be more difficult than you would think. So we went to the other extreme. We bought wigs that were nothing at all like our own hair. I was a sleekly cropped strawberry blonde, Ally a longer-haired honey blonde which, with her pale skin, looked more probable than you might have thought. Kath hadn't changed her color—she was still brunette, every other shade she'd tried on had looked just ludicrous—but she'd gone for short and curly, which opened up her face, made her cheekbones more prominent. When she'd first tried it on, before we'd actually shaved our heads, we'd all said more or less in unison something like, "Wow." We'd said maybe she should cut her hair short, and she'd smiled—a big white smile in her uncovered face—and said, "I'm planning to, don't you know? I'm thinking *mighty* short."

We didn't need to get further than the hallway outside Linda's hotel room to know what we'd done in Kath's hotel bathroom was worth it. Her expression when she answered our knock was the funniest thing I'd seen in ages. *Who are you?* it said. *I was expecting Kath and Ally and Frankie.*

She laughed so delightedly when she realized it was us that she sounded almost healthy again. "Why are you guys wearing wigs?" she said.

We shrugged and said we were ready for a change.

"New city, new night, new look," Kath said. "A girl's got a right to turn loose every now and again."

Linda said she had fixed on Ally when she'd opened the door, and she knew she should know her but she couldn't for the life of her place her. She figured she was someone from back in Connecticut, someone she'd grown up with who'd tracked her down here, though she couldn't imagine who or how or why. Then she'd realized it was Ally.

"You look foxy as a blonde, Ally," she said. "But I'm glad it's a wig. That much bleach would destroy that wonderful hair of yours."

The way Ally touched her wig made me remember Kath's words when we'd first looked at ourselves in the mirror that afternoon, after we'd shaved our heads: "You don't miss the water till the well runs dry." But none of us said a word to Linda about no longer having hair to destroy.

We set off for the show and took our seats and waited impatiently, talking about Brett sitting backstage. Chip was with her—we were glad for that. He'd brought her to the show and was going to stay with her until she went on, then slip into the audience to watch her. He was flying home right afterward, so they wouldn't have to leave Sarah and Mark with anyone for the whole night. We all were reluctant to leave our children in someone else's care for any period of time now. Linda being vulnerable made us all feel vulnerable, made our world suddenly tenuous and fragile.

The music started—Doc Severinsen and the NBC Orchestra—and Ed McMahon appeared, and it was no time before he was saying, "Heeeeeere's Johnny!" And there he was indeed, coming through the curtains in chocolate slacks and a gray blazer, white shirt, wide red tie. The curtain swayed behind him, all blue and green and gold. *This is it,* we thought. *This is happening for Brett tonight and it is going to happen for all of us, we have worked together to make this happen and even we sometimes didn't believe it ever would, but here we are.* And Linda was clapping as wildly as I was, as Ally and Kath were, as I imagined Brett, watching a television monitor backstage, was, too. We weren't clapping for Johnny, though. We were clapping for each other, for those women who'd arisen from that coffin almost four years ago now.

Johnny went right into his monologue, quieting us, moving the show along. He was always current, and since this was the Friday night before the Miss America Pageant, he lobbed up some funny jokes at Bert Parks's expense. Well, not very funny, actually. I laughed at first, but my heart wasn't in it. I thought I was just too worried for Brett. But the laughter all around me was forced, too—not just Kath and Ally, but the two fellows behind me, and the woman with the flower in her hair in the first row. Only Linda was genuinely laughing, her laughter so lovely that part of me just wanted to sit quietly and drink it in.

The band started playing "Tea for Two"—their your-monologue-is-flopping-Johnny tune—and Johnny said, "Wait a minute, wait a minute, Doc. This lovely blonde in the third row thinks I'm funny even if no one else does."

The camera panned to Linda sitting beside me. She waved at the lens and called out, "Hi Jeff! Hi, Jamie and Julie! Hi, J.J.!"—words you can't hear on the film clip, although you can read her lips. My hand went involuntarily to my glasses, then touched the odd texture of something that was not my hair.

Doc Severinsen—in a turtleneck and very loud jacket—led his gang into "Tea for Two" again, and Johnny, looking chagrined, started his okay-I-admit-this-monologue-is-flopping dance. The crowd laughed—real laughter now. And then Johnny was talking about the guests who would join him: someone who was going to teach him how to break a board in half with his head, then Brett, then Ron Howard and Harrison Ford, who were starring in *American Graffiti*, a new movie we all wanted to see although we couldn't imagine how the cute little redheaded lisper from *The Music Man* and *The Andy Griffith Show* could possibly have grown up.

No animal high jinks tonight. No oversized bug to crawl up Johnny's arm. No furry little critter to perch on his head. Which was a good thing, I figured, because those exotic animals really stole the show sometimes. They were so funny—or Johnny reacting to them was—that they might be a hard act to follow for Brett. Humor was not her forte.

Johnny did his trademark phantom golf swing, aimed at stage left where the band was, and I was glad it was the Friday before the Miss America Pageant and not the Monday after; Monday was often guest-host night, and I couldn't imagine Brett getting through this with anyone but Johnny, anyone who might find humor at her expense rather than at his own.

He did his Carnac the Magnificent gig, wearing his extravagantly feathered and beaded red turban and his cape. He held the sealed envelope to his forehead, saying, "Sis boom bah," and tearing and blowing open the envelope as Ed McMahon repeated, "Sis boom bah." Johnny gave him the look and pulled out the paper. "What is the sound of a sheep exploding?" At which the crowd around me laughed genuinely.

Usually I loved Carnac, he was my favorite Carson routine, though I liked Aunt Blabby, too. But I was impatient for Brett.

The breaking-the-board bit was funny, too, with Johnny succeeding, and then Ed McMahon pointing him in the direction of the camera and saying—while Johnny blubbered in exaggerated pain—that they'd be right back with the latest literary sensation, Mrs. Brett Tyler. *After* these commercial messages.

And then we were back on the air and there was Johnny, talking about his next guest, Mrs. Brett Tyler, and her new book, *The Mrs. Americas,* and then there Brett was, coming through the curtain. They'd done her hair wrong somehow, it looked too poufy, but I thought maybe that was the effect of her earrings: oversized globes that, together with the oversized buttons on her jacket, emphasized her smallness in a way that made her look fashionably adorable. It had been the last of a million jackets she'd tried on—all of us crowded into the dressing room. The last of a million earrings.

Johnny stood to shake her gloved hand. "*The Mrs. Americas,* those would be my ex-wives you're writing about?" he said—he was on wife number three by that time—and the audience laughed.

Brett sat in the guest chair and Johnny began asking her about her book and her experience publishing it. She answered easily, articulately, as though she really might be Harper Lee after all. I was so very proud of her. We all were.

And then somehow she got on the topic of us—of the Wednesday Sisters. She started explaining how important the Wednesday Sisters were to her and how she couldn't ever have gotten the novel done, much less published, without us. Right there, on Johnny Carson!

Johnny was all over that. "The Wednesday Sisters?"

He loved that.

And it just got better and better.

"So they're your sisters?"

"No."

"Not your sisters?"

"Friends. Writing friends. The Wednesday Sisters Writing Society, we like to call ourselves. But we're more than that, too. So much more than that."

"So you write together?" Johnny asked.

"Not anymore. We started out writing together. On a picnic table in the park one Wednesday morning. The Wednesday morning after the Miss America Pageant five years ago, in fact. That's when we decided to write together, while we were watching the Miss America Pageant the year all those women protested out on the boardwalk."

"The bra burners?" Johnny said, and Brett said right, except that they didn't actually burn any bras, they hadn't been able to get a permit to burn anything.

"Now we write at home, though," Brett said, "so we can spend our time together critiquing each other's work."

"You don't write together but you do watch the Miss America Pageant?"

"Right."

"And you meet on Wednesdays?"

"No."

One of those funny Johnny looks. "You don't meet on Wednesdays?"

"We meet on Sunday mornings. At sunrise."

Johnny laughed and laughed at that, which was something. If you could make Johnny laugh like that, then you knew half the households in America were laughing, too.

"But you do all wear white gloves?" he said when he'd recovered.

I swear, you could hear the intake of breath in our four seats as if it were the wind howling through downtown Chicago just before a thunderstorm. You could see our faces imagining the wavy skin under those gloves and the curled little finger, and the young girl stepping up to her brother's awful dare all those years ago, and succeeding.

Brett touched one gloved hand to her strawberry blond hair as if she would run her fingers through it and mess it up, but then she didn't. She simply said, smooth as anything, "No, that's my own little oddity."

As though it was nothing at all.

She was telling him about me getting my novel published then, and about the coffin, about Linda dragging us to the funeral home and making us lie down in that coffin and imagine what we would think of our lives if we were dying, and she was pulling something from her purse. Johnny looked at it, and you could tell by the delight in his blue eyes that all those people watching at home were about to get a peek. He held it up for the camera to move in on: the coffin photo, Brett playing dead in the coffin with the four of us lined up behind her, grinning as if we'd all seen this moment with Johnny Carson in a crystal ball.

The five of us on national television, and only Linda with her hair combed.

Johnny was looking at the photograph again himself, pointing to one of us in the photo and saying, "Haven't I seen this woman somewhere before?" He looked to Brett. "Is this the other friend—the other Wednesday Sister—who's already published a novel? Maybe I've seen her book?"

"Frankie?" Brett said. "No, Frankie is the other blonde, the one in the glasses. That one is Linda."

"Linda," Johnny repeated.

"She's the lovely blonde in the third row who liked your monologue when no one else did."

"Ouch!" Johnny said, again with a comic face, while the band played a few spontaneous notes of "Tea for Two." "Are you Wednesday Sisters this brutal when you critique each other's work?" Johnny asked.

Brett smiled what Kath calls "a big ol' smile" whenever she tells the story, and you could tell she was thinking, *"When in doubt, tell the truth."*

"Let's just say that monologue wouldn't have made it beyond the picnic table," she said.

Johnny laughed and laughed. "They're all here, all of the Wednesday Sisters?" he asked, and the next thing you know, he was inviting us all to come up onstage, and Brett was pointing to us, saying, "They're right there."

The camera panned to us: no stage makeup like Brett had, and you can see if you watch the tape how flustered we look: *Us?* our faces say. And we stood—I don't even remember this part, us sliding out into the aisle, although obviously we did, you can see us there on the film. I don't remember slipping my glasses off or tripping on my way up the stairs, either, though you can see that on the clip, too. The first thing I do remember—and even this did not seem the least bit real—is standing there in front of Johnny, who'd gotten up to welcome us, as had Brett.

Standing there on the Carson show, the most watched talk show on television, wearing a wig that hadn't looked great to start with and was now slightly askew.

That flustered even Johnny. You can see in his eyes on the film that he wanted to reach up and straighten it. Every time I watch the clip I want to straighten it myself, but as I stood on that stage I had no idea the thing had shifted when I'd tripped. I was too busy trying not to look out at the fuzzy blur of colors that was the audience, sure that if I did, my knees would rattle even more and I'd collapse.

Brett reached one hand toward her hair, but then stopped at one of those wonderful globe earrings and smiled easily. "This is Ally Tantry. Kath Montgomery. Linda Mason," she said, indicating each in turn. "And this is Frankie O'Mara. M. F. O'Mara. Her novel, *Michelangelo's Ghost,* is terrific."

"*Michelangelo's Ghost,*" Johnny repeated. "I like that title, don't you, Ed?" he said, and Ed said he did, he liked that, *Michelangelo's Ghost.* And me half thinking, *My title mentioned not once but three times on* The Tonight Show! and half trying to determine if Linda was really shooting me a funny look or if it was just that I couldn't quite see without my glasses.

"And the book is even better than the title," Brett said. Then to the audience, "If you haven't read it yet, you should get up from your seat right now and rush out to your local bookstore to buy a copy."

Johnny faked leaving, heading toward the curtain for a moment before turning back to us.

Then Linda, suddenly reaching toward me, said, "Frankie's real hair looks better anyway," and before I knew what she was doing, she'd pulled off my wig. There was a startled Oh! in her eyes, one that echoed the intake of breath throughout the audience as she stood with the long, smooth strawberry-blond length of my wig in her hand.

She looked down at it, then back to me, to the funny arc of my ears, to my eyes and nose and lips and high, high forehead unsoftened by the drape of all that dead protein (which even on the most humid days, I'd seen the moment I'd shaved it off, had been beautiful).

"Frankie!" Linda said, looking confusedly from the wig in her hand to my bald, bald head. "You didn't—?"

The audience exhaled a stir of *Oh my God*s and *What in the world*s as Linda, too stunned to think to hand the wig back to me, and I, too mortified to move, just stood there.

Sweet Jesus, my mother, watching from her couch at home, reportedly said.

Somehow, I managed the smallest little bit of smile (a nice smile, really; you can see it on the clip). "I'm afraid I did," I said. Or croaked, actually, to tell the truth.

"Lordy, Lordy, life sure doesn't give us all the practice we need," Kath murmured, the *What is happening here?* expression in her big brown eyes in her big-chinned face working its way into a big, self-conscious smile. I felt her hand taking mine, her palm as damp as my own. Then heard the audience again as Kath slipped off her brunette curls.

That's when Linda started laughing. No doubt about it.

Ally, muttering "Heavens to Betsy," eased off her long blond locks just as Brett, slipping her free hand into Ally's, touched her white-gloved fingers to her overly poufy strawberry coif and removed her hair, too.

Linda, laughing so hard by then that tears were rolling down her cheeks, pulled off her own wig. She dropped it, and mine as well, and as they flumped onto the floor she linked hands with Ally and me, and we stood there in front of the whole world, bald-headed and together and proud.

Johnny, quick on his feet, pulled on his own hair. It didn't come off, of course, but the crowd certainly laughed.

"Look out, world," he said. "The Wednesday Sisters are coming. They're not sisters and they don't meet on Wednesdays, and for reasons I'm sure we'll come to understand because I'm sure we're going to hear a lot about *all* these ladies, they shave their heads together—though only one of them wears gloves!"

46

DID WE WATCH the Miss America Pageant the night after the Carson show, when we were in Los Angeles with so many other things to do? Well, we thought we wouldn't. We were sure that would be the year we'd let go. But then it seemed it might jinx us, what with the great success of *The Mrs. Americas,* a title Kath never would have thought of and Brett never would have agreed to without those Saturday nights in September spent with just us girls.

Or that was the excuse we used, anyway.

We watched Colorado's Rebecca King be crowned Miss America for the next year, 1974. She was not your typical Miss America, though, which somehow made it all right to watch her win: she'd entered for the scholarship money, which she would use to attend law school, and her vocal pro-choice stance would get nationwide publicity in a country as torn over *Roe* v. *Wade* as it is now.

The country just tore and tore that fall. It started lightly, with Billie Jean King defeating Bobby Riggs in the Battle of the Sexes with more than fifty million people watching on TV (a smaller thing than King refusing to play the U.S. Open that year unless they paid equal prize money to women, which they then did, but the match with Riggs got more attention). Within months things got more serious. Vice President Agnew resigned, OPEC started its first oil embargo, and Congress passed the War Powers Act over the president's veto, limiting his power to make war. By the next Miss America Pageant, Nixon would have resigned, and the following spring the last Americans in Vietnam would be evacuated by helicopter from a rooftop as Saigon became Ho Chi Minh City, a retreat from a mistake we never really would admit.

And the Wednesday Sisters?

As you can imagine, there isn't much that could get more attention than five bald women appearing together on *The Tonight Show*—which sure didn't hurt our writing careers. True, Kath never has published a word—she just keeps on editing ours—and Ally, when it came down to it, said selling the novel she'd written for Hope seemed too much like sharing with others the gift she'd made for her daughter; she didn't want to publish it. But *The Mrs. Americas* made it as far as number ten on the bestseller list, *Michelangelo's Ghost* came back from the dead to haunt bookstores again, and Linda began selling to magazines: the pieces she'd written that summer about searching for mastectomy photos, cutting off her braid, and saying good-bye to her kids, as well as a new piece about her own mother's death, one she developed from those exquisite few paragraphs about the key and the girl and the dead mother she didn't want to share, that five minutes of her writing from that first time the Wednesday Sisters had gathered to write, when she'd spilled the contents of her purse on the picnic table and directed us to start moving our pens. Pieces she would, at Kath's suggestion, eventually collect in a single volume, a book dedicated to her mom.

That Carson show seemed a sort of turning point for the Wednesday Sisters in other ways as well. Brett started talking to surgeons about her hands later that same September, the September I started classes at Stanford, where I did not graduate valedictorian as Danny and Brett had, but where I acquitted myself pretty well for a mother of two who was writing novels while she attended school. English literature, that was my major. No physics. No math. No graduate school. But my life isn't over yet.

By year end, Ally was pregnant with a baby she again miscarried. She was as devastated as she had been before Hope was born, but she held herself together, for Hope's sake. Three years later, she would give birth to a son she and Jim named Santosh Amar—Santosh meaning "happiness" and Amar "forever." Sam's birth was nearly as premature as his sister's, but in the interim, corticosteroids had been introduced to speed lung development of babies likely to be born prematurely. Like Hope, Sam wasn't allowed stuffed animals in intensive care, but he was born breathing on his own, and he wasn't even all that small.

As for Kath, no, she didn't divorce Lee, and Lee didn't move back in. But there was a shift in their relationship, a little of a letting go by Kath. I think she might actually have left him back then but for the children, but Linda says no, Kath will never leave Lee, hard as Linda has tried over the years to make her. "'Life and livin' aren't the same,'" those conversations always end, Linda throwing one of our favorite Kathisms right back at the source. Kath has had her reasons over the years. Health insurance is the one she touts most often now, which is ridiculous, of course, because she has her own health insurance, through her publishing house. But if you point that out to her, you get back that you never know when a girl might be fired, and anyway, she's fixin' to leave publishing to write her own novel any day. Never mind that she now heads up the West Coast office. Never mind that she's thrown out that "fixin' to leave" line for years, without ever once meaning it.

"You never know," she says. "I might could just up and quit tomorrow."

And we're talking about the woman who rammed her husband's car while speeding down the freeway, the one who, when the rest of us were hesitating in that hotel room, set the electric shears to her hairline right smack-dab at the peak of her forehead and cleared a path across the top of her head before she could lose her nerve. Yes,

Kath "might could" do just about anything. She "might could" even divorce Lee someday.

And Linda?

Well, Linda is a survivor, going on thirty-five years now. But then, she always was.

We all were, it turns out.

Acknowledgments

I am grateful beyond words for the support of my husband, Mac Clayton—without his belief that my Wednesday Sisters were something special, this book would be in the proverbial drawer—and for that of Brenda Rickman Vantrease; both read and reread, listened at every turn, and inspired me. They are truly my Wednesday Sisters, even if one is male and our little writing group met on Tuesdays rather than Wednesdays.

I can't say enough about the newest sisters on my team: Marly Rusoff, who took this manuscript under her amazing wing when no sane person would have done so, and über-editors Robin Rolewicz and Anika Streitfeld, my own two dear and wonderful Kaths. The early enthusiasm and unflagging efforts of Libby McGuire, Kim Hovey, and Brian McLendon have been an author's dream, as has the care Beth Pearson has taken in helping me get the words just right. The great kindness of the entire Ballantine team has been remarkable; thanks especially to Kate Blum, Katie O'Callaghan, Robbin Schiff, Victoria Allen, Victoria Wong, Nancy Field, Christine Cabello, Margaret Wimberger, Kate Norris, and Jillian Quint. Thanks, too, to everyone at the Rusoff Agency, especially Anna Lvovsky and the wonderfully spirited Michael Radulescu, whose good cheer even through the great flood is one for the books.

As befitting an ensemble novel, I have an ensemble of others to thank for their help and support: Leslie Berlin, Adrienne Defendi, Harriet Scott Chessman, Casey Feutsch, Leslie Lytle, Liza MacMorris, Carol Markson, Kirsten Moss, Madeleine Mysko, and Manjiri Subhash (who gave me the gift of Ally's meddling mother-in-law). WOMBA, Ellen Sussman, and my Monday night poker gang were touchstones throughout, as was the entire Waite/Clayton family, including my own never-meddling mom-in-law, Page Clayton. Special thanks to my sons, Chris and Nick, who provided all of the charm and originality of the Wednesday Sisters' children, as well as more joy than any mother could hope for.

The list of sources I relied on would be, I fear, longer than the book itself, but Leslie Berlin's wonderful *The Man Behind the Microchip: Robert Noyce and the Invention of Silicon Valley*, Ward Winslow's *Palo Alto: A Centennial History*, and Dorothea Lynch's heartbreaking *Exploding into Life* deserve particular mention. My apologies to the folks at Intel for the imposition of my fictional Danny upon them, and for the other liberties I took with their history. Thanks, too, to Steven Staiger and everyone at the Palo Alto Historical Association (without whom the old mansion might not exist), and to the Palo Alto Public Library staff and volunteers, who retrieved old magazines, called up books, and answered questions with amazing patience and cheer.

My mom, Anna Tyler Waite, and her many friends in the many places we lived in my youth were invaluable examples to me of what friendship can be; thanks to all of them, and especially to Dritha Ethel Pearson McCoy, Ginna Kanaga, Joyce Lindamood, and Elsie Minor. And although I am blessed with too many friends who have supported me over the years to list them here (you know who you are, and thank you all!), I want to thank in particular Jennifer Belt DuChene, who taught me to laugh at myself and led me, by her incredible friendship, to the heart of this book.

The
Wednesday
Sisters

MEG WAITE CLAYTON

A READER'S GUIDE

A Conversation Between Meg Waite Clayton and Brenda Rickman Vantrease

Meg Waite Clayton and Brenda Rickman Vantrease, author of The Mercy Seller, *have been writing partners and close friends for more than a decade. They first met at an open writing group that gathered monthly at a Nashville library, but they really came to know each other as part of a more closely focused splinter group much like the Wednesday Sisters. Their small group met weekly at local coffee shops, commenting on one another's work and improving as a result, and eventually all four members published articles, essays, and stories. Seven years after this writing group formed, Meg sold her first novel,* The Language of Light, *and a year later Brenda sold* The Illuminator. *Although they now live nearly a continent apart, Meg and Brenda continue to critique each other's work, and the friendship that began in that first tentative sharing of manuscript pages now encompasses every aspect of their lives. Brenda and Meg enjoyed reminiscing about their early work together, reflecting on how friendship inspires writing, and exploring how much of* The Wednesday Sisters *is drawn from real life.*

Brenda Rickman Vantrease: There is so much I love about *The Wednesday Sisters*—I mean, it's a beautifully written novel about writing and about friendship, which is as necessary to the human experience as breath. So what is not to love, right? But being a writer of historical fiction, I especially admire the way you integrate the historical setting with the lives of your characters. This story, these characters, could not exist apart from their time and place. That's not an easy thing to do. What drew you to that time and place? Why the late 1960s? Why California?

Meg Waite Clayton: I wanted to write a novel about women who have dreams for themselves that they are struggling to reach for, that they don't really begin to reach for until their friends urge them to. I originally set out to write a contemporary story, but I worried that women coming of age today have no great excuse for hesitating to reach for their dreams. We still do hesitate—it's a scary thing to reach for a dream, because what do you do if you come away empty-handed?—but women today are open to the charge that we're just cowards, and it's hard to make a coward a sympathetic character. If you put those same women in the 1960s, though, when there were real societal barriers to women reaching for dreams . . .

The answer to "Why California?" starts with the fact that I live just a few blocks from the park the Wednesday Sisters meet in, so it was a short walk to see what, for example, the trees look like when I needed to describe them. And the more I poked around, the more I came to realize that Palo Alto in the 1960s was, as a community, divided in a way that paralleled the divide in the country as a whole: it was a fairly conservative community set next to a college with a liberal student body, a dynamic point of contact between the old world and the new. The city council minutes from the time are full of wonderful gnashing of teeth over the hippies taking over the streets, and the newspaper was full of photos and stories about student occupations of university buildings and bombings of local bookstores, and ideas about how the community should be dealing with the chaos. I didn't have to concoct some scheme to drag the Sisters to a women's rights demonstration elsewhere because the women's rights gathering described in the book actually occurred right on University Avenue.

Brenda: Since Kath, Linda, Brett, Ally, and Frankie are in traditional roles as wives and mothers, they are slower to recognize and embrace the evolution in women's lives that began in the late 1960s and early 1970s. For example, they are reluctant to let go of the Miss America Pageant, and they harbor secret ambitions for which they seem almost ashamed—like Brett's desire to be an astronaut. They have to be pushed by Linda to attend the feminist rally, sort of tiptoeing into the water as they walk on the fringes of a peace march. We see them being changed by the times, not trying to change the times themselves. Was that a deliberate choice on your part? Did you ever consider including an unmarried woman in the group or a strident, card-carrying feminist?

Meg: The choice of five traditional women was a deliberate one that I think comes out of an "aha" moment I had at Michigan Law School, when my friend Liza Yntema dragged me to see some old class photos in Hutchins Hall, to show me how few women there were in classes not many years before us. I don't think I had a clue what a difference the women's movement had made in my life before that. That was definitely something I became more and more interested in exploring as I wrote *The Wednesday Sisters:* the shift the movement provoked in the way women—many women or maybe even all women, not just those who would call themselves feminists—think of themselves. I wanted to have my characters pretty well settled in more traditional women's roles when the women's movement really became visible in part to spotlight the real differences in our lives now: We run marathons. We attend colleges where the doors used to be closed to us. We can support ourselves financially; no one is requiring us to leave our jobs because we've gotten married or had children. I think a lot of young women coming of age today—and even those of us who aren't so young—don't fully realize how much more restricted women's lives used to be, or have lost sight of that.

I'm guilty of that myself: I remember thinking when Sandra Day O'Connor was appointed to the Supreme Court that it was really cool, but I wasn't emotionally overwhelmed by the moment. I thought it was something that ought to happen and so of course it had. The same with Sally Ride going into space. I was a lot younger then, and considerably more naïve about how quickly the world changes. By contrast, by the time Nancy Pelosi was sworn in as Speaker of the House, I was basically bawling my eyes out, because that next round of barrier-breaking seemed to take such a long time. I was also interested in exploring the extent to which the way we judge ourselves as women still has some distance to go.

Brenda: You evoke the 1960s so well. Would you say something about your research methods? (You can't be old enough to remember Johnny Carson!)

Meg: Alas, I was in law school when Johnny retired from hosting *The Tonight Show;* I used to try to finish studying in time to catch his monologue. The lunar landing happened when I was eleven, so I remember it, too—although admittedly not well enough to deliver the lunar landing scene even after being steeped in the 1960s as a history major at the University of Michigan. I did a lot of research on the particulars, turning to 1960s bestseller lists and fashion photos, articles on the state of medicine, the Olympics, and women's marches, and Miss America photos and quotes. I read old magazines and talked to people and—this part was really fun—watched the footage of the lunar landing, and old clips of *The Tonight Show* from the days when Johnny Carson was the host.

What I discovered was that women's lives were even more limited than I'd imagined: even Stanford had no women's track team; new mothers were often required to forfeit their jobs; want ads were separated by gender; there were actually men's-only flights; and my own high school yearbook, when I was a freshman—1972—listed only six girls' sports teams (no track there, either!), all after the many, many pages of the many, many boys' teams. I think of myself as coming of age on the other side of the women's movement from the Wednesday Sisters, but I see in retrospect how long it has taken—and is still taking—for the world to change.

Brenda: While the Wednesday Sisters are women of their time, there is universality in their experiences that transcends the time in which they live, like the love they have for their children, Linda's breast cancer, Kath's struggle with her husband's infidelity, Ally's desire for children, their awareness of body flaws such as small breasts or big feet. In what ways do you see yourself as different from the Wednesday Sisters? In what ways are you similar?

Meg: Women of the Wednesday Sisters' generation—my mom's generation—certainly had more limited choices than women of my generation did, despite the few years between us. It's one thing to go to law school, as I did, with a substantial number of women students, and another thing entirely to decide you're going to law school when most schools don't even admit women and those that do have no more than a handful in each class. Similarly, women just a few years younger than I am, who came of age after Title IX was fully implemented, take things for granted that I didn't: playing soccer, for example, or being able to attend Ivy League colleges and become engineers.

But even among our different generations, there are experiences that are universal. We still care deeply about our children: it's interesting to see how many young women today choose to leave careers to have families. We choose perhaps as badly as we ever have in love, and stay with unfaithful husbands even when we have the financial freedom to leave. Beyond these universal issues, there are other ways in which I am individually very similar to the Wednesday Sisters, little pieces of me embedded in each of them: Linda's fear—for her children and for herself—is definitely my fear: my mom is a breast cancer survivor and my grandma didn't survive. Brett's tortured relationship with her "unfeminine intellect" draws its emotional roots from my inner math-science geek. Kath's darkest moments draw from a relationship of mine that didn't end well. Frankie's self-doubt and her chubby phases are mine, as is her experience with her first novel. Even quiet Ally is me in her middle-of-the-night journey back to the neonatal intensive care unit, where her daughter, Hope, is tethered to life by the same tubes and wires my own son Nick once was.

Brenda: There was one scene—I think I told you this the first time I read it—that was hard for me to read. I can better understand the Kath on the freeway than the Kath who begs her philandering husband for affection. It was painful to watch her humiliation. Was there any scene that was particularly hard for you to write?

Meg: That's the one scene I point parents to when they ask if the book would be appropriate for their teenage daughters, not because it's graphic, but because it presents a level of humiliation that I hate to imagine young readers knowing might exist. That was definitely one of the hardest scenes to write, although for me there are at least two scenes that were emotionally harder to write: the scene where Ally goes to the hospital in the middle of the night—because that is drawn from real life—and the scene where Linda tells her children she is going into the hospital, because I suppose my greatest fear is dying before my children could survive my death relatively unscarred.

Brenda: I know you've said that the story of *The Wednesday Sisters* emerged from an image of a woman with a blond ponytail who walked across your field of vision one day. She would later become Linda. How did you birth the other characters? Did anybody else come as easily as Linda?

Meg: All five characters came to me that same morning. I've told this story so many times, but I was quite seriously having a pity party for myself and the impending death of my writing career when that woman walked by; then within hours I had the guts of *The Wednesday Sisters* mapped out in my journal. They really came to me in a gang, all five of them, with Frankie telling their stories.

That having been said, Kath and Linda came more easily than the others. And I had a struggle with Ally and Brett. Even after I sold the novel, my editor suggested merging them into a single character because they were bleeding together. I think—hope—they seem to be very different personalities in the final book, because I put a lot of work into making them distinct. I revised and brainstormed and revised some more. And more. And more. One of the things that I think helped was adding Ally's mother-in-law, which was a suggestion of a friend of mine from India. I remember reading somewhere that one of the best ways to characterize someone is to show them through another character's eyes.

Brenda: Let's talk about friendship and writers. There are probably more examples in literary history of friends who have fallen out over writing than friendships that are strengthened because of it. Our love of writing was the shared interest that brought us together. The Wednesday Sisters seem to discover their common interest in writing *after* they become friends. They are initially brought together by their loneliness and their children. The discussion about books is more of a conversation opener for Frankie than a desire to form a reading or writing group. Do you think friendship has a positive or negative influence on the kind of feedback writers get from one another in a work group setting?

Meg: I think true friendship is a huge positive for writers. True friends really care about each other, and if you really care about someone, you're going to do everything you can for them. If they want to improve as writers, what you can do for them is tell them what you honestly think. True friends will speak gently, because they love, but they will also make sure they are heard—again, because they love. And then they will step back and let their writer-friend make his or her own choices, because another crucial element of true friendship is respect.

Brenda: When you're speaking "gently," that's the time I really listen because I know that desire not to hurt comes not just from friendship but a real concern about a problem with the writing.

Meg: I feel the same way. I think those fallings out seem to happen mostly as a result of jealousy, don't you? You and I—as much as we might envy each other's successes—have stayed so close because we have been able to draw inspiration from them. I remember when your ad for *The Illuminator* appeared in *The New York Times Book Review*. Have I ever told you this? I taped it onto the glass on a framed photo hanging on the wall of my office right beside my desk. I still have the ad, although I've moved it to my middle desk drawer now. But I used to look at it and think, *Dang, Brenda can do it and I know she's only human, so maybe I can, too.*

Brenda: I felt the same way when you were the first to sell a novel. I was a little jealous—okay, a *lot* jealous—but at the same time I was so happy for you. I knew how hard you'd worked on that book, writing and rewriting to get it just right. You'd worked harder than any of us, and you deserved to be the first. And when I held that book in my hand, I teared up with a fierce pride not only in you but in us. It was a shot of mental adrenaline. I was determined that you might be the first, but you wouldn't be the only.

Meg: It still kind of amazes me that our books sit together on my bookshelf—and with Leslie's book now, too [Leslie Lytle, Brenda and Meg's fellow writing group member]. One of the nicest afternoons I've ever spent was that day we visited Nashville bookstores together and signed our books.

Brenda: We used to meet over coffee each week and faithfully exchange manuscripts and ideas with a seriousness that would indicate we thought we would someday actually write something that somebody else would not only want to read but pay to read. I'll confess it all seemed like an impossible dream to me, but I was enjoying the process and the dream. However, I always had the sense that you were sure it was going to happen. Was that true? Where did that confidence come from?

Meg: Don't tell my poker gang, but I bluff well in poker, too.

Honestly, I don't know that I was any surer it would happen than you were, Brenda. What I *was* sure of was that if it *didn't* ever happen, it wasn't going to be because I hadn't tried as hard as I could. I actually went through a period—inspired by Scott Adams, who draws the Dilbert cartoons—where I would write in my journal "I will get my novel published" not just once, but fifteen times every day. It was good for me, because it kept me focused on the future, on the possibility that I *could* reach that dream. Almost everyone I know who has been published—including you!—has a long history of sticking to it when no sane person would continue to do so.

Brenda: Now that that dream has come true what has been the most surprising thing you've learned? What have you learned that you wish you had known when we were so earnestly swapping pages and picking one another's brains for tips on the most effective query letter, the best kind of opening line, the appropriate point of view?

Meg: I think the most surprising thing has been how much better I've come to know myself through my writing. And I wish I'd known to hold tightly to the story I wanted to tell. I've come to see that's where my best writing comes from, but there were definitely times along the way where I was so intent on being published that I lost my center in trying to please.

And I suppose I wish I'd really understood that flawed characters are more compelling than perfect ones, that sometimes the most grammatically correct sentence isn't the best one, and that point of view is richer and more complicated than I once thought.

Brenda: Speaking of point of view, this seems to be a real pitfall for some writers. I know you have experimented with other points of view but in the end chose to have Frankie narrate all of the Sisters' stories. Can you tell us a little bit about why you chose her point of view?

Meg: When I first began imagining the story, it came to me in Frankie's voice. I spent a lot of time poking around looking at points of view in the early stages, though, because I had these five stories to tell, and Frankie wasn't going to be, for example, in Kath's and Lee's bedroom; a traditional first-person point of view wasn't exactly going to work. But maybe because my storytelling roots are in listening to my family tell stories on itself, I feel much more comfortable in first person. Honestly, even the third-person stories I've published have for the most part been written in first person and then converted to third. So I finally decided that, because it's retrospective and because these are friends who are so close that they know one another's stories well enough to tell them even if they weren't there every moment, I could get away with Frankie narrating scenes she isn't in—even that awful Kath bedroom scene. It allows me the benefit of one unifying narrative voice, and yet it also allows me to tell all the stories from a very intimate point of view.

Brenda: I have always envied your energy and discipline as a writer. Would you say something about your writing process, for instance, your typical routine?

Meg: Two thousand words or 2:00 P.M. when I'm writing a first draft. I sit down to write at 8:00 every morning, and if I've got 2,000 words by 9:30, I can do whatever I want for the rest of the day. But if I have 2,000 words even by 2:00, I'm reluctant to get up from that chair, because that's a really good writing day.

I do sit down to write each weekday morning almost as surely as if I had to punch a clock. I figure what I lack in talent maybe I can make up in discipline.

Revision is the sweet spot of writing for me, where the awful cocktail party at which I know not a soul starts feeling more like a gathering of friends. I go through draft after draft. I'm only guessing, but I'd say at least twenty for *The Wednesday Sisters*. I did an entire draft focused on making Brett and Ally more memorable. I did a dialogue draft, looking only at dialogue to make sure each of the five characters' voices is distinct. And each draft isn't necessarily better than the last, either. At one point for this novel, I returned to a draft from six months earlier, did a redline of all the changes since and—starting from the earlier draft—picked the few good changes and left everything else on the cutting-room floor. I'd like to think there is a more efficient way to write, but it seems I sometimes have to go down a wrong road far enough to see it's a dead end before I can find the open path.

Brenda: I'm almost as excited about your next book, *The Ms. Bradwells*, as I am about my own third novel. I wish you were here so we could workshop both of them over coffee the way we used to. I know your new one is a friendship story, too. Can you tell us a little about it?

Meg: I like to call *The Ms. Bradwells* my "law school story" to make my pals from law school nervous, though in fact it's about four women who first meet at the University of Michigan Law School a few years before our class was there. I'm in the early stages, so I'm less articulate than I'd like to be on the subject of what it's "about," but my explanations tend to include the terms "friendship," "motherhood," "that first wave of women entering historically male professions in substantial numbers," and "the consequences of the choices we make." The four friends in the story—Betts, Lainey, Ginger, and Mia—come together years after their law school graduation, expecting to spend a long weekend celebrating Betts's appointment to the D.C. Court of Appeals. But a question raised at her confirmation hearing about an unexplained death during their law school days sends them fleeing to an isolated Chesapeake Bay island family home Ginger has just inherited from her mom—the very place where the death occurred. Over the three days they spend together, the friends reconsider the truths they may have buried in the wake of that death. They also begin to make sense of the very different career and life choices each has made in the intervening years, the effects their mothers' dreams and expectations have had on who they have become, and the world their daughters will inherit from them.

At least, that's what I think it is going to be about. I do look forward to having you read it, though, as I always learn so much about what I'm *really* writing—as opposed to what I *think* I'm writing—from your critique!

A Wednesday Sisters Reading List

In Cold Blood by Truman Capote
Third Girl by Agatha Christie
To Kill a Mockingbird by Harper Lee
Great Expectations by Charles Dickens
The Great Gatsby by F. Scott Fitzgerald
The Bell Jar by Sylvia Plath*
Rebecca by Daphne du Maurier
Couples by John Updike
Charlotte's Web by E. B. White*
Pride and Prejudice by Jane Austen*
Aspects of the Novel by E. M. Forster
Middlemarch by George Eliot*
Breakfast at Tiffany's by Truman Capote*
Portnoy's Complaint by Philip Roth
A Passage to India by E. M. Forster
Love Story by Erich Segal
The French Lieutenant's Woman by John Fowles

Some of Meg's Favorites the Sisters Might Read Today:
Excellent Women by Barbara Pym
The Heart of the Matter by Graham Greene
Charming Billy by Alice McDermott
A Thousand Acres by Jane Smiley
Last Orders by Graham Swift
A Lesson Before Dying by Ernest Gaines
Bel Canto by Ann Patchett
Empire Falls by Richard Russo
Back When We Were Grownups by Anne Tyler
Inventing the Abbots and Other Stories by Sue Miller
Alias Grace by Margaret Atwood

*Meg's thoughts on these "model books" appear on the following pages.

The Model Books

FRANKIE'S MODEL BOOK: *Middlemarch* by George Eliot

Middlemarch is such a rich and complex novel that it doesn't succumb easily to a single tagline. It's a portrait of the ordinary lives in a provincial English town in the 1830s, with a focus on the unconventional and idealistic Dorothea Brooke. Thomas Wolfe, among others, has named it as one of the greatest books of all time. Eliot delivers a broad and wonderful cast of characters, all of whom breathe as if they were real.

Like Frankie, I came to *Middlemarch* late and through the insistence of someone else: an English teacher—not mine!—I met while I was passing the time at one of my son's chess tournaments by reading a Jane Austen novel. He described it as "like Jane Austen, only better." I've reread it several times, and it is probably my desert-island book. I particularly love Dorothea, in part because she has ambitions to do some good in this world, and in part because she's so sure she knows what is best for her, and she turns out to be so dreadfully wrong. And I love pretty much everything about the way Eliot writes.

Frankie is the only Wednesday Sister who changes model books in the course of the novel. She initially chooses *Rebecca* by Daphne du Maurier, which is a wonderfully gothic exploration of insecurity, something the insecure Frankie would be drawn to. But as Frankie gains confidence through her friendships and her writing, she outgrows *Rebecca,* which, much as I love it, I don't think holds a candle to *Middlemarch* in terms of the quality of the writing and the complexity of the characters. She reaches toward more challenging literature, and finds in Eliot's Dorothea a reflection of herself: a woman who wants to be more than women are supposed to be.

KATH'S MODEL BOOK: *Pride and Prejudice* by Jane Austen

Pride and Prejudice is a comedy of manners and a wonderful love story that I read again and again. The spirited Elizabeth Bennet spars with the rich and proud Mr. Darcy while her sister Jane and the shy Mr. Bingley conduct a parallel romantic dance—all under the looming prospect of the five Bennet sisters losing their home to the obsequious Mr. Collins when their father dies.

I came to Austen through a friend of mine, the poet and fiction writer Madeleine Mysko, who remarked about an early few pages of the first draft of my first novel (then titled *Emma* after one of the two main characters, Emma Crofton), "But of course you can't call it *Emma*!" I'm not sure I'd even heard of Austen at the time—this was before Hollywood brought her back in fashion—and I didn't read *Emma* until after I'd finished the draft of my novel. But then I went through all Austen's novels, as Kath would say, in two shakes of a sheep's tail. Still, Lizzy Bennet remains my favorite Austen woman, and I agree with Eudora Welty's assessment that *Pride and Prejudice* is "irresistible and as nearly flawless as any fiction could be."

I think when Kath looks in the mirror, she wants to see Lizzy. In many ways, she is like Lizzy: she speaks her mind, and she has standards, and she's impulsive in ways that don't always make her life easier. She's smart, and she cares deeply about her family, despite her frustrations with them. But in other ways, she only *presents* herself as a Lizzy because that's what she wants the world to see.

LINDA'S MODEL BOOK: *The Bell Jar* by Sylvia Plath
The Bell Jar is Sylvia Plath's novel about a scholarship student and aspiring writer on an internship with a women's magazine in New York. The novel is autobiographical enough that it was originally published under the pseudonym Victoria Lucas and was not meant to be published in the United States until after Plath's mother died, although ultimately it was. Plath didn't live to enjoy her success: she committed suicide within weeks of the publication of this, her only novel.

I first read *The Bell Jar* as a teenager, not long after it was first published here in 1972. It's definitely one of the books that left me longing to write myself. I identified both with Esther's dream of writing and with her emotional isolation in a world in which she didn't feel she belonged. Part of the reason I love this novel is because Plath uses humor so brilliantly to allow us to sink into this tale of mental illness and despair.

Linda chooses *The Bell Jar* as her model book because she, too, identifies with Esther's dream of writing and her sense of being different from other young women. Linda's apartness comes largely as a result of her mother's illness and early death and the defense mechanisms Linda has adopted to survive. I imagine her coming to Plath through her poetry, welcoming words that reflect a depth of emotion and loneliness that she feels but that it seems no one else in her life understands.

BRETT'S MODEL BOOK: *Breakfast at Tiffany's* by Truman Capote
Holly Golightly is one of my favorite characters in literature: an elegant extrovert who seems to party her way through a trouble-free life, only to turn out to be a much deeper person than that. Like Brett, I admire the boldness of Holly walking away from her past and creating a future for herself that is all about who she is now rather than who she has been, even if I don't agree with all the things Holly does.

I suppose Brett's choice of *Breakfast* as her model book is the choice I'm least happy with. They *do* share the wearing of gloves—though the gloves are much more visible in the Audrey Hepburn movie than in the Truman Capote novel—and Brett does admire Holly's attitude, and envies her social ease. Brett *thinks* she'd like to be more like Holly than she is. But I see Holly as primarily a social being, and Brett as primarily an intellectual one. Maybe that's why Brett struggles so to get her own novel to work, because her model book is tied to what she thinks she wants to be instead of who she is. I might have chosen one of Margaret Atwood's wonderful novels for Brett's model book, but her first, *The Edible Woman,* wasn't published until 1969, after the sisters had chosen their model books.

ALLY'S MODEL BOOK: *Charlotte's Web* by E. B. White
What child who moves as many times as I did wouldn't identify with eight-year-old Fern's friendship with Wilbur the pig and Charlotte the spider? My mom read *Charlotte's Web* to me as a child, and when I read it to my own children, I was barely able to get the words out at the end without crying. It is one of the few children's stories I know that is even more moving to read as an adult.

Ally's choice of this as her model book has everything to do with her longing to have children; she writes children's stories for the child she hopes to have. But I chose this particular children's book for her because it also has this lovely theme of different beings finding love for one another despite how different they appear, just as Ally and her husband, Jim, who come from different cultures, form what is probably the strongest marriage and closest family in *The Wednesday Sisters.*

In retrospect, I see that *Charlotte's Web* was an inspiration for *The Wednesday Sisters,* that it was perhaps a model book for me as I wrote, albeit an unconscious one. Characters who don't appear to have a lot in common become as close as friends can be. They work together toward a common end. And they support one another in ways that allow them each whatever it is that they need to become whole.

Reading Group Questions and Topics for Discussion

1. What do you think draws the women together in the opening scenes of *The Wednesday Sisters*? Is it, as Linda suggests, a shared love of books, or is it a shared fascination with Brett's white gloves, or is it both or something else?

2. Twice in the novel, Linda attempts to ask about Brett's gloves, but she is cut off by one of the other Sisters. Why are they reluctant to cross that line? What do you think the gloves symbolize? Do you think young women meeting Brett today would be as gentle about her gloves? Are there generational differences in the ways women relate?

3. Ally enters the group in part based on an unspoken assumption that Carrie is her daughter, when the child is in fact her niece. Why do you think Frankie keeps this secret rather than sharing it with the others? Do you think Ally's life would be different today, given the existence of fertility treatments and support groups?

4. Why does Kath go so far in trying to win Lee back? Did this surprise you? Do you think she would have acted differently if the success of her marriage weren't so important to her parents? If divorce had been as prevalent then as it is now? If she had been able to provide for herself financially? Would you, like Kath's friends, be reluctant to counsel her to leave her husband? Or can you imagine giving her different advice?

5. Linda's breast cancer and Ally's fertility issues cause each to doubt her own femininity, and leave their friends at a loss as to how to help them. Have you or a friend ever been through a similar crisis? What has helped you hold on to your sense of self through tough times? How have your friendships affected this experience?

6. Why do you think Frankie finds it so difficult to tell Danny she's writing a book, when she has no trouble at all confiding this fact to her husband's boss? Why are we sometimes reluctant to admit we have dreams?

7. The old abandoned mansion—"a Miss Havisham house," as Frankie's husband, Danny, calls it, after the moldering mansion in Dickens's *Great Expectations*—is a haunting presence through most of the novel. What does this house seem to symbolize? Does it mean something different to each of the Sisters? What does its destruction mean?

8. Published books are mentioned throughout the novel—from *The Great Gatsby* to *The Bell Jar* to *To Kill a Mockingbird*. What role do these titles play in *The Wednesday Sisters*? Why do you think each of the Sisters chooses the "model book" she does? What model book might you choose yourself?

9. The writing group the Sisters form in *The Wednesday Sisters* helps its members grow in self-awareness and self-confidence. Have you been a part of a group—perhaps even a reading or writing group—that has had a similar effect on you? What do you think of the author's message that writing doesn't have to culminate in a book deal; that it can feed the soul of anyone who works hard at it; that with hard work, it is possible to get better; and that writing can help one make sense of one's life?

10. In one memorable scene, the Wednesday Sisters gather in a funeral parlor and imagine what they can accomplish in their lives that will not perish with their deaths. Did this make you think about writing in a new light? What about motherhood?

11. The women's movement provides an evolving backdrop to the lives of the women in *The Wednesday Sisters*. How did you relate the experiences of the Wednesday Sisters to events in your own life or in the lives of women you know who lived at that time?

12. The Wednesday Sisters make a tradition of watching the Miss America Pageant every year. How do their reactions to the pageant change over time, and why? How does the pageant itself change?

13. If the Miss America Pageant is one recurring motif in the novel, the space program is another. What similarities and differences do you see in the way the author uses these two iconic slices of Americana?

14. Brett's novel, *The Mrs. Americas,* posits a future in which a spaceship crewed by women and carrying a cargo of frozen sperm takes off on a mission to propagate the human race beyond the confines of our solar system. Why do you think Clayton chose to have Brett write this particular novel?

15. In addition to exploring the empowerment of women and the prevalence of sexism, *The Wednesday Sisters* addresses other social issues. In what ways are race and class raised in the novel? What did you think of the Sisters' reactions to the fact that Ally's husband, Jim, was from India?

16. Why do you think the author chose to set the climax of her novel on the set of *The Tonight Show with Johnny Carson*? How does this scene compare to the Miss America Pageants described in the novel?

17. Throughout the novel, the Wednesday Sisters' friendships are complex, constantly evolving, and occasionally downright messy. Yet even as their bonds are tested, the group endures and grows stronger. What do you think keeps their friendships growing stronger rather than breaking apart?

18. In an interview, author Meg Waite Clayton once said, "If an author makes me weep, I am theirs—though why so many of us like books that make us cry puzzles me to no end." Do you share this sentiment? Why do you think readers respond to novels that make them cry?

MEG WAITE CLAYTON's first novel, *The Language of Light*, was a finalist for the Bellwether Prize. Her stories and essays have appeared in *Runner's World, Writer's Digest*, and numerous literary magazines. She is a graduate of the University of Michigan Law School and was a Tennessee Williams Scholar at the Sewanee Writer's Conference. She lives in Palo Alto, California, with her husband and their two sons.

www.megwaiteclayton.com